Where The Stream and Creek Collide

Sarah Lashbrook

Spire Publishing - August 2011

Copyright © Sarah Lashbrook
This book is sold subject to the condition that it shall not,
by way of trade or otherwise, be lent, resold, hired out, or
otherwise circulated without the publisher's prior consent
in any form of binding or cover other than that in which it
was published and without a similar condition including this
condition being imposed on the subsequent publisher.

The moral right of Sarah Lashbrook
to be identified as the author of this work has been asserted.

First published in Canada and the UK 2011
by Spire Publishing Ltd.

*A cataloguing record for this book is available from the Library and
Archives Canada.*
Visit www.collectionscanada.ca/amicus/index-e.html

Designed in Salt Spring, Canada
by Spire Publishing Ltd.

www.spirepublishing.com

Printed and bound in the USA or the UK
by Lightning Source Ltd.

ISBN: 978-1-926635-61-3

With all cheese and loyalty
This book is for you Shawna Rose
You are the best friend one could ask for
And for that, I thank you!

A promise is a promise!!!

Acknowledgements

First and foremost I would like to thank my beautiful better half. I would be lost without you. It amazes me that you can put up with a writers life with the patience and grace that you do. I am truly blessed.

I would also like to thank my draft readers. I needed your input and you gladly gave it. To Shawna, Jen, Shana, Judith, Bill and Tina (who read it twice and forced the finish) – I owe you. You were my first audience, my first praise and most important - you were my first criticism. For those who read a page or a paragraph – those little edits made big differences - my gratitude goes to you as well.

To Sgt. Ted Beaudry and Const. Gord Goddard - thank you for your resourcefulness.

To my mom – you have inspired me in more ways than you know. I am appreciative beyond words.

Cecile Goddard – you know what you did. Thank you.

My cover art would be a leaf taped to a piece of paper if it wasn't for Ms. Laura Aubertin and Ms. Ashley Miller.

Laura - I must say that your creative genius, your passion for photography and your patience for me is astounding. You are unique. Thank you.

Ashley – at AEM Designs – my beautiful British bestie and go to graphics girl. I haven't seen the final product yet - but I know it's good. You always have my back. I am a lucky girl.

Lastly to my kids: be creative, be inspired - and most importantly – be yourself. Never let anything or anyone stand between you and your dreams. Thank you for being a part of my life and my dreams. Let's hope that somewhere down the line this career will send you to all the far off lands you wish to visit.

I have three wishes for this book. First - to be read. Second - to evoke emotion. And third - to give a relatable character to a minority group that seems to lack just that in the literary world.

And of course, to one day have Ms. Helena Bonham Carter read my work.

PROLOGUE

The pain is gone. How could the pain be gone? It hurt so much just a minute ago. Don't breathe, he's coming. Don't breathe.
"You alive bitch?"
Don't breathe. Don't breathe. Get your grubby hands off me. Please just go away.
"Sadie, come on girl, you in there?"
I needed air. I tried to slowly breathe through my nose but couldn't. A sensation to gasp was inevitable. Keep it together, Sadie. He reached down and touched my neck.
"Good, dead. Just like your mother. You still have the money I gave you?" He paused and lightly kicked my shoulder. "Ah, staying silent are you? I guess you're putting new meaning to being my silent partner?" His evil laugh vibrated through the room. "Keep it. It was worth it."

Silence followed the echo of the front door slamming shut. I stayed still. I expected Tim to come back but a revving car engine told me he was gone. I need to see my mother. I need to get to her. She needs me too. Where are my legs? There was no feeling, just numbness. Was my mother okay? Where the fuck are my legs? Lifting my top half up, I expected my legs to follow but they wouldn't move. What is happening? I tried to make them move, to feel them but nothing. Nothing!

The front door opened. I stiffened, pressing my body back down to the ground. Holding my breath, I felt my heart beat quickly against the hard wooden floor. He came back. What if he notices that I moved? Damn!

"Hello, Charlie? You here?" A voice called out. "Sadie, Sadie, are you okay? You're hurt?" Mr. Gordini, my mother's accountant bent down over me. "What happened? Where's your mother?"

"She's dead." I cried. "Mom's dead, and it is all my fault."

-1-

WHEN THE BOUGH BREAKS

As a small child I used to play on a large elm tree in the front yard. Father and I built wooden steps up the tree trunk for easier access. Although it was father's project, mother was the one that spent the most time exploring with me between its thick branches. I would be outside playing, when mother would poke her head up into the tree, with a napkin full of chocolate chip cookies, and two margarine containers full of milk. We would eat, drink, and laugh until dad returned home from work. Now, looking out of the window, I can still see the steps, though weather worn and scratched, they are still attached to the big elm tree. As I stare, a dry leaf falls, passing the steps in its slow journey to the ground. I wonder if it was pushed away by the branch, or if it was just too weak to hang on? Did the tree have too many leaves, and thought it could spare one before the fall? Or did the leaf try with all its might to be part of a bigger mission, just to lose the battle in the end? I contemplated both thoughts, though I knew it was neither.

I lost mother when I was 17. She was good, kind, and in hindsight, more importantly – she was all mine. She ably made my boyfriends forgettable, my tears lessons, and most of my fear's fun. I loved her a lot. I remember once, in a playground somewhere, a little boy pushed me off of the slide, after telling me I was too ugly to be a queen in his castle. Harmless maybe, but I still recall the feelings of rejection and inferiority. I had started to cry and mother came rushing over, tissue in one hand, and a butterscotch candy in the other. Bending down, she swept me up in comforting arms, and explained to me that any King, who would not let the most beautiful girl in the world into his castle, was not a worthy King that I should want to rule with. And furthermore, a good Queen would recognize a false King, walk away, and return when the Kingdom had fallen and they were now looking for a kind, and fair Queen to guide them. Sucking on the scotch candy, mother asked me if I thought she was beautiful. I said yes. She pulled out a compact mirror and aimed it at my face. "That is my nose," she said, "and my eyes, and my smile…

you see," she would continue, "if I am beautiful, then you must be too." She was so convincing to me at that age. I did miss her. Like I knew the tree would eventually miss that leaf. You see the leaf was not weak, or hated, and it did not just fall. The leaf left as part of its natural progression in life. It was time. And as far as I can see, time takes away everything. It's a callous cycle really. The evolutions are as cold as the window separating us.

I could not help the pause this morning. Mother seemed present in my room. She always did on the first day back to school, no matter the grade. The truth was she had not been present for 6 years.

I spent the first 3 years wanting mother back, and the second 3 wanting to replace her. Torn between the desire for a mother figure and the fear of loving someone that much again. It was a contrast that could only hold guilt, pain, and fear in between. I saw her every time I looked in a mirror, and heard her every time I spoke to a small child. She was alive inside of me, yet very much dead.

The days of her memory being emotionally paralyzing are now gone. Six years have passed, and my life has been kicked into full tilt. It was August, the third year of College was about to start, and I didn't have a damn thing to wear. Almost everything I owned in clothes was packed and at residence. I already tried on the Khaki shorts with the blue and red polo top, it was too preppy. I tried the jeans and the pink baby t-shirt, it was too casual.

"Sadie, your breakfast is ready," Father chimed from the kitchen. I pushed away from the window. I could smell the waft of burnt eggs gliding through the air. I knew I had about 5 minutes before Jackie, father's girlfriend, came to my room to fetch me. She liked things timely, precise, and routine. She calls herself organized, others called her anal. Jackie was a cat-like woman, moody and bossy. She sat around grooming herself all day, only allowing herself to be touched, when she felt it was right. Today she was more catty than usual. For not only was I off to school, she was off to Spain for 6 months. It was an exchange offered through her work. She would go there, and a therapist from Spain would come and work here. Jackie jumped at the opportunity, without consulting father or her daughter Madison. Jackie and father have been fighting a lot lately, so I did not think dad minded at all that she didn't talk to him about it, or that she was leaving, for that matter.

I decided on the jeans and the polo shirt and slid out of my wheelchair and onto my bed to get dressed. I have had this bed since I was a child. It was always warm and inviting; a comfort in times of need. It still had Barbie stickers on the back metal frame. I ran my fingers over one with such elation; the memories of our trip still so vivid in my mind. When I was 10, my parents took me to New York for the long weekend. We went to a Broadway show, to the Macey's Thanksgiving-day parade, and then, and most exciting for me, we went to the huge Toys R Us store in the middle of Times Square. They had more toys than I could have ever imagined one store to have. I picked up a Barbie as my souvenir. She came with a plastic hair dryer, a mirror, and a myriad of clothes to change her into. She also came with stickers. Within minutes of returning from our trip, I placed the stickers on the back of my bed frame. Every night before I went to sleep, I would look at them and remember what a fun time we had. What a perfect family we were. Sometimes now, the elation turns to melancholy, but I couldn't bring myself to remove the stickers. They are too important to the bed, and the bed was too important to me. The bed was one of the only things left from our old house decor. I refused to give it up. After mother died, father boxed everything we owned and put it in storage. He took the books, the ornaments, the furniture, and even the kitchen utensils. Nothing was left. It was hard for him to look at anything she once touched. I am surprised that I am not sitting in that storage unit as well.

"Sadie Coleman, did you not hear your father call you for breakfast?" Jackie said, as she barged into my room.

"I have no shirt on Jackie, I can't come down undressed!" I yelled, as I scrambled to find my shirt. Jackie moved herself further into the room. She was dressed in a white laced frilly skirt, with her favourite matching Gucci tunic top. Her board straight blond hair, freshly brushed, was up in a pony tail, with a big white flower held hostage to the elastic band in the back.

Jackie stared at me. Her perfectly tanned yet very leathery face was all squished up with a look that read 'I will have to teach you about life.' "Is that what you are wearing for you first day back? The first impression is the most important you know. And we both know that girls like you need to look extra nice so others notice them first, and not the wheelchair!"

Jackie was my latest and last attempt to find a replacement wife for father. Precisely, she was attempt number 7. Last year I had physiotherapy for 4 months after I pulled the muscles in my back playing basketball. Jackie was my therapist. When I would show up for my time, she would act like she had been awaiting my arrival all day. And now that I had come, her day was made. I instantly liked her smell, her class, and her bluntness. A bluntness I must admit, that I now see as rather pointless, insensitive babble, but I digress.

During one of my sessions Jackie mentioned that my back could get worse before it got better. I took this information as a way to put a plan into action, a way I could keep Jackie in our life forever. Slowly over the next few days I claimed my back was getting worse. I asked father for help with everything. I tried to balance showing him an excessive need for assistance and shyness for a father's – a male's – help; all this leading up to a carefully planned and scripted breakdown of how I needed a woman around to assist me. I added an 'it's not fair,' and 'I wish Mom were alive,' and a long story short, I convinced father to pay Jackie to come into our home and work with me privately. I manipulated them into several talks, and after one short month, they were dating. And now a year later, she spends most nights here although she has never officially moved in. She ended up not being the greatest match for father, or for me.

"What do you mean 'girls like me', Jackie?" I replied with as much assertiveness as I could congregate. Personally I thought it sounded quite pragmatic. I pulled my shirt over my head. The collar got stuck on my elastic band. Like a building getting demolished, I crumbled over in my bed. Deflated. Deflated before I even started. The funny thing was I could see the face she was making even though my eyes were covered in polo-shirt fluff. She often did this to me with her presence. She knows where my buttons are. Jackie dislikes me. Who could blame her? Most days I dislike myself. And my shirt, evidently, hates me as well. It's unanimous.

"Well don't take offence." She retorted with a condescending laugh. "The fact is that girls in wheelchairs need to have that little extra to get people's attention. I know you don't like to hear that, but I don't like saying it either. It is just a fact Sadie. Society will look at you as a young, helpless, disabled girl, and not as a healthy, vibrant, classy woman. You have to show them who you are the minute you enter a room. Otherwise they will assume first and find truth later."

Yawn. The sad thing was she actually believed what she said. I think I rolled my eyes because she continued with a little more conviction in her tone.

"You'll be working more closely with Lonny this year won't you?"

"Yes."

She smiled a crooked smile, the one where one side of your lip sinks into your cheek, while on the opposite side of your face, an eyebrow lifts. Oddly, the same expression a dog makes, when cleaning the sides of his mouth after eating a potato chip.

"Well! It has been two years of close quarters and you guys are still not dating. He calls you all summer, you are stuck together all year at school, yet you are best friends? What is wrong here Sadie, I know you like him a lot, you told me such."

"Geez! Don't hold back there Jackie! Next time tell me what you're really thinking?" She stood quiet, but still my sarcasm was not lost on her. I took a deep breath before forcing my next sentence out. "First of all, I enjoy being his best friend. And yes, I do like him a lot. But I would rather be his friend than nothing at all. Second, he has a girlfriend, and has for several years. I wouldn't want to ruin that."

Jackie walked over to my dresser. She picked up my bottle of Satsuma perfume, sprayed her wrist, smelt it.

"Orange citrus, who the hell likes that smell on a person?" She was mumbling, but she made sure I could understand each word. I ignored her. She tossed the bottle into the garbage bin.

"That all sounds like a bunch of excuses if you ask me. In a normal world you two would be a couple already." Her voice now back at full volume.

"It isn't excuses, and I didn't ask you. And…actually, I am not discussing this matter with you anymore. It is none of your business."

Her face remained the same - condescending. I am sure she had heard my last line several times before from many others. It did not seem like it was news to her that her opinion was not always wanted. She dogmatized everything she thought. If I saw it, others must have as well. I continued.

"Now would you please let me finish getting ready so I can go down to breakfast?"

Unfortunately this came out more like I was begging her to leave and not demanding it like I hoped it would sound. But she still obliged.

She spun around on one foot, her skirt swaying high, her face not looking at me, or saying another thing. She shut the door behind her.

Bitch! Who the hell did she think she was? I went over to my dresser, and looked into the mirror. My face was as red as it felt. I hated it when she got me upset. I didn't like to give her that satisfaction. I grabbed my perfume out of the garbage bin. I sprayed it. I sprayed my neck, and chest, my wrist, and any other place that would hold a scent. I placed it back on the dresser and went for

12

breakfast. And to think, seven used to be my lucky number.

* * * * * * * * * * *

"I can't believe your father puts up with that woman. Seriously, Sadie, can you imagine dating her? I think I would rather poke myself continuously in the eye until it bleeds. It would be less painful than conversing with her." Piety steered the car slowly off my street and onto the highway. Father and Jackie were still standing at the end of the driveway. Father was waving goodbye, and Jackie, just standing, swaying her skirt back and forth, was retouching her lipstick.

I laughed.

"Poking yourself in the eyes really would be more pleasant, believe me. She leaves today anyway. Hopefully she likes it so much, she stays."

Piety smiled. First it was soft, then evil. "I wonder what she is like during sex. Do you think she paints her nails or reads a book while your father does all the work? Or do you think she beats the hell out of your dad?"

I became squeamish. "I don't want to know." I threw up in my mouth a little just thinking of it.

Piety Chilton and I have been friends since we were in grade ten. I had just started at Rachelle High, and Piety was the first student I met. We sat together in Mrs. Polly's English class. Piety had short red spiky hair that week, and wore gothic style clothing, black with lace. We were the two outsiders in the class. Jimmy Milken, captain of the debate team, came over to us on that first day, pointed, and said to the whole class, that he had just found out where the losers' corner was. Now, you know you are in trouble at a new school, when the debate team captain calls you a loser, and the class laughs. We both, in unison, told him to go fuck himself, and that was when we bonded – well actually, it was a little later, in detention.

Piety's Gothic days are long over. Her hair today was long, curly, and brunette. She has a never ending supply of jeans and baby t-shirts, and loves to shop for shoes. All of which are against true gothic garb standards. We remain the best of friends. In fact, we both applied to the same Colleges, both decided on Greenbury, and both entered Film and Television Production. The only difference was that for the past year, and now this one, I worked as a residence assistant, and she worked for house keeping. Working allowed us both to still live in residence after our first year of College.

"Trust me, if I didn't need to go home to get the rest of my stuff, I wouldn't have gone for the night. I would have stayed to finish my bulletin boards, or have gone to your house. What time will Hal be there?"

Hal Bartolli was a Resident Assistant like me. He was also Piety's boyfriend.

"He is getting a ride from his mother, so probably not until after lunch. You know Nancy?" Piety made a motion with her hand to imitate a person drinking out of a bottle. "The lush never rises before 11."

"Let's hope today she does. Alex gave us the option to go home for the night. She wasn't supposed to. The only stipulation was that we needed to arrive back by 9 am. Not a good way to start off his first year on the job."

Alex was new to being my boss. Up until this year – the residence which was divided into two buildings – also had two Resident Life Coordinators, Alex Ward and Kent Luopa. I have always been in the Allen building which was Kent's building. Over the summer the Resident Manager and the Dean of Student Services decided that there was no need for two RLC's, so Alex, who had more seniority, stayed, while Kent moved on to another school. I have lived and worked with Alex over the past three years, but this was our first official year as boss and employee. I was very excited for the change. I had always got along with Alex, and never had with Kent. Years ago, Alex knew my father, and although they hadn't really seen each other in years, their former bond seemed to help my present one a little. She already knew about my life and never really intruded upon it too much like others seemed to do.

We pulled into the Residence drive at 8:30 am. The building looked smaller this year. The parking lot was full. It was a concrete pool of mini-vans. Students had already begun to arrive. The Mothers looked completely exhausted and traumatised, carrying numerous boxes and bags across the parking lot. The Fathers looked elated and in a rush to have their kids stuff moved in - carrying as many packages as humanly possible in one load. Alex was outside by the popcorn machine, greeting families as they came up the walk. She noticed us pulling in, and came running over.

"Hey Sadie, Piety, glad to see you gals. They are arriving early this year." She took a quick look around the parking lot. "Thanks for helping us out today Piety. I have the pamphlets for you to hand out in my office. The pink ones on my desk. Sadie, when you get a

moment, can you come find me?"
Piety nodded in acknowledgement.
A 'sure can' was my response. And as quickly as she arrived, she rushed off.
"What is that all about?" Piety asked.
"Beat's me." We got out of the car and grabbed our things from the trunk. I only had a back pack. "I'll catch up with you later Piety. Thanks for the lift."

Rushing through the doors, I heard a mother explain to her daughter that the lavender curtains from home would go much better in her dorm room than the green ones provided by the College. In the hall, there was a father in a serious talk with his son, the son's face totally red, the father's stern, athletic looking face businesslike, as he handed over a box of condoms. Unknowingly to him each Resident Assistant had a year's supply of condoms tucked in his or her dorm room, for when they would be needed by any student.

"Sadie, in here!" Alex's head was peaking out of the R.A. office. Her hair was down, just clipped back. Jeans, a white t-shirt, and her blue Residence Life Coordinator vest on. She threw my work vest at me, "put it on" she said. I obeyed, and then rolled into the room. To say the room was colourful would be an understatement. To the right was the kitchen area which included a miniature fridge, a sink, and a long green corner counter. Straight ahead was a red futon, with matching red bean bag chairs on either side. The furniture was separated only by two old wooden school desks masquerading as side tables. The wall behind the couch, and encompassing most of the room, was blue, matching the carpet. To the left were the mailboxes, a photocopy machine, arts and crafts supplies, a shift board listing our next scheduled work time, and a computer, all which sat neatly on top of orange tables. In the far corner was a second entrance to Alex's office. It was the only one used by staff. Finally, the highlight of the whole room was the 2 foot wide cement pillar in the middle, painted a bright shade of yellow. Despite the fact that it looked like a had thrown up in the room, it all blended really well.

"How are you doing Alex?" I asked, as she dropped herself down on the futon. She let out a loud exasperated sigh which blew her bangs straight up in the air. She looked like she needed a nap.

"I thought I would have another hour or two to get ready for this. I guess parents are anxious this year to let their little darlings go." I transferred onto the futon beside her. I smiled. She reached over and gave me a one armed hug. She continued to talk. "I wanted to let you know that I had to put Jack on your floor. I had to move a girl off of yours, whose parents wanted her on a quiet floor instead. They were adamant that she move today. He was the only one I could put into her old room. And he was all too willing to move off of the quiet floor."

My smile faded. Shit! Jack DeGraff on my floor. Even his name annoyed me. Jack had been at the residence for three years now. He was one of the only students ever allowed into residence more than one year. Residence was usually only for the students in their first year of college, and if you stayed after that, it was because you were staff. Jack; however, was the exception to the rule. Jack was a handful. He was hyper, cocky, and drunk most of the time. He was also filthy rich, being the son of Robert DeGraff – the Owner, original chef, and namesake of Degraffs, the largest Italian fine dining restaurant in Canada and the United States. The restaurant was the hot spot for any celebrities visiting Toronto, Vancouver, and New York, to name a few, and has a two month waiting list for the general public. Robert works out of the Toronto restaurant but occasionally makes appearances in all of the hot spots.

The other problem with Jack was that he was also the nephew of Cathy Degraff, the Dean of Student Services. I think my face was expressing all that my mouth couldn't, because Alex spoke again.

"He isn't that bad Sadie. He still has to follow all the same rules as everyone else. You treat him as you would the rest of your students."

I trusted her residence advice. I have since my first year. She has yet to steer me wrong. But this decision, I questioned.

"Alex, I am a senior R.A. this year, in my last year of school, and now you are saying that I will have the most obnoxious, idiotic, self-centered, spoiled, asshole on my floor! He is always ready and willing to run to his aunt with any problem he has with any rule in residence. You got to be joking."

She wasn't.

The town of Greenbury was in the heart of the Muskoka's in Northern Ontario. It hid just outside of Port Sydney on highway 141. The Muskoka District consisted of a group of regions including Huntsville, Bracebridge, Port Carling, Port Sidney, and Gravenhurst, and several other towns and townships. Located in its twenty five hundred square miles are waterfalls, cliffs, and over sixteen hundred lakes, along with many other tourist attractions and resorts. It had over fifty thousand permanent residents, and over ninety thousand seasonal residents. The area had come to be known for holding beauty, serenity, and the summer homes of Hollywood's rich and famous. It was Ontario's answer to New York's, Hamptons. Because of this, several high-class, rich, somewhat snobbish students came to Greenbury. Some are, needless to say, more spoiled than others. On top of that, a lot of parents of students pay for additions and programs at the College as well, giving the already snobbish spoiled students the feeling that they have more of a right to be at the school than others. It all never really sat well with me. Jack was one of these students.

She looked a little taken aback, but she sat up and took my hand. I pulled mine away. She swallowed hard. "I know, but I am fully confident that you can handle him. You are great with the students. As we saw last year, he does have a silent respect for you, more so than the other staff members. Between us, I can't afford to not have him happy and safe this year. His aunt is my boss. And, well, you are the best chance I have for keeping him alive throughout his last year. So please, go into this with your chin up. He is already in the room getting settled. Besides, you'd be doing me a huge favour."

My head was screaming no. But my eyes took one look at her pleading face and my heart knew that I had to agree. It was already done. Besides, it was sort of flattering that she trusted me with him, considering the degree of consequences she would face should anything go wrong. I smiled, took a deep breath, and looked at her, "let's do it." As she hugged me in relief, I wondered if she knew who exactly she was leaving her trust in. She wanted him to stay safe and alive. So she gave him to me. The one person who, six years ago, got her mother murdered.

-2-

BREATHLESS

"There will be no smoking on this floor. No cigarettes, no pot, no bongs, no drugs period. If you want to drink, you will have to drink in your room, or in the lounge. No glass bottles are allowed in the halls of residence. Therefore, you must pour your drinks into plastic bottles, or cups, or buy cans. For transporting, please use a spill proof cup. It has to have a lid on it for transporting in the hall. If it is a can, keep it unopened." I looked at all the upset faces staring back at me. They were not impressed. "And when I say lid, I mean that you need to have something secure enough to be able to turn your drink upside down and have nothing spill out. Got it?"

They nodded.

"And remember, people, especially those from out of the Province. This is Ontario, the legal drinking age is 19. At Greenbury we take this law very seriously. There is a zero tolerance to underage drinking."

It was the first floor meeting, and things were not going too badly. Fifty-six of our seventy-two students showed up to hear Ashlyn and I go over the Code of Conduct. This was by far, the worst meeting of the year for them. Most students were excited for their first year of College, because for most of them, it also represented their first year of freedom. To hear the number of rules they would have to follow for the next nine months didn't exactly make a lot of people happy.

"Now, there will be no weapons of any kind. From the obvious of no guns, to the not-so obvious – no knives, swords, wood carving kits, darts, etcetera. Nothing that is sharp and or harmful. Any questions?"

One tall kid standing in the back raised his hand. Rather quiet, he asked, "I am in culinary classes, I will have a set of knives, will I have to keep them at school then?" Jack DeGraff decided to field this one before I could. He quickly piped in, "No dude, they are part of your course, you are allowed to have them, and they can't stop you. I have had my knives here all three years."

Ashlyn clearly had less patience than I did.

"Well while most people won't have their knives in res. three years, yes they are allowed to be here. Just remember though, you are responsible for them, and for whatever happens with them. So, keep them somewhere that is safe."

Jack smirked, sat back on his chair, and put his feet up on the lounge table. He had short sandy blond hair that hung long in the front, just enough to get into his eyes. This was a shame because the one good thing about Jack was that he had the most amazing glacier blue eyes. He chewed on a tooth pick that drooped from his mouth, the piece of wood trying desperately to escape the grip of his perfectly straight white teeth that illuminated from his busy mouth.

"The rest of the Code of Conduct is your responsibility to read. I know you all have a copy in your room. There is also one online. Ignorance will not be an excuse for breaking a rule. Other than that, if you have any questions, Ashlyn's room is at the far end of the hall." I pointed to the left. "And mine is at the other." I pointed right. "We are your R.A.'s, we are here for any of your Academic, Educational, and Social needs. Please feel free to knock on our door at any time."

Jack stood up. "And if you want to hear what they are going to say, but don't want to hear it from them, please knock on my door. I will be glad to fill you in." There were a couple of chuckles in the crowd. Jack looked like he felt quite proud of himself. I wasn't about to let him set a standard for running over Ashlyn and I on the first day. That was the mistake his R.A. made last year, and never could recover from it. Jack practically ran the floor.

"Thanks for your input Jack." I said rather sarcastically to him. Then to the others, "everyone, this is Jack. Jack has lived in residence for 3 years now. Normally people would not be here that long, but his daddy is someone pretty, let's say, special. So if he seems to know all the rules, that's because he has heard them several times. He should almost work here as an R.A., oh, but that's right - he applied twice, but didn't get it. It was your marks or something right Jack? Or was it attitude?"

Jack tried to give a cocky look, but his face read embarrassment. Ashlyn looked afraid. Everything stayed quiet for a moment. I spoke up first.

"Now one last thing, this is the 5th floor and it is a co-ed floor. So remember ladies and gentlemen, all washrooms and showers are also co-ed. Please don't take advantage of that. Spare all of us on the floor from having to listen to any 'extra curricular activities' going on behind the shower curtains. Now if the guys wouldn't mind coming with me, and the girls going with Ashlyn, we can go over the safe words for this year. I see the confused looks so let me elaborate. A safe word is a word that we decide on that can be used if any of you need our help trying to get out of a situation, and feel you can't directly ask us to assist. You say this word and we will know to remove you from the situation you are in. The girls and guys will have separate words. Then, once that is done, you are free for the evening."

Forty five minutes later, I was in my room. I had exactly one hour before our staff meeting, which would quickly lead into the busy evening of Frosh Week Pub Night number one. It was a night of no sleep, drunken jocks, and half dressed girls parading around the halls. Awesome!

I was becoming a little bummed. I had been back at the school for exactly 12 hours, and I had yet to see Lonny. He was stationed in the McGregor building. I was in the Allen. Really there wasn't much separating the two buildings, just a short hallway maybe 60 ft long. However, when it comes to Lonny, the room beside me is too far. Lonny and I have been friends since we were 5. His mother and mine were close friends. We had play dates together. We laugh, because even now, in our older years, we make sure we have a 'play date' at least once a month. I love him. Not many people have a guy in their life that they can genuinely say that they are totally in love with when they had never dated at all – yet! Over the past few years, being here at College together, we have gotten even closer. I want him. Unfortunately it seems he wants Jessica, his high school sweetheart and girlfriend of 6 years. She was a petite red head that was athletic and smart - and dearly loved by many. She seems to know when to smile, when to be sympathetic, and when to walk away, impressing everyone who crosses her path. Lucky for me, she goes to Jansen College. Three hours away.

I grabbed my best and tightest Levi's, put them on with my baby blue t-shirt with a frog on it asking quite playfully 'your pad or mine?' I hesitated. Took one last glance at my outfit, and then sadly covered it all with my ever so hot blue work vest. I decided to wear my hair up today. I loved it at this length, just long enough that the ponytail perks in a perfect V behind my head. The highlights light and dark brown, blended with a tinted red, mixed throughout the curls. I liked it, today at least.

Heading into the conference room, I couldn't help but feel like one of 19 lemmings that had gathered to find out the next bridge we were all going to toss ourselves off of. We all matched in clothes, and in exhausted facial expressions, except of course for Jen Lee, a 2nd year R.A, who always runs on high gear. We called her Mary Katherine Gallagher – after Molly Shannon's character on Saturday Night Live. Mary Katherine was a cheerleader that was always excited, jumping around haphazardly. The two characters are quite a match I tell you.

"Hey! Sade. Got your seat right here." Lonny said, patting the chair next to him. He kept us at the top of the oval table, so I could easily pop out of my chair and into an office seat. All the R.A.'s sat waiting, chatting amongst themselves, in no hurry to have this meeting started.

The door opened again and in walked Alex. With her was Elizabeth Warrender, the Residence Counsellor. Elizabeth was in charge of training us on such issues as sexual assault, drug addictions, suicide, grief and loss, and crisis management. Once a month she gives us a different session so that we are better trained to help our students with whatever situations come up. She was, in my opinion, one of the only people that can keep us interested, and willing to learn for several hours, with us wanting more when it was over. She was also in charge of counselling for all of our residence students, under almost any circumstance. The college integrated a one counsellor rule about five years ago. The rule kept one person in the know alleviating all other professional opinions. It was a 'too many cooks spoil the pot' kind of theory. She even counselled the staff, including me. The only way another counsellor would get involved was if we specifically needed a male therapist. Then Carl came over.

Elizabeth had it all. She was smart, she had a good job, she owned her own house, and she was beautiful. Possibly because of her job, she was also kind, empathetic, and interested. Interested in how you are and who you are. She was the perfect woman; the charismatic man's doll. That was why I felt that it was my year this year to set her up with father. She would be a perfect match for him - out with the old, in with the new. Father always told me that mistakes were okay to be made, as long as you corrected them somehow. Well, Jackie was my mistake, and I would correct that, not sure how, but I would. On his advice too, can't get any better than that.

Elizabeth always treated me like a friend. Which, in her case, being my counsellor, was probably not the best idea, but we managed. On my birthdays she would take me out for dinner. She would advise me on matters both on a professional level and on a personal level. Take Lonny for instance. She would always tell me the spiel about how two staff members could not date. She would then listen to me talk. Later she would tell me her opinion on how I could find out exactly my chances in regards to making him my boyfriend, and what she thought he was really thinking. It was wonderful. I had a great co-worker, and a great friend. Father had worked at the College for 16 years as a professor in the Athletics department. Elizabeth even counselled father after mother was killed. Well, not officially counselled, they went for dinner a lot, to 'talk.' I wanted another love for father, and I wanted it to be her.

"I'm tired, how about you guys?" Alex had a smile despite her question. In unison, we all responded with different answers to her question. She ignored the indifference and went on. "Most of you all know Elizabeth from last year. Even those of you who were students last year should know her." We all nodded and said hello. Lemmings I tell you.

"Elizabeth is here to get us prepared for tonight. It is the first pub night of the new school year, so we have a lot to cover." Elizabeth took the seat between Alex and I. I felt a bit nervous, breathless. My stomach twisted. Already I felt excitement over trying to set her up with father.

We sat in our meeting circle eating pizza and going over issues like under age drinking, the code of conduct, how to potentially spot the date rape drug in someone, and bullying - apparently it wasn't just for high school anymore. Two hours later we were done, and we were on our own. It was just us and the seven hundred energy sucking teenagers who would soon be feasting off the thrill of their first night on their own, in a college dorm.

* * * * * * * * * *

Every time I heard the elevator ding, I thought I would puke. With the ding, came an elevator full of drunken students, most likely carrying bottles we'd have to take and dump into an exceptionally large bucket that we lugged around with us. When they were stupid enough to come down with bottles, we were to take their whole drink and dump it, keeping the bottle as well. Once dumped, we would then usher the students outside through the front lobby door. Fun! Each time it took every ounce of strength not to grab the bottle and down its contents. It was Ashlyn and I at the lobby elevators in the McGregor building catching all the kids before they headed out to the bar. Last year we made almost eighty dollars in bottle returns, which we used for the end of the year social for the residents. We had Jen and Hal stationed in front of the Allen building elevators. We saw everyone who came from the Allen building since they had to pass us to get outside. We could tell some of the students that had their drink taken away. They weren't pleasant to us as they passed. Being disliked was a given with the job. Some students hated us without knowing us. Tonight, being the elevator police didn't help that fact, nor did the job of the other staff members who were busy walking the floors carrying the same large bucket as us.

The elevator doors opened again. Four girls and six guys climbed off. A smell came wafting out of the small enclosed space.

Ashlyn winced, and then smiled tightly "Old spice! Nice job guys, way to pick up the laaddiees." The tall guy punched the short one in his stubby arm. "I told you man." They all laughed. The short guy not showing any signs of embarrassment, replied, "Dude, that is how my father picked up my mother." We all laughed as they walked away.

"Man, Sadie, did you see that quiet one in the back? That dimple, how cute was he? He looks like that singer from Sum."

He did actually.

With the next crowd came Jack DeGraff, his younger brother Jefferson DeGraff, and three very young girls. None of the females, I would guess, were 19. Only the guys were carrying booze, nicely stored in plastic water bottles. All legal, so we let them pass. They stayed nearby informing us that they were waiting for others to come down and join them. We allowed them to stay in the lobby a little while. It was easier than fighting them to keep moving.

"Hey Sadie! Nice to see you back." It was J.P., one of the cleaning staff from the outside company the school hires to clean most of the residence. They took the bathrooms, kitchens, and office areas, while the student cleaners do the floors, carpets, walls, and windows. J.P. was kind, gentle, and patient. Many students teased him because he was different. He seemed a little slow with his thoughts, he got overly excited over small things, and had a tendency to talk in a very loud and toothy voice; spitting on most S's and T's in his sentence.

"Thanks J.P., you too. Working tonight eh? I hope you are well equipped. It is going to be a long night." I smiled at him.

"Don't worry Sadie, I am all set. I bought a new mop just for tonight." He laughed. "You should come by and see it later if you get some time. It's yellow."

"I will try to catch up with you later J.P. I can't say I ever saw a yellow mop." I gave him a wink and a nod that was meant to read the end of the conversation and turned my interest back to the dinging elevator in front of me and the two new bottles of beer I needed to dump.

Behind me Jack grabbed the one girl's arm, not hard enough to make her pull away, but hard enough to get my attention. I watched.

"Take this back up to your room, I will see you there later, when I return."

She stepped back a bit from Jack and laughed. "Do you think you own me now?"

"Don't I?"

She stared at him. What an ass! I wanted to scream to her encouraging words in support of hitting him! But I didn't. I sat and stewed. Did Jack really think that girls liked a guy who spoke to them in the way that he just did? No girl would put up with that.

The girl looked at him. She laughed again. Here it comes, would it be a right hook or a left jab?

"You can own me if you want to." She finally said smiling playfully, twisting a pinkie finger through her hair.

I was lost. I checked my ears for any abandoned cotton balls - none were present. She stepped into him, gave him a kiss, and said she would see him later, and then walked away.

"Bridgette, before you go, just be a good little girl and take this to your room for me. I will get it later." He handed her his drink. She took it, twirled around, and left towards the Allen Building hallway. The guys looked at Jack with adoration. His brother slapped him on his back. "She'll be nice and warmed up by the time you get back." And with that, they were gone. Not bothering anymore with the friends that they were waiting for. I just looked at Ashlyn. She shrugged her shoulder and mouthed 'whatever.'

Ding! The elevator sang again. I whipped around to see what came next, but instead of beer bearing students, it was him. It was Lonny and some of the students from his floor. My stomach dropped. This stomach dropping thing was getting annoying. Even more annoying was the fact that I wanted to grab him, pull him closer, and kiss him hard, long, and fast until he was out of breath – and I couldn't. I couldn't even kiss his lips.

"Hey Babe!" Or maybe I could. He stepped out of the elevator then leaned over and kissed my cheek. I had to settle this time.

He smiled probably one of the best smiles I ever saw. "I just got the new Johnny Depp and Helena Bonham Carter movie. Monday night, when this is all over, want to snuggle up with me and watch it?" I thought for a moment. The yes, yes, hell yes answer that I was screaming inside was not the one I wanted to leak out. So I grinned and replied, "Sure, sounds great."

"It's a date then, I'll bring the Nachos and Salsa." He walked away. I stared at his ass. I couldn't help it. I stared until he rounded the corner, or until Ashlyn spoke, not sure which one came first.

"Think you'll ever date him?"

"I sure hope so."

"Me too, get it over with will ya. Is he still with Jessica?" My eyebrow raise and head nod answered that for her.

We continued our elevator dance for another hour. The students waltzed out of the metal box, we glided for their drink, dumped it in the bucket, they swayed away. When that ended, we settled onto our floors entertaining the sober students who stayed, and awaiting the return of the drunken ones who'd left. Ashlyn and I relaxed in the lounge to watch some of the girls play Cranium. There were others in the hall playing dimes. Music was blaring from a dorm room but it was so loud we couldn't make out the artist. It was hard to enjoy. Kind of like being the only sober one at a rave party. The music and the fun just sounded like noise. It was several minutes before we heard it; loud agonizing shouting coming from the far hall.

"Did you hear that?" I asked. Ashlyn quickly stood up to go to the lounge door. I looked at her from a few feet away. All I could see was her boney hand wrapped around the door frame.

"Sadie, I think someone is yelling for help." She put her head back into the room with a slight deer caught in the headlights look on her face. "Do you want to go or should I?"

I immediately moved towards the door. "Lets both go."

I pushed myself down the hall as fast as I could. Ashlyn was trailing closely behind me. Now that we were far from the room with the blaring music the yelling seemed louder and more desperate. We rounded the corner to see a girl lying in the hallway on the floor. Two people who said that they had just arrived were surrounding her. A third was doing CPR. I jumped out of my chair and onto the floor. The girl was grey in the face with several scratches that looked fairly fresh. What the hell was going on? My heart was racing. My body was shaking. Please don't be dead. Please don't die. I asked the crowd to back up. Ashlyn pushed them back further. "What happened here? When did she go down?" I asked. No one knew. The crowd was bigger now. The Cranium girls had just joined the group to see what was going on. Others had come out of their rooms. I could still hear the music from down the hall. Although fainter, the voice was clear now. It was Marilynn Manson singing Beautiful People. I felt for a pulse, there was none. I checked her throat; it didn't look like anything was lodged inside. She seemed to have scratches on her arms, and one on her right cheek. Her cheek still bleeding a little, the skin was red and puffy.

"What do you need me to do?" Ashlyn asked.

"I need you to go get the Automatic Defibulator from the 3rd floor. It is in the white box on the wall. With the sign, you know, that has a heart with a lightening bolt in it? We can attach the machine to her and try to shock her heart back into beating."

"Yah, I know what you're talking about. I'll be back in a second."

"I always wondered what that was for." One of the cranium girls said to the other.

"Who has a cell phone?" I yelled. I didn't have mine on me.

One of the girls standing pulled hers out. "I do."

"Good. Your name?"

"Heather."

"Okay Heather. I need you to call 9-1-1."

I began two-person CPR assisting the other student who had already started it. Ashlyn was back in less than a minute. I attached the pads to her chest as per the instructions. The machine instructed people to move away from the body, and then instructed me to press the button to initiate the shock. I did.

I heard Heather relating the situation to the dispatcher on the phone.

"Do you know if she has any major allergies or medical conditions Sadie?"

"I wasn't told of any, and usually we are if they are serious."

"They want to know if she has a pulse?"

"No!" We were doing CPR for fuck's sakes. But I held my sarcasm in. "Tell them we have an AED and we are about to shock her heart for a second time."

She related my message. Three shocks later, her heart was beating again but her breaths were shallow and almost non-existent. I continued the assistive breathing part of CPR. Between breaths I looked at Ashlyn, "Call Alex. Tell her where we are, and that we called 9-1-1." I gave two more breaths. "Let her know she stopped breathing, and had no pulse, we are still doing CPR." I gave two more. "Tell Alex, that she is from our floor. Not sure of her last name right now, but the girl's first name is Bridgette."

MIRROR, MIRROR ON THE WALL

Red and Blue lights flashed off of Alex's face. Through my tear induced kaleidoscopic view I could see she was crying as well. Alex grabbed my hand. I squeezed hers then pulled my hand away. We stayed there, starring as the ambulance left. She wiped her face and spoke first.

"We better get in and fill out that report. We should have the papers done before Ashlyn returns from the hospital later. Good work tonight Sadie. You got her heart beating again. Saved that girls life, kid." She petted my head. "Do you know what happened?"

I took a deep breath. I was relieved, angry, and sad, all at the same time. "Not just me, one of my students too. Karen, I think her name is, started and assisted me with the CPR. As for what happened, I have an idea that is all."

She looked confused. "Care to elaborate?" She asked.

"Jack Degraff. He…" she cut me off at his name.

"Let's go into my office to finish this conversation." She turned and walked through the doors. I followed. Her walk was slow and deliberate in hopes of showing calmness to those still clearly upset over the night's events. Once inside, she had to address the crowd of students, informing them that the excitement was over for the night, that all would be addressed at a floor meeting the next day, and that the student would be fine. She stopped, talked to security, and talked briefly to the residence manager who was called in. When all information was both gathered and spread, she ushered me into her office.

It was dark inside. Just the lamp in the corner was leaking light into her office. The desk was the first thing to see entering the room. When she sat at it, her back was to the staff entrance door. The chairs for the students sat at the far wall. The black one was for the students meeting for assistance. The white one was reserved for all the students who came for disciplinary action. That chair was missing a peg. When the kids sat down, they would feel off balance. Alex believed this gave her a psychological advantage over them.

I tended to agree. Other than her chair, her office was organized, well decorated, and besides the secret evils of the white chair - quite inviting. I loved it.

"How are you?" She looked worried.

"I am okay." Not believing it myself.

"That was pretty wild, Sadie. You just started a heart."

I told her about what we saw when we got to the girl. How we did CPR on her and used the AED, until her pulse came back. I told her about what Ashlyn and I saw at the elevator an hour before we were called to her lifeless body on the ground. I also informed her about Jack, and how he had treated her, including the words they exchanged.

"And then?" She was hungry for more information.

"And then nothing." Wasn't that enough? "He caused this Alex." I told her about the scratches on her face and arm, and how they were fresh and still bleeding.

"Okay, Sadie, I'll admit the guy is a creep, but you didn't give me anything that would prove it was him. Did he give her drugs in front of you? Did she look intoxicated? Did you see them fight? You saw him leave, how could he have caused those scratches?"

"No, no, no and I don't know!"

I found her expression painful. She looked sorry for me. "I trust your instincts, really I do. I believe what you are feeling. But I am sorry Sadie, I will talk to him, but unless he admits something, I can't accuse him of this. Besides, we are not even sure what happened to Bridgette tonight."

I appreciated what she was saying. My head understood it. But I wanted him held responsible. I just knew it was him. It had to have been. At least I think it was. Arrghh! There was a knock on the door. Alex got up and answered it. It was Elizabeth.

I recognized my time to leave, "I'll get out," I said.

"No. She is here for you."

This was curious. Why for me? "Why?" I asked.

Alex sat down in her chair again. Elizabeth went to sit on the white chair.

"No" we both yelled. After a short explanation she happily took the black chair.

"I thought you could use someone to talk to. You have had a big night." Alex said.

"It wasn't that big. Besides this is what you've trained us for. Of course it was bound to happen at some point, to someone right?"

I rubbed my eyes. I wanted to dig a tunnel and crawl out of the room. A spoon, I needed a spoon. Alex always kept one in her desk drawer. I would reach for it. I would reach it and dig my way out. Just through to the other side of the wall – to the outside. That was fine. Fresh air would do me good. Great plan I. Except not only would they see me attempt this great challenge and wonder what the hell I was doing, but they would probably be retired and on their way to Florida or some other hot destination for the winter, by the time I have a decent size hole to crawl out of. Considering I would also have to fit my wheelchair through the opening. Shit!

I looked up. They were both giving me a look of pity. They seemed lost. They seemed lost in their own conversation. They were waiting for me to speak. I didn't. Alex put her head in her hands for a moment, sighed, and then lifted her head slowly. Her hands slid down her face, as if the pressure from the words she was speaking were what drew her head up from the pits of her hands.

"Sadie, I am worried about you. It is the first night and you already had someone die, and come back to life. From the moment the ambulance arrived and took over, you have been in an almost Zombie like state, a million miles away. I know you zone out. You told me as much last year. That is okay. That is how you deal. But if you need to zone, that means you are struggling with something. Am I right?"

I wasn't sure if she was asking me or Elizabeth, but I answered.

"You said it yourself Alex - that was a big thing. I am just reacting. I wouldn't be human if I didn't react. I am okay, I promise." I wasn't only trying to convince them. I was trying to convince myself. It wasn't working for them or me, and I knew it. What I didn't really know though, was how I felt. I just knew how I wanted to feel.

It was Elizabeth's turn.

"Sadie, all we are asking is that you just talk to us about this for a little while. We don't need to get in too deep. We just want to see where you stand on what happened. We understand, more than anyone else, what this situation might mean to you."

In an instant, this meeting made sense.

"If you want, I can leave so you and Elizabeth can talk privately. It doesn't bother me if you need some privacy." Alex was sincere. She meant well, but I didn't want her to go.

"No, you can stay. I just need a moment." We dropped into silence mode again. All three of us shifted in our seats within seconds of each other; chain shifting. Alex even began to re-organize the already perfectly placed papers on her desk.

The phone rang. Alex answered. She informed who ever was on the phone that she would be out in ten minutes and hung up.

"You have to go." I said relieved.

"Not yet." She replied.

Damn it! I thought this intervention, or whatever the hell they were going to call it, was over. If they really cared they would back off. This was so frustrating. Seriously, were they going to stay here until I cried, or yelled, or told them that I was damaged for life? What did I need to do to end this?

"Listen, I am okay. I just need to sit on what happened tonight. I need to let it sink in. Then I will talk, I promise." My face started to feel hot. I had to concentrate on my breathing pattern. "I wish you wouldn't treat me like I am so damn fragile. Would you do this to Ashlyn? Hal? Jen? Or is it just the disabled staff members that get the preferential treatment?"

"Now that isn't fair Sadie. Alex and I are worried about you. We care about *you*. It has nothing to do with you being in a wheelchair."

"But?"

"But it does have everything to do with your accident. The others don't have the past that you do. At least not that we know of."

The phone rang again. This time with a little less patience, Alex informed the caller that she would be out shortly, when she was finished doing what she was doing. She hung the phone up a little harder than last time, sat back and crossed one leg over the other.

"I fell down the stairs and broke my back. That is all MY accident was. Not related. Neither Bridgette nor I had stairs around us. I am good. She will be good. Alex needs to leave, and you need to go home." I pointed to each of them respectively. There! Over, I started towards the door.

"Not so fast," said Alex. "You are my first priority right now. I am not going anywhere." She leaned forward for emphasis. "And we all know that that is not the part of the accident we are talking about. I am talking about what happened to your mother in the situation."

It was like seeing the bus before it ran over you. I knew where this talk was headed. This wasn't the time. I didn't want to discuss it. They knew what I did, didn't they? I have always suspected that they had known, and now there was no denying it. It had caught up with me. Did father know too? Did he tell them? Images of the night my mother was murdered flashed through my head. The meeting I had with the stranger in the park and our exchange of money. The

31

door bell ringing, me letting him in. My mother screaming, and then her silence. And finally myself fleeing the scene, running from the man I invited home. Running and falling down the stairs. It pained me to remember. Why are they bringing this up? I wanted to hit them. Hurt them. Hug them. Cry inconsolably and tell them how very sorry I was that it happened. How since that night, I have been trying to make up for my mistakes. How I will never, ever, forgive myself. I wanted to beg them not to hate me. But the truth was - I hated myself.

"Please." I had a crying voice barely audible through gasping, sobbing breaths. Alex stood up and grabbed my face. Her hands were cold and clammy. She was shaking. Her opal ring was backwards on her finger. The gem felt warm against my cheek. She kissed my forehead. One of her tears dripped onto my eyebrow. I felt Elizabeth's hand on my back. They didn't hate me yet. They couldn't know. They still cared. I had to get out of there before they changed their minds. Before they asked more questions, and got more answers. It was one thing to know I killed my mother; it was another to know how.

"That is it. I am out of here." I pushed Alex away. I was crying harder now. I felt slightly panicked "This isn't about how I am doing. This is about your own curiosity. And it isn't about how I saved a girls' life. It is about how my Mother died. It's been six years, let her be dead. I'm trying to."

I pushed toward the exit. I chose the door that led to the R.A. staff room. I grabbed the handle and ripped the door open. The blinds on the tiny window crashed hard. It was as if they knew the effect I needed. They obliged my anger by hitting something for me. I owed the blinds a debt of gratitude.

"Sadie!" Alex called after me.

I kept going. I was free of them. Free of my past taking any more of my future. Alex was my boss and my friend and would stay that way as long as she didn't know. And Elizabeth would hopefully be father's future wife. She would never want to be if she knew the truth. They wouldn't.

The last thing I heard as I left the staff room was Elizabeth's soft voice. "No Alex, let her go. She'll be okay."

-4-

HE LOVES ME, HE LOVES ME NOT.

Have you ever spent an evening holding onto someone you love? More than that even, someone you desire. You lay together, snuggled, you in their armpit, their arms wrapped around you. A perfect fit. You felt how perfect it was by the sensations in your body. It was in the jumpiness that arose in your stomach. It was in the thrill of the sensation of something crawling up your spine, leaving goose-bumps in its wake. It was in the way, that no matter how hard you tried, you could not get close enough or hold tight enough to that person. It was perfect. Every fibre of your being wanted to look up and kiss the one you were with. Their neck, or their cheek, or their mouth, you didn't care. Because eventually, when the night was through, you would have wanted to take them all in, every ounce. You stopped yourself several times from looking up. You had to. If you were to look, you would not be able to reject the urge to kiss them. You were not that strong. You couldn't kiss them. They were taken, or you were. Maybe they were not interested in more than friendship, or maybe you could not bear the thought of rejection. That would hurt more than suffocating the craving. So you stayed still. You talked to them through mumbles, careful not to lift your head. You grabbed them tighter, to keep yourself sheltered. Deep inside you knew that having them, would be as likely as winning the Lotto; 1 in 13,983,816. That was how many combinations of the 6 number slots there could be. And see, you had so much time not kissing them that these were the things you figured out. That was how I spent my Monday evening with Lonny.

The movie had just ended. I sat up. "Johnny is so hot. I want one of the t-shirts that say 'Mrs. Depp' on it. Think people will believe it?"

Lonny laughed mockingly. I hit him in the arm with my long circular body pillow. He grabbed me, pulled me down to his chest, and rubbed his fist in my hair. I felt like his little sister. Not what I was going for.

"Did you see the product placement in that movie? I mean, holy crap, you would think they would all have the worst kidneys in the world. All they drank was Coke."

He sat up this time. Scratched his head and turned to me. "Did you know that Coca-Cola use to have cocaine in it? In the late 1800's."

"Shut up. It did not." I shouted. He cracked me up.

"Seriously, at first it was sold as a cure for sore throats, headaches, colds, sleeplessness, nervousness, and shit. It was a medicine and the patent had a small amount of cocaine. Like many other medicines at that time." He sat up straighter. He looked seriously excited to share his knowledge. I thought I could have eaten him up he looked so cute. He brushed his hair back. It was short. His brushing was more for emphasis than for actual benefit.

"Really?" Was all I could muster up.

"Yes. By the early 1900's, when the company found out about the dangers around cocaine use, the company immediately eliminated it from the drink. Eventually it became a soda, and well, you know how popular it is now."

"And drug free." I added, a little more than slightly sarcastic. "How did you find that out Mr. Know-it-all?"

He gave me an archaic smile. "My Uncle Tom!"

I couldn't hold my laugh in. I laughed harder than I had all summer. "Doesn't your uncle Tom have a bullet in his head? Which, might I add, he believes was implanted into him during World War Two by aliens."

"We weren't there. It could have happened." He retorted. We both collapsed onto the bed, our cackles louder now. I loved my time with Lonny. It was refreshing. Especially after the long week we had. The rest of Frosh Week was a lot calmer than the first night. Of course, nothing, in regards to Jack, was done about what happened with Bridgette. The doctors said she had an overdose of ecstasy, a common drug used by College students. We couldn't trace where she got it from, and we found no others on her or in her room. We were allowed to search due to our no drug policy. Unfortunately we could not search Jack's room, like I wanted, only Bridgette's. She was not talking about it either, beyond denying ever consciously taking the drug. Alex couldn't evict her from residence because there was no proof that she wasn't telling the truth. Until we could trace where the drug came from, she was a victim. Which was fine with me because I never believed it was hers in the first place. I didn't necessarily believe that she was forced to take it, but I didn't think she sat alone in her room, with her own stash, popping ecstasy pills for kicks either. Maybe I was naïve, time would tell.

As for the situation between Alex, Elizabeth, and I, well, none of us even mentioned it again. When our talk ended that night, it really ended. I completed my reports in my room alone that night, and slipped them under her door for her in the morning.

"What time do you want to do our first rounds?" Lonny asked, standing to put on his vest. We were on call together and had to do rounds around both buildings three times. We were making sure the rules were being followed and giving the other R.A.'s a chance to do things like sleep, and not worry about what was happening on their floors.

"Nine thirty? That's in twenty minutes or so. Are you leaving?" I was sad. Although I had the whole night ahead to see and spend time with him, I didn't want to see him leave now.

"Just running to the little boy's room, then down for a soda. Want anything? A Coke perhaps?" He asked with a giggle.

"No thanks."

"I'll grab the walkie-talkies and give one to security. Then I'll be back." He leaned over and kissed my cheek. Butterflies! "See you in a few." He turned to the door, opened it, and before exiting, smiled and winked in my direction. He was so hot. Bloody hell, I wanted him, crazy uncle and all!

* * * * * * * * * * *

All was quiet on the first and second round. Before the third round, we stopped into Hal's room and visited him and Piety. They were fighting over the lyrics to a James Brown song. We always tried not to get involved in their debates.

Entering Hal's room was like entering the 70's. His room was dark, with a coloured disco light turning in the far corner. It was slow to spin the red, yellow, and blue colours onto the wall. His bed was made up of sheets only, brown and yellow in colour. His wall hosted three posters. One of Jimmy Hendrix on stage, one of Janice Joplin getting onto a motorcycle, I think it was one of her album covers. The third was a rainbow coloured smiley face holding up a peace sign. His room was otherwise bare. He had a fridge that held no magnets. He had frames that held no pictures. And his counters were clean with not a lot of papers or books, just a computer and socks to decorate it.

"How are rounds going tonight?" Hal asked.

"Pretty good. Quiet." Lonny answered. "Most people got a little dose of reality when they started their classes this morning. Realized that partying is not all they are here for."

"Did you hear about Hal's rounds last night?" Piety asked as she got up from the bed and sat on Hal's lap. He was sitting in his desk chair. She smirked at him and wrapped her arms around his neck.

"No, what happened?" I asked.

She was all too willing to fill me in. She sat up straighter, her full body aimed in my direction. She smiled, her excitement surrounding the story was energizing. I felt like a school girl about to hear what the boy she had a crush on, just said about her.

"Okay, so you remember Cynthia from move in day?" Lonny and I looked at each other. I shrugged. "Was she the one with the over-bearing mother?" I asked.

"Close but no, it was an over-bearing Father. She was the over dressed one, jeans and sweatshirt, on a hot August day. Remember she was attached to her parents at the hip a goody-goody daddy's girl."

A bell went off in my head, a flashback to that day. "Oh yes, she is the one that cried for her parents not to leave right? Then when they started to, she got angry with them and said they didn't love her."

Piety got excited. Clapped her hands and did a slight momentary bounce up off of Hal's lap. "Yes, that's her." She continued to stand. "Okay, well, remember she like cried for three days or something. Upset that her parents had left her here. She was such a suck. Although I think her dad even asked Jen to call him if his daughter ever needed anything. Sad really. I mean, she's in College now. Don't you think that would be the perfect time to take the nipple out of the mouth? I mean come on. Kids these days don't know how to function on their own. Can you imagine that a century ago girls were married at age fourteen! They crossed towns with their family on foot. Now they can't even go a half an hour away from home without needing Daddy to move in next door."

Piety had a way of running away with a story. I tried to steer her back. "So what happened with her last night?"

It worked. She sat back down again and kicked a leg up onto Hal's lap. She was going for effect. She spoke slower.

"Weeelll. Guess who Hal caught in a room, macking with three different guys, on three separate occasions?"

I didn't get it. "What?"

Lonny apparently understood. He elaborated, but politely directed his comments to Hal. "So each round, you found her in a different guy's room, with a different guy?" He laughed. "This is good."

Ah, now I got it. Slow on the up-take, but I got it. "If only daddy could see her now. Maybe we should get Jen to call him and give him the news." We all chuckled. We shouldn't have. I felt slightly remorseful but in this job, you have to find your kicks where you can. "So nine thirty, eleven thirty, and one, busy girl. Who were the guys?"

Hal shrugged. "Not sure, not so good with names yet. Do you remember the jocks that like to hang out in the lobby to watch the others return from the bar? One of those guys."

Before I could answer him, and clarify who he was talking about, I heard the *beep-beep* of the walkie-talkie, and Alex's voice speaking through.

"Lonny? Sadie? Are you there?"

"We're here." I answered. She must have been at the security desk using their two-ways.

"When you get a second, can you come to my room please?"

"Be there in five." I responded.

"So will I. Actually make it ten, I have something to grab before I get there." She replied.

Ten minutes later, Lonny got up from the bed. "Sorry guys, we have to run." They didn't care. I think they were spending some alone time before we showed up anyway. I had a feeling that as soon as we left, they would continue their quest. Not sure why, but the thought of them spending time alone together really irritated me. They snuggled, and it led to a relationship. Lonny and I snuggled and it led to nothing. Maybe not irritation, maybe it was jealousy. I couldn't decide.

-5-

THREE TO GET READY.

Alex's room was on the 3rd floor of the Allen building. It was important that the Resident Life Coordinator remained on campus as much as possible. She was the first point of contact in a crisis, after the R.A.'s. That was why most R.L.C.'s were single. They get a small one bedroom apartment, in the middle of a residence that houses almost 800 students. At least that was how it was at Greenbury. This year, her neighbour right across the hall was Madison Harmen, father's, current girlfriend's daughter. Joyous! I didn't like her. I tried to convince Alex to continuously bang three times on Madison's door, at every hour of the night on weeknights to wake her up, just because she could. But sadly she said no.

I knocked on Alex's door. A cute sign was placed on the door's middle. It said 'only those who are challenged in some way may enter this room. I invite difference only, I reject perfection.' She opened her door. She was in her fluffy and very comfortable looking pyjamas. Her pants were red, with white polka dots on them. Her top had a rabbit with a large tail, matching the polka dots and it read: *somebunny loves me*. It was cute.

"Thanks for coming guys, mind the jammies. I needed to get comfy. Bet I am your first boss you have ever seen in her p.j.'s."

"Surprisingly no, but that is a whole different story." Lonny confessed. We smiled. I playfully slapped him in the hip. I didn't want to know the rest.

We walked into her room. It was very cool looking, for reconstructed dorm rooms. Three different rooms went into making this one. They knocked down the walls and rebuilt. She had a bathroom that was big enough for a shower, a sink, and a toilet. No tub would fit. The living room hosted her 32 inch flat screen television, a stand for DVD's, and a stereo. The couch was placed in the middle of the room. Behind the couch, in the left-over space, was a make-shift dinning room with a table that was set for four. The wall behind the table was actually half windows, half being the top half of the wall. To the far left was her kitchen. It was small but it served its purpose. Her bedroom was to your immediate right upon entering the room. The bedroom doors were closet style doors. They were made of small pieces of wood that fanned from the top of the frame to the floor. All her walls were light blue, very faint in colour.

    I wheeled in. She moved a large fake green plant so I had room. I plopped myself down on the couch. It was comfortable. It was inviting. It felt like it could easily become someone's favourite hide out from the residence and all its inhabitants. I could see myself being one of those 'someone's'. I already wanted to stay and hide out. Lonny took my wheelchair as a seat.

    "What's up?" I asked.

    "I need some help with a couple of things. First the Residence Life Conference this year is in January at Jansen College, just west of Toronto." We both nodded. We were familiar with the College because of Jessica, Lonny's girlfriend. "I can only bring twelve of you. That means seven have to stay. Not sure how to pick who should come and who shouldn't. So any future thoughts there would be helpful." She coughed a little then grabbed her cup of tea from the side table, took a sip, and placed it back down. The whole time she held a hand up to notify us there was more to her talk. It was coming. Lonny stayed silent and still. I looked around the room. After a moment, and a hard swallow, she continued. My attention came back to her. "When it comes to you both, one will have to stay behind being that you two are the two senior staff members. Especially since Elizabeth will not be at the school either, she will be with us on conference. Security will take my place. So we need to think about who will stay and who will go."

    We looked at each other. Initially I wanted to go if Lonny went. Stay if he stayed. But that wouldn't work. I put that thought aside, and my stomach instantly said that I wanted to go. I verbalized that. Unfortunately, so did Lonny, especially since it was Jessica's college that was holding the conference.

    "Guess we have a fight on our hands eh, Sade. Race you for it, by foot." He giggled. He was proud of that one.

    "Sure, then we race in chairs after for the real winner. You can have the kitchen chair." I felt equally as proud. Alex seemed to be enjoying our banter because she held her cup to her mouth to take a drink, yet she hadn't. She just held it up, and peeked her eyes over the edge. She seemed to be watching a tennis match because both her eyes bounced from Lonny to me, and back again.

    "Well, we can both prepare a presentation, and the one that gets accepted into the conference, is the one of us that gets to go. How does that sound?" I offered.

"That works," replied Lonny.

"And what if both or neither one of you gets accepted?" Alex asked, always the devils advocate.

"Then it is back to the races I guess," was the only suggestion I had. We could cross the other bridge when we got to it. Meanwhile, I would put together the best damn presentation I could, so I could go. I enjoyed the conference.

"Did you know that the first wheelchair was built over 4 centuries ago for some Phillip the Second for Italy or Spain or something like that," Lonny shared.

"How would you know this?"

"I looked it up"

"You mean made it up?" I laughed.

"No. I looked it up. It was called the invalids chair." He defended himself.

"Ugh! I hate that name. How awful!"

"I'm just saying," he laughed.

Alex got up and went to the kitchen. "There is more to discuss. Do either of you want a tea?" She poured another one for herself. I said yes. She grabbed me a mug from her cupboard. A Greenbury College mug, how fitting. She brought over my tea, the milk and sugar already in; she knew how I took it. She returned to the kitchen. Lonny and I thumbed through her photo album we found on the side table nearest us. There were pictures of Alex from her younger years. Also inside, were pictures of her parents, her brother, his wife and their three kids. The book also included many pictures of her and her friends.

"Is that your father?" Lonny asked me perplexed.

"Yes. Alex and my father were high school sweethearts. They dated for like four years, before my father met my mother. They broke up when they went to college. Alex went to Alberta for school."

She came back and handed us a plate of double stuffed Oreo cookies.

"I didn't know that you and Jason knew each other from before." He said to Alex. "How did I not know this Sade, I know everything about you. So I thought."

"Maybe, but this isn't about me, it is about my dad."

"Well he is your dad, it affects you."

I shrugged realizing he was trying hard to make his point.

"I'm an international woman of mystery, I guess."

"We were going to try to get through the four years of College and then rekindle our old romance, but..." Alex added and then trailed off on.

"But my dad fell in love with my mother. Right?"

A strained smiled crossed her face. "Right. I don't blame him. It was hard being so far away." Her face wasn't as convincing as her words.

She shifted and grabbed her tea from the side table. "Now, not this weekend, but the one after, on Saturday, I need to throw a dinner party for the Residence Manager and his wife, the Dean of Student Services and her husband, and the head of International Student Affairs." She was trying to change the subject. It worked. "I must have been drunk at the time, but I told them I would cook, and fit them into this small room. I need your help. I will be in a meeting earlier that day. I need some help to get things prepared."

"Count us in." I said stuffing another cookie into my mouth. Feeling honoured that she asked. Although technically she didn't.

"Great! It is a late dinner. Can you be here for six? They are showing up at seven thirty."

"I have a great recipe for a vanilla walnut cake. My mother used to always make it for my birthday. If you want, I can come make it for you for that night?"

She seemed shocked. I was insulted. I could cook. I mean I once burnt water, and I always cook my eggs too hard. But cake I can do. Believe me.

"Err...how about giving me the recipe and I can make it early? Then the room won't get so hot. Besides I need your help with getting this place organized." I had a feeling she was making it up as she went, like trying to fake confidence in my skills to spare my feelings. But I obliged by nodding okay. "Speaking of cake, your birthday is coming up isn't it?" Alex asked me.

"Two weeks, today actually. It's a Tuesday."

"Remind me when it is close." She said. "We will go have lunch."

We agreed to a time for us to show up that Saturday and then finished our tea and cookies. It was almost time for our next rounds. As we left I thought about the great presentation I was about to create, and how I could use it to get father and Elizabeth together. I had done a match-up before, with other women. I knew I could do it again. Number eight had to be the one. Elizabeth was already going to the conference. I just had to figure out a way to get father there. And I knew just who to ask for help with that.

* * * * * * * * * * *

The next day after my 9 a.m. telecommunications class, I returned to the residence to see Alex. I went the route through the R.A. office to get to her door. She was in with the student that Lonny and I had caught smoking in his dorm room the night before. He was seated in the white chair. Hopefully he wouldn't get her in a mood. I needed her fresh and happy to help me with my endeavour. I grabbed my mail from the mailbox, sat on the couch, and read it. Jen Lee came in, danced in actually.

"Hey Mary Katherine, how she be?" I asked.

"Alright I guess. Things are like, so crazy right now. All my classes are giving out major homework already. Seriously, like isn't there enough days left in the year that they can do that? Give me a break. It is the first week." She really was a whiner.

"It's funny how they want you to learn and all eh?" I couldn't help myself. I laughed so she wouldn't feel my quick jab at her. She laughed back.

"The bastards." She teased back.

Jen grabbed her mail and sat next to me.

"Did you see the new floor reports we have to do? There is a part for maintenance, for washroom cleanliness, and for security checks. I think it is so great." She stretched out the word so, so it sounded like sooooo. "We can actually, like put in our own input now."

Please shoot me. "I did see that, that's great." I said through clenched teeth. I got back into my chair and looked into Alex's office. The kid was still there. Tristen and Sandy came into the room. I said a quick and silent prayer to God, thanking him for the distraction of others, then said hello. I couldn't handle another five minutes of hearing the word 'like'. She was a great girl, but my goodness, I enjoyed her more when she was silent. For a short little girl, with a shaved head, she sure commands a presence when she was in a room.

"Wad up?" Tristen announced to the room, to no one in particular.

"Alex busy?"

"Yes. And I am next." I didn't want to wait too long to get my plan going.

The R.A. door opened again. Ashlyn came in, receiving her

books from a guy in the hall.

"Thanks Phillip, I will be sure to pass it on to Alex." She shut the door behind her then looked at me. "Quite handy, that little fellow. Already wants to be an R.A. next year. Asked if I could pass that on to Alex. I think I could play this out a little. Have a little helper all year. If he wants to kiss an ass, I'll be glad to bend over." We all laughed.

Tristen placed his chubby hand on Ashlyn's shoulder. "I may need to get in on this action a little." He said.

"No way man, he's all mine."

There was a rap on the door. Sandy answered it. "Ashlyn it is for you. It is Jack and Jefferson DeGraff."

Why was he here? Why was he asking for Ashlyn? She looked at me confused. I shrugged my shoulders. I had no clue. She got up and stepped into the hall to talk to him. I didn't like the guy. I didn't trust the guy. He was always up to something. His brother seemed to be his opposite. Jefferson was new to the school this year. He was a first year. He seemed quiet, and shy. He had his moments, when he was around his brother and their friends when he joked and spoke louder than his norm. But other than that, he seemed a little reserved. They looked alike, except Jefferson was very blond, and had less bulging muscle. Jefferson I could handle. Jack, I was so over. Ashlyn returned after five minutes.

"What was that all about?" I asked.

She waited until the door shut fully. Her face was long and still. "Jack wanted to know how Bridgette was."

"Like he even cares." I was unimpressed.

"He also wants us to let him decorate her room for when she returns." Said Ashlyn.

"Like that is going to happen." I knew we didn't have to worry about appeasing him on that request. We wouldn't be allowed to let him in, even if we did want to.

Ashlyn grabbed her mail and headed back towards the door. "Remind me please, if I am ever in a debate over why women should swallow, that I should take his picture for my argument. Cause his momma should have swallowed him." She opened the door and left. The room instantly erupted in laughter.

Alex was still in with the student. "She's all yours Tristen. I am out of here. I'll try again later." I opened the door to catch up with Ashlyn. I had to get to my room. In Jen's words: I had like a ton of planning to do, like before my next class.

43

-6-

DON'T FORGET THE TURKEY DROP.

Twenty four hours later I found myself in the same position that I left the RA lounge in - waiting for Alex to be done with a student. This time though, I was alone in the room. My Film Production class was cancelled, so it left me with a 2 hour block of time. I had been thinking all night about what I was going to do to get father on the trip to the conference with us, providing of course that my presentation got accepted. That was the problem, to think of a topic good enough that the conference committee would approve me to come be a part of the presentations, but also include an element that would get my father involved. The one idea I came up with was a presentation on disabilities in residence, where the first portion could be on educational information that offered awareness on different disabilities; with enlightenment on both disabled students and co-workers perspectives. The second portion would include an obstacle course where able bodied people, R.A's from all Residences, would try to manoeuvre around several items in the course, to get an idea of what it might be like to be in a wheelchair doing daily tasks. This was where I would include father. I would get him to create the obstacle course, mostly by adding a home-built ramp and posts for people to manoeuvre the chair around. Hopefully father would see the importance of him coming to bring the course hardware and to set it up for us before our presentation time. The idea was that we couldn't travel with it put together.

    I decided to sit down on the couch and stretch my legs by placing them up on my wheelchair cushion. The surest way of getting into an appointment or getting to see someone arrive quicker I thought, was to make myself less easily available. Several times I have been waiting for someone to call or come over, and the phone or door bell didn't ring until I got on the toilet to pee, or decided to change my clothes. I was hoping I would have the same luck by removing myself from my chair.

    I leaned my head straight back and let out a large sigh. I was tired. Between school, Jack, Lonny, this presentation, and my father, my head was full. Full and exhausted from thinking. I needed it all to be done. I spent a moment imagining my perfect world of Jack leaving residence, Lonny leaving Jessica, my presentation being accepted and a hit, and father of course, seeing Elizabeth as the same intelligent, beautiful match that I did. I wanted them together. They would be good together. I was sure father would see it. I just had to get him to open his eyes.

The back door to Alex's office swung open. "Come on in Sadie, I am free."

I went in and sat on the black chair after declining Alex's offer of removing it to make more room for me in my chair. I would rather be comfortable in a plush office chair and push my wheelchair to the corner than sit in it and have her furniture hanging outside the room.

"You look stressed. Are you okay?" I asked Alex. Her face was stretched down. She wore her coat over her shoulders in an attempt to warm up. Alex usually felt cold when she was frustrated or tired. It was almost as if her emotions could solely stop her circulation.

"I am. It's two things really. First, I just had a meeting with one of Wanda's students, a young girl who is having a lot of problems with cutting her arms - mostly just scratches right now. Wanda has been counselling Calista up to today, but the kid seems to be getting worse which tells me she is in the height of whatever she is trying to cope with. Last night Wanda went to check up on her after she had a fight with another student, and Calista was bleeding all down her arm. Nothing deep or fatally dangerous but worse than it has previously been."

"Scary stuff. It just takes the wrong cut in the wrong area, with a little more pressure then you realize and you're in a lot of trouble." I added. "Is she seeing Elizabeth in counselling?"

Alex sat back in her chair and cracked her neck on either side. "Well that is what I was talking to her about. I had to inform her that I was aware of the situation and that I felt she would need to go to see Elizabeth at least twice a week. Up to now we just took her word for it that she was going. Now it has to be mandatory to stay in residence. Elizabeth won't share with me what they talked about but she will keep me abreast of her appointment adherence."

"Good!" I agreed, "I think that is exactly what is needed."

She sucked in the left corner of her bottom lip with a look that said she wasn't as sure as I was that this would be enough to help this young girl. "Well, according to Elizabeth, mandatory counselling doesn't work. You can make a kid show up but you can't make them talk. But this way, at least I know she is going and has a chance of talking. Elizabeth did inform me though that if Calista just wants her to sign the paper than she will. She is the expert in this so I won't argue. I am not as informed on cutters as I should be, I would like to set up a workshop for us to educate ourselves a little more."

I smiled and nodded approval, not that she needed it. "What's the other thing?"

"The other what?" She asked puzzled.

"You said there were two things stressing you out. What is the other?"

She smiled. "Right, sorry. The other thing is this potential strike with the College support workers. It looks like they may go on strike. There is still three months on their contracts but the negotiation doesn't seem to be going all to well. By Christmas they could be on the picket line."

"Wow, that's big. How will that affect us here at residence?"

"Well," she sighed. "It will mean that our cafeteria staff will be on strike, leaving the students to run things in the kitchen. It would also mean the cleaning staff are out, again leaving students in charge of all the housekeeping."

"A little scary, doncha think?" I laughed lightly.

"A little yes. But I am sure you are not here to discuss co-workers nor students. How can I help you out?"

I pulled open my backpack and pulled out my writing pad. "I want to discuss the conference with you. I also need your help with something and I am hoping I could talk to you about it not as a boss, but as someone I trust and respect." I winced with a little fear of her response.

Alex smiled. She offered me an oatmeal cookie from the half eaten, open package on her desk. "Now there's a loaded sentence. I am both flattered and a little concerned." She laughed. It was nice to see her relaxing. I did the same.

"Don't be afraid." I took the snack. "I just wanted to know if my father is able to come to the conference with us?"

She looked at me with confusion. "I am sure he can. I need to have a few staff members to drive the vans, two per vehicle, so I can add him on. May I ask why?"

I debated if I should tell her all about how I wanted to try to set up my father and Elizabeth together, how I planned on getting both of them down there to the conference in hopes of them spending some much needed fun time with each other. They were friends already so they would hang out. I was confident of that. I wasn't sure how Alex would react but I decided to share it all anyways. I also deliberated telling her the real story about what happened to mother. My deepest secret of how I was responsible for her murder. I needed her to know this so she would understand just how important it was to me to get my father happy and in love with another woman. Not like he was with Jackie, I was looking for him to have something more healthy and loving. I decided to share just the former and not the latter. Baby steps I thought. First see how she reacted to my plan and then maybe I would share the rest.

"So you want to set up your father with Elizabeth. Isn't your father dating someone?" She looked half disinterested half amused.

"Sort of. She's a bitch, even dad thinks so. You know Madison? Well she is a mini Jackie." Alex nodded understanding. "Jackie is also gone on an exchange for work to Spain. She won't be back until March. That gives me plenty of time to help him find someone better."

"You have listened to yourself right Sadie?" Her face changed from amused to concern.

"I need you to understand how important this is to me Alex. He needs someone. He needs a caring, loving woman in that house." I sounded almost desperate, I knew it, yet I kept going. "You know my father. You know how much in love he was with my Mother." I stopped. They look on Alex's face told me I had just hit an emotional spot. Years ago, father ended his long term relationship with Alex because he was so in love with my mother. "I forgot. Sorry."

She leaned forward. Her eyes wet a little and her mouth softened. "That's okay. It was twenty some years ago. And yes, I do know how much he loved her. But she is gone now, and he is a grown man Sadie. He should be capable of making his own decisions." She sat back again. "You're playing with peoples lives here." I was positive now that I would not share with her the rest of my secret. She would not understand. She would call me a murderer and a manipulator and never speak to me again. She would tell my father and he would never forgive me, nor would he ever fall in love again. We would all end up alone, and it would be my fault. I would never be able to make up for any past errors. I made a mistake even now in telling Alex this much. I was sure of that, until Alex finished her speech.

"However," She smiled. "If this is what you want to do. And if it is that important to you, then I am behind you one hundred percent."

I smiled in relief. "Thank you."

She returned my grin. "You're welcome." She paused. "I will not lie or manipulate though. That is not my game. We will have to do this the honest way, okay?"

"Deal." I got back into my chair and wheeled to her side. Wrapping my arms around her neck I gave her a huge hug. "You won't regret this, I promise. My dad will be happy, and that is all that is important."

"Well, you better get working on that presentation and hope that it gets accepted to the conference. That is your step number one. Your proposal is due this Friday."

I knew that was my main obstacle at the moment. Unfortunately it was also an obstacle I had to compete with Lonny for. It saddened me that he could not be a part of the conference if I was.

"Thanks Alex. I knew I could count on you." I smiled and left her office. I had some presentation work to do, and a father to convince to build a ramp or two.

* * * * * * * * * *

"The important thing to remember is that the majority of kids who become 'cutters' are not suicidal. They cut to punish, to relieve, and to express pain or emotions they can't get out other ways. Some do it for attention, but not most. Most do it to cope."

It was Friday night, a week later and we were having our residence workshop with counselling. Elizabeth comes in with a different topic every month. This month, due to recent events, was about Cutters. Cutters are kids who would express their anger or hurt by marking up their arms mostly, or other body parts, with a knife, safety pin, protractor, razor, etcetera, with ambitions of feeling better internally. Some kids would explain it was like a punishment they could give themselves. Others said it was quite simply a need to get the outside pain to reflect the inside pain, a validation of sorts. Whatever the reason, to the individual it was not something that was easily solved. The reasoning behind each case was relative to the person.

"So, you say that they are not suicidal, how is that possible? They are cutting themselves, mostly drawing blood, and quite typically right around their wrist area. How is that not being suicidal?" Ashlyn directed these questions to Elizabeth. "And if they aren't really suicidal, what is the main concern?"

Elizabeth sat down. Up until then she had been standing to get better range with her voice. She seemed very presentation-like in her demeanour. Now she was relaxed. She was in thought. She was serious.

"Some may be suicidal. Without treatment, cutting may not be enough, and they may get more and more into hurting themselves. They may need more punishment, which could mean suicide. But that isn't why cutters are cutters." She paused for affect. "Cutters want to express, to hurt. Death is not the result they are searching for. The fear we have, as people who are in direct contact with these kids, who work with them on a more personal level, and who see them everyday, is that just once, they will cut the wrong place, or press too hard and do some potentially damaging and fatal cuts. I remember once I asked a girl who was a cutter how she had the courage to cut, to hurt her self. I told her that I could see that it would hurt. She replied to me by saying, you should see how much it hurts inside when I don't cut."

She stood back up again. "The counselling for these kids should come from professionals, like me; however, as I said, you guys will be the first on the scene if anything goes wrong. You need to know where their emotional state may be, and have a little understanding into why they do what they do."

"That sounds a little scary for us to be dealing with. How many kids on average are cutters?" Wanda asked.

"More than you would expect," replied Elizabeth. "A lot of kids will exhibit cutting in a mild form sometime over their teen years. Only a few bring it to a dangerous or habitual level. But you have to also remember another problem. A lot of times kids are cutting with materials that are not sterile and probably more times than not, are dirty."

"I get all that, I guess," said Hal, "but what about the students who are just doing it for the attention? How do we deal with them?"

"Well just looking for attention is a problem too right? If they are looking for it, it must mean that they need it and are not getting it from their own supports. We need to help them just the same. It is a cry for help and not everyone can ask for it. Sometimes they have to make you see their needs, not hear them."

The talk went on for another hour so we could cover prevention and assistance in helping kids to find other distractions to deal with their sadness and stress. It was an informative meeting, Wanda of course also helped with sharing some of what she had been dealing with, with Calista.

When the cutting workshop was over Elizabeth covered one more topic - turkey drop. Turkey drop was the famously coined expression for the week after Thanksgiving. Most of the students went home for the holiday which was their first time back to their towns since they started school in August. A lot of these students had boyfriends or girlfriends back home when they left. Every year several boys and girls return home to their loved ones to find that they have been dumped, or replaced by their not so loyal other half. The week after Thanksgiving was traditionally one of the highest ranking weeks for drug and alcohol abuse, counselling, school drop outs, and even suicide attempts, among college residents over any other academic week. This was mostly due to the number of students who got dropped over the holidays – hence the name - turkey drop. Thanksgiving was a week away, preparation time was now.

"I guess that about sums it all up. Thanks guys for spending your Friday night with Elizabeth and I, and please don't forget to hand me your presentation proposals for this years conference. I will be driving them up to the courier tomorrow so they make it to Toronto on time for Tuesday." Alex shook Elizabeth's hand and thanked her.

Before handing in his proposal Lonny ribbed me a little about hoping the best 'man' wins. I chuckled but informed him that I wasn't worried at all. I knew that this 'woman,' was going to do just fine.

I handed mine over to Alex. She smiled and said that she was excited to read it over. "Don't forget tomorrow, Sadie. You and Lonny said you could come over to help me with that dinner. We are still on, right?"

"Absolutely," I answered, and headed out the door of the meeting room. I only got a few pushes in when I came face to face with my dad.

"Hey Tootie! I have perfect timing I see."

"Dad!" I reached up and gave him a hug. I was happy to see him. My father had called me Tootie since I was a child. I use to love trains. I was more than a little obsessed with them. I would go around the house crying toot-toot as I held my train in the air. That was it, that was what started the nickname, and I haven't lost it since - with my family at least.

"I know this is last minute, but I was hoping I could borrow you for the rest of the evening. Maybe we could go for a drink and a late bar snack?"

"Sure, that sounds great. How did you know I was here?"

Father explained how Elizabeth had informed him that she would be with us tonight to do the workshop, and how he figured it would be a great time to come over and spend some time with me. I didn't buy the fact that he wanted to just spend some time with me, considering it was a Friday evening; however, I could not concentrate on other reasons that it could have been. My mind was too busy focusing on the fact that obviously he and Elizabeth had been talking together or even spending time together earlier. That excited me most of all. I was in the middle of picturing their perfect afternoon together when I was interrupted by Alex leaving the room.

"Hi Jason! Long time no see. I heard you were working at the North Campus this year." She hesitated then said slowly. "You look really good, how have you been?"

My dad seemed a little squeamish. He cracked an awkward smile. "Thank you, you look great yourself Graham. I have been quite great, and loving the new job. It's great. Just here taking Sadie out for a drink tonight for some father daughter time." Alex smiled, "that's…er…great…Jason, nice to see you. You two have fun tonight." With that she was off. We watched her walk down the hall. I had many questions, the name Graham for one, but little time to ask.

"First day talking dad? Could you have said great anymore times in that sentence?" I laughed. He smirked.

"That bad eh?" I said yes, and then we laughed and left.

* * * * * * * * * * *

We walked across the parking lot to the Blue Pig, a restaurant and pub at Greenbury. It was busy in the bar part but pretty free in the dinner table area. That was where we sat. Father drank a rye on the rocks and I had a Coors light in the bottle. I was not a draft girl at all.

"So what's really up Dad?" I asked as I munched on the Spinach and Cheese dip we ordered.

"Am I that obvious? I thought that maybe I could get away with just casually adding my news into the conversation." He looked almost impish in the face.

"Ha! I know you better than you think. Now spill it old man."

What came out of my father's mouth next was nothing I would have ever guessed would have happened so soon. But it did. He explained to me how he and Jackie had called it quits already. She called him last night and informed him that she had fallen in love with a physical therapist from Spain, and she and he were planning a future together. She went on to tell Dad that they just didn't have the spark to get them any further than where they were, and that this was best for both of them.

"What did you say to that?"

"What do you say Sadie? I am not someone's second choice. Besides, as great as she is, was, she's not my type. We didn't enjoy the same things. You and your happiness is all we had in common."

I almost choked on the last line but I tried to keep my thoughts just that, thoughts. "I am sorry dad."

"Thanks. But no need to worry, I'll be fine. This is for the good anyway. I just wanted to make sure I told you before you heard it from Madison. I am not sure when she is going to be told by her mother."

I appreciated that, but was still pretty shocked that father really had no idea how Jackie and I felt about each other over the last few months. We loathed each other, constantly fighting over every little thing - both of us, obviously deserving an Emmy for our award winning acting abilities in front of my dad.

I gave my dad my best 'keep your chin up' look. "Just remember dad that every new beginning comes at the expense of an old new beginnings end."

And the new beginning I had in mind for him, for us, was not one with Jackie in it.

-7-

IT'S MY PARTY AND I WILL CRY IF I WANT TO.

The next morning I called Alex before her meeting just to make double sure that she didn't want me to come over and make mother's walnut cake. She declined again. Fair enough. I got myself showered, dressed, and called Piety to go out to the mall for awhile. An hour later she was knocking at my door.

"Your car or mine?" She inquired.

We decided that I would drive, and set off for a few hours of shopping and good ole fashioned girl talk. At the mall I bought a pair of jeans and a handbag. Piety indulged herself in some Clinique make-up and shoes from Transit. We topped the day off by going to the Cinnamon Joint and stuffing our faces with mini caramel pecan frosted buns.

I kept my eye on the time while we were gone. I had a date to meet Lonny just before we went to Alex's party. I didn't want to be late to see him. I knew that I might never have a chance to be with him romantically; however, that didn't mean I was going to waste the time that I could be around him.

"Would you stop looking at your watch?" Piety scolded.

"I can't help it. I just want to make sure that I get everything done on time. You know what it is like when it comes to Lonny."

Piety did. She was the only one who knew how I really felt about Lonny. Everyone thought that we should be together because of how much time we spent together, but I would always counter that with a comment on us being just friends and Lonny being with Jessica for the past 6 years. That would be acceptable for the individual asking the question. Piety knew different. She knew that I was completely in love with him. She knew that I wanted him and Jessica to break up. She also knew that every time I said we were just friends, my nose grew a little.

"Things will be fine Sadie, believe me. Now let's run before it is too late. I thought you wanted to stop and pick up some beer before we get back to res.?"

It was 5:15 and I was on my way over to Lonny's room when the

53

phone rang. I picked it up to hear Lonny's voice on the other end. "Change of plans slightly Sade. Looks like we will have to dress up a little instead of wearing our scrubs to cook. Alex called and asked if we would also stay for dinner. She is a little nervous and could use the extra back up conversation from people she is more comfortable with. Some people being us. I spoke for you and said we would be there, I hope you don't mind."

"Of course, I don't. That's fine. I am in. I will change and be right down. I am going to make a stop at Piety's room to grab my six pack of beer that she picked up earlier for me for Alex's, and then I will be there. Do you think that would be trashy to the College biggies if I showed up with a case of beer?"

"It's a six pack, Sade. I think your reputation will survive."

I hung up the phone and immediately started to fuss over the state of my hair. I changed into my best dinner dress, put on a necklace and black leathered boots as accessories, and headed out on my way.

Lonny and I had a drink in his room before we went to Alex's. He offered me a bottle of Vodka to bring with us since Piety was not in her room or in Hal's to pass me my case of Coors. I declined. I always thought of beer representing wanting to have a few social drinks, while hard liqueur was more of a representation of wanting to get smashed. Not an image I want others to have of me.

"What are we cooking tonight, do you know?" I asked Lonny. He was speaking to Alex this morning.

"I think that she has a lasagne on and we are to help her with the appetizers, salads, cheese and pickle plates, you know, shit like that."

"So, no cooking at all then, just prepping for the big dinner."

"Looks like it, and organizing I think." Lonny said as he knocked on Alex's door. "It's us Alex," he called out.

She yelled at us to come on in and Lonny opened the door. It was dark in side.

"Cooking in the dark there Alex?" I shouted as I reached for the light switch. I turned it on to see a barrage of friends and loved ones staring right back at me.

"Surprise!!" they all yelled. Alex came walking over, kissed my cheek. "Happy Birthday kid. Are you surprised?"

Surprised was an under statement. I was shocked. I was elated, yet stunned.

"I am. Thank you Alex, this means a lot." I couldn't help the tears that were falling down my face. I was speechless.

Where the stream and creek collide

* * * * * * * * * * *

I had been at the party for about six hours. Or 7 beers, whatever way you wanted to count it. Piety was there with my case of beer and some more. All the R.A's were present, including the two that were on duty tonight. My father and Elizabeth were there and so was Reggie Austin the Front Desk Manager and Martin Ewell, the manager of House Keeping. Some of the students who worked for the front desk and house keeping came out as well. It was a great party. People were slowly starting to peter out now that it was midnight.

"So you will be happy to know that I got your father and Elizabeth to work together on the signs and decorations. I made sure to ask them for home made ones so they had to spend time together." Alex had pulled me aside in the kitchen to inform me of her assistance in my plan.

"Really, thank you. And thank you for the party. I love it."

She smiled. "You're welcome, for both. I have a present for you. I will give it to you before you leave. You can open it when you have a moment alone, okay."

"My curiosity is piqued. I am excited."

"Excited about what?" Father asked as he slid his way over to us.

"Excited to see you dad, what else."

"Sure, sure," he said. "Nice party Graham." Alex smiled and nodded her head in reply.

"Why do you call Alex, Graham?" I asked to either one who would answer.

My father told me of how they were in high school around grade ten, when they had Alex's parents' house all to themselves for a Saturday night. They decided to throw a party and invite half the neighbourhood. They had one rule on the night – that was that no damage was to come to any part of the house. Their friends were pretty good with respecting that request. What happened near the end of the night with the phone jack was purely accidental. One of the girls tripped over the wire and pulled the jack right out of the wall cracking the face plate in half. Somehow Alex fixed it with Duck tape, Styrofoam, and White Out. Father said that you couldn't even tell that it had been broken.

"Why didn't you just go buy a new face plate?" I asked.

Alex and my father laughed. "We were too drunk and too

panicked to think of that at the time. We would have been able to pick one up the next day. My parents didn't return until dinner time."

I was laughing now. "And the nickname because?"

"The nickname was because she fixed the phone jack." Father added and then waited for my response. I only had one of slight confusion.

"Alexander Graham Bell, you see the connection."

I laughed. "Very cute, I like that story."

"Me too," Alex said to what seemed like no one in particular.

Father, now slipping back into his slight awkwardness, said that he was leaving to go home, thanked Alex for the party, she thanked him for the help, and then he kissed my cheek and went over to Elizabeth, who in turn came over and said her good byes as well.

"You are leaving together?" Alex inquired.

"Yes, I had too much to drink. Jason is going to give me a ride home tonight. I will come for my car tomorrow."

I was thrilled. "Thanks for coming Elizabeth. And thank you for the journal. I will use it well."

She kissed my cheek as well and said good night. Moments later they were gone. By now, most of the people were gone, just a few close co-workers, including Ashlyn, Lonny, and Piety. Lonny called us over to the middle table.

"Round of Tequila shots for everyone." We clanged glasses together, licked the salt, drank the drink, and then sucked the lemon. I was getting really drunk.

Before I left Alex handed me a small package with a card attached underneath. "Remember open this when you have a moment alone." She winked.

"I will and thanks again. I had such a good time. You made me happier than I have been in a while." I was starting to slur and talk the mushy drunk talk that I usually get after 7 too many.

"My pleasure kid," she said as we hugged. Lonny came to my side. "Are you ready lady? I will walk you home."

"An invitation like that how can I not be ready? We should help clean up first though."

"No need. Ashlyn and Piety are staying to help. Let's go."

With that we were out the door. Lonny decided he was going to push me to my room. Usually when guys are drinking and they decide they are going to push my chair I get the race car game which involves tight corners, fast speeds, and sound effects from a foot behind my head. Tonight and Lonny was no exception.

Where the stream and creek collide

Once we exited the elevator and landed on my floor, Lonny seemed braver than he had been on the previous ones. Maybe it was a mix of the altitude and the alcohol that clouded his judgement on the slowness required to round the last bend because when we took it my chair went tumbling over rolling me flat on my face with Lonny landing on top of my mid section.

"Oh my goodness, are you okay?" Lonny asked nervously.

I moved slowly. Surprising I felt no pain at all. I told him that.

His face was only inches from mine. We looked in to each others eyes and laughed. We laughed until we cried, trying to be as quiet at both as we could; shushing each other several times. We did not want to wake up any of the students that were there for the weekend. We laughed for almost ten minutes before he assisted me up and back into my chair. Reaching my dorm room door, I opened it with one hand and turned to Lonny with the other side of my body. "Have a good night. Thanks for everything."

He didn't respond immediately, he just looked at me with a hesitant look. And before I could ask him what was wrong, his lips where pressed against mine. His hand was wrapped around the back of my head and as he pushed me closer into his kiss, into his mouth. It took a moment, but eventually I joined in with full vigour. All I could think about was why he was kissing me. I was shocked. My stomach was flipping upside down. Goose bumps came popping up in several places. My heart was beating exceptionally fast, and my right eye began to twitch. The kiss ended. He touched my lips with his thumb, and then rubbed across the bottom one while he looked me in the eyes. He gave me a smile before he walked away. No goodnights were said. None were needed. I was not destined for sleep that night.

-8-

KISS AND TELL.

I spent the next few weeks in a haze. I thought about that kiss over and over again. I talked to Piety about it who was more than a little excited for me. She made me go over the details several times. She also told me over and over how she knew we were destined to be together and this was the first sign that she was right. I also shared it with Ashlyn, who had a slightly less enthusiastic response saying simply that it was about time. I talked to Elizabeth about it who replied by hugging me. We talked for an entire hour like two pubescent teens at a slumber party – giggles and all.

I shared my news with father as well who in turn gave me the 'be careful of guys intentions' speech and who also kindly reminded me that he was already in a relationship, one that was 6 years old. He was the only one to do so. I wanted to talk to Alex about it but she was really busy. She promised me a few moments of her time as soon as things settled down. I was okay with that. The kiss already happened and was going nowhere, and I wanted more than a second of interrupted time from her.

Besides Alex, the only person those weeks that I didn't seem to talk to about the kiss was Lonny. We were both avoiding each other. At least I was avoiding him and realized pretty quickly through our accidental bump-in moments, that he was making no efforts to stop me from doing so. That was okay with me. We were coming up to Thanksgiving weekend which would give me a lot of time to think about what happened and where I wanted to go with it, before talking to him. I needed to think about if I thought of the kiss as a drunken moment during which a lapse of judgement occurred or as more of a passionate desire that had been a ticking time bomb just waiting to burst open and release itself. I wished guys came with manuals. Well at least one guy. I think Lonny was the only guy I ever loved. I have had crushes but nothing long lasting. Yes a manual for him would be nice, maybe a manual for Jack as well.

Jack DeGraff had been quiet lately but that was only temporary I was sure. Although on the outside he had seemed to have settled down, I remained pretty confident that he was always up to something when working and when playing. He had that look about him. Not just when he wore jeans with white collar working clothes like business suits and ties on his top half, or when he had a pipe in his mouth with no tobacco in it. But also in the way he talked to people, calling everyone his bro, or his dog. Not to mention his approach to women when he could slap almost any girl, at any time, on the ass, and they just giggled and winked in his direction.

He was up to something and I knew it. I didn't trust him. Silent or not, he was up to something. I often wondered how he could be so different from his brother Jefferson. Jefferson was quiet and shy. He knew when to talk, and was oddly comfortable with girls and other friends of his brothers. He was respectful for the most part, and kept to himself. He seemed like he knew that he was here first for school, and second for a social life. He was enrolled in the law and justice course. Jefferson told me one afternoon that he was looking to become a lawyer. He was going to finish his Greenbury course, go on to University for Law School and then hopefully one day pass the bar exam to be able to practice law in Canada. He was unsure if he would have to take some other course in University first before Law School or if he could apply right after college. I told him I would look into that for him. I was planning on doing that this weekend. I was not going home for Thanksgiving. Father was actually going out of province to see my Grandmother – my Mothers' mom - for the holiday. She had asked him to come down and spend the week with her to help her go through some of her things in the house. She was moving to an old age home and thought that father might want some of the old pictures and childhood keepsakes of mothers. Father asked me to go with him but I declined. I pushed him to go. I reminded him that she was a lonely woman and needed someone there with her. Mother was her only child so no other kids could assist her. Besides I wanted a weekend alone to think, to catch up, and to sleep. There would barely be any students in the residence over the weekend. And because some students were staying around, some of us would have to stay and work the weekend anyway. I was more than happy to be one of those workers. I also had a lot of schoolwork to do. I was working with Piety on a movie script for class. We needed to do some research.

It was Thursday night and I was in the middle of planning my weekend agenda. A lot of my friends laughed at my lists but I couldn't help it. I functioned a lot better when I had a plan. If I wrote it down, I at least had a chance of getting half of it done, whereas if I didn't, I usually only managed one task to completion. I was trying hard to concentrate on all I wanted to get done but it was hard. I had several interrupting thoughts of Lonny, my friends, my father, the students. My head was full. Or I was procrastinating. The jury was still out.

At 8 pm Julie Dabble showed up at my door, exactly to the minute of when she said she would. Julie was a first year student who had a lot to deal with. She came to me the second week of school and told me that she had dealt with an eating disorder for most of her life. She said she was better now but had some relapses now and then when stressed. Her therapist had encouraged her to tell one of her R.A.'s about this problem so that if she needed anything we could help. She chose me, and I was honoured. She also told me that her mother had died about three years ago and she hadn't been the same since. I empathised with her and told her that my mother had died as well. Neither of us went in to any detail of their deaths. We didn't have to. We had a common bond when it was simply kept.

I opened my door, "Come on in Jules, I have those papers for you right here." Julie was an energetic, enthusiastic, beautiful young woman who wanted to fill the gap in her schedule with some kind of working position within the college. She also said she needed the money for her tuition. I didn't quite understand the financial part of it knowing how much money her father must have made. But that wasn't my business. We did have an opening for a residence social coordinator so I suggested she should apply and she did. She was offered the position just this week and needed to get the permission papers signed by her father.

She helped herself into the room and sat on my bed. One of her boney fingers did a perfect figure eight in a strand of her blond hair. "I still don't really understand why I need a guardian to sign permissions forms for me to take this job. I am 18."

"Yes, but this is an educational institution and they require a permission form to be signed, so they don't get into any trouble - in the case that you do. You will be dealing with events that will involve setting up a bar at the dance or graduation, or events that will be at a pub already. You are underage Julie. There is no way around this. I am sorry."

"No big deal, my father will be okay with it. He is cool that way. I just think it is a little silly, that is all. Are you ready for the weekend? Where are you going?"

I finished signing my portion of the forms and passed them to her to bring home. "I am staying here actually. It is my weekend to work. And you?"

"That sucks."

"Someone has to work, why not me. Where are you going?" I asked again.

"I am going to Harvey's parent's house for Saturday night. I will see my father tomorrow night before he leaves to Vegas with his new girlfriend. He likes to spoil the ladies in his life. But I guess when you have his money, why not? They invited me to go for the holidays but I wanted to stay with Harvey. He is close to his family and I am starting to be close as well." She stood up now. Her petite frame barely made a dent in the mattress. She continued to talk as she usually does. "He and I have been dating two years now and I am yet to spend a full holiday with him and his family. It will be nice to be there the whole time. I barely see him now that we're in school. His University schedule is a lot different from my College one."

"It usually is. Well you have fun, and come fill me in when you return, okay?"

She agreed, and then left. Her spandex pants and rubber running shoes allowed her to leave with a swishing sound that followed her all the way to the corner and beyond. She had a presence that was for sure.

* * * * * * * * * * *

Most of the students were gone by lunch on Friday, many skipping their last classes in the day. For most, this was their first time home since they left to come here at the end of August. I was glad that things were quiet. It was nice. By the next morning it was even more silent. We had a total of thirty four students stay. Some because of work, others lived too far away to go home. For the students that were left, the residence was holding a Turkey dinner with all the traditional side dishes in the cafeteria for dinner tonight. For about a dozen of them, this would be their first Thanksgiving dinner. They would have had similar holidays back in their countries, but not one like the North American holiday that we celebrate here. The other Resident Assistant that stayed was Emanual. We called him Manny. He grew up in Africa and moved here through an exchange program only two years ago. I didn't know too much about him, just that he worked really hard at school and at his job. The International Students Department suggested we let him interview for a position. They offered to help with his pay due to international laws. Long story short, he passed the tests and interviews with flying colours and the ISD worked out his payroll issues. He had no family here so he was not celebrating Thanksgiving with anyone. He was free to stay the weekend and work with me. Manny was excited for the residence dinner. He wanted to experience part of the holiday. He was already in the R.A. lounge waiting for me when I got there.

"You ready to start decorating?"

He jumped from the couch and picked up the box with the construction papered turkeys and the orange and yellow streamers.

"Let's go, have you seen Alex? She is supposed to come help us."

"Yeah," He said as he opened the door, placed the box on my lap, and pushed me through the doorway all in one swoop. "She is already in the cafeteria waiting for us. She took the table cloths and the center pieces about 20 minutes ago. She is probably already done."

When we entered through the cafeteria doors, the tables were in fact fully decorated and the buffet table was out and loaded with the metal buffet trays. All they were missing was the food.

"Hey guys, thanks for your help. I thought we should get this done this afternoon so we are not rushing minutes before the students arrive. You both have the time?"

We answered yes and got right to work. The college had a daycare and we asked them to get the kids to make construction paper turkeys for us to hang up. We also had signs reminding us of the holiday name, and a few cute posters like one that had a picture of 3 alive holiday birds with signs claiming they were on strike.

I went over to where Alex was folding napkins.

"Do you have some time to talk with me between this and dinner?"

"I do. I have the whole time in between," she smiled. "Where and when?"

"Well I thought that maybe after we are done here, we can go grab our jackets and I can take you for a walk to my thinking spot and we can talk there."

"Okay, secret thinking spot huh? Sounds intense. You okay?"

"I am great."

"I have to run to my room for a moment. I will grab my jacket.

Do you need me to grab you one?"

"Yes please."

"Can I leave you with the napkins?"

I said she could, and Manny came over to help me finish them. There was a lot to get done.

"Tell me more about yourself Manny." I said as he sat down.

"What do you want to know?"

"Where in Africa are you from?"

"Northern Africa." He seemed hesitant. I wasn't sure if he was nervous or not interested in sharing.

"More specific?" I pushed a little further.

"Sudan."

"What part? What was it like for you growing up?"

"I am from many places."

"And?"

"And what? And life was what it was." He didn't look up at me, just continued to fold napkins.

"You don't want to tell me, do you?"

"No, I don't mind telling you – just a lot of people don't really want to hear about it. Or they're unhappy that I told them once they know. I come from a very different world than you Sadie. It was bad."

"Tell me about it, if you are okay with it. I want to know. I think hearing other people's stories is what keeps us in check. Maybe something you tell me about your life will teach me something about mine. You never know. Besides, my mother was a criminal lawyer. I have heard and seen a lot."

"Okay, but remember that I forewarned you." He sat down. "My home village was called Tawilah in North Darfur."

"Isn't Darfur the dangerous part of Sudan? Full of war and political strife?"

He laughed almost mockingly. "Depends who you ask. The Sudan government would say that it is an area full of war torn criminals with political and religious agendas. The people of Darfur say they are victims of a Government who sides with the Arabs over the Africans."

"Wow, so that would mean the Government is a part of all the killings that are going on there; directly or indirectly. Are they?" We were done folding napkins but we stayed sitting at the table anyway. I finally had him talking. I was interested in what he had to say.

"In my opinion they are. Have you heard of the Janjaweed army?"

I shook my head no.

"They are the army responsible for all of the genocide and rapes and looting in the Darfur region. We believe that the Government was responsible for giving them weapons and funding to rid the country of its African population. It is the Nomac tribes fighting the African farmers."

"That must have been so hard for you growing up in that. Did you see any of the war?"

"See it, Sadie, I lived it. You can't avoid stuff like that. It is everywhere. They raided my village when I was 15." His eyes were wide yet emotionless.

"Really, what did they do? Can I ask?" Not sure if I would be over stepping any boundaries we may have had.

"Sure. They came in to our village with their guns and they shot all of our strong men. They killed all boys under 5, and took all girls under 16. They beat and raped the women in our village. My mother had my brother in her arms when they beat her. The beating killed him." He showed a bit of emotion when he bowed his head.

"Manny that is awful."

"He was 4. He would have died anyway."

I wasn't sure if I was more shocked at what he was saying or how easy it was for him to say.

"Your mom? Can I ask?"

"Sure, it doesn't bother me. She is still alive. At least was the last time I saw her."

"Before you came here?"

"No, before that. We were separated. We had to go to a camp that was for refugees, sort of. For people that had their villages burnt and destroyed, or taken over by the Janjaweed. It was a place we felt protected. The UN could come in and bring us food, and supplies. Things we wouldn't have gotten otherwise." He shifted in his seat. "My mother and I joined the rebel army there. We learned how to shoot a gun, how to fight and hide, and how to kill without remorse. That was the easiest part."

"Joining the army?"

"No, killing without remorse."

"Oh!"

"I sound awful to you don't I?"

"Err...not at all." I knew I hesitated. I instantly regretted it.

"You're lying."

"I'm not, sorry. I just can't imagine this life. It is hard for me to picture that you are not talking about a movie but instead, your childhood. I couldn't imagine being 15 and being trained, alongside my mother, to do my first kill."

"I wasn't."

"You just said you both joined the rebel army."

"Yes, but not for my first kill. I had my first kill when I was 8. But that is another story." He laughed.

Again I was speechless not for his words but for his demeanour. I could see just how much this was his norm, and how little it was mine.

"Do you want me to go on?"

"You can't leave me here Manny. There is obviously a happier ending to this story because you are in front of me, here in Canada."

"Yes, but it gets a little worse before it gets better." He made circles on the table with his pointer finger.

"Okay. Maybe just give me the skinny of it then. I am not sure I want a lot of details. I am not as brave as you."

"Sure you are. You are plenty brave. You can't comprehend what life I have lived because it is not how you grew up. You think you would have died, been murdered, or killed yourself instead of fighting like I did. You think that because of that, because I learned how to kill to get out, that I am brave. But for me that is a way of life."

"And that makes me not as brave."

"Ah, but it is how you look at it. In my country, with the resources and my experiences, I think I would have died, been murdered, or killed myself if I was in a wheelchair. To me, you are braver than I. Perspective is everything. My familiarity with dealing with murder and death is just as easy or hard as yours with dealing with paraplegia. You understand."

I smiled. "I may need to sit with it a little while to get full understanding but I think I got it."

"Good." He relaxed his hands on his lap under the table.

"I still just want the brief version though."

"Okay." He smiled. "I ended up in the army and when the Janjaweed came to fight us I fought. Then came a moment where I was in a secluded area with my mother and a friend of hers. We also had two other guys with us. One guy was 17 and the other 21. They came up from behind while we were on a time out. It was our time to eat and refresh. I was the only one holding a gun. I had finished eating first and just picked it back up. They shot Danbewa, the 21 year old. Then one of the militia took my mothers friend off to the side at the edge of the bush. He was going to take her into the woods and rape her. Because she was in the rebel army, he would have killed her right after. She was a gun holding woman. I yelled at him to stop or I would kill him. The other guy he was with said I and Ugundy, the 17 year old, had a choice, to die or to be one of them. To be a Janjaweed."

"Really, they wanted you to be one of them?"

"That's what they said. We were young and boys. We were perfect for their army."

"What did you do?"

"I aimed my gun towards the militia man and my mother's friend and I shot her. I shot her before they did."

I gasped.

"Awful I know. But it saved my mother, and it brought me here. They took me and Ugundy away, my mother's cries were humiliation enough for them to be satisfied. They put me through school. They brought us to Northern Kurdofan and enrolled us into the University of Kurdofan. I was able to get into an exchange program there and viola, here I am in Canada."

"Wow," I paused. "Wow." I whispered again. I couldn't get anything else out.

"Do you regret asking?" He laughed. Looking at my face and what I could imagine was a completely horrified look.

"No. I am glad I did. What now for you. You have to go back don't you?"

"I am hoping to stay here long enough to get a law degree and then specialize in International Law so I can properly help out the people there. Stop the genocide, the murders and rapes."

"Will they let you stay that long?"

"Well that is up to the Canadian government now."

"And if they try to send you back?"

"Well I am counting on you to marry me, Sadie." He teased and stood up.

"I will save myself for you Manny." I joked back, getting back into my wheelchair.

"I knew I could count on you. One question for you now."

"Sure." I heard the door open, and Alex walk in.

"Did you learn anything about your life from mine?"

"I learned that I am glad I live in Canada." I winked, he nodded in response. "I am sure that I have learned a lot more than that, it just hasn't set in yet. You gave me a lot to sift through."

"Okay, good. Do you consider me a murderer now?" Alex stopped once she reached us. It was obvious she had only heard the last part of his sentence by the perplexed look on her face.

"No. A survivor."

"Thanks. Remember what I said about being brave and perspective." He smiled and touched my shoulder.

"I will for sure Manny, thank you!"

"We are all done here, Alex. Excuse me. I am going to go freshen up before dinner tonight." He said to her and then headed to the door before waiting for an answer.

"Thanks Manny! Go ahead." Alex yelled to him anyway.

It took us about 15 more minutes to complete the last minute preparations and then we shut the door behind us and put on the jackets Alex brought. Moments later we were on our way through the arboretum and nearing my favourite spot along the stream. I loved the arboretum. There were very few of them in Ontario. They were pieces of land that the government and school held onto as an area in which their students could do research and studies in an environment that was natural and protected. The arboretum was a great asset to Greenbury.

"It's beautiful in here isn't it? The trees, the grass, the water, it is pure nature wrapped around us. Where are we headed?"

"To the stream. There is a bench there that we can sit on. Not my favourite spot but close. I will show you. Do you know about Manny's past?"

"Not from him personally, but I have been educated on a lot of what he has gone through. Makes you feel a little lucky to be who you are doesn't it?"

I agreed.

We sat down on the bench. It was a beautiful spot facing the stream. Since it was fall, the trees had shed most of their leaves leaving the ground covered in an array of red, yellow, and orange. The sound of the stream was louder than usually. The water must have been high.

"So, I am sure we are not out here for the scenery," she said with a small laugh. "What's going on Sadie?"

"Lonny and I kissed." I paused. I needed to see her facial reaction. There wasn't really one. I continued. "It was last weekend after my birthday party, when he walked me to my room."

"Was it a long kiss? An awkward one? What was the feeling after?"

I explained how it happened - the events leading up to it. I also

67

explained the feeling of shock. That he initiated it at first but I responded. That we were both completely intoxicated and that we hadn't spoken of the kiss since.

"How are you feeling now?" She was still looking straight ahead.

"Seriously Alex. That is what you are going to say to me? You are just going to respond by asking me questions that will get me to talk and work it out myself. I know what you are doing. I have had those workshops too remember." I stopped for a moment. She looked at me. "This is what I waited all week for? It's me, Sadie. I am not a student that you are counselling. You can show an opinion with me. Please show an opinion with me. I wanted to talk with you for a reason."

She squirmed a little in her spot. Sucked in her bottom lip. "Okay, fair enough. I think that you are going to get hurt. I think that he is already in a relationship that he has been in for a while. I think this kiss probably confused him. I believe that he cares about you very much and probably wanted to kiss you really bad. But I don't see how this could have a good ending."

I was taken aback. Not sure how I felt about what she was saying. "Please elaborate." I insisted.

"In my opinion," she emphasized the word opinion, "there are three possible outcomes here. One, it stays at just a kiss and he stays with, ah, Jessica, is it?" I nodded. "Two, he leaves her for you. In which case, you better hope it works really well between you both, or he will blame you forever for standing in between him and what could have been his true love. Or three, you guys continue a secret affair in which he stays with her and you at the same time. But you are better than that. You are not the mistress type."

I wasn't. But the other two options could happen. I appreciated her honesty but felt a little bummed. "Do you really believe that is it? That we are doomed to never be together. That this will never work. I think that there is a good possibility that this will work out."

"I didn't say never, Sadie. Just going about it this way won't work. It's just - I have been there. I know how it works. It is really tough."

"With my father?"

She hesitated before going further. "Yes. Except I was the Jessica in this situation."

"No offence when I say this, but it worked out between my father and my mother. They got married, had me, and lived happily."

She was quiet again.

"Talk to me Alex. I need experience here. I have none in this area."

She looked at me with uncertainty. "You know how your parents started their marriage right?"

"You mean they got engaged because my mother was pregnant. Yes I know. With my brother, Carter. He died at child birth. I know that her pregnancy was why they decided to get married so quickly after only a year of dating."

"I always believed that your father was the love of my life, the one person I was meant to be with. Then he called me to tell me that he met someone else. I believed your father that he never cheated on me with her, I still do. He broke it off with me first." She shifted again and looked out ahead of her. "Anyways, a year later I went to visit him because I really wanted to try to get him back. That is when he told me he was engaged, and why. He told me he loved your mother very much and that he would always keep me in his heart. That he wanted to stay friends. Your mother came home early from her law class, yelled at me for being there, and kicked me out of their apartment. I didn't blame her. I was, after all, there to break them up."

"But you didn't. They stayed together."

"Yes they did. And they were happy."

I wanted to say that she had proven my point that it may work but I wasn't completely confident that she was finished her story. I was right.

"What I am getting at Sadie is this. I will always wonder if your father was my soul mate. I think your mother always wondered that as well."

"Wondered if she was or if you were?"

"If I was, well both, I guess. She called me a week later, after kicking me out. She said that she wanted me out of his life. That he would not be calling me, nor would we continue to be friends. She said that I was to be out of his life for good. She begged me, woman to woman. I obliged."

"So my parents stayed together because you decided to let them?" It came out way more sarcastic than I hoped.

Alex had small tears in her eyes. "You know that is not what I am saying. Your parents loved each other very much. And when Carter died, that brought them even closer. They were inseparable. But it isn't a life to have Sadie when you are always wondering the 'what ifs', and if you are actually the second choice not the first. It is also

69

hard to think that you have done that to another woman as well."

I took a deep breath. I got it. I nodded to her in understanding. "So what do you suggest?"

She wiped her face clear of tears. "I suggest you have a long talk with Lonny. You tell him that he needs to think about what he wants. If he decides to break it off with Jessica than great. Take your time, stay friends for a few months and slowly work into a real 'first' kiss."

"I knew I was talking to you for a reason. Thank you for sharing with me."

She smiled. "So, did you open my present?"

I told her no, and I pulled it out of my sweater pocket. It was still wrapped. "I wanted to wait until I was with you to open it."

She liked that idea. "That is good. Because I have something to add when you have opened it and completed its requirements."

"Sounds cryptic, my interest is piqued."

I opened the small box to find a black roped necklace that had a small silver vial attached to the middle. "It's beautiful. Thanks."

"Open the vial."

I did. Inside was a little piece of blank white paper. "What is it?"

"This is a secret keeper. What it is meant to do is to allow a person to write their deepest darkest secret down on a paper, and then keep it in the vial around their neck. It is a cathartic exercise; a way to help you get something that you never told anyone, out of your system and out into the world, in a safe way. I have one, see." She pulled it out from around her neck. "I have had it for a year. It has helped."

What a great idea. I knew exactly what I would write. I would write about mother's murder. I would write my guilt and shame down. I would write what I never told anyone before.

"Thank you."

"You're very welcome. Now, I have a question for you. Tomorrow I am going to my parents for turkey dinner. I want you to come join me. I could use them having someone to interrogate other than me. Plus, I say we both could use some time away from this place. What do you say?"

"I'm in," and with that we got up and left. We only had ten minutes before the residence dinner started.

-9-

SECRET, SECRET, I GOT A SECRET...

I murdered my mother.
The man gave me money to let him in.
He said just to talk. I believed him.
I honestly didn't know he was a hit man.
He came over the next day and I let him in.
He went upstairs and beat up my mother in front of me.
Then when he tried to attack me, she fought him.
He shot her in the head, and then went after me again.
For the first time since the attack started, I moved.
I ran away and fell down the stairs.
He thought I was dead. I pretended I was. He left.
Not only did I help to set up her murder.
I never protected her from him.
I didn't keep her alive. I ran.
I failed her in every way.
I still remember what he looks like.

    I rolled up the piece of paper and placed it in the vial. It wasn't very big. I thought about adding the article from the newspaper that told how mother lost Armando Vitalli's case, the suspected mob boss and now was going to spend the rest of his life in jail. It was only her second loss since she started on high profile cases. Her murder was covered nationally. No one knew who did it. They suspected it was someone connected to Vitalli. They were right. I claimed that I never saw his face. In reality, if I wanted to or not, I could see his face every time I closed my eyes. I told no one of any of our prior meetings. They would blame me. I blamed me. I just never meant for it to happen. I didn't think anyone would believe that. I wouldn't if someone had told me my story.
    I looked in the mirror. My eyes were red and puffy, a direct consequence of crying for hours. It felt good. It had been a long time since I cried about what happened. The vial was probably the best gift I ever received for a birthday.

I showered, got dressed, and put my new necklace over my head. I was ready to take my secret out into the world. It was funny, even though it was safely around my neck and hidden in a metal vial, I was a little nervous. I was nervous to lose it.

"Are you ready? It takes about an hour and a half to two hours to get there, so you may want to pee, or grab a drink, one last time before we go."

Ten minutes later we were on our way to Sudbury, a small city North of Greenbury. I was happy to go. I was set to visit Sudbury with Piety in two weeks to interview the Sudbury Police for our script assignment for class. This way I could find my way around a little better to see where the station was. I have visited the city a few times but Alex grew up there. She told me all sorts of funny stories on the way to her parents. A lot of stories included my father.

"Thank you for sharing what you did about my parents yesterday. I appreciated the honesty." I changed the subject slightly, but needed to say it.

"I am glad you were open to hearing it. I am sorry if I made your mother look different from what you imagined. It was not my intention. She was a wonderful woman. Every situation is relative, and I was hurt back then. I can't help but be a little biased when talking about those days."

"I understand. My mother was young too. I think no less of any one. Not you, my mother, nor my father. I do realize now though how awful it was of me to ask you to help get my father and Elizabeth together."

"You didn't know."

"No, I didn't. But now I do. So, no more helping, I will work alone."

Alex smiled. "I appreciate that. But you know if you need anything, just ask."

"I will."

We moved the subject to Bridgette and how she was doing. She had decided not to come back to residence and classes until after Thanksgiving. Up until now she was at home doing work that was sent to her from her teachers. As of Tuesday, she would be back. Alex was torn on the situation. Bridgette returning questioned the no tolerance to drugs rule in residence but it was hard to prove what happened. She had no drugs on her, just in her. We discussed it for the rest of the ride. Before we knew it, we were pulling into the rocky city of Sudbury, and moments later, into her parent's driveway.

"Okay, here is what to expect. My parents will have dinner promptly at 5. That leaves two hours of uncomfortable talk beforehand. They will probably share mine and my sister's whole childhood with you, including all of our embarrassing moments. They tend to idolize my sister Jennifer because she is the baby. At least that is how I see it and if you notice that I am wrong in that assumption, please keep it to yourself. I prefer to keep myself in the dark." She stopped to take a few breaths. I could hear a little nervousness in her voice.

"Your sister is married with 2 children right?"

"Yes. You will hear a lot about that. She married her high school sweetheart right out of college, had twins, one boy, one girl. An almost perfect life don't you think?"

"I don't believe anyone has a perfect life. We all have ghosts in our closet."

"Maybe so, but if she has any ghosts, they are deep in her closet. Anyways after dinner comes dessert, then we can leave. I plan on using the fact that kids would be returning to the residence as a reason to leave. Go with me on that."

I laughed. "I got your back partner." I saluted her. Not fitting but it worked.

* * * * * * * * * * *

"So that is when Alexandra decided that dressing up and looking like a lady was not something that was going to be in her future. She was a tomboy through and through. Only jeans and t-shirts for her. Women's pantsuits for work. That is it. Can you believe?" Her mother asked me with conviction and not seemingly really interested in a response.

Connie Ward was a short and plump woman only about 5 ft tall. She had short grey hair in a permanent tight curl. Connie, as I am told, had her hair curled in a permanent once a month, despite that her hair was already naturally curly. She was a bit of a bossy lady. I got the impression that she knew what she wanted, when she wanted it, and just how she wanted it to be done. In my mind I placed her somewhere between brilliant and bitch.

"I have seen Alex dressed up."

"Alexandra." Connie corrected me.

"Sorry. I thought I said Alex." I was confused.

"You did dear. Her name is Alexandra."

"Mom, everyone calls me Alex." Alex interrupted.

"Well they shouldn't. I didn't name you Alex. I named you proper."

"Mom!" Alex argued.

I corrected myself before they started arguing stronger. "Sorry Connie, I meant to say that I have seen Alexandra dressed up and she looks quite nice and lady like in my opinion." Connie smiled and nodded at me. Alex took a deep breath.

"How much did you pay her?' Jennifer asked her sister with a smirk.

I was about to respond but Alex grabbed my arm. I looked at her. Calmly she just smiled and shook her head. You could tell this was nothing new to her. It was obvious that there was a lot of love in their family, but there were also a lot of opinions where they were not always needed or wanted. Perfect Jennifer, who married her high school sweetheart, and had twins, one girl and one boy, also had her Mother's attitude. They were two peas in a pod. I wasn't sure how to handle them exactly, all I knew was that that was one end of the Thanksgiving dinner table that I didn't want to be on.

"Would you like to see my favourite picture of Alexandra, Sadie?"

"Dad! Enough pictures of me."

Her father, the complete opposite of her mother, tall and slender, decided that one more picture was needed. He went upstairs and came back with a 5x8 picture frame. Mrs. Ward and Jennifer got up to go into the kitchen to get supper on the table. Alex joined them and left me alone with her father Michael. He was a kind, soft spoken man. His white hair was smooth. His face had many wrinkles, evidence of the many years spent in the sun as a construction worker.

"She was 7 years old. We went to the lake together. I rented a cabin every year when the girls were younger. Jennifer always went to socialize and sun tan. That was her thing. Alexandra liked to get dirty. She liked fishing and boating. This particular day, she had a rough afternoon of being teased by the other kids for not being as girl-like as they thought she should. We went fishing together to try to get her mind off of things."

"Did it work?"

"You tell me," he replied. He handed me the picture. She had long hair hanging down. A pink dress with grass stains all over it, rubber boots, and a large fish held up by a chain. She had a huge smile on her face with one front tooth missing.

"I say it did." I smiled. The picture was so funny, and so much like the Alex I knew.

"She insisted that she hold the rod herself for the first time that day. I hesitated but said okay. She caught this fish herself. I just helped net it. It was a day of emotional growth for both of us."

"She is a good person. She has helped me a lot."

He smiled. "She is a good girl. A special gift. Just as I am sure you are. Now let's get ourselves into that kitchen for some turkey, before those ladies start calling. Connie cooks one hell of a dinner."

He was right. The dinner was amazing. We had a moist tanned coloured bird which I was told stayed that way because she oiled the skin and cooked it on really high for the first hour, dropping the temperature a little every half hour after that. Inside the bird was a stuffing made with apples, not potatoes, and a mix of whole wheat and white bread. We also had mashed potatoes, turnip, crusty butter rolls, meat pie, home-made cranberry sauce and a tossed salad. It was a feast. We topped it off with blueberry and pumpkin pie for dessert.

After dinner I helped bring the dishes into the kitchen. Alex was asked to put the food away and fill the Brita while Mrs. Ward and Jennifer did the dishes. The twins Calvin and Carly went off downstairs to watch a movie. The men, Mr. Ward, and Jennifer's husband Lloyd went to the sitting room with a bottle of whiskey. I offered to help. I thought that I would fill the Brita for them, but was quickly stopped when I was about to put tap water into the container.

"She only uses bottled water," Alex whispered into my ear.

"Bottled water?" I replied a little louder than I should have because Alex shushed me then shrugged her shoulders.

I continued. "Bottled water for a filtered container? Really? How..."

"Odd," she finished for me, lifting one eyebrow. "I don't get it myself. You should see when she gets on the flavoured water kick. She has to constantly buy new filters because the flavouring syrup clogs the Brita up."

We looked at each other and cracked up laughing. Giggling on and off until all the food was put away. It took us longer to do that than it did for the other ladies to wash the dishes. We met them in the sitting room for tea when we were done.

"So, you were Jason's daughter?"

"Yes." I didn't realize until then that they probably knew my father and all about his and Alex's past.

"And still is." Alex added with a mocking smile.

"Interesting! We thought that he was the one that would actually marry my sister, but we were wrong. We really hope it will happen soon, poor Lloyd and Father want another male companion for these family to do's."

Alex stayed silent. I just nodded and drank my tea. At this point I didn't think I would say anything nice to Jennifer, so I stayed silent. To my surprise Jennifer did not adopt the same code.

"But that would require Alexandra to trust someone, and well she doesn't even trust her own family."

"Jen, enough, really, I know how you feel." Alex finally said, rolling her eyes while speaking.

"You just don't take my advice though do you?" Jen retorted with a snotty tone.

"Well that would imply that I thought you were right in your advice. And I don't. You think you have this perfect life but you don't. You have what you *think* is what life is about. But you don't have what I feel is important."

"So a husband and kids is not what you feel is important." She said with an insulting laugh.

"I won't just settle for anyone." Alex was starting to shout.

"You think I settled? Did you hear that Lloyd. Apparently I settled on you."

"She didn't say necessarily that you were the one that settled!" I piped in. Alex was running off a cliff and I decided to run shotgun. She gave me a small smile and giggle.

"Well…" Jennifer responded with a huff. She didn't finish her sentence she just stood up.

"Enough all of you, leave each other alone." Mr. Ward replied waving his hand in their direction.

"Alex - andra," I added not wanting to insult any more family members. "I am not feeling so good. I think the dinner tasted so well I ate too much. Would you mind taking me home?" I asked.

She was more than happy to say yes, and within minutes we had said our goodbyes and were out the door, on the road back to the school.

"How are you feeling now?" She asked.

"I am better thank you. I just needed air I think."

"Or out of there?" she smiled.

"Was I that obvious?" I asked not really needing an answer.

"I appreciate the way you stuck up for me." She winked. "I wanted out as well. Sorry to put you through that."

Where the stream and creek collide

"Don't be. I had a great time. I really like your family, I just don't like the way they talk to you."

"Thanks, kid. I appreciate that, but Jennifer is just being a typical pain in the ass sister. And my mother, well, she is a mother. I know I should tell them exactly how I feel, and some may see it as a weakness that I don't but really I just don't want to give them any more of my energy. Not in response to their negative opinions anyways. It isn't worth my stress. Besides, any comments I would make would bring me down to her level. I would much rather wait for her to come up to mine. Tonight is the farthest I have ever gone in responding to her."

"Well, kudos to you. I wouldn't be that strong."

She showed me where the police station was. We spent the rest of the ride talking about different workshops we would like to see this year in our meetings. We decided on grief and loss, and common drugs. We needed three more topics but thought we should see what other people were thinking about in terms of what they are dealing with. We also talked about the potential support staff strike that seemed more and more possible. Residence talk was always a good subject when trying to avoid other uncomfortable talk - like family. The ride home seemed much quicker than the ride there. The parking lot had a lot more cars than when we had left it.

"It looks like a lot of students are back already."

"Yeah, most have classes in the morning. Alex, I have been thinking," I paused for a moment. "What your sister said about trust. You know I trust you right?"

"Yes of course, and I trust you Sadie." She took the keys out of the ignition and reached for her door handle, not making any eye contact with me.

"Wait," I asked grabbing her arm. She turned and looked at me. "Trade me then," I said.

"Trade you what?"

"Necklaces. Trade me necklaces." I almost felt like I was having an out of body experience. My hands were shaking. "I wrote in mine my deepest darkest secret. One that is very painful to me and that no one knows. It's a secret that I want no one to know, including you." I continued to look her in the eyes to show my sincerity. "I trust that you won't look at it. Trade me. Give me yours and I will give you mine."

"Sadie, I don't know what to say. I am both honoured and terrified."

I swallowed hard. And just before I could tell her that I took it

77

back and that maybe we should think about it for a while first, she grabbed her vial from around her neck, lifted it over her head and said okay. We traded, both adding a disclaimer; no opening each other's vial.

-10-

ALL FATHERS IN THE WORLD, WE SALUTE YOU... WITH THE FINGER!

"Okay everyone, we all know that we need to decide this tonight. So every one throw out some ideas, Hal if you don't mind can you write them on the chalk board?"

It took us a while but we narrowed down our workshops for the rest of this year: Drug Use, Grief and Loss, Burn Out, Eating Disorders, and Sexual Assault. We also had to do Crisis Management which taught us to deal with things such as protecting ourselves against an aggressive student and using our body language to diffuse a high tempered situation. Crisis Management was part of both orientation training that we already had and an up-training that we would receive after Christmas – the second half of the school year. The up-training at Christmas also gave us a quick refresher on a few other topics. The most common needing refreshed were sexual assault courses and drugs and alcohol. This focus was followed because laws changed, and new street drugs became popular. We needed to be updated on these subjects.

Our meeting was on the Monday this week, due to the Thanksgiving holiday. Lonny was the only one not there. He was still out of town. Other topics we discussed were our students. I shared the information I knew on Julie and her mother's death, her eating disorder, and of course her acceptance of the social coordinator position. I always felt bad that we had to share the student's confidences with the other R.A.'s but understood the importance of it. If anything were to happen while I was gone, it would help if the others were aware of the situations.

Wanda talked about Calista. She said that she was doing better with the cutting. She would call Wanda when she felt like hurting herself and Wanda would make herself free to do something to help her get her mind off of it. Not a great long term strategy she knew, but it worked right now.

Ashlyn talked about Bridgette's return which was pretty quiet and a day early. She had a lot of friends that spent time with her.

Jack brought in a welcome back cake to the lounge and they had a mini party going on as we spoke.

Once all of our student issues were brought to the table, we shared a little about our weekend's home. I of course, kept mine to talking solely about the residence dinner, which we also discussed. We talked a lot of how the students ate so much that they slept for most of that evening. No food was left. The kitchen staff gave all the leftovers to the students on paper plates so that they could take it up to rooms.

Last we talked about turkey drop, and no one yet, had any problems there. Some had students with break ups but nothing too dramatic. Then we were done. I was on duty with Wanda, and had an hour and a half before our second set of rounds. Before we left the meeting room I informed her that I would meet her downstairs at 11 and took the pager in case she needed me. I had to go to Jefferson's room to talk to him about what I learned about Law School requirements. He was waiting for me in his room.

"Come on in," he said. "I am just unpacking. I didn't go to my classes today. I spent an extra night with my girlfriend." He had an impish yet confident look that offered no apologies for missing classes.

"Well, as long as you had fun. I got that information for you. It is all on this paper. Do you want to go over it with me?"

He did. I went into his room. It was hard for me to fit. He had clothes, papers, and movies all over the floor. Not what I would expect from Jefferson at all. He reached down and threw things to the side, giving me room to get it.

"Sorry about the mess," he said still moving things to the side. "I haven't had much time to clean lately."

"Wow," I replied. "This is like the physical picture form of what I imagine my life would look like." He laughed at my attempt to make light of the mess.

"So you have that information?"

I told him that he would have to go to University. That some Law Schools require at least a two year course from University but most want a completed undergrad. The diploma he gets here at Greenbury would help him possibly enter a University in its second year rather than starting from the beginning. In University he just had to take a course that helped him with rational and critical thinking, Law, English, etcetera.

Once he had completed his undergrad he would need to write

his LSAT (Law School Admissions Test) and apply to law schools using his score and his profile. A profile would include reference letters, work history, educational back ground. He would have to decide before applying if he wanted to study civil or common law and the answer would determine what school he would apply to.

After 3 years at Law School, he would then get a job for a minimum of ten months working with a Lawyer before he could write the bar admission course. Jefferson listened. He asked a few questions here and there, I answered them. He seemed frustrated by the end.

"What's going on in that head of yours Jefferson?"

He sat on his bed. "That's a lot of work."

"Yes it is."

"Your mother was a lawyer right? Do you mind me asking?"

I didn't. "No, I don't mind. She was a criminal lawyer. She represented a lot of people accused of organized crime."

"Did she make a lot of money doing it?"

"Yes. A lot. She was a private lawyer, worked on her own and had a lot of business."

"Like 6 digits kind of money?" He was persistent.

"Yes, over two hundred thousand when she was with the firm. Not sure privately," I conceded.

He smiled. "That's what I like to hear. Then I wouldn't have to rely on my father at all. Was the job hard? Like I mean, I am okay with having to work but how hard was it?"

"Well, hard." I didn't want to sugar coat it for him. "She had very long hours. She worked with some pretty scary people who for the most part lacked a moral compass, so we never knew what to expect from her clients. And well, lots of times she was trying to get guilty men free and that is hard on your psyche."

"Wow! That sounds tough. It doesn't stop after the schooling does it?"

"No, but the money was good. The fame she liked. The lifestyle again she had no complaints. The work just comes with the territory. If you want it, you can do it."

Almost under his breath he whispered, "If I want it."

"You don't?"

"I do and I don't. I want to work for my father. But the only way I can work in his establishment is either as a lawyer or an accountant. I hate math, at least enough to not want it to be the only thing I excel at."

He looked defeated. "Why can't you be a cook like your brother?"

"Ah, yes my brother. You see, my father has an old fashioned way of thinking. He prides himself on his success and his offsprings' success. The oldest, he follows the father's footsteps and the youngest kids are to get a different respectable job. A lawyer, a doctor, an accountant, you know. And only a few of those would get me into the restaurant business with him."

"That's too bad. What if you wanted to be a chef? What then?"

"I am on my own then. I would be his competition only. Not ever his co-worker or replacement. It's a good thing I don't want to be a chef eh?" He smiled. I didn't believe the smile.

"You want to be a chef don't you?"

He stood up and continued to unpack. "It doesn't really matter what I want."

I felt slightly bad for the guy. In his family of rich and powerful members, it was his birth order that was going to hold him back. For most of my students it was the money and the power that stopped them. Although I didn't feel too bad, he was probably going to end up a very rich and powerful lawyer, most likely making most of his money representing his brother.

"Want to know the shitty thing? Jack doesn't even want it. He is in just as much of a bad state as I am. He would be happy just living a bachelor's life, with Daddy's money of course." He laughed through his nose.

"I can see him filling that role well." He smiled a more believable smile this time.

"I can too."

"Listen, I have to go do my rounds now. I will be up until at least 2 a.m. if you think of any more questions or just something else you want to say, okay?"

He agreed. It's funny how two brothers who grew up in the same house with the same people, could turn out so opposite of each other. Their differences kept me in thought most of the evening.

* * * * * * * * * * *

"Sadie, it's Lonny, we need to talk. Please call me back when you are in. Better yet, come by my room. I'll be there studying."

I had to admit, I was a little relieved that I didn't answer the phone. It was accidental that I picked this call to ignore and continue on with my homework when I answered the previous three calls.

Where the stream and creek collide

However it could have also been some sort of telepathy talent that I have not quite tapped into yet. Not sure. I did want to talk with him, but at the same time there was something to be said about ignorance being bliss. I was done classes now. They had ended for the day at 2 p.m. I decided to make my way down to the office and handle the call back later. I had to hand in the incident reports from last night. The reports were mostly just quiet hour violations. I had two students on two separate floors decide that it was okay to start playing their music at 3 and 4 in the morning, just because they were still awake. Quiet hours started at 11. Normally I would just ask the student to turn it off, in assumption that they were just drunk, but in these particular cases they were students that had already had several chances and warnings and were completely sober.

The lounge had its usual cast of characters, Hal, Sandy, Wanda, and Tristen. They were all hanging on the couch talking about Hal and Piety's interesting weekend with his not quite sane mother. He made light of it, I personally felt a little bad for the guy.

"Here to meet your father Sadie?" Tristen asked. His dreadlocks were standing straight up today. He did this every once in a while for effect. His face was chubby, so when his dreads were spiked it made his head look exceptionally large.

"My father? What do you mean?"

"Father - the male parent in the house."

"That would be assuming of course, that both parents are of opposite sex. It is the 21st Century, Trist, we gay people are starting families now, too," Wanda chimed in.

"Ah, yes, good point, even through all the sarcasm."

"Guys! Back to my father, is he here?" I asked.

"He is in with Alex. Has been for about 20 minutes," Hal informed me.

I went over to the door to knock. I heard them laughing inside. I rapped my hands on the door. Alex opened it up.

"Am I interrupting anything?"

"No, come on in." I was shocked to find them in good spirits, especially after what I had heard over the past few days.

"We were just talking about the conference. Alex asked me to come and help drive one of the trucks. I said I would be happy to go."

"Great," I smiled. "And to help with my ramp right?"

"Of course that too, if you are accepted to do your presentation," father reminded me.

"I know."

I handed Alex the reports from last night. My father got up, said his good byes, gave me a hug, and left.

"I hope I didn't chase him out of here?" I was curious to know more of his visit, but my curiosity would have to wait. Alex just replied with a 'no, we were done' comment.

Back in the lounge, the door was open and most of the R.A.'s were starring out to the entrance way. "Look at the boys with J.P." Sandy said. "Let's open the window."

I looked out of Alex's office window. Jack, Jefferson, and Tucker Palmer, a self proclaimed bad boy, were talking with J.P. A lot of slaps on the back were going on, as well as some knuckle punches. 'You're my dog, I heard Jack tell J.P.'

"Please, this can't be good." I spoke out loud. Maybe it was my own stereotypes in play here, but I didn't think that this was innocent at all. Were they up to something, or just getting kicks out of teasing J.P. behind his back?

I went outside when the boys left.

"J.P., How are you?"

"I am good, thanks. I just stopped for a while to talk to my friends, and now I am afraid I am a little behind. I am going to lose the J in my name."

"The J? What do you mean?"

"Didn't I ever tell you? J.P stands for Janitor Pierre. My name is Pierre and I am a janitor, get it?"

I was shocked. I never knew this. I assumed his name was Jean – Pierre, or something to that effect.

"Wow, how long have you had that nickname?"

He shuffled his feet while scratching his head. His longer than usual hair was in disarray.

"Well, I started the name when I first started here about 8 years ago. It caught on and now that is all people know me as." He spit many times in his sentences. I tried not to wince. It was hard when one droplet of saliva landed in my mouth.

"Very cool, J.P., what a great story." I paused for effect. "Anyways, I shouldn't keep you any longer from your work; you're going to be really behind soon. Although, I am quite confident that you would catch it up just fine. You are good at what you do." I knew I was borderline on patronising him, and I really didn't mean to, but it came out that way, and I couldn't really be bothered correcting it today.

"I am. Thanks, Sadie for noticing."
"See you later, Pierre." I needed to go. I needed to talk to Lonny. I went to his room instead of calling him back. I thought it was time for us to talk. I wasn't sure what we were going to say, but I was sure that the format of our discussion would work itself out. I was more right about that than I could have ever imagined.

-11-

LOVE ISN'T BLIND, IT'S DEBILITATING!

"How many fucken people did you tell, Sadie, the whole residence? You shouldn't have even told one person. This is nobody's business. I didn't think you had that much of a big mouth. Fuck!" He was pacing. He was pacing and while he was, he was also rambling on about many things. I had never seen him so angry, at least not at me. I could not respond to his harsh words. I was speechless. I had gone to his room and after knocking on his door just once, he whipped the door open to reveal a very angry, very red faced, Lonny. "Come in," was actually the first thing he said. I did. The door closed. The shouting began.

"I can't believe this, I can't fucking believe this. A kiss, a drunken goodnight kiss and you tell everyone. Everyone, Sadie" he seemed to be talking to the wall. His last word, my name, came out very slow. I held up my right hand in sort of a cup position, shrugging my shoulders for emphasis. My face said what my mouth couldn't – what?

He bent down and got really close to my face, his right pointer finger coming awfully close to my nose. His left hand was resting on my left tire. "Do you realize that Jessica has friends here? Do you realize that the people you talk to are big mouthed immature girls that go running to their friends, who go running to other friends, to tell them what again is OUR business." He stood up and backed away.

"Do you really think we are that interesting Lonny? That, that many people would want to know *our* business? Friends of friends? Believe me, we are not that exciting." I finally responded to him. I had nothing else. My emotions were bouncing back and forth between being upset and being pissed off.

"That is not my point and you know it."

"Then what is your point, because I am really not hearing one."

"My point is that you talked to someone about our kiss didn't you?"

"Don't you mean the *drunken kiss*, yes, of course I did. I talked to Ashlyn, Piety, and Alex." I felt no need to mention Elizabeth since she can't tell anything I talked to her about to anyone anyways due to confidentiality issues. Unless she wanted to break an oath and I am pretty positive she would not risk her job for a silly little kiss that happened in a college residence.

"Three people, nice job, Sadie. This isn't high school anymore you know. Those days are long gone. We are adults now, not teenagers."

"What is this about Lonny? Are you paranoid that Jessica is going to find out that you stuck your tongue down my throat?" I knew I was pushing his buttons. I didn't really care at this point. My mood had made a decision to balance out nicely at upsettingly pissed off.

He went red again. He looked me in the eyes with a little more conviction than he previously showed.

"Paranoid that she is going to find out, Sadie? She knows. She knows, she knows, she knows. She called me this morning crying because one of her friends informed her that she heard that we kissed. She was freaking out. I have never before heard her as upset as this. She knows Sadie." He sat down on his bed.

"Gee Lonny, by any chance does she know?"

"This is not funny." He spoke through gritted teeth. "She is thinking of breaking up with me. Six years down the tube. I am fighting for my life with her right now."

"I am sorry Lonny." I didn't know what else to say. My stomach started to turn. He was very upset. I was hurt. Not a good mix. Did he really blame me and only me for this? I wanted to try to slow the yelling down. "What did you say to her?"

"I told her that it was nothing. That it was just a Happy Birthday kiss that didn't mean anything to either of us. I told her that we will always be just friends."

Pop! There went my balloon. I had a feeling that that was a statement for me as well as for her. I suddenly felt more confident than I had all the past week. It all became clear to me; my feelings, my wishes, my reality. Something about feeling the bottom underneath your feet that does that to you.

"That's what it meant to you, nothing. Just a Birthday kiss was all? Okay."

He paused for what seemed like ten minutes, but was more like 10 seconds. He looked at his feet. "That's all it was, Sadie."

"Okay." I paused, "point taken. Nothing! Just two friends celebrating a birthday with a kiss, hooray!" I took a deep breath.

I felt like I was speaking with assertiveness not sarcasm. Lonny apparently felt different.

"Don't be so childish."

"Childish! Because of how I am reacting; how should I react to this Lonny?" My assertion was short lived. "Do you want me to cry, because believe me it is coming. I thought it meant more to you than that?"

"What do you want me to say?"

I wanted him to say he meant that kiss. That he wanted more. That he thought of me every moment, and that he was glad she now knew so that we could be together. The truth was, I wanted him to say this more than anything, but I knew he wouldn't.

"Say we are done here. Say that this," I paused and pulled his chin up so that he was looking at me again. I made circular motions with my hand. "That this thing here, the circles we are going through, whatever it is, is over, done."

He didn't respond. He didn't have to. Instead he stood up and moved between me and the door.

"Come on Lonny. First of all, I doubt Piety or Ashlyn are the reason she found out. If you recall, we fell in the hall right before it happened, and probably woke up many students. Second, I sure didn't plan it to happen."

"Neither did I, you know? It meant nothing." He interrupted.

"Yeah, nothing, I got that."

He remained quiet so I kept going.

"Are we going to get over this Lonny?" I wasn't sure I wanted to know the answer. To my surprise he not only replied but he was calmer when he did so. He leaned in towards me again. This time with both hands on my wheels.

"I am sure we will. We have been through a lot. You are my best friend. But I have to make things right with Jessica. That is the most important part. You may not see it now, but you will see it in time; it really was nothing. You will probably even forget about it very soon."

I passed him and opened the door to leave. I had a sudden burst of either guts or resignation, I wasn't sure, but whatever it was, it made me turn back in his direction.

"Alright Lonny, but just for the record, it wasn't 'nothing' to me. When the guy I love more than any other guy I have ever met, kisses me the way you kissed me that night. It means something. And, no, I won't see that any different in time, and I won't forget about it. Nor will I forget the way you talked to me tonight." I turned around and left, pushing my chair faster than I have in a while. I needed to get to the elevator before the onset of the many tears I felt building inside myself came flooding out.

But it was too late. Before the ding of the bell rang out, I tasted the salt of my tears.

-12-

PLANS, LIKE PIMPLES, JUST POP WHEN THEIR READY.

"It's kind of like landing on the moon, isn't it?"

"What do you mean?" I asked Ashlyn who was filling in for Piety on this interview. Piety and I were doing a movie script together for class, but she had to work today, and the police officer we were interviewing was not able to reschedule in any time frame that would have been conducive our project due date.

"Driving into Sudbury. The black rock that surrounds us."

Sudbury, a large mining town in Northern Ontario, with a population of over one hundred and fifty thousand, was believed to be the remnants of a 1.8 billion year old meteorite crater. Basically, the city was built in the big hole of rock that the crater left after impact. In the late 1800's when the community was known by its previous name, Sainte-Anne-des-Pins, blasting and excavation during the building of the Canadian Pacific Railroad, revealed high concentrations of nickel, copper, and ore, on the edge of the Sudbury Basin. These minerals were believed to also be remnants of the meteorite crater.

"It is a little daunting isn't it?" I agreed.

We drove into the city through its South end. Turning right onto Paris Street we followed the road past Ramsey Lake, Science North, and the Bridge of Nations - a bridge that crosses over many railroad tracks and holds flags along its sides from over 70 different countries and cultural groups. A moment later we were driving into Tom Davies Square, on Brady Street, the government building that housed the Greater Sudbury Police station.

"Do you know where we are going in here?" Ashlyn asked as she pulled my chair out of the back seat of my car. It was always easier for my passenger to get my chair for me when I was driving with someone because my chair went in the back seat. When I drove alone, I kept it beside me in the front - an easy place for me to reach it to lift out. I made sure my wheelchairs were light-weight and compactable, so that getting out of vehicles was less time consuming.

"Well, I know I need to go inside. After that, no clue."

"Awesome."

We were able to park right in front of the main doors so when we entered the building it was apparent where we needed to go first. We needed to go to the information desk located directly in front of anyone taking their first few steps inside the station.

"Can I help you?" A middle-aged blond officer asked. She was in a booth and remained seated at her desk as we approached.

"Yes, I, ah, sorry…we have an interview with Staff Sergeant Bob Gunushy." I spoke through the small opening in the very large piece of glass that separated us.

"Let me call him out here for you." She smiled and then picked up her phone.

"Seriously, that's his name? And you are just telling me this now? I could have had a lot of fun with that name on the drive down. I would have entertained you a lot more with that information than my stupid dog stories."

I laughed, "But I liked your stupid dog stories."

Ashlyn just sighed from her nose and smiled at me. "Sure, sure."

"Sergeant Gunushy will be right out."

"Thank you."

We only had time to look at one of the Greater Sudbury Police history displays in the front lobby when Sergeant Gunushy came out to meet us.

"You must be Sadie and Piety?" He asked as he walked over to us, hand extended for a handshake. I shook his hand first, Ashlyn followed behind.

"Actually Piety couldn't make it. I am her stand in sir, Ashlyn."

"Well, stand in, nice to meet you. You both can call me Bob."

He was a tall man, slim but muscular. His hair was in a buzz cut, military style and he sported a dark haired goatee on his chin. Most interesting though was his piercing yellow green eyes. They seemed to sing. His walk was fast and deliberate. It took us left behind the information booth, past a series of desks, and down a hall. We followed behind ambitiously. At one point, Ashlyn grabbed on to the back of my chair and started pushing. I wasn't sure if it was to speed me up or to hold her up. Finally he opened up a door and guided us in.

"We can meet in here ladies," he said as he turned on the ceiling lights to reveal an 8 seat table in a very dark boardroom. It had no windows, yellow walls, brown carpet, and a mountain of boxes in the back of the space. As if reading our mind he educated us on the reasons for the state of the room. "It's an old boardroom that we don't use very often anymore, except to store supplies. We have newer rooms now, but this one will do for us today, don't you think?"

We agreed with him.

"Now, this is for school correct?"

"Yes. Piety and I are in film, and for our writing class we have to write a script for a short movie, 40 minutes in length or less. We are doing ours on the life of a man named Gerald, who works on a Tactical unit and finds himself in a gun standoff at work with his own Sergeant, who has recently suffered a great loss." Ashlyn placed her hands under her face, resting her chin on her finger tips, and smiled a fake smile, when I said Piety and I. It was her little joke to remind the Sergeant that she was a stand in.

"Okay. Interesting! So what exactly are we here to talk about today?" He asked.

"We need to know things like hierarchy in the police force, protocol for these types of situations, insights into some losses that an officer can experience, job related of course, that would drive him or her to a gun standoff reaction. Basically any insight you can give us will be greatly appreciated."

"Sure, no problem." There was a knock on the door. "Come in!" Officer Gunushy shouted. The door opened and an extremely cute, blond haired, blue eyed officer, dressed in uniform, gun and handcuffs included, walked in. "Ladies, this is Officer Craig Hales. He now works with the Boating Unit, patrolling the lakes and waters around the city. But he was also on the tactical team and has had a lot of experience he could maybe share later."

"Hi ladies!" He greeted us.

"Hello," we replied in unison. We were both immediately taken with his looks.

"I need you to sign these papers Sergeant." He bent down and showed Officer Gunushy the papers and had a short discussion with him about the contents.

I looked at Ashlyn. "Holy shit!" I mouthed.

"I know." She mouthed back.

"Hot!" I continued to talk without volume.

She nodded.

When they were done with the papers, Officer Gunushy explained to Officer Hales the reason for our visit. Officer Hales agreed to come back in 5 minutes and assist with the interview. He did. Ashlyn and I talked to the officers for over an hour about various situations they had been in, various stresses on the job, and why they did what they did. They told us about protocol in a hostage situation as well for domestic disputes. I found it most interesting when they talked about how it affected their families. For Officer Gunushy, he talked about how hard it was on his wife for him to be gone for such long shifts. How it became more critical that he take fewer hours, once the kids came along. For Officer Hale, who to our delight, had no wife and kids, talked about how it troubled his parents and siblings. It was a great insight for us to have considering we were writing about an officer on a personal level as well as a professional one.

Ashlyn asked some really great questions. I was surprised at that considering she was only debriefed on our script idea this morning.

"Well I guess that pretty much does it. I can't think of any more questions or you." I said closing my notebook. "Thanks so much for your time."

"You're very welcome. I was just in doing paperwork today. This broke my day up nicely."

"And I was just doing the same before heading back out to the docks." Officer Hale added.

"Are you guys patrolling today?" Gunushy asked.

"No, the weekend."

"So what exactly do you do on the water this time of the year, it is the middle of October? We don't have any large waters around here." I asked Officer Hale. I felt my cheeks blush a little warmly as I presented him with the question.

"You would be surprised how much action the lakes still have. There are a lot of end of the year fishing parties going out. People don't think the waters are being patrolled because of the season, so they drink more while boating. They also tend to forget their life jackets because of the amount of clothing they are wearing. We need to always be ready to go on a moment's notice. If people fall in, we have to be ready to go. Boat and water rescue is a huge part of my job."

"I find that so fascinating." I responded, trying slightly to sound flirtatious.

"Fascinating, eh? You like boating?" He asked.

"No. She likes being rescued." Ashlyn answered for me. I

elbowed her in the arm.

"Shut up!" I felt the blushing return.

The Officers tried to stifle their laughs unsuccessfully.

We talked with them a few more minutes before we left the station and returned to my car.

"Thanks a lot for embarrassing me in front of the hottest guy in the world." I smiled yet chided Ashlyn as she sank herself into the front passenger seat.

"No problem. Thought I would help Lonny out by not letting you get hooked up while out on an interview. You wouldn't want to do anything to hurt that budding romance would you?"

"I am afraid you are too late for that."

"What happened? Already?"

The whole ride home I filled her in on my conversation with Lonny. The ride home went quicker than the ride to Sudbury. Anything connected to Lonny did that – suck time away from me. That should have been my first sign of the impending doom that was about to be my love life.

* * * * * * * * * * *

The weeks went by slowly and before I knew it, the end of November was here and we were starting to wrap up before the Christmas holidays. I had not been in a great mood all month. School was starting to get more intense with homework that kept me behind a computer for most of my evening time, at least the evening time that wasn't already taken up with meetings or on-call shifts.

We were busy hiring students for extra jobs. The support staff contract negotiations were in the final hours of talks, with neither side willing to budge. The Full time staff wanted more hours with better benefits. As of now the part time staff, who were all students, were getting a lot more hours for less pay and no benefits. The full timers felt that they were slowly being pushed out for cheaper labour. The painfully ironic thing in the situation was that the resident staff talked the culinary teachers into allowing their students to work in the cafeteria for their required placement hours should a strike arise. This would start after the holidays if we needed the staff. I was positive that it would not go over well.

Also with November came the return of Jack's troublesome nature. Within the past few weeks he started with the parties and the constant drinking again. This for the most part was normal happenings in residence, but he seemed to push it to the extreme. One evening I went to his room on a noise complaint from one of the students living down the hall from him. When I got there, he had the music really loud and two other people in his room. I asked him to turn the music off. He said he would. Several minutes later I was called back to the room. I again knocked on his door to get him to turn the music down. This time when he opened the door there was 5 people, besides him, inside his room. I kicked them out and again asked him to turn the music down. A half hour later I was called back to his room to find the music on again and 6 people now in his room, 4 of which I just kicked out. He just laughed in my face every time. This kept going until I wrote every last one of them up on an incident form, including Jack. This of course kept me up until 5 in the morning on a Thursday night. I was not impressed - he was thrilled.

Many other R.A.'s complained about his behaviour as well. Jack was always throwing parties, going to bars, coming back smashed and he always had a huge following while doing it. We guessed that it wasn't his natural charm that led people to be friends with him, but more so his money. He would always buy rounds at the bar, he provided the booze and we assumed the drugs, for all his dorm room parties, and he would occasionally bring out groups of friends to dinner at his father's restaurant in Toronto, splurging for the limousine and the hotel rooms to sleep everyone afterward.

I was not surprised to see Bridgette back in his circle of friends. She was around Jack 24-7. My guess was that she had not yet learned all she needed to from Jack, because not only was she hanging around him, but every time he got in trouble, she seemed to be in trouble as well. Weekly she would come show me her newest necklace, or a bracelet she had received as a gift. Finally one day when I asked her why she was getting all these gifts, she replied – sounding rather insulted by my question – that they were dating and he thought she deserved it. I left it at that with a smile and a nod. Who was I to judge considering how my love life was going.

Lonny and I had seen each other several times since our fight. It was really awkward at first. I wasn't sure if that was due to our exchange of words, our kiss, or the fact that I told him that I loved him in a way that was more than just friends. We still did things relatively the same, but there was no joking, no talking beyond superficial crap, and there was definitely no touching. Our distance was bitter sweet for me. Probably more bitter than sweet, because I missed him, but I couldn't hide the fact that I was still pissed off at how he handled it.

I talked to Alex after leaving Lonny's room that night. I had called her from my cell phone right after, to see if she would meet me in either my room or hers. She came to my room only taking 5 minutes to get there. She greeted me with a big hug before sitting down to listen to me whine.

After many hurt-filled sentences, Alex suggested that he was probably reacting the way he thought he should, with his head, not his heart. He wasn't responding to kissing me, he was responding to cheating on Jessica. The feelings of that indiscretion over-rode all other feelings he was experiencing. I wasn't sure I agreed with her, but her assertion made me feel better about the situation. The last thing she told me was 'the opposite of love is not hate, it is apathy. As long as he is angry it means he still cares. People don't get angry over things they don't care about. We are generally a lazy society. We don't exhaust efforts where we don't have to.' I believed this. I just wished we had skipped the whole moral dilemma thing.

She ended our talk with me assenting to see Elizabeth about the situation. Then we determined ice cream was a necessity. Alex needed to finish up a little work, and I needed to shower the day off of my self. We called Piety to come with us. We all met downstairs in the lounge an hour later.

"Yes, that sounds nice. I would too. Dinner tomorrow sounds great to go over the details." Alex giggled like a young teenager. She seemed to wrap her pointer finger a million times around a long strand of her light brown hair. She winded the strand up with enough gumption to let it unravel for at least ten seconds with out stopping. I was in the R.A. office, just outside her door. Her door was cracked open just slightly. Piety had not yet shown up.

"Alright then," she again laughed with a slight giggle. "Ah, Jason? Thanks a lot for your help. I appreciate it. I probably should have let Sadie tell you what's going on, but since we were on the subject."

Jason? Sadie? Why was she talking to my father? And why was she talking about me? Telling him what about what was going on? What was going on? She couldn't have told him what we were talking about. My stomach started to shake. I entered the room with both extreme caution and regret, presumably like I would enter a room that I was told had a bomb in it. I had obviously startled her, because I interrupted her sentence and she spun around rather quickly in my direction. I had a curious look on my face, I knew it, but I couldn't stop it.

"Listen, Sadie is here. I should let you go," she said with her arm held out towards me. "I will see you tomorrow then. Bye." She hung up the phone and turned to me. "That was you father on the phone."

"I gathered that. What did he want? What did you tell him that I should have?"

She didn't seem to be bothered with my intrusion of her privacy. I sensed she got where I was going with my question. "I was calling him about the conference, Sadie."

"Oh! You called him?"

"Yes, I did."

"Are you friends again?"

Alex took a deep breath then blew the air up to make the short strands of her bangs fly high.

"We have always been friends Sadie. We just haven't been able to get over what happened before. Now we are better at forgetting it, or moving on with it if you may."

"I see." I didn't but I also didn't want to discuss it further right now.

"Anyways, I was saying that we were talking about the conference. Two proposals were accepted, Tristen's and yours. I have to send a list off in two days to let them know who is coming in regards to both students and volunteers."

I sighed, relieved. "Cool. That is very exciting." I tried to change my tone quickly to mask the confusion I was feeling prior to being privy to their conversation. I was excited about the proposal but the earlier little scare hadn't left my system yet.

"And is he coming?"

"Your father, yes, he said he wouldn't miss it."

It all started to fall into place. I smiled. Alex smiled back, hers probably for a different reason than mine.

"Who is all going for the volunteers?"

Alex replied with telling me my father, Candice, the residence secretary, and Elizabeth would be going. It would be an interesting trip I thought. I had Elizabeth who I wanted to get together with my father, Alex, who was going to help me, and Candice whom I could get to assist as well, if needed. Candice was an older women and a secretary that worked at the residence for many years and she was always willing to help me out with anything I needed. When it came to residence fees, she helped me postpone dates to get my payments in on time. She would help me get information for students when I was trying to help them and the school records office wouldn't talk to me thanks to my small position at the school. Candice told me that she had my concern in mind always. It was possible that I was going to need to put that concern to test at the conference.

"Knock, knock." Piety said as she opened the door. "Are we ready for ice cream?"

"I am so ready," I replied. I needed to celebrate. My plans on one front at least, were falling exactly into place. A weight felt lifted. "Bring on the ice cream."

-13-

CRAZY SHOULD BE A FOUR LETTER WORD.

"Alright guys, as you know we are now two weeks away from Holiday break. All of the students are wrapping up their classes and will slowly be leaving residence over the next 14 days."

It was our last meeting before the holidays. We had ordered Chinese food to munch on while we talked. I ate a plate full of Cantonese noodles, beef and vegetables, and breaded shrimp. We always ordered from King's China on the last meeting of the calendar year. We couldn't call it a Christmas meeting because not all of our employees celebrated the holiday. It was the residence way of being politically correct. We couldn't say Merry Christmas, we said Happy Holidays. Just like we couldn't ask about a student's boyfriend or girlfriend by that title unless we knew what sex they were. We had to say partner, to not exclude those in same sex relationships. Of course on both accounts, we all slipped from time to time.

Elizabeth had joined us for our meeting and I was sitting nicely in between her and Lonny. I felt a little awkward still around him. Small talk used to be okay when it was meaningful. Now it was just small talk because that was all we could think about saying to each other that wasn't said with a hurtful or angry tone. And we couldn't stay silent for some reason. For me, I think silence made my feelings more intense. At least if I allowed myself to have small snippets of anger come out over time, it would stop me from completely exploding all at once in a volatile way. I hadn't spoken to Elizabeth about the situation as I said I would. I didn't have the time, nor did I feel like I really needed to talk about it anymore. The only downside I was now seeing was that I would have to put up with the many looks of confusion from Elizabeth. These looks came when she had spoken to both Lonny and I in one sentence and received a very short answer from either one or the other of us, and never both. She knew this was not a common occurrence. We usually finished each other's sentences, and every one knew it. In fact, every one almost expected it.

"So Manny and Wendy are staying in residence over the holiday, but Wendy will be gone the evening of the 24th." She paused and looked over in Wendy's direction for confirmation. Wendy nodded.

"Of course, I will be here for the most part. When I am not here I will just be at my parent's house, and available on the pager. They live in Sudbury so I will never be more than an hour and a half away. And on those days that I am in Sudbury, I will have someone with a pager closer to the residence just in case of an emergency. So what are everyone's plans for the holidays?"

We all shared what our plans were. Six of us had not finished shopping yet, including me, and four of the six had not even started. Many of us just planned on seeing family and relaxing at home. I said that I was looking forward to spending time with my father, and Lonny made sure to add that he was excited about seeing his girlfriend. Alex, as though reading my angst, changed the subject, for me I believe, at the end of Lonny's proclamation.

"I have one last order of business before we end our meetings for this year." We were starting to get restless and talk over each other. "I have received the results of the proposals for the conference. We do have two people who have had their proposals accepted." People were getting up to throw their plates in the garbage, but this information had them scampering back to their seats, garbage still in hand. Only one or two continued over to the plastic barrel of rubbish. And Tristen, who wasn't headed for the garbage but rather for the food to replenish his plate a third time, didn't sit down for her to continue at all.

"I got your attention haven't I? Thought that would do it. Well our two lucky presenters are Sadie and Tristen." I smiled and Tristen shouted and spitted whoo-hoo with a mouth full of chicken fried rice.

"I don't fucken believe this." Lonny whispered. I heard him, and was pretty sure Elizabeth did as well, as she turned to look at him with slightly shocked and annoyed expression.

"Sorry Lonny, I know you wanted to go.' I said to him unsure of why I was really apologizing.

"You're not sorry Sadie, you wanted it badly." I shrugged. He was right. "That isn't why I am upset anyway, not like you care," he said as he stood to leave.

"I do care Lonny," I replied.

He grunted in return.

"Not yet Lonny, I'm not done." Alex added unaware of the conversation we were having. Or lack of it I guess. Oblivious that she was keeping Lonny from running out on me as much as from her. "There are 19 of you. Lonny can't go because I need a senior R.A. here, and Tristen and Sadie are obviously going already. That leaves 16 left, and I said I would take about half or a little more of you, so let's go with 10, besides the two presenters. This year I have decided that both presenters can decide who is coming to the conference by deciding who they want to help them with their presentation." There were a lot of sighs, some smiles. "Sadie you will pick three boys and two girls to assist you with your presentation, and Tristen you will do the same, but opposite on the number of girls and boys. I want names in to me by tomorrow night. That gives you 24 hours to decide. Sound good?" We both nodded. I liked the idea of picking who would be working with me on my project and who would be coming with us on the conference. The conferences were always a blast, so you wanted friends to be there with you.

"Works for me, I'm in," Tristen said.

"Me too," I also replied.

"Can we leave now?" Lonny begged.

A little bit sympathetic, Alex responded with a yes and asked everyone to make sure they said bye to her before leaving for the holidays. With that, he was gone.

"He okay?" Alex mouthed to me.

I made a face that required my mouth to be sucked in at each corner where one lip met the other. My shoulders shrugged up, my right hand lifted palm side up, as I broke my lip hold only to mouth back "not sure." Don't really care anymore, I added only in thought.

Besides I didn't. I had no idea why he was so upset. I knew that he was angry with me already, and I knew he wanted to go, I just didn't realize he wanted to go 'tantrum worthy' bad.

I went straight to my room after helping Alex clean up the food. We put it all in the fridge in the resident assistant lounge. We were fairly confident that the food would be eaten up over the next day or so by the R.A.'s. It usually did.

Neither of us knew what was going on with Lonny. Of course we had guesses. I did tell her about what he said when she said that my proposal was accepted not his. To be a little disappointed would be normal, even expected, but not to be pissed.

When I arrived to my room, there was a pink stick-it note on my door. It was in Lonny's hand writing. *Jessica will be at the conference. If you really do care, you will avoid her.*

Mystery solved.

* * * * * * * * * * *

I exited my room to toss out the garbage from under my bed. I was trying to tidy up before I left for the holidays. My room had gotten out of control and I needed to once again have power over the mess. I dumped my bags into the garbage and quite literally bumped right into Harvey Boom when turning around from the can.

"Here to pick up Julie?" Harvey was Julie's boyfriend. He came here once and a while for the night. Julie had told us that he was coming to get her. He was a cute guy. He had brown eyes and slightly lengthy, yet still short cut, brown hair. He always had a scruff growing for a beard, never fully shaved yet never fully grown in. And his left ear held an oversized round red tube earring, one designed to stretch out the earlobe over time wearing it. Harvey seemed to be fairly consistent when it came to his jewellery. He also always wore a necklace that he claimed was a shark's tooth that his uncle had once pulled from a shark's mouth himself.

"Yes I am. I'm whisking her away for Christmas. You, are you getting out of here soon?"

"I am. And I can't wait to get home. I leave tomorrow. Do you two live close?"

He leaned against the wall and picked at his nails. "The same town, Cambrian, not far from each other. Just a half hour drive through traffic. This year we are going to spend the first part of the holidays at my parent's house, and the second part between her father's and her mother's house."

I was confused. "Oh, I didn't realize that her parents lived separately from each other before she died. Sorry if I am being nosey, but does someone still live at her mother's house?"

He laughed. It was his turn to look confused. "Her parents separated about 3 years ago. Her mother lives in Ayre, just outside Cambrian. And no one died, just the marriage maybe."

"Her mother's alive?"

"Yes."

"Are you sure?"

"Yup, unless she died sometime between now and the last phone conversation I had with Julie 15 minutes ago."

We both jumped to the noise of Julie opening her door.

"There you are. When did you get here?" She bounced out of her room, jumped into his arms and kissed him on the cheek. "Whacha two talking about?"

Harvey snickered. I felt uncomfortable. I scratched my head to hide my face. I didn't really want to get into this with her right now. "Did you tell Sadie that your mother is dead?"

She looked at him, then at me. "Yup, I told the truth, now let's leave." She grabbed him by the arm and led him into the room. Her blond locks flew up in the air and dropped slowly back down. Her strands of hair seemed to be in less of a rush than her body. He looked back and shrugged in my direction before disappearing behind the heavy dorm room door. Other than the fact that she vanished in about 5 seconds flat, Julie didn't look phased at all by the latest update on her life. That was what interested me. It wasn't everyday someone's mother came back to life. Heaven knew I had been trying for 6 plus years to have mine come back, to no avail, yet here she managed to have hers return in a matter of seconds.

I was a little pissed that she would make up something so important for what? Attention? A friend? A job? Bizarre. How could she tell me such a sob story about her mother when it wasn't true at all? Especially when she knew that my mother had died as well, and how I felt about it. What a bitch. I went back in my room to finish cleaning. I couldn't stay out in the hall in case she came out of her room. I didn't think that I could face her and stay civil at the same time.

Two hours later I was done cleaning. The only thing left to do was to pull down the gifts from the top shelf that I had already wrapped and stored. Lonny was supposed to get a ride home with me, so he would have reached them down and packed them into the vehicle, but he made other arrangements to get home. Avoidance was his communication of choice these days. He claimed he wanted to leave a day earlier and didn't think I would want to, so he just went ahead and asked his buddy Tom to drive him home. His alternate plans were quite fine by me. An awkward ride home was not one that I was particularly looking forward to. The only thing right now that sucked about the whole situation was these damn wrapped gifts stuck on my top shelf.

I opened the door to see what students were available in the hall to help me reach them down. To my delight, Jefferson was there. He was just about to get onto the elevator when I called him to my door. He was happy to help me.

"So when are you out of res. Jefferson?"

He removed his black trench coat and laid it on the bed.

"I leave tonight with Jack. Well as soon as he returns from his date with Bridgette that is. I have knocked on his door three times now, and he still has not returned. He drives me nuts." Jefferson replied with frustration in his voice. He pulled down the first two gifts. "Where do you want these?"

I pointed to the end of the bed. "There is fine." I didn't want to interrupt him. He sounded like he needed to vent and I needed to focus on someone else besides my mother, Lonny, and Julie.

"How many people did you buy for, the town?"

I laughed. "Three."

"Must be three much loved people. Who evidently need every thing?" He smiled. I returned the facial expression but his question I left unanswered.

"You may not want to hear this, but that gives you and Jack something in common." He was right. I winced at the thought. "My brother will buy 7 or 8 gifts per person in his life. I prefer to buy one really special, really thought out gift for every one. I don't think the giving should be about what they need as opposed to what they wish for or desire. Am I making sense or sounding like a sissy?"

It was refreshing to see a DeGraff in a loveable light. Jefferson was so much more relatable for me then his brother. "Definitely not sounding like a sissy. I think that it sounds rather nice. And if I were a recipient of one of those gifts, I would be honoured to receive just one because it is a wished or desired for present."

He stopped. Looked me in the eye. "So if you think about how it would feel to receive a gift like that, imagine now how it feels to be the one who gets to give that feeling to someone. It's euphoric, truly it is."

A laugh came out almost hysterically. He was back to lifting boxes down.

"What's so funny," he inquired.

"I just find it ironic that you are the one who talks like this and your brother is the one that gets all the ladies."

He smiled. "My brother gets all the ladies because he prefers to. He samples everything on the buffet table, whereas I would rather order just one dish and hope that it becomes my regular. Corny, but you get my idea."

"Yes on both."

We laughed together. "So do you guys have a big family get together planned over the holidays?"

The gifts were all placed on the bed. He picked up his coat and sat down in the spot that it had just occupied.

"Yea, we always have a big family to-do. Usually everyone gawks over my father and his misguided and oldest son and heir. Not that I mind, I really don't appreciate that kind of attention." His face didn't really say the same thing his mouth had. He continued.

"They usually last days. Italian families you know. They are big and proud. They love to spend time with each other and eat, drink, and share. You know, the Italian way." He said the last part with a fake accent, while he held all his finger tips together in one hand and kissed them.

"I make fun but I do enjoy the Urn of Fate tradition." I showed him my curiosity so he continued to explain. "We all put a small wrapped gift into a large bowl and then later that evening we get to take turns grabbing one out to unwrap. It is nice. For the most part, that is all we get. Well, lately these past years we have become more commercialized and given other gifts. Like I said, Jack gets 7 or 8 per person. I just get one extra besides the Urn of Fate gifts." I shrugged and nodded in understanding.

Loud giggles came from the hallway. Most of the students had left, leaving little possibilities of bodies behind the voices. Both Jefferson and I were pretty convinced of who they belonged to. Jefferson lifted his eyebrows, grabbed his jacket and stood up. "Thanks for the chat. It sounds like it is time for me to finally get out of this place for the holidays." He smiled a seemingly sincere smile.

"It's me that needs to say thanks. You got all my packages down for me. Thank you."

"My pleasure," he said while he opened the door to leave. He froze in the door way.

"Un-fucken-believable! You were there the whole time?" Jefferson shouted out the hall.

"What's wrong?" I asked as I went to the doorway to see. Jefferson had entered the hall and was about a foot away from Jack's face. Jack was naked, yet covered, with his hand in the most appropriate spot. Bridgette, who stood in the hall, was wrapped in a bed sheet and nothing else, her eyes bloodshot, her make up smeared, and her hair in disarray. She giggled uncontrollably the whole time.

"I asked you a question?" Jefferson reiterated while slapping his brother in the head. "Were you fucking here the whole time?"

Jack laughed. Bridgette just laughed louder.

"What's so funny asshole?"

"I was just thinking. I wasn't fucking here the whole time. I was here fucking, the whole time." His laughter got heartier. Bridgette was now bent over in laughter.

"Fucking, that's funny." She gasped for air. "Because we were. So funny," she ended her sentence on an up tone. She was obviously totally stoned by the way she spoke, not that her look didn't also scream 'I'm high.' She couldn't even stand back up. I had to help her.

Jefferson was red. He wasn't anywhere as subdued as he was just 10 minutes ago in my bedroom. "Why didn't you say something one of the three times I knocked on your door?"

"I was busy bro. Do you usually answer the door when you are getting busy? Or do you remember that far back?"

Jefferson turned around, started to walk away, and then turned back to face Jack. The whole time he had his pointer finger up to his mouth and nose area. He shook his finger towards Jack, then rested it back on his nose.

"I am not even going to reward your wit with a response. Just get your ass in that room and get dressed. I will meet you down stairs in 20 minutes." He turned to Bridgette, "And you, you little dorm room whore, you will have to deal by yourself for a few weeks, if at all possible. Maybe sober up a little."

"Easy there Jefferson." I said. He backed away a bit, in what I saw as resignation to this particular part of the argument.

Bridgette straightened up to full height, not as resigned as Jefferson to the situation. "Who the hell are you to speak to me that way?" Her finger was twisting in small circles while pointing in Jefferson's direction. I imagined it was moving to mimic the circles her head was doing. "Now if I could just throw up, I would feel so much better." She bent over again. I went to her side and held onto her. She leaned on me, her butt taking a seat on my tire rim.

"I'll take her to her room. I need to talk with her." Jefferson said, taking a few steps towards us.

"Sorry, I need to take her. She is too impaired. I can not let her go off with another student, even you Jefferson."

"You don't trust me? She does, ask her. She is my brother's girlfriend."

Bridgette squeezed my hand a little but did not move or say a thing. I wasn't as convinced as Jefferson was, that she wanted to go anywhere with anyone. She squeezed again when Jack offered the same escort.

"Sorry boys, she is staying with me, it is my job as both a resident assistant and a female. Cheesy as that sounds, now Jack, what has she taken?" I asked a little concerned.

"She is just drunk, that is all."

"I doubt that. What have you taken Bridgette?"

"Nothing I told you." Jack quickly replied.

"I was talking to her Jack."

"Nothing," Bridgette finally answered.

"Well, let's hope." I turned to Jack. "Because if I feel that she is not coming out of this properly then I will send her back to the hospital, and I can promise you, that neither of you two are going to like the consequences of that trip." I looked back at Jefferson. "I am taking her to her room. Thanks again. I hope your holiday starts to pick up a little."

"Thanks. Same to you Sadie," he said giving Bridgette and I one last glare before he turned to the elevator. "Get dressed Jack." He yelled over his shoulder.

I walked with Bridgette to her room. She used my wheelchair like a walker.

"Honestly Bridgette, what did you take tonight?" She was lying on her bed. I grabbed her face and tilted it to mine, forcing her to look me in the eye.

"I am fine. I took nothing too harmful." She closed her eyes and passed out.

She took nothing too harmful? I think anything that would cause you to sleep with Jack Degraff after knowing full well how he treats women, was plenty harmful enough, if you asked me. I delayed my trip home one more night. I couldn't leave her alone.

-14-

THE FIRST ONE UNDER THE MISTLETOE HAS TO BURN IT!

"So, Julie's mother is alive? Really? Didn't you say that she spent many hours in your room over several nights talking to you about her feelings of her mother's death?" Father and I were sitting at our kitchen table drinking hot chocolate loaded with marshmallows and catching up on each other's life. It was the 22nd of December, in the evening. And it was the only time that I would have father to myself over the holidays. We were in for a montage of visits from different family members. Both mother and father's side were headed to our house to celebrate Christmas. Father's parents were the ones that were staying for Christmas morning. Mother's parents were visiting just after.

"Well, she did. It took her many weeks to decide to talk too. She had this whole elaborate story of how her mother died from a car accident. She said it took two weeks for her to actually pass away. Dad, she went into detail on how gruelling the days and nights were to go through. She cried for Pete's sake."

He laughed a little. "Some people have the knack of storytelling. Do you think it is a possibility that the boyfriend is lying?"

I thought for a second then told him what I had concluded before when I thought of this possibility myself.

"Well, she did say when he asked her if she told me her mother died, that she said it because it was the truth. But don't you think that if it was the truth, and the boyfriend was clearly lying about her being alive, that Julie would have defended herself more, called him out on the issue, or at the very least, looked upset that he lied about something so important? I sure would be pissed if someone close to me told someone else that I was lying about my mother's death. That just isn't right."

"Or sane," father added.

"Exactly," I furthered for emphasis.

We drank in silence for awhile. Besides the clock ticking the only noise you could hear in the kitchen was the sucking sound of us pulling the marshmallows out of our drink. Father had designed the kitchen himself. It was an old fashioned looking space that held both a cooking area and a dining spot. The wood was old and rustic looking. The counters and the cupboards shared the same type of lumber. It was a greyish coloured wood, with gold metal flower handles on all of the cupboard and drawer fronts. The counter tops looked as though you could get a splinter if you ran your hand over it, yet funny, no one ever had. The majority of the remaining décor was found at yard-sales visited over the summer by Dad and myself. He had an old cuckoo clock on the wall that looked a lot like a birdfeeder. The little yellow bird was stuck on the outside of the house. No more coo-coos for him. Father vowed to fix it one day but had yet to get around to it.

The table that we both sat at was also wooden. It was a large red painted wood picnic bench style table. In fact, the back side that sat against the wall was a large bench for people to sit on. We could seat twelve comfortably around the whole thing.

Our kitchen also included an apartment freezer, a black fridge and stove, several plants which father nurtured religiously, and many simple paintings in, - surprise - wooden frames. Looking around the room made me think of Jackie. She always hated this kitchen. She said it reminded her of a cottage. We wouldn't have to hear how much anymore.

"Awfully quiet here without Jackie?"

Father chuckled and added, "awfully nice too."

I was shocked. "Well, well father, what is this we are admitting to? Are you finally ready to say that she was nuts?"

"Calling her nuts is a little harsh, high maintenance maybe. Really high maintenance, that is."

I just smiled a knowing smile.

"Listen, don't even go there or I will start asking you about your love life and why there is no mention of Lonny being anywhere near this house over the holidays." My smile faded.

"Things are just a little tense between us right now." I didn't want to lie to him, but I wasn't about to get into it either.

"Okay, I'll accept that, for now."

I went to the counter and refreshed my hot chocolate; father declined a second cup. He was tired and wanted to head to bed. I kissed him good-night.

"Don't stay up too late, kid, we have a busy morning."

I grabbed my mug and went into the living room. I transferred into the recliner and popped on the television. A re-run of the Golden Girls was playing. It was the episode where Rose inherited a pig from her dead relative. I enjoyed this one. I had only settled into about ten minutes of the episode when the phone rang. The call display said that it was Greenbury College. I answered it.

"Sadie, glad you are there. You made it home safely." Alex's voice was kind.

"Of course I did. What's up?"

I stretched back on the recliner and turned the volume down on the television.

"I wanted to ask you a question. Off the records, with the complete understanding that you can of course say no at any time, without fear of disappointing me or anyone else." She paused for my response.

"Okay," was all I could come up with.

"I was really hoping that one of the R.A.'s picked by you or Tristen would have been Manny. I think that it is really important for him to go to the conference, to see the presentations, and to experience what it is like to have so many strangers be united in this way. You know, to see the residence community. You went to the conference before so, you know what I am talking about."

"I do. And I agree. May I ask a question back? And before you answer know that I am already totally willing to change one of my assistants for Manny. I haven't told Wanda or Jacob that I picked them yet, so since he is a guy, I will trade him for Jacob."

Her voice was relieved and happy. "Thanks Sade, I really appreciate it. So very much. Now what is your question?"

"Is the need for him coming really from what you want or because of pressure from above?"

"A little of both reasons actually, but not above, more of a sideways push." She giggled.

"Fair enough," I also laughed. "Put the trade in. I am game. Besides, you know that if you need it done, I am more than willing to help you out if I can. It's a sort of a 'I got your back, you've got mine' thing."

We talked for 15 more minutes about the holidays and our plans with family. We even saved a minute or two to complain about certain relatives. When we were done, I settled in for another show. Golden Girls was over, but Reba was now playing. A few minutes after the show ended the phone rang again. I looked at the call display, it was another Greenbury College call, and it had a star beside the name.

That only happens when the number calling was the same as the last number that called the line. In short, it meant that it was Alex again. She must have changed her mind about calling because it stopped ringing after two rings.

I thought about our conversation. I had no problem having Manny on my team. It would be fun. I did enjoy his company even though his stories of home scared the crap out of me. Jacob would have no idea that I picked him. I didn't see him after I made my choices on who would be assisting me. Almost every assistant said that they wanted to go so Tristen and I knew that we didn't really have to ask them if they were interested. We could just pick who we thought would be the best asset to our presenting team. The Resident Life conference was not only an educational event but a competition for the presentations. The top presentations went on to the National conference to present to the Resident Managers from across Canada. Everyone wanted to go there. The Nationals were one wicked-ass party.

I started to yawn so much that tears fell down my face. I needed to go to bed. The heat of the hot chocolate started to have its affect on me. I got into my chair and then into the elevator. I was a little concerned that the sound would wake father up. As I got closer to the top floor I realized how unconcerned I needed to be. I could hear father laughing hysterically. He seemed to be in a conversation. I opened the elevator door and looked in. He was on the phone. I smiled. It was nice to hear him laughing again. Chances are he was talking to a woman. I knew that he had been talking on the phone to Elizabeth again lately, it was probably her.

I wheeled by the room and whispered in a 'good night again' to my dad. He returned the salutation, and then returned to his conversation.

In my room I could still hear him talk. His voice would rise up at parts of the conversation he found particularly exciting, that was usually followed next by a bout of laughter. I had not meant to eavesdrop when I got into bed, but I couldn't help but want to hear the rest of the conversation once I heard father say, 'you crack me up Graham.' I guess Alex didn't call back and hang up on the second ring after all. Father had answered, and Alex had finally reached the Coleman she was really calling for.

* * * * * * * * * * *

My Grandparents arrived around 4:30 in the afternoon on Christmas Eve. They called us from their cell phone every hour from 1 pm on to let us know where they were on the road and how fast they were driving. They really didn't like showing up unexpected.

When they arrived, they each had a suitcase. They informed us over dinner that they had long passed the days of sharing each others' things. They had their own likes and dislikes, their own personal products, and most importantly their own way of packing. My Grandfather liked to roll his clothes up to give more space in the suitcase, so he could add more clothes to the pile just in case the weather becomes, in his terms, schizophrenic. My Grandmother, who agreed with my Grandfather about the need for more clothes, preferred to fold half of her clothes regularly, while the other half stayed pressed in a garment bag that she hung in the closet of whatever room she was staying in. They were both committed to their concept on packing, and less concerned with the need to be unified in their travels. This was quite a change in their relationship from the earlier days.

I remember when I was young my Grandparents use to take me on a summer vacation with them for a week every year. One particular trip, when I was 9, they took me to Niagara Falls. We stayed at one of their friend's cottages in Niagara on the Lake. My Grandparents were so adamant that all of our stuff fit together in the same suitcase that even my clothes had to go in with theirs. They said that when families vacation jointly in every sense, it brings them closer together. My Grandfather even went as far as going out to buy an extra large purse for my Grandmother, so that we could all fit our daily things into it. The large pink purse was more like a carry-all bag. Every once in a while Grandma would get tired of carrying it and Grandpa would step in. He would walk around the streets with a huge pink purse on his shoulder, unaware of the looks and snickers he received in return, some of which came from Grandma and I. That trip, I took a whole roll of pictures of Grandpa and his pink purse.

"Pass the peas please," Grandma asked as she scraped up the last of the potatoes onto her plate. She was a skinny woman who ate like a growing teenage boy. She still dyed her hair brown. She would say that she knew most people would figure it was a dye job sooner or later but if she could fool just one person, it would be worth it. I passed the peas to her, and she finished them off too.

"Anything else Grandma? There is another piece of chicken," I offered.

"No thanks. Just more vegetables dear, I don't need any more protein." Her voice had the old lady shakiness to it.

"So what happened to that Janet lady Jason?" Grandfather asked my dad.

Father was caught off guard. When he was uncomfortable with a question he first responds by putting his hand up to stifle a cough that still comes out, while looking at the person lifting just one eyebrow. He did this to Grandfather.

"You mean Jackie, Dad. And we are no longer together. We broke up a few months ago."

"That's too bad. I liked her. Didn't you Sadie?"

"I did," I said in the most convincing voice I could find. Father, I'm sure, didn't buy it, but he knew better anyway.

"A young woman needs a mother Jason; you should find someone pretty steady soon for Sadie's sake."

"I am fine Grandma. I am 22 years old. I don't need a mother anymore. I had one, she did a good job. She gave me a foundation to build on. And Dad, well he is mother and father. No offence Dad." I tried to add a laugh at the end.

"None taken honey," he smiled back.

"That's nice dear," Grandma added in what I believed was a very unintentionally patronising tone. "But sometimes you don't know what you need until it is too late. Not to take anything away from Charlie, your mother, she was great. But she is gone, and you are not. A girl needs a mother, period. And a father can't do it all despite wanting to." She pointed her fork, prong side up, towards father for emphasis.

I wanted to shrink. I wanted to shrink just small enough to slide under the table and through a set of chair legs so I could get the hell out of this room.

"You need to remarry Jason. I know Emilio and Stacey's daughter is single again. We should give you her number. You can invite her over one night. The holidays are the best time to meet someone new. There's always mistletoe around somewhere. Great way to get over the first kiss jitters."

Father shifted in his seat. I grabbed the last piece of chicken. I didn't figure I was going any where any time soon. I wished I was, say, maybe falling off the face of the earth or drowning in my own vomit causing me to slowly fade away. But no, here I was, eating more chicken, listening to my Grandparents, whom I love very much; dissipate the life choices of my father and I.

"I think Sadie is doing very well," he said as he nodded his head in my direction. "I do agree a woman figure in Sadie's life is important; however, more important than that would be to make sure it is someone that is going to understand where she has come from, enrich our life and make me happy, and stay with both of us for a very long time. Until I find a proper candidate for that we will continue to do the great job that we are already doing on our own." He smiled at the end.

Although I agreed with her on the idea of father remarrying I worried about the thought of having another parental figure in the house. The last thing I would want would be to make foolish decisions again and cause another person I cared about to die. Not just die but to be murdered in such a brutal fashion like mother was.

"Now you leave them alone, Jamie. They are doing well. And there is no mistletoe in this house. So I guess you will just have to keep that phone number in your purse for a little while longer." He winked in my direction.

"Thanks Grandpa. I know you mean only the best for us Grandma, but really, we are doing well." I squeezed her hand quickly before moving to put my plate away in the sink.

She gave me a sceptical look, but changed the subject anyway. We spent dessert talking about Christmas's from the past. We laughed, we remembered, and once we even cried. We also talked about the holiday parties that we had coming up. My grandparents on mother's side were coming down two days after Christmas, the same day that my now visiting grandparents were leaving. My other grandparents, my father, and I were all going to my aunts, mother's sister's house, for dinner and board games.

New Year's Eve was at our house this year. Father decided that after a week straight of family, it would be nice to have a group of friends attend our house. Since last year had been all about Jackie and sharing things with her family, New Years was a welcomed change for me and dad. We were both looking forward to it. Some old friends and new friends, work friends and play friends were all expected to attend. We just had to get through the rest of the days first.

That night I spent the first few hours not sleeping but thinking instead. I thought about all the things I should have done differently in my life. Mostly in regards to my mother, my father, school, Lonny, etcetera. You name it, I regretted something about it. My grandmother was right, dad did need to remarry. But dad was also right. He had to be the one to make that decision. He had to be happy, and enriched by the choice he made. I just wasn't sure I could wait around to watch the process unfold without interfering. I would be too afraid that he wouldn't make a choice. That he would miss something and stay alone for the rest of his life. If that happened, I don't think I would be able to deal with it. I think that that would probably be the end of me, at least the end of the 'me' that I liked. Death to Sadie.

-15-

NEW YEARS RESOLUTION: TO BE LESS RESOLUTE.

Most people believe that we all have a soul mate out there. I don't. I believe we have many. To think that only one person in this entire world could be what your soul is searching for is illogical. Soul mates come as lovers, friends and sometimes as family. It's all in what you stay open to and what you act on.

Finding a soul mate is easy - we chose our mate out of a handful friends and lovers. No magic to that. What is magical – is that every morning soul mates wake up and choose each others souls again and again. Despite meeting other matches and other connections, despite having other desires and other wants, they stay together. That's where the magic comes in. But for Lonny and I, this magic will never come. We will never get the chance to choose each other every morning. For this, I am sad.

Piety was over early and we were preparing the kitchen with all the snacks for the evening's event. We thought it would be best to put out some snacks now, before everyone drank. We wanted to give them a good base in their stomachs to soak up some of the alcohol. We had many types of crackers with various cheeses, a vegetable platter, and a fruit plate. Then at midnight we would put out the rest of the food, like the salads and hot dishes to again help people sober up a little before going home, not that it mattered too much. Father had arranged for two youth from his church to be at our house from 1 am until 3 am. They were not to drink at all, which according to them they didn't do in their daily life anyway. They were just there to drive people home when they were ready to leave. One would drive the guest's car and one would drive my father's. This way the guest would get home safely with their own vehicle and the youth would drive back to our house to wait for the next guest to want to leave. It was a great gig. My dad was paying them $300 each for the night.

"So, how many people are supposed to come?"

"Not sure. Dad invited around 45 people. He didn't ask them

to R.S.V.P., he just said to show up if they wanted to. I think at least 20 some have told him that they were coming. But only 5 said they weren't." I shrugged my shoulders. "It's up in the air on the attendance." I grabbed a chunk of Garden Vegetable Havarti cheese and popped it into my mouth.

"Are any of our teachers coming?" Piety was washing the counter with the wash cloth cleaning up the mess from cutting the watermelon.

"Just one that I know of, Malick. That is it. Although, Hanton is coming as well, the coordinator, but we barely know him so it won't be that awkward. Most people you will recognize and not know. The only others you will know from school are Elizabeth and Alex."

"Okay." She nodded.

"What time are your parents coming?" I started to pull out all the crackers from the boxes. Laying them on the tray became an art form for me.

"Around 10, Lonny's parents are coming aren't they?"

"Yes. He's not though. At least I doubt he would. He is barely speaking to me."

Piety put the trays out on the table. "What wine am I grabbing?" I showed her where the wine was and added that she could put one of all the kinds out. On her way back into the kitchen she paused with a confused look on her face. "That is so silly Sadie. He truly acts like he is the victim of a forced kiss. Like really, he is just as much to do with that kiss as you are. One cannot do it alone."

"I know. But what can I say. He is convinced that I did it on purpose, when in fact, if he sat and thought about it a little he would realize that he was the one who kissed me. I kissed back, but I did not start it." I ate some more cheese.

"So why is he so angry? Does he remember it differently?"

"It seems that way. I think he is angry because Jessica knows. He thinks I told her, or told someone who told her."

"Did you?" She asked as she went back to the cellar for more bottles of wine.

"No!" I said, spitting out cheese by accident. I wiped my mouth with my sleeve. I waited until she returned before finishing. "I don't know how she found out. People in the hall did see us kiss. Maybe someone she knows saw us. Who knows, did you tell her?" I smiled mischievously.

"Yes, at our weekly dinner together, I spilled my guts. Sorry, didn't mean to ruin your life." We laughed.

"What's so funny?" My dad walked in trying to fix his tie.

"Life. Need some help Mr. Coleman? I do my father's tie all the time. I am a pro by now."

He walked over towards Piety. "I would actually. I have always been spoiled with a woman to help me tie it. Sadie does it for me now," he laughed. "But I am sure she could use a break."

Piety was half way through the tie when the door bell rang. I went to answer it. It was my aunt Hope, my dad's sister. She had come with her boyfriend Matt. They had brought some banana bread which she handed to me after a hug and kiss for a greeting. "Happy New Year sweetheart."

"Thanks." I put the bread down on the table with a knife for cutting. "Excuse me. Piety and I have to run upstairs and get ready." I looked at Piety and nodded.

"Excuse me." She wiped her hands on the dish towel and followed me to the elevator.

I had a cute little pink sundress to wear for the evening. I grabbed a white cardigan sweater to wear open on top.

"How does this skirt look on me? Do I look fat in the hips?" She twirled around in front of the mirror, moving from side to side to see her butt from different angles.

"You weigh like what 120 pounds and you're 5'8"? No, you don't look fat. That's not possible. You are just not used to looking at yourself outside of jeans and t-shirts."

I wheeled to the mirror myself. My makeup and hairspray were over on the counter. "Mind if I get in here tubby?" I kidded. She slapped my shoulder.

"Not funny. How can you wear that shit? It is bad for your skin."

"Really? You really just said that to me?" I giggled, almost poking myself in the eye with the mascara. "You, the girl who dressed in gothic wear for years. Didn't you smear white make-up on your face every day?"

"Yes, and I caused a lot of damage to my skin." First using her hands to smooth her dress to her bottom, she found a spot on the bed and sat down. "I am just trying to save you from my mistake that's all."

"Yes, thanks mama. I will keep that in mind."

There was a knock at the door. "Come in."

It was Elizabeth. "Hi ladies! There is a really handsome man downstairs awaiting his wonderful girlfriend." She pointed out.

"That would be for you Piety," I said with a little disappointment.

She got up and left to get him. I explained to her before she left that my dad was still one of those old fashioned guys that no matter my age, would not allow boys to be in my room. She said she would say hi to him, then return back upstairs.

"Your dad is a doll, Sadie. He's a really nice man. You know he only says things like that because he wants to keep you safe."

"Yes, I know. It doesn't bother me. I really have not felt the need to have a boy up here yet." I lied, but what does she care right now. Besides, if anything, she was at the very least, good friends with my father, and hopefully would pass that last sentence on to him for me. It never hurts to get bonus points with your father.

"Are you coming down?"

"Yup. I am just going to finish my hair and then I will be down, ten minutes maybe. You look great. I like that shirt."

She was wearing a pale green and white tunic shirt over white skinny jeans. Her high heeled shoes were pale green as well. It looked really nice with her reddish brown hair and green eyes. She looked as though she stepped out of a movie premier.

"Thanks," she gave me a hug. "I'll see you down there." She patted my back. "You look good kid."

"Thanks."

She left the room and in her place walked Alex. The two women exchanged their hellos before Alex walked in and shut the door behind her.

"You still want to set up her and your father?" She stood behind me and took over brushing my hair. "You mind?" She lifted the brush up so I could see it in the reflection.

"No. I don't mind." We were talking to each other looking through the mirror. "And I am not sure on the set up. I want them together. I am just not sure I want to be the catalyst behind it."

"Gotcha! So what is the plan then? Or is that the point – no plan. Do you have an elastic band? You wanted a pony tail right?"

"Yes. Thanks. Here." I handed her the pink one from around my wrist. "That's where I am at, at this point. No plans, just opportunities. If they get together great, if they don't then they remain friends. Either way, she is in his life."

"Then what?" She was busy pulling back some unforgiving strands and capturing them with bobby pins.

"Then nothing. I have no plans as of now. I am feeling a little deflated in this area at the moment." That usually happened after a week of grandparents visiting. She finished playing with my hair and knelt down beside me.

"Why?"

"Not a big deal. Just my grandparents being here over the holidays really drove me nuts. I love them to death, but all father's parents talked about were my father's remarrying plans. All my mother's parent's talks were about how she, my mother, will always be irreplaceable to father and me." I looked at her directly. "I am just pooped out on the matter. I am spent." I sucked in my bottom lip to try to suppress tears. "My father is spent on the subject, too."

"You know, it isn't your job to find happiness for your father. He is a grown man. He can do that himself when he is ready. Don't put so much pressure on yourself."

"You don't understand."

"Maybe not. You can help me understand? I have a lot of time. All night in fact."

"I appreciate that." And I did. I bit my bottom lip harder. I was suddenly nervous. I didn't want to go any further, yet I did. She obviously didn't break her word and read my necklace vial. "But not tonight, maybe some other time."

"Okay. Just hang in there and let me know if there is anything I can do." She gave me a hug. "Look at it this way - you wouldn't want him picking out your husband would you?"

I laughed. A tear fell from my eye when I did. "Why do I have a habit of crying around you?"

"Oh my, I hope that reputation doesn't supersede the one I have going." She stood behind me again and placed her hands on my shoulders. "You look like a queen. Let's get downstairs. I have a Christmas present for you."

Happily I replied, "I have one for you too."

* * * * * * * * * * *

The party was a hit. There were around forty people at our house. Every one was dressed up in their best clothes. They mingled all throughout the rooms. Father had instrumental music playing in the back ground, and the television on mute playing in the living room. He wanted to keep it on so that we wouldn't miss the New Year count down. Ashlyn showed up and so did Wanda. Jen Lee and Jacob Landry went back to work at residence for New Years. It gave Wanda a night out, and a chance to really celebrate one of the holiday eves.

The five of us had gone in the kitchen to munch on the food. We had originally gone in there to hide from the adults for a while, but found ourselves really enjoying our time. The laughter was incredible. I didn't remember the last time I laughed this much for this long of a time. The wine helped a little.

I had already exchanged gifts with those whom I had ones for. The lights on the tree were turned on and the mistletoe was up in the doorway between the kitchen and living room. Every time someone came in to refresh their drinks, or grab a plate of food, they would make a comment. We heard things like, 'I am glad I walked through alone' or 'boy, one more kiss and I will be labelled a naughty girl.' My favourite of course was when Nixon, our next door neighbour, who was openly gay, came through at the same time as Mrs. Crampton, a 3rd year Law teacher. He took one look at her and said: 'you are the most beautiful woman here, but if you kiss me, I may have to run away screaming.' Then she leaned over and informed him that normally she would have kissed him anyway, but considering he complimented her with such kind and gracious truthfulness, she would let him go 'kiss free' this time. They both laughed hysterically, ending only because Mrs. Crampton was about to pee herself.

I had seen father kiss almost every female at the party. The ones I didn't see happened when he took the mistletoe down and brought it around the room to make sure that he kissed the women he missed when passing under it. As a joke, he even brought it over to Nixon who playfully abided with dad's humour and kissed him on the cheek. By the time the count down came around, every one was sounding and acting quite drunk. We counted down the last 10 seconds, we sang the traditional 'Ole Lang Sine', and we hugged and kissed and shouted 'Happy New Year,' and then we put out the hot food and we ate. The evening was wonderful. That was until quarter to one in the morning. When the doorbell rang and Wanda came walking into the living room with a very sad and a very drunk Lonny in hand.

"Sadie, I needed to see you. Can we talk?"

-16-

HE DRINKS, HE DRANK, HE'S DRUNK...
SAY THAT THREE TIMES FAST.

"Hey Lonny, it's about time you got here. Happy New Year! Come on in and grab some food." Father shouted across the kitchen. He and most of the college guests were in the kitchen filling their plates with lasagne and chicken.

Elizabeth was beside him. I hadn't updated her yet with the latest drama in Lonny's and my life. She must have read into the looks on the faces of me and my friends, because she leaned her head to the side with a curious look, then with sudden enlightenment she grabbed my father's arm and hushed him quiet. He mouthed 'what' to her.

Alex walked over to me. "Would you like me to get the boys to drive Lonny home? I could also walk him home I guess. He isn't far away is he?"

"Thanks Alex, but no and no. We need to talk, so why not now. Sometimes people are more honest when they are drunk, right?" I purposely looked up at him and said that last part loud enough for him to hear.

"Okay, but if you can, do me a favour, stay in my sight will you? I would feel a lot better. I don't trust a drunk on anyone."

I was honoured. I agreed for that fact only.

"Come on, let's go to the porch." I rolled past him, he turned to follow. Our porch was off the kitchen entrance. With the door shut we could not be heard. But, as Alex had asked we were visible through the glass windows that separated the porch from the kitchen.

"I thought you weren't talking to me? Why did you come?"

He sat down on one of the chairs. "I told you, I needed to see you."

"Well, here I am, see? You can leave now." I wasn't sure what to say to him. I was angry, I was hurt, I was elated, and I was hopeful. But mostly I was scared.

"Come on Sadie, you know what I mean. We need to talk." He started to rock back and forth on the chair. "I hate fighting with you.

I miss my friend. I miss you."

"I miss you too, Lonny. We need to talk about what happened. If we don't, nothing is going to change between us." I looked into the kitchen. Alex, Piety, Hal, Ashlyn, Wanda, and Jacob were all still there. They had started some card game. Alex and Ashlyn had a view straight out to the porch. I felt safer with all them there. Not that Lonny worried me by threatening my physical safety; it was more my emotional state that I was worried about. I was afraid to lose myself in front of him. I was afraid I would end up kissing him or wanting to, again. The last time I did it became my Pandora's Box. It started a whole bunch of terrible moments that I didn't want to go through again.

"This whole holiday, all I think of is you. Every time I close my eyes I see you leaving my room. I hear what you said to me when leaving. And every time I kissed Jessica," I winced at that part. "Bear with me," he continued holding a hand up in a way of saying stop. "Every time I kissed Jessica I wanted to be kissing you, again."

"Well there's a start. You actually admitting that we kissed."

"Is that all that you got from that?" He leaned forward in the chair. His hands held his head up as his elbows rested on his knees.

"You're drunk Lonny. I find it hard to get too excited when you are sloshed out of your tree." I felt bad for saying it, but I had to be honest. "If you remember this tomorrow, and I hope you do, then I will be thrilled beyond what you can imagine. Now I should get inside."

He stood up and moved to the seat right beside me. He moved my chair so I was facing him. My legs sat in between his.

"Sadie, I mean it. I want to be with you. I want to break it off with Jessica and be with you. Truly! She and I are done. We have been for a while." He grabbed my hands. I let him for a moment then let them go. I didn't like holding hands with anyone. With two limbs already not working, I hated giving up a third. I felt defenceless and exposed. He sighed. "I love you Sadie, you know that. I just had a hard time with the idea of breaking off a 6 year relationship. That's scary. I hope you would want me to not take something that big, lightly." He wiped his brow and took a deep breath.

"Of course not, Lonny, but don't put that on me. I love you as well. I just." I stopped to try to find my words. He found them for me.

"You just need some time to digest what I am saying, right?"

"Right." I backed away from his space.

"Okay, well I am going to break it off with her tomorrow. When we get back to school, we can talk then about how we go ahead with our relationship."

My head was shaking back and forth at its own volition. I opened my mouth to protest. He spoke first.

"I am breaking up with her no matter what. We will go from there. Okay?"

"Okay." He leaned over and kissed me. I kissed him back. I couldn't help it. My body just responded to him.

He left out the door, and I sat for a moment before entering the kitchen area. I hoped he was being truthful.

I went inside. Everyone at the table wanted to know what had been said. I informed them of the whole conversation. They had a ton of questions all of which I planned on answering. I needed to talk. The rest of the night was like a spontaneous slumber party. We ended up in my room all talking about the drama of guys - and girls for Wanda's sake. The only change to the audience was when Hal had left and Elizabeth had joined us. We talked a little bit about work. I informed everyone what had happened with Julie and Harvey before I left residence. They found it as interesting as I did. We even coined a new nickname for her. She was now Crazy Julie. Not to be used in her presence of course.

The last person left at 3 in the morning. Ashlyn spent the night. In the morning I awoke with a message written on my bedroom door sketch pad. *Lonny called, he said that 'he remembers and that the plans are going ahead as promised. Take the time you need.'*

-17-

WE ALL HAVE SKELETONS IN OUR CLOSET.

Getting back to residence was a welcomed change. Holidays were great but after that many days with your family, you were ready for people who didn't know all of your childhood learning curves.

The strike had gone from a threat to a reality. All of the affected employees walked out and were now planted on the front lawn of both the residence and the College, their picket signs strong and very noticeable to everyone returning.

School hadn't started back yet. It was only Sunday afternoon and classes didn't resume until Tuesday. Most students headed back to their dorm rooms today and consequently a planned day to relax became one of work. We had to make sure that we were around to greet the parents who were there to drop their kids off. Most parents had questions for us. Others had comments, like Cynthia Dorset's dad. Cynthia was our daddy's girl turned party animal. Her father went up to Ashlyn and thanked her for awarding Cynthia with the resident of the year certificate. He continued to say that he was very proud of her and her college accomplishments. He hung this certificate in his office with all the others to show everyone who entered just what a talented child he had. Ashlyn went with the idea of course, but when the father left, she confronted Cynthia about the lie. Cynthia, unapologetically said that she randomly printed off certificates for her father, to make him happy. It was a small joy that she could give him. Ashlyn said that her delivery in the explanation was one that resembled an all important Miss Universe throne speech. Somehow, I could see her making one of those speeches for real in the near future. Cynthia that was, not Ashlyn. Ashlyn would rather chew her toe nails off, than run for Miss Universe or make a speech for that matter; unless she was doing it as a joke.

I was on call for the evening with Hal, who had also just returned to residence. I was glad to work that evening. I had a lot in my head that I didn't want to think about. Keeping busy was a good way to avoid that for a night. Temporary avoidance never hurt anyone. Although, that, I was not entirely certain of - but I was willing to take a chance.

I decided to use my afternoon to get my presentation ready. I had already worked out the obstacle course and was working on my part of the verbal presentation. We had one hour to showcase all of our information. We were spending the first half hour on speaking to the crowd, and the second half hour doing the course. For the first part of the presentation, I would speak on my experience as a Resident Assistant and how students typically responded to me, especially in regards to disciplinary actions and enforcements of the code of conduct. The second part we planned to show a video of a student who was disabled, and how they related to their R.A. in terms of physical assistance and emotional support. Last, we would hand out a package that included many bullet-point informative flyers on different common disabilities and on what medical conditions and general issues typically came with them.

Ashlyn was doing the video, Wanda was working on the package, and Hal along with Manny helped my father build the obstacle course that so far included a steep ramp, pennies to pick up from the floor, and a tray of water glasses to carry on their lap while pushing over a flat rug. I was writing my part of the presentation and working on getting the wheelchairs to bring for the obstacle course. I was also going to be doing most of the speaking come the conference day so I had the least amount of prep work of the four of us. I wrote for about two hours before I put my residence work vest on and headed down to the R.A. lounge to wait for Hal. It was quarter to 7 and our first round wasn't for a few hours. The 7 pm meeting was usually just to get our thoughts together and to decide the exact time for our first rounds later. It would be a busy drinking night considering most students were back and classes were cancelled for tomorrow.

Hal came in at 7 on the dot carrying both of our walkie-talkies.

"Here ya go lady," he said, handing me a walkie-talkie.

"Thank you, sir," I replied, taking the instrument from his hand. "When do you want to start rounds tonight, nine or so?"

"Sorry kid, but we have to start now. We have a complaint on your floor, Jack's room. Front desk got a call from someone saying they saw him coming in with a keg. Not sure if it is real or just someone playing a joke on him, either way, we have to check it out."

"Wow! Not sure I want to see this. When did the call come in? I was just there." I checked the channel that my walkie-talkie was set on. "You on channel 9?"

"Ya! The call was like a minute ago. I was there when the phone rang." He went to his mail box to check for any memos. There weren't any.

"That is odd. I was just up there. I must have just missed him."

Hal moved towards the door and opened it. He held the door for me to go through. "Probably when you were in the elevator. Apparently he took it up the stairs. The person said that he wasn't alone. He had a guy and a girl with him."

I went through the door way. "Well let's go see." We headed through the connector wing.

"So, have you spoken to Lonny yet?"

"No, why?"

"Just curious that's all." He gave a little impish smile. He walked beside me. His hands seemed to move furiously from front to back when he walked. He did this often. Piety called him her speed demon. It was odd that he walked so fast considering every other aspect of his life seemed to be very Zen-like. He liked Bob Marley and Pink Floyd, marijuana, and yoga. He spoke slowly, he thought slowly – considered everything through thorough, and he laughed slowly. Yet, he walked like his ass was on fire.

"I haven't seen him yet. Not sure if he is back. I need another day or so alone anyway so I don't mind."

"Well he is here. I saw him come in around dinner time. We just said hi because he was in a hurry. He was carrying a very large box. Christmas presents, I assume."

The elevator came quickly. We went in. "Probably."

"What do you need more time for? Isn't he breaking up with Jessica and then you two are getting together?"

A loud ha escaped my throat. "Not quite that simple. He is, or I guess did, break up with her over the holidays. The last we spoke, we were going to talk about possibly starting to date after we come back here. But it can't be that simple."

"Guess not. But it isn't like you two don't know each other well. You guys know each other as much as you know yourselves."

I laughed again. "Man, Piety has you trained. No offence but I feel like I am talking with one of the girls." I smiled and winked in his direction when I finished speaking.

"Yea, well no offence taken. I like gossip; probably more than Piety does."

"Well here is all I know. I know that we are supposed to start working on having a relationship now that the holidays are over. We are in love, and he is breaking up with her, so we can be together. Will it happen right away, possibly not? But at the very least, we will start developing something."

"So that means yes, you will be dating now that the holidays are over."

I just smiled and left it at that. He may have been trained well by Piety, but he was still a guy. Simple was best. We were outside of Jack's door. I could hear the people inside talking.

"Do you want to knock or shall I?" Hal asked already holding his fist up to the door.

"By all means, be my guest," I replied holding my hand towards the room and sliding it side ways. It was my best Vanna White impression to date.

He knocked. We heard Jack say that it was probably Jefferson at the door, *answer it* he shouted. The door opened and Bridgette was face to face with us. "Oh, look, it's R.A.'s. What can we do you for chaps?" Jack laughed in the back ground. I ignored her blatant attempt to rattle us.

"We are told you guys are having a party tonight?"

Jack stepped up to the door behind Bridgette putting his arm around her neck. "Sadie, when has a little residence celebration been any of your concern? Unless you want to come?"

I smiled as sarcastically as I could. "No thanks. But I am interested in the beverages that you are serving tonight. I hear there is a keg already in res."

Jack gave his pretty boy smile, flashing all 16 of his front, vibrantly white teeth in our direction. "Really? Where? Maybe we should cancel our soiree and go to that one." The room laughed behind him. I could hear several voices but couldn't see who was in the room. Jack and Bridgette were blocking the view.

Hal decided it was his turn to join the conversation. "Nice try. Where's the keg Jack?"

"Come on in hippie, and see for yourself. We don't have anything like, what did you call it, a Craig?"

"Funny guy, my name is Hal, not hippie, and we will come in. Thanks." Hal pushed his way past the two in the doorway. He looked around the room and under the bed that was sitting high thanks to the 8 egg crates sitting under the frame. There were 2 at each corner. I followed behind doing a search of my own. Jack's room was surprisingly clean. Immaculately clean actually. His bed was made, with his blue comforter perfectly ironed out across the mattress. His carpet was vacuumed. His counters were completely free of any clutter, just a small kid's plastic cup filled with pens and pencils. I found a lot of things to suggest that Jack was possibly hiring a maid, but I didn't find a thing that was of any importance in regards to the keg party. I did; however, find something of great interest when I opened the closet. There, facing me was a very familiar face. He held his hand to his mouth and with one finger he shushed me. He was holding a bottle of beer in the other hand. Stunned as I was, I closed the door, turned around and addressed the crowd with my warnings about what could happen if they did have a keg party. Jack gave me a knowing look. I nodded to Hal and we left.

"Well, that was useless. We didn't find a thing. But they were all a little strange, don-cha think?" Hal said as he hit the elevator button to go down.

"Strange! Yes," I let out a large sigh. "Hal, I didn't find a keg, but I did find something as important,"

"Oh, yea, what?" He asked as we walked onto the elevator. I followed behind and filled him in on what I saw in the closet. Neither of us could understand why J.P., the custodian was in Jack's room, but we both agreed that nothing good could possibly be going on.

* * * * * * * * * * * *

Hal and I had decided that we needed to go to Alex and inform her of J.P.'s visit to Jack's room. He was striking earlier that afternoon so he was now on his own time, but Hal and I weren't convinced that he was really supposed to be partying with the students. I wanted to talk to him first and get his side of the story, but Hal thought that was not my job. I concurred. I liked J.P. and I didn't want to get him into any trouble, but I did want to save him from some. I knew that J.P. getting in a little mess for spending time with Jack was better than the big mess that could happen if J.P., as impressionable as he seemed, started taking on a bit of Jack's personality.

We tried calling Alex's room but there was no answer. We also had front desk try her pager but she had not yet answered, so Hal and I hung around the R.A. lounge for awhile. We both sat on the couch which gave us front row seats for when Wanda came in singing at the top of her lungs. She flung the door open, her eyes wide as she belted a Broadway verse of 'Life a Many Splendour' into the room, flailing her arms up in audience acknowledgement. We clapped when she finished. She bowed in front of us both saying thanks for our praises. When her performance was over, she sat down on the couch, inching her way in between us, bouncing between the side of

Hal's lap and mine. Hal asked her why she was so happy.

"Oh, that would be life and love my friend, what more do we need? And speaking of love how is Lonny?" She answered the first part to the air in front of her, and turned in my direction to ask the second half of her sentence.

"Haven't spoken to him yet. I haven't seen him. I know he is here because Hal has seen him. I will go to his room later I suppose."

"You suppose! What does that mean?" She moved her butt to the front of the couch. "You are about to reconnect with the guy you have longed for most of your life, and you just suppose you will go see him."

"She has reservations." Hal answered for me.

Wanda never turned her eyes away from me. "Do you have reservations or is it fear? You are finally going to experience what you have been wondering about forever. That is scary. You just have to jump in Sadie." She put her hand up to my shoulder and squeezed it.

"Holy psychoanalyzing me and my movements, Wanda. Man, you guys make me laugh, but maybe you are right." I said in response to please her. I wasn't sure she was right. I knew fear, this wasn't fear, it was my gut. Then again, fear came from the gut as well. Especially when I have been telling that gut to leave things alone for the past 10 or more years when it kept telling me to lean over and kiss the guy.

"Of course I am. I am always right. The sooner you realize this, the faster we will get along magically," she smiled. She was joking of course, so I smiled back.

"You're right again, see! I already feel the magic." I laughed. "Maybe I should go see him before our rounds."

"There we go, that is my girl, only one problem - you were beckoned elsewhere. I was on my way in here from front desk. They said that Alex had just returned your page and is in her room now if you need her."

Twenty minutes later we were outside Alex's door knocking to get in. And as if the world was in perfect sync today to cause me irreversible nervous twitches from opening doors - ta-da - my father answered.

"Hey Kid, come on in," he said swaying his arm out to show all the space there was to fit through the doorway. "Alex is at the table." He pointed toward her. She was at the table writing. There were tons of papers on her small table. There were also two glasses of wine as well.

"Dad, what are you doing here?" Hal and I went into the room.

"Hi guys," Alex looked up from her work. "Just give me a second to have this paragraph filled out." She looked back down and continued writing.

"I am here helping Alex fill out the papers for the conference. We leave next week and there is a lot that has to be worked out. The strike has taken most of her time, so this is the last minute push to have it completed." He sat back down at the table. "Busy night?"

"A little bit." I was upset with his change of subject. I didn't feel like he properly explained his presence to me. "When did you get here?" I didn't give up my questioning.

"Umm, two hours ago maybe." He was answering me in a tone I was all too accustomed to. His tone that said 'not that I, as your father, need to clarify but.' I knew what he was thinking. I could tell that he felt interrogated, and he probably should have. I noticed Hal and Alex were now both looking at me with the same curious look. He finished. "Not sure, something like that at least. We had a meeting and now we are working on the papers. It has been a while."

"You were here the whole time and didn't answer your phone, and you were just working on papers?" My voice was rising, and so was my body temperature; my face felt hot.

Alex poured another glass of wine. "We were in a meeting with Elizabeth and Candice, the other two chaperones. I did not answer my phone in the meeting. I don't usually, you know that." She put the bottle down and took a drink of her Shiraz. "I did answer your page though." I had a feeling she was only explaining to me to be polite. Both of them were. Their eyes were burning a hole in me, awaiting my response.

I took a page from father's book and changed the subject. "We are having problems with Jack again."

Alex put down the pen. "Shit! What now?"

Hal sat down on the arm of the couch. He went on from my sentence. "Front desk received a call from someone who said they saw Jack come in to res. with a keg. So we went up to his room to look for it."

"To look for the keg? You can't go in the student's room to look for a keg? You can ask but."

I interrupted her. I was getting annoyed again. "We didn't go there to go in. We went to ask. He invited us in to look."

"Doesn't matter, you have to see it first and you should have security with you when it happens." She took a large breath. "Not sure I want to know but did you find anything?" Alex asked. Father excused himself to go to the bathroom.

"Well, not a keg, but we found something else. Someone else." I paused. Even though I knew I was going to tell her, and that I couldn't turn back now, I still felt a little nervous to rat J.P. out. I didn't want to get him fired. Alex just sat there waiting for me to tell her who, but Hal did. "J.P. was there."

"J.P.? The janitor?"

"Yes. The odd thing though is that Sadie found him hiding in the closet. He was holding a beer."

Alex got up and paced. She was whispering the information she was just told, while she worked it out in her head. "Did he say anything Sadie?"

"No, just shushed me. I froze and closed the door. We weren't sure what to do. That is why we are here."

My father came out of the bathroom. "Everything okay?" He asked with concern. Alex sat back down. "Yes." She took her left hand and rubbed her eyebrows. Her thumb moved across the left brow, while the other fingers massaged her right.

"Well, we will just have to keep an eye on things and see what develops. Hopefully he is just looking to bond with these boys and that is all. Maybe he will find that he doesn't like them and moves on."

"That's it?" I asked. "What about their influence over him? What about what they could get him to do? What about Jack and what he is up to?" I was moving close to Alex, and to the table.

"He is a grown man. Besides their influence on him is not what I am concerned with Sadie. Nor what Jack is up to. You don't get this do you? Honey, first of all J.P. will get written up over this; over drinking with those boys. He knows that, that is why he was hiding in the closet. That is why he asked you to keep quiet. Not because they are up to something."

"I hope you are right."

"And second…" There was a knock at the door. It was Ashlyn and Piety. Hal let them in, kissing his girlfriend when she approached him.

"Sorry for the interruption. Sadie we need to talk to you. It's pretty important." They looked as though they had just returned from a funeral.

"What's up?" I inquired.

"Can we go to your room? It is kind of private." Ashlyn answered.

Dad stood up. "Are you girls okay?"

"Fine Mr. Coleman. Just need to talk to your daughter."

I looked at Alex. She looked relieved that we were interrupted. "We can finish this talk later tonight if you want. I have a lot of papers to fill out. I will either be here or in my office."

I left with Hal, Sadie, and Ashlyn. Wanda was in the hall. "Give me your vest."

"Excuse me?"

"Give me your vest. I will do your shift for you tonight."

"Why would I want you to do my shift for me? Why are you guys here? What's going on?" I started wheeling down the hall away from them. They followed in pursuit. I was becoming more and more certain that I didn't want to hear what they had to say.

"Just thought you would want to spend some time with Lonny tonight, you know, talking."

Ah, I finally got it. It was an intervention. They wanted me to talk with Lonny and get the relationship going. I wanted the same, nerves and all.

"Okay. But I will take one of your shifts later this month. Deal?"

She agreed. I gave her my vest. "Let's go to my room ladies, you can help me prepare."

Ahslyn and Piety followed me to my room. "So what shall I wear?" I asked as I searched hard through my closet. "Jeans or a skirt? I should actually call him first shouldn't I?" My head was buried in the closet. The girls were sitting on my bed. "I should call him first shouldn't I?" I said louder and then lifted up due to their silence. "Cat got your tongues?" Lifting up I could see their faces. They weren't smiling. The phone rang. "I should answer that. It may be Lonny finally."

"Don't answer it," Ashlyn asked.

"What's wrong?" The phone kept ringing.

Ashlyn spoke first. "Dude, we didn't come to talk to you to get you prepared for what you think. We have something to tell you." The phone finally stopped for a few seconds, then started ringing again.

"This doesn't sound good."

"It isn't." Piety stayed silent. Ashlyn was the only one talking. She continued. "Sadie, we just saw Lonny in the lounge. He seemed very quiet and to himself. I started talking to him and then saw it. A ring on his ring finger, left hand."

"What do you mean?" I was confused.

She put her hand out in front and pointed to the ring finger again. "He is wearing a ring Sadie, a new ring. An engagement ring. One he wasn't wearing before."

I swallowed hard. The phone stopped ringing. "So he was wearing a ring. What does that matter? Guys don't wear engagement rings. He probably had to move his pointer finger ring because of the holiday weight we all put on. It happens to me every year."

She smiled but shook her head no. "Sadie, I asked him about it." My cell phone began to ring. "Don't tell me this Ashlyn." I said feeling tears well up in my eyes. My voice was cracked. Piety started to cry as well.

"Sorry, Sadie. I asked him who he was engaged to and if it was with you. He just hid the hand in his pants. He said nothing; just left the room. The look on his face said it all."

"So he didn't say he was engaged to her. He wouldn't be. He was breaking up with her." I answered with as much confidence as the tears would allow.

"Well, is he engaged to you?"

"Screw you!" I was sorry the minute I said it. She was forgiving. "Sadie, he didn't break up with her, he got engaged to her."

My heart felt like it was being yanked from my body like a hooked fish coming out of the water. "But…"

Piety finally spoke. "Sorry Sade. It's true."

I leaned forward, my elbows on my knees and my hands holding up my head. "I don't believe this. How could he?"

I lifted my head. That fucking jerk was going to get a piece of me. Tears fell uncontrollably. I tried to wipe them away. My efforts slower than the speed they fell.

"Just take a moment before you go downstairs. You need to talk to him, not freak out."

Ashlyn was right of course. But I couldn't wait. Lonny needed to hear what I had to say, and he needed to hear it now!!

-18-

FOR SALE: ONE FRESHLY FALLEN PIECE OF SKY. ~CHICKEN LITTLE.

It took me about half the time it usually takes to get to Lonny's room. And that wasn't long considering I have wheels. I knocked so hard my knuckles turned red. He opened the door and let me in. We didn't speak. He just stood in the middle of his room. His legs were snug in his ripped jeans and his top half was adorned in a black t-shirt. He had a silver chain around his neck.

I wheeled to him and grabbed his hand, lifting it close to my face. There it was in front of me. A silver braided band enveloping his left ring finger. I was lost for words. I just stared at his hand not sure of what I was going to say. Considering his instant burst of tears and lack of explanation, he couldn't have been sure either.

I decided not to say a thing. I turned to leave. I reached the door when Lonny decided to speak.

"Don't go," he whispered.

"A ring Lonny. You're wearing a fucking ring! Is it an engagement ring? Since when does a guy wear an engagement ring?"

"Sadie!" He ignored my question and my insult.

I sighed through my nose. "What's it matter really, Lonny?"

"We haven't talked yet."

"What is there to say? Your finger already tells me everything I need to know." I tried to turn back to face him, but I just wanted to leave. I could hear Piety and Ashlyn hanging out outside his door.

Lonny sat down on his bed. "Fuck! Sadie. How did it get this far?" He laid himself back and put his arm over his eyes to cover the tears.

"Not my job to help you figure that out Lon. I'm done here. I am done with you."

"Sadie, I went there to break up with her and next thing you know she was proposing. She gave me the ring. I couldn't say no. I couldn't break up with her then. I will, but not then. I was a coward."

"Your words not mine."

"What was I supposed to do? Say no then and hurt her?"

Yes. Yes. Yes!! I was blown away by his way of thinking. "Really Lonny, you didn't want to hurt her by saying no when she proposes, so you chose to instead say yes. Sounds great to me, wait until she tells all her family and friends that you two are getting married, and then break her heart. Smart. Really freaken smart of ya."

He sat up. "I really messed this one up didn't I?"

I just shook my head. "Whatever." I waved my hand towards him. "I'm so done." My tears started going again.

"I am going to break up with her. I am. I want to be with you."

"You have a really fucked up way of showing that. Most guys, when they like a girl, don't get engaged to another." He had a box of tissues on top of his mini fridge by the door. I grabbed one out of the box. He asked for one as well. I threw the box at him, hitting him in the chest.

"You're mad, I know. But soon I will break it off and we can work this out."

I laughed. "Oh Lonny, mad doesn't even begin to cover it. There is so much to work on here that I don't even want to start. I mean it. I am done with you."

I turned to leave.

"So you are done with us?"

"There was no 'us' Lonny. We didn't get a chance. And even if there was, you chose to break my heart and not hers. That, my boy, is you choosing to be done with us as well."

"No more friends even? That's it? Our whole life of friendship gone? You would do that?"

"Don't put this on me Lonny. I am not the bad guy. That's your role."

He stood up and came over to the door. "It wasn't too long ago that you sat at this door telling me that you loved me. Yelling at me for not recognizing a kiss for what it was. And now we're through? I told you Sadie, I made a mistake. I will fix it, I promise." His right arm stretched down and grabbed my face. He leaned in and started kissing me. I couldn't kiss back. My lips were trembling too much.

"Lonny, stop!" I was begging him. My lips wisped against his as I talked. I couldn't take it anymore. If he didn't stop I would start kissing him back. My heart was breaking. I felt like I was losing my best friend. I was losing my best friend. I wanted him. But I didn't want to be his second choice. And that was what I was.

"I love you." He said to me looking straight into my eyes.

"I know you do. I love you too. That's why this hurts so much.

Where the stream and creek collide

Good-bye Lonny." My eyes now totally flooded.

"Don't go." He whispered again. "I'm sorry." I grabbed the door to open it.

"Sadie!" Lonny called. He had desperation in his voice. I didn't want to hear him beg. I didn't want this to continue. His arm reached up over my head and held the door closed.

"Sadie, don't say anything to Jessica at the conference please. She is volunteering for the 3 days. It isn't her fault, it's mine." His face showed that he knew the gravity of what he had just said.

The thundering sound in the background was either the earth swallowing us in, or my heart crashing into my stomach, shattering as it fell. What was worse, I wasn't sure - that Jessica was not only at that school but now a volunteer at the event, or that Lonny felt the need to again put her first, and remind me to watch for her feelings.

I couldn't address him. I turned, opened the door, and wheeled out. He let me this time. "Are you okay?" Piety said as she stood up from her crouch.

I couldn't speak. I could only cry.

We walked down to my room. As we rounded the corner towards the long straight hallway to my door, Alex was walking towards us. "Hey, what's going on?" She looked concerned but I didn't care. I was angry at her. I was mad. She was the one who had warned me about getting too close to him, about trusting him, so she obviously knew this would happen. Why didn't she warn me harder, louder? She could have saved me all this trouble with Lonny.

Alex got down low to my eye level. "You're crying. What's going on Sadie?"

"What's it matter to you?"

She attempted a step back. She was crouching, so it proved to be a little more difficult than what she expected because she almost fell over, her hand catching her fall.

"Did I do something?"

"No, Lonny did." Piety answered her.

I pushed my chair so it went past her. "I don't want to be in the hall." I wheeled towards my room. They all followed. I turned around. "Thanks for telling me guys. I appreciate that, and I appreciate you coming to make sure I am okay. But I need some alone time." Ashlyn and Piety nodded.

"Can I come and talk with you for a while?" Alex asked.

"No. I don't want to hear any 'I told you so's from you," I turned again towards my room.

137

"Sadie. You won't hear any. I am concerned, that is all." She moved a chunk of hair from the front of her face to behind her ear. "I want to help."

"You've done enough. You suggested that this would happen and it did. Are you happy? Maybe if you spent less time playing house with my father and more time trying to convince me of your gut instincts, than maybe you could have helped. Now it's just too late."

Alex walked towards me. Her voice lowered, I knew, in attempt to get me to lower mine as well.

"Okay, that was harsh, but this isn't my fault. And it isn't your fault."

"Then who's fault is it, Alex? Someone is to blame here." I paused. My head felt like it was 20 pounds heavier. I tilted my head back to get the snot to run to the back of my throat instead of down my face. "I just need some time alone. That's all. Please, I know you care, so care enough to let me go into my room and freak out all by myself."

"Okay. Can I give you a hug?"

I put up my hand in a stop sign type position. "No, please don't touch me. I can't handle that right now." I turned and wheeled towards my room.

"Call me if you need anything," she called to my back.

I didn't turn to face her nor did I answer. I just kept wheeling to my door. I needed to be alone with my thoughts; alone and broken. It was my Humpty-Dumpty moment and I didn't want or need any of the King's men to try to fix me tonight.

* * * * * * * * * * *

The ride to the conference was long. I rode in the van that my father and Elizabeth were driving. The other van had Candice and Alex as co-pilots. Candice and Alex got along really well, and when the two of them got together, the surroundings tended to get loud. That was the main reason why I chose father's van. I needed down time, quiet time. I was not prepared to see Jessica up close at the conference. I knew she was attending that school, but she wasn't an R.A. It didn't occur to me that she would be volunteering.

Our arrival came before my conclusions to the questions of what I was going to do when I first saw Jessica face to face. I was now sitting in my dorm room for the weekend. People from the visiting colleges were put up in the new hall at Jansen. It housed nearly eight hundred students, five to a room. In my room were Ashlyn Miles, Wanda Needham, Jen Lee, and Sandy Mull, all the girls that came. We all decided on arrival to take some time to freshen up. We wanted to change before meeting downstairs to have dinner. It was the opening night of the conference. Jansen, this year, held a casino theme. There was a dice logo on all the t-shirts and cups in their registration package with a slogan that read 'bet on life in residence.' Our opening dinner was at 7, with a casino night and fake money to follow after at 9. I had already seen Jessica once, from afar, when we registered. She looked my way but made no attempt to make contact. That was good for me. I still hadn't decided how to handle things.

I wanted to tell her the truth myself. I wanted to explain that we were in love. That Lonny and I had always been in love. We were soul mates, and destined for each other. I wanted her to know that he was going to go there and break up with her, and he only accepted her proposal out of fear of hurting her feelings.

That's what I wanted to say every hour on the hour.

The time in between, well, that was when I considered telling her that he was a no good son of a bitch. I wanted to tell her that Lonny was a liar, a user, and probably would never really fully commit to her. And if he did ever make it down the aisle, that she should watch him because he would never, ever, stay faithful. I struggled with both of these thoughts. I had two difficulties with them. One, I wasn't sure which way I looked at Lonny at this point – if I loved him, or if I hated him? So I couldn't decide which way to go. Two, I wasn't convinced that I thought either of my points to be true. I wasn't sure I wanted to be with him or if I believed him when he said that he was going to break up with her that night. But I also wasn't sure he was a complete ass. He very well could have just chickened out trying not to hurt either of us.

"Knock, knock. Can I come in?" Ashlyn said. She knocked on my door as she opened it.

"Sure, just sitting here taking a moment. Are you ready to go?"

"Yea. What you going to do if you see Jessica tonight?"

"Reading thoughts now are we? I was just wondering the same thing."

She sat down beside me on the bed, passed me my shoes from the floor. I put them on.

"Do I pick assholes as guys to love?"

Ashlyn laughed. "No!"

"So then I make them assholes by liking them?"

She laughed again. "No!"

"It has to be one or the other, because they are assholes when the relationship ends. So do I pick them or do I create them?"

She didn't laugh this time. "I think love creates assholes. In all of us, at random times, throughout a relationship. You just have to try not to be assholes at the same time, and try not to become such an asshole that you forget about the feelings of the one you love."

"You calling me an asshole?"

"No. That is not necessarily what I am saying. I am saying that he forgot about you, when he was breaking up with Jessica, and you forgot about him when trying to understand why he did what he did."

"Are you seriously saying this is my fault?" I was starting to get defensive.

"No, Sadie. I am not. I mean that he was an asshole, for sure, one hundred percent, but he was in a tough situation. Not an excuse, but a reason." She paused and put her hand on my arm.

"I am just saying that you shouldn't accept being second as you say, and you shouldn't accept the position he put you in. That isn't the way to start off any relationship. It won't work. You two together now won't work. But don't hate him for what he did. Life is too short to go around with those types of feelings. It wasn't out of malice that he got engaged to her; it was out of stupidity."

"Humph! A lot of stupidity. You're right. I can't hate him. I don't even think that is possible anyway, but fuck, why did he have to do this to…" I started to cry again, a common occurrence these days.

"Why did he have to do this to you?" She completed my sentence, "why not you? Who are you to be exempt from heartache and assholes?"

"You do know you are a complete bitch right?" I asked her laughing as best as I could.

"That is why you love me, Sade. Would you expect anything else but honesty?"

"No." I wiped my eyes with my sleeves. "Let's go down to eat."

"Did you decide what you are going to say if you see Jessica?"

"Probably nothing," I got in my chair and grabbed my wallet. "Just don't let me drink too much." We laughed together.

At our table in the dinning hall was our whole crew from Greenbury. We were sitting with the Hamilton group. I was thrilled to see father sitting beside Elizabeth. She looked beautiful tonight.

Her dress was long, black, and form fitting. Her hair was tied back in a ponytail, and her eyes were circled with black mascara, making them pop like they were about to leave her head. She smelt fresh like her shower was only seconds before now. My father and she seemed to be having a wonderful time. They were laughing together, talking, and even touching every once in awhile with a shoulder tap here, and a hand grab there. It was wonderful to see my father happy. It had been a long time since I had seen this. Jackie never evoked such emotion from him.

There was a spot saved in front of them for Ashlyn and I. Jen and Wanda were closer to the middle of the table with the rest of the group ending with Alex and Candice – who separated us from the Hamilton R.A.'s. The tables were pushed together fitting several of us in a row.

"You know your dad here, seems to think that he is a funny guy." Elizabeth nudged her shoulder into his after her sentenced ended.

"Yes. I have that trouble too. Not sure how to break it to him."

Father made a mocking face. "Okay you two. Maybe I will share my enlightenment and my wit with Ashlyn from now on. She will appreciate it."

"Sure will Mr. Coleman."

"Although, I am a better dancer than comedian. Can I take you for a spin around the dance floor before we eat?" My father was looking at me.

"Not right now dad, maybe Elizabeth would like to." We both looked at her. She finished the sip of rye and ginger she was taking, wiped her mouth with her napkin, and then said "sure, why not."

For dinner we had chicken, pasta, and salad, the staple opening dinner at many conferences. The only difference tonight was the type of pasta; it was penne with a bacon and tomato sauce. The evening was going well until Jessica and her friends came over to say 'hi'.

"Hey Mr. Coleman, really nice to see you here. I hope you have a great time at Jansen." She was blowing smoke up my father's ass and he didn't even know it. My stomach was in knots. I was afraid of what she was going to say.

"Thank you, and nice to see you as well Jessica. I think the last time I saw you was when you and Lonny came over, the New Years before last, right?"

"Yes, that was the first place we met you know. One of your New Year's Eve parties 5 years ago."

"Really, that long ago, eh?"

"That's right. The infamous New Years party at your house."

"How are you these days?"

"I am great. Didn't Sadie tell you? Lonny and I are engaged." She pointed her hand towards dad's face to show him her ring. "He proposed to me just a week or so ago. He was very romantic. But that's Lonny. If I didn't know better, I would think that Sadie, or some girl, helped him out with it." She looked over at me and smiled. The evil bitch! I wanted to grab my fork and jab it into my arm just to end this meeting. I couldn't tell if she was egging me on or lying about the proposal. Either way, I knew she was trying to get me upset. It was working, but I wasn't going to let her see it. Besides, Ashlyn was right, neither Lonny nor I paid attention to each other's feelings. Maybe we weren't right for each other as a couple. Maybe 'conniving Jessica' and 'lying Lonny' were meant to be together after all. Especially if she was being truthful about who proposed.

"You got me. I was definitely a part of the proposal and more so the answer." I smiled my best evil smile back.

"Listen, we were just wondering if you wanted to come with us. We are pulling one representative from each college to come participate in an on stage welcome presentation. We thought you would be great."

"Hey, that sounds right up your alley Sadie, you should do it," father said as he looked at me with an excited grin.

"Ah, sure! Where do you want me to go? And when?"

They informed me that I would be leaving with them now. I didn't want to go. I wasn't sure I could keep my tongue still much longer. I gave Ashlyn my very best, "this didn't take long" look that I could, and got ready to leave the table.

"Careful," Ashlyn said with the last words before I went with them. "I've watched this movie. If they call you Carrie, run. I am pretty sure they pour pig blood on you before the night is over." She winked as I left with my new posse.

-19-

I CONFIRM, THE CONFERENCE IS CONFINING...

There was no pig blood, but there was definitely a blood bath. The girls had swept me away to the outer hall where people were lining up. They of course, immediately questioned me about my involvement with Lonny. There was a short and a tall brunette, a fat and a skinny blond, and a very fiery red head that looked like she could chew me up and spit me out with one fallow swoop. Last, there was my dear nemesis, Jessica.

When I told them that Lonny and I we were just friends, and now were no longer – as requested by Jessica, the red head smiled and informed me that that was the way I was to keep it if I liked my face. And I did like my face, so I agreed. The fat blond one was the most aggressive. This I knew, by the way she constantly slapped her fist into her hand as the other girls spoke. And yes, it was the other girls that spoke, tubby, being the true enforcer that she was, kept silent. All brawn, no brain I suspected. I wasn't about to argue with the likes of her. Besides, becoming friends with Lonny again was not exactly on the top of my to-do list. In fact, it didn't even hit my list of things to do in the future. I kindly smiled, knowing I was completely out numbered, and asked if there was anything else. I looked at Jessica as I posed the question. She just lifted her eyebrows and shook her head no. The short brunette handed me a homemade Greenbury flag made out of cardboard, slapped me in the back, and said, "all right we have an understanding then, let's get this opening parade going," and we joined the rest of the group at the other end of the hallway.

Ten minutes later I was paraded up on stage where I was to show my school flag, share the highlights of our residence and educate on the number of employees and students. Then when done, I was to step back and let the next student enlighten everyone on their school. The whole process took about forty minutes. From the stage I had a great view of the hall. It looked as though there where around five hundred people there, which was the typical registration with these conferences.

When I returned to the table I got a lot of enthusiastic congratulations from everyone and of course a rather sarcastic one from Ashlyn who knew the real reason why I had been asked to the front. She knew something else I didn't also.

"Dude, they gave you an extra flag," Ashlyn informed me as she reached behind my back and pulled off an orange square paper that said 'kick me.' "I figure it isn't part of your wardrobe?"

"That Jessica has always been a kidder," father laughed.

"Yup, a real joker," I replied. "My goodness, are we still in high school?"

"Relax Sade, it is just a joke. You haven't lost your sense of humour have you?"

"No dad, I haven't. It's just…" I looked at his face. He seemed almost shocked at my reaction. The truth was he had no idea the real velocity of the Lonny situation. He knew there were slight problems but he didn't know how things had progressed. He only knew that we were fighting slightly and that he was now engaged. Father was never one to add 2 and 2 and make 4. Not that he couldn't come to a proper conclusion, he just would avoid it for not feeling like he needed to know the answer. "It's just that I am tired that is all. I need some sleep to lighten myself up."

After we finished with dessert, they had a casino night and dance. Half of the gym was filled with black jack and poker tables, two roulette tables, and a dice game that no one was really familiar with. The other half had a dance floor and a DJ that played music loud enough to dance to, but quiet enough to not interrupt the casino area too much. The night didn't go too late due to early presentations.

Our presentation was at 10 a.m., and Tristen's was around 4. Father and Elizabeth were helping Hal and Manny set up the obstacle course. I enjoyed watching my dad and Elizabeth work together. They laughed and giggled at the most appropriate times. Alex came by for a moment to make sure I was all set up and ready for the presentation. I was working on the chalk board with Wanda at the time.

"I am just fine thank you. Dad and Elizabeth are here helping."

"I see that. Can I do anything?"

"No. I think it is all under control."

"I see that too. I am asking if I can help, not if you need my help."

"I don't see anything left to help with." I went back to work on the chalk board. I felt pretty confident in what I was doing and saying until she left without another word, and Wanda asked me what was going on.

"To be honest, I am not sure." I dropped the chalk on the board's shelf. It was true, I had no idea what that was all about, but I did know that I didn't feel good about it. Why was I angry at Alex to the point of hardly speaking to her? And more importantly, why had I stopped caring about Jessica and her friends, and the little games that they were playing? I was angry with the one I cared about, and didn't care about the ones I was angry with. Who knew!

* * * * * * * * * * *

The presentation went well. We had some pretty positive feedback. All participants were asked to fill out a small questionnaire with ratings out of ten. The questions were generated by Jansen, and were the same for everyone. We capped out at 30 people, the most allowed in one session, and scored an average of 87% for our questionnaire. The top rated presentations would go on to the National conference in June. We thought we were in contention until later on that afternoon, we found out that Tristen and his crew scored a 94% on their presentation titled Dealing with Anger in Residence. We would have to wait and see the results at the closing banquet. It was a fast conference - arriving one day, presenting the next, with closing ceremonies the same evening. The next morning, a key note speaker would present to all of the attendees at once, then lunch, and on to home after that.

The closing banquet was a lot like the opening, except we had roast beef, carrots, and potatoes. After dinner was the same casino offerings and dance. The group of us decided to stay around the dance floor. We all sat at a table just to the left, and got up quite often to dance. I sat with my presentation group and my father. Tristen's group was next, and then the ladies, Candice, Alex, and Elizabeth sat at the end laughing and gossiping. Gossiping of course was the exact opposite of what they were trying to educate staff about at a residence life conference, but everyone still did it in their own respective groups. Ours was no exception.

For most of the night I was watched by the fat blond who periodically would slap her fist into her hand for effect whenever I looked over. The two brunettes would always make sure to come close to me whenever I would get up on the dance floor with my friends. Jessica made sure that she told her engagement story to anyone that would listen, and she told it within 5 feet from where I was at any time. If I was farther she would squeal loudly with her ring hand in a position that made it obvious what she was talking about. I really didn't care anymore. It seemed like the gauntlet of emotions had ended.

"I think I need to dance with my daughter, what do you say kid?"

"Let's do it." I pushed out from the table. Father grabbed my hand and he swung me around the dance floor. Everyone seemed to stop and watch. That was what usually happened when the 'girl in the wheelchair' got up to dance, especially when she got up to partner dance with her father. I even saw Elizabeth, Alex, and Candice stop their conversation to watch us. With the exception of those 3, I was quite annoyed at the eyeing that was going on. People stared for their own curiosity, and I hated it. I hated it with a passion. That was the one thing that really bothered me about being in the wheelchair, no moments were my own. The lack of privacy was enormous. Everyone looked to see if either I was okay, if I was able to do 'it', or in amazement that I could do something they thought not possible. I gave kudos to all of them for satiating a need to gain knowledge, but shitty for me for enduring their blatant curiosity and ignorance. They had no idea of what I had to deal with on a daily basis and they probably didn't even care. They also didn't seem to care too much that I might not have wanted to be stared at the whole time, nor clapped at for completing a dance, which many able bodied people did at the end of the song.

When the dance, and the clapping ended, father grabbed Alex, who was standing up walking towards the dance floor at the time, and asked her to dance. It was a slow song that came on. She looked at me and shrugged her shoulders then accepted the invitation. I decided to leave the banquet. I needed air more than I needed to hear a soppy love song.

The wind felt nice on my face. It was freeing. I needed some freedom. I was usually in my own little zone when it came to Residence Life Conferences, enjoying every minute of the weekend, but not this year. This year was different. This year was at Jansen. This year was without Lonny, who, normally outside of our current type of position, made me feel better. And lastly, this year had father involved. My father being there was of course my request, and I was glad he came, but I didn't realize how much extra it would put on me. I had to think about my presentation, about Jessica and her gang, about my feelings for the situation with Lonny, and on top of all that, about trying to make sure father was happy and having a good time. It was a lot. I moved over to a set of steps that led to an upstairs in the building. I got out of my chair and placed myself on the second stair. It was cold on the hands, it felt nice.

A deep breath helped me to relax a little further. There was too much going on. It was more than I could comfortably handle. I did this to myself a lot. It was as though I liked to inflict as much pain, heartache and emotion as I possibly could on myself at any given time. If I started to feel better with one situation, then I would have to mess up some other area of my life to balance it out.

"Penny for your thoughts?" I heard a soft voice come from around the corner. I lifted my head to see Elizabeth standing there.

"You'd have change coming back. I am just out to get some air."

"Mind if I join you?" I informed her that I didn't. She sat down two steps up from where my butt sat. "Nice night."

I nodded.

"So you were thinking about nothing?"

"Nothing important," I lied.

"Hmm, okay." She crossed her legs and looked up at the sky, leaning back on to her elbows. We sat in silence for a minute or two.

"Can I ask you a question, Sadie?"

"Yes."

She looked away from the sky, bringing her focus to mine. "Are you trying to set me up with your father?"

I was taken a back. There were many questions I was expecting but that that was not one of them. I didn't know what to say. How did she know? Did Alex tell her? Was I that obvious?

"Why do you think that?"

"By the way you are always encouraging us to spend time together. How you push us to be in the same room. You are always telling me how wonderful he is, and so I hear, vice versa."

"That doesn't mean anything." I was stalling.

"Well, it kind of does young lady." She put her hand on my head and patted. "Your father and I are friends and we talk. We have both come to this conclusion." She smiled at the end lightening up the feeling of interrogation I was starting to feel.

"That obvious huh? I mean if my dad is figuring it out." We both laughed. "Sorry!"

She bent down and kissed the top of my head. "Don't apologise, I am flattered."

"Did any of my efforts work at least?"

"No. We are friends, and we always will be. He doesn't love me that way, and I don't love him passionately either." She squeezed my shoulder. "Can't make romantic love happen. I will always be in yours and your father's life."

"I know. I just want to see him happy. I want him to have another wife; not that my mother is replaceable, because she isn't, but he needs someone."

"It is not your job to make sure of that Sadie. He is a big boy."

"I know. But sometimes he gets too busy."

"Maybe that is his way of dealing with your mother's death. Maybe he isn't ready."

I was getting a little agitated. "That is a lot of maybes. I know he is a big boy, but sometimes big boys need a wake up call. They need to see what is in front of them."

"Listen to yourself. You have become so focused on your father's happiness. Why Sadie?"

"Because he is my father, I am concerned."

She uncrossed her legs and leaned in towards me. "Is that it? Are you sure?"

"Yes I am sure." I was starting to shout.

"Okay, I believe you." Elizabeth started to whisper.

"I am sure. I just want him happy." I whispered as well.

She sat up straighter. "Okay. There's nothing wrong with that."

"No there isn't. Really, that is all. I just want him to have another mother – I mean wife…sorry."

"Now we are getting somewhere."

I sat up straighter, defensively. "What do you mean now we are getting somewhere?"

She moved down two steps until she was snuggled in beside me. "This is also about getting a mother for you isn't it?" She put her arms around my shoulders.

"No!"

"Are you being honest with yourself?"

"Yes, I am in my 20's. I am too old for needing a mother. I had one, she was great, and I don't need another."

"Everyone needs a mother, at any age Sadie."

I was yelling now. "No, everyone needs their mother at any age, but no one needs a replacement mother after they are grown up. Especially not after they killed their own mother."

I seemed to have surprised myself more with what I said then I did her. Shit! She grabbed my hands, I pulled them away. She settled hers on my knees. "That is a little warped honey. How could you have killed your mother? Do you feel responsible?"

I needed to give her an answer. My face felt hot. I was shaking. I didn't want her to figure out my lie. I took a deep breath to try and slow my heart beat down a little before I passed out.

"I didn't save her that is all. It was a slip. Something I am working on."

"I hope so. It wasn't your fault. She was a grown up, and couldn't save herself. So you - as a kid - didn't have a great chance."

"I know that in my head." I was trying to give her something so that she would believe me. I needed to show some inner struggle. I hoped it was working. It must have, because she continued on, on a slightly different topic.

"We'll go there later." She paused for a moment. "I could go through many reasons why you would need and would be looking for someone to be a mother figure to you. For starters, you were young when your mother was taken away, and you needed one, and you obviously want one. That is what this is about isn't it, not just someone for your father but someone for you as well?"

I tried the best I could to look her in the eyes. I was shaking trying to keep myself steady. I was worried she would read wrongly into how I was feeling. "I slipped with my wording, honestly, that isn't what it is about. I loved my mother; I don't need another mother figure. This isn't about me it is about my father. I am sorry I got you involved, I just thought good friends also made good partners."

"Well they do but not in this case. Your father and I don't love each other in that way. And again, no need to say sorry. I am flattered." She leaned forward and kissed my forehead.

"Okay."

"Okay," she smiled. "Now let's get inside and get this weekend over with, shall we?"

"Yes, please." I got into my chair with a little help. Not that I needed it, it just speeds things up a little.

"Just remember one thing Sadie, no matter what, if you ever need anything, I am always here. And I will always be on your side, okay? I may push you, but I am behind you…always."

"Thanks."

We walked in through the double doors. The second set was held open by Elizabeth for me to go through. We looked ahead to see Alex talking with Jessica's tubby friend. The fat one pointed in our direction. Alex nodded and walked in our direction.

"Hey, there you are. I was wondering where you two went off to, glad you were together. Are you okay?"

149

"Yeah, just needed some air."

We all walked into the dance area side by side.

"That girl was nice. I described you and she knew exactly where you were. Imagine that."

"Yes. A real surprise for sure." I looked over at tubby who was now standing talking to Jessica. We exchange glances briefly and then we both went on with what we were doing. It was amazing to me. This all would have been avoided if Lonny had given me half as much attention and effort as his girlfriend did.

-20-

JACK BE NIMBLE, JACK BE QUICK...

When you work in a college, every time you go home for a visit, you come back to residence and some kind of teenage crisis. Usually, it was a party that caused a lot of damage, or a fight that resulted in someone being injured. No matter what it was, it was always something that needed your immediate attention. That was the life of a Resident Assistant. This time was no exception. Upon turning the corner of the hall towards my dorm room, I saw three girls hanging out outside my door, with a fourth one on the floor crying.

"Hey guys, what's going on?"

"Hey Sadie!" The three girls standing said in unison.

They backed away for me to see crazy Julie on the floor with big crocodile tears coming down her perfectly snowy white face.

"Hey Julie. You okay?"

"She needs to talk to you," shared the tall friend who I recognised but didn't remember the name of. I knew the other two girls names, Natalie and Ginny.

"Come on inside." I said to Julie, than looked at her friends, "I got her ladies. Thanks for staying with her."

Julie stood up. "I want them to stay if that is okay?" She was almost hysterical in talking, taking large breaths in between words. Her blond hair was tear-soaked and stuck to her face.

"Of course it is." I liked to assume that students didn't want their friends with them so they didn't feel awkward in telling them to leave.

We all came into my room. I put my stuff down in the kitchenette area and motioned for them to have a seat on either my bed or my floor. Julie sat at the edge of my bed still crying her eyes out, and her friends took up the floor space by the radiator. It was horrible, but my initial thought was that maybe this time Julie's mother actually did die. I went over to her and put my hand on her shoulder.

"What's going on Julie?" She wiped her eyes and sat up a little straighter. "Jack," she looked down again, "Jack, assaulted me last night."

What! Assaulted her, how? Where?

"How did he assault you?" I asked with hesitation, not sure I could handle the answer.

"Physically, mostly," the tall friend whose name escaped me answered for her again. "Show them your back."

Julie just looked at me hesitantly. She was nervous, I could see. I was instantly angry. What did mostly mean? I knew this asshole was no good but I never thought he would go this far. This guy was completely out of control and we let him be. I took a deep breath. I needed to stay the calm one.

"Okay, start from the beginning and tell me what happened."

"It was last night. We were all at the pub and he was flirting with me like crazy. Me and Harvey are fighting, and word is that Jack and Bridgette are open when it comes to other people." That didn't surprise me.

"So I flirted with him back." She started crying again. "This is so hard." This time it was Natalie who helped. She jumped up on the bed and gave her a big hug.

"Okay, listen, you are going to have to tell this to Alex as well, due to the nature of the subject. Because you are telling me, I assume you are going to want to go further with this, than just me, correct?"

She nodded her head. "Well, maybe."

"Okay, then let me get Alex now. That will save you from telling the story twice, especially considering how hard it is for you to get this out once." Another nod from Julie, the girlfriends agreed with me.

I went over to my desk to dial Alex's room. She answered. I explained to her the situation, and she quickly agreed to come up and meet us to hear the story as well. While we waited, I got all the girls a drink of juice, and opened some windows to let new air into the room. The weekend away had resulted in the room air going stale. I had four of the five windows opened when Alex arrived. Ginny, the third of the friends, opened the door to let her in. She went straight to my empty office chair, sat in it, and wheeled herself over toward Julie. She made sure she was far enough away that she had some space, but close enough to give her, her full attention.

"I hear you had a pretty rough weekend huh?" She leaned in towards Julie, her voice softening. "Do you want to be alone?" She looked around at her friends.

"No, I would like them to stay."

"Okay, talk to me then. I want to help make this better."

Julie fell back on to the bed. I felt bad that it was not made, although I was sure she could care less. Her head landed on top of my already worn pink penguin pyjamas. She put her arm up to cover her eyes and took two deep sighs.

"It was Saturday night, and it started at the bar." Ginny had informed Alex from her space on the floor. Alex just smiled and looked back at Julie.

"I know this is tough, but you need to let me know what happened that night Julie. And I need to hear it from you sweetheart."

I handed Julie a tissue, placed the rest of the box beside her. I handed one to Alex as well, who was starting to tear a little. That was one of Alex's best features – she knew how to empathize with a student. She could really put herself in their shoes. Julie wiped her face, blew her nose, and sat up. "Okay," she whispered. "Just give me a moment."

After taking a quick bathroom break, and returning looking freshened up and calmer, Julie began her story.

"We were at the Blue Pig all night. Jack started flirting with me and I was flirting back."

"Did you go to the pub with him, or did you meet him there?"

"No, we didn't have any plans to see him or be around him. I could take or leave Jack, really. But I was drinking and he was flirting with me. Harvey and I are fighting and I was hurt and angry and I didn't mean to get together with him at the bar, and I know I was flirting but I didn't want to be with him, I promise. I didn't mean to tease him and piss him off. That wasn't my intention. I know it looks bad but…" Julie started to cry again. Her words were babbled and no longer formed.

"Whoa, slow down kid. Its' okay. I don't think flirting with someone is a crime, nor do I think it is an invite to anything more physical." Alex grabbed Julie's hands and held them. There were more tears in Alex's eyes. She let go with her left hand and wiped her face. "Tell me the rest."

Julie kept her right hand holding onto Alex's.

"We were flirting all night. I thought for a while that he might be trying to get Bridgette jealous but nothing happened. It must be true that they have a loose relationship because she didn't really seem to care that he was there flirting with me. She just sat at the table with his friends and his brother Jefferson."

Alex asked for some paper. I passed her a pad and a pen. I was sitting in the kitchen area. I wasn't sure what to say. Alex seemed to have the situation under control so I just sat and listened. I couldn't get involved. I didn't feel objective enough. I was angry. I hadn't even heard the story yet and I already had an ending; an ending for both her story and his punishment. The latter of course involving me, a tire iron, and a dark alley. Not that I could physically follow through but it was a nice thought. It didn't matter much. The situation and his punishment were two things I had absolutely no control of.

"We stayed until the bar closed and then came back to residence and went up to his room. We were in the hall for a while with some of his friends."

"Who was there?"

"Umm, there was Jack, Ginny, Natalie and Callie." She looked over at her friends.

Callie Francis was the other girl, now I remembered her. She was on the College basketball team as a point guard. She was good. Here on a scholarship.

"There were some of his guy friends like Pete, Chris, Jacob, Liam, Miles, I don't know any of their last names. Sorry."

Alex looked up at me. "I know them. They always hang out with him. I will get you their last names later," I said answering the question she didn't need to ask. Alex nodded in acknowledgement.

"We were kicked out of the hall by Tanya and Joel who were on call that night. They said there was a noise complaint. I went into Jack's room with him; the guys went into Pete's room."

"We went back to Callie's room," Natalie added.

"Why would you leave her alone with Jack if she did not want to be with him?"

They were shocked at my question, guilty perhaps. I was appalled that they would leave her with him. Alex gave me a look that I read as a 'back off a little' look. Julie answered my question anyway.

"This is the hard part."

"Go on." Alex was encouraging.

"They left because I wanted them to. I wanted to sleep with Jack. I was drunk, I was hurt, and I wanted to have sex with someone who could care less if I was there in the morning. No one better than Jack, right?"

We didn't answer. I was surprised at her candidness. I was also confused as to where this was going.

"Anyways, things started going on, you know what I mean, and it got to the point where I was nearly naked, and he was in his jeans and undershirt." She was talking with her head down towards the ground. Large tears were flowing down her face.

Alex tightened her grip on Julie's hands. I kept where I was. The tension in the room was incredible. No one but Alex seemed to know how to act and speak.

"Go on."

"I am a little embarrassed."

"Don't be. You are talking to people who care about you right now. The important thing is that you are talking about it, and telling us. Go on, please."

Julie smiled a small nervous smile then continued. "After a little bit of foreplay, he got up and went to the washroom."

Alex asked for more details about the moments prior to the washroom break and Julie gave them. Alex wrote it down.

"Sorry, but be as specific as you can from here on in okay. You are doing great. So you were on the bed when he left?"

"Yes, and I stayed there until he returned from the washroom. He was back after about 5 minutes. He came back with two ecstasy pills, we took them and then we started to kiss and make out again. He had a marker in his hand. He said he wanted to write on my stomach. He wanted to brand me as his for the night. For some stupid reason, I let him."

"Where did he get the pills?"

Julie shook her head and shrugged her shoulders.

Alex left it there. "What did he write?"

She answered by lifting her shirt to show her stomach. It read: Jackman's dirty whore.

Holy shit! I thought, but I stopped myself from saying what I was thinking. I didn't think now was the time to tell her how stupid she was, or how bad her judgement and taste in men were. Not to mention how completely sick this was, that she would let him do this to her. What the hell was it that Jack did to get these girls to let him do whatever he wanted to them? Really, I wanted to know this. She put her shirt back down and went on with her story.

"I was trying to take off his undershirt when I saw over his shoulder that the door was still open."

Alex made a curious face. Julie elaborated. "The lock was out so the door didn't shut tight. It looked closed but it wasn't. Like this." She got up and went to my door to demonstrate by twisting the lock so the bar came out. She let the door attempt to close, but it stayed open a fraction due to the lock bar hitting the side of the door frame. She closed it properly afterward, and then sat back down on the bed.

She was shaking. "I told him and he said it was okay. No one was around anyway and it will be fun to do it knowing we could get caught. I said okay at first, kissed him again, but then chickened out. I told him I wanted to leave. That I wasn't in to it anymore. He said fine. He was upset but was alright with it. When he got up I looked at the door again and thought I saw someone looking in. I told him so." She stopped and started to gasp as she cried.

"Someone was there, right?"

She nodded her head. "Yes." She whispered.

Alex grabbed her hands again. "Who was it? What happened?"

Julie went on. "He grabbed my arm, stood me up and pressed me to him. My back was against his chest, and we were both facing the door. I didn't know what to think. I thought maybe I was wrong because I couldn't see anyone there anymore. Jack then said…" She stopped and cried harder. "I can't."

"Yes you can Julie, and you need to, for your self, and for other girls." I said my first words to her since she started to tell the story. I broke the first rule of not making the situation about anyone but the victim, but she continued without harm.

"He said he would stop but that I was a tease. I had no right to do this to him. He pushed me against his desk and I hit my back." She then showed us her bruises on her right shoulder blade. "He grabbed my hands and tied them together. I had little strength thanks to the Ecstasy and the pain so I wasn't really fighting. He placed my arms up and hooked them around his neck. Like a backwards hug. Briefly, I thought it was nice, arousing. The door still bothered me a lot. But I was back into it." She cried louder. "I feel so dirty explaining this. I am sorry. I feel awful."

Alex replied to her concerns. "Don't be. We all have our secrets. We have all been sexual. Continue on."

"I stayed in that position. He lifted his leg and held mine against him."

"Now, just to clarify, at this point you are still on board with him right?"

"Yes, but hesitantly. It all happened so fast. But this is the point where it changes." Her head went down to the floor again. She continued from that position. "At this point, he yelled, 'come on in boys' and the door opened to his friends, clapping and cheering. They took a picture."

"What friends?" Alex asked shocked.

Julie named the boys she mentioned that were in the hall earlier. I felt odd to not be shocked over the way this was going down. It felt typical of Jack's personality to do things this way. I was convinced, just for that fact alone, that he was guilty.

"Did they touch you?" Alex asked angrily.

"No, they just came in and took turns taking a picture of me, still wrapped around Jack with his hands all over me. Jack was saying nice things like 'they just wanted to see the perfect body', or 'c'mon baby, just pose with me, not many girls get to be this close to the Jackman.' The guys said some pretty nasty things about me, and encouraged Jack to move me into different positions, but they never touched me. Again, I couldn't fight it much because I was pretty high from the E. I just giggled every time I tried to open my mouth to fight it. It was like my head and my body had two different personalities." Julie pulled her knees up to her chest and hugged herself as she finished her sentence.

"I am really sorry Julie." Alex said, touching her hand to Julies shoulder. Julie backed up away from her touch, no longer willing to have that connection with Alex.

"How did you get out of there?" I asked.

She looked up at me. "I asked. After they took a picture they left. Jack unhooked my arms from his neck, untied me, and stuffed fifty dollars into my mouth. He said thanks for the good time slut, and told me the money was half of what he won in the bet. He said he knew I was easy enough to be the one to win it on. He threw my clothes at me and told me to get dressed, unless I wanted to stay and finish what we started. I said no, got dressed and left."

"I am glad you got out of there."

"That is when she came and talked to us," Natalie informed us. "We convinced her to come and talk to you, Sadie."

Alex faced the girls and answered for me. "We are happy that you did. You are great friends. We need to call the police Julie, and tell them what happened."

"The police, why the police?" She had fear in her voice.

"Because what he did was horrible and illegal," I answered.

"I know, I just never thought I would have to talk to the police. Besides, I was on board with it for the most part. And they can't do a rape kit, I already showered."

"But you said that he never penetrated you. Did he?" Alex asked.

"No. Sorry! I'm just really shaken. I guess I just watched one too many Law and Order's."

"I understand. I will call them and they will come in to get a statement from you and from him. He had no right doing this to you and taking pictures. He wronged you. And he was physical with you as well. That is a crime. Not your fault."

"This is a little scary."

"Understandable. But we will be with you for whatever you need." Alex stood up. "I need to go call them. I will also have to talk to the Residence Manager and the Dean of Students, you understand that right?"

She nodded. "What about Jack?" Callie asked.

"Well, the police may arrest him. I can't kick him out officially until there has been an investigation, and he is found guilty. I can put a disciplinary sanction on him so he can't go near you. He will be moved to a motel until this is over."

"Okay. Please do that. I may go home for a few days. Just to get my thoughts together. I need to be able to think without crying."

"Do your parents know?"

"Not yet. I will tell them."

I noticed Julie used the word "them", not "him".

"You need to talk to someone. Can I call in Elizabeth our residence counsellor to come in to talk to you tonight? I think it would be really important."

Julie agreed to see Elizabeth.

"I will call your program co-ordinator to make arrangements so you can miss classes without negative consequences. Just let me know how long you will be home when you know. I will also get your work for you,' I offered.

She agreed again, and she and the girls got up to leave.

"Where will you be?" Alex asked.

"Callie's room." She answered.

"Alright, when Elizabeth gets here I will bring her to you. Is that okay?"

Alex told Julie that she would check in with her later. Once they were gone, Alex moved to the bed to sit. "Need a drink?" I asked.

"I am not supposed to."

"I won't tell a soul, besides a little red wine won't hurt anyone."

I poured her a glass of my red while she made some phone calls. She called the police, Rodney Maigny, the Residence Manager, and Elizabeth to inform them all on what had gone on over the weekend. Elizabeth and the police were on their way. Rodney was coming in the morning.

"You know this is really against all the rules right?"

"No worries, just relax a moment, you have a long night ahead. Can you not kick him out tonight?"

"I can't. When it comes to assault it is a 'he said she said' situation. Chances are he won't admit to anything. At least not anything that will put him at fault. I need proof before I can kick him out. I can remove him temporarily only because of the nature of the accusation. This situation has been addressed in residences across Ontario, the victim's rights versus the accused rights to being innocent until proven otherwise. It's difficult when they both live under the same roof."

I jumped onto the bed beside her after handing her my glass of wine. Once settled I grabbed it back and took a big gulp. "That sucks. I think he needs to be removed from residence."

"Yup! Me too. But what if her version is far from the truth?"

"Really? Do you not think this happened? She has the marks."

"Yes, but that doesn't mean that her version is the only one."

I shrugged. "What about the drugs?" I asked.

"I can't prove that at all. If I saw the drugs, or someone else saw them that would be different. Again, unless he admits to having them, nothing I can do."

"But *she* admitted to the drugs, why she would put herself in jeopardy like that if it was not telling the truth is beyond me."

"I agree. But the flip of that is that it is hard to say that what she remembers is exactly how it is, since she was self admittedly high. Then it also has to be proven who brought the drugs. And again, he wouldn't admit that, so it would be another he said she said. Just being the devils advocate here. What a mess." She blew her hair straight up as she sighed.

We sat together in silence for a few minutes. Just sitting on the bed and drinking our wine. Alex broke the silence first.

"You had therapy after your attack, right?"

"Yes," was all I responded in answer to her question. I was surprised.

"For long?"

"Just while I was in rehab. It was part of my recovery. They had a therapist at the hospital. I had appointments with her as much as I had appointments with physio."

"Did it help you cope?"

"I guess. I am here aren't I? Didn't off myself yet."

Alex messed my hair with her hand. She was smiling. "Don't say that again. That isn't funny."

"You're giggling." I smiled back. She refilled our glasses. I continued. "It did help. Someone listened. But I always thought of it as a joke. I felt like I was always the one with the control. She wanted to know how I was feeling, and I told her what I thought she wanted to hear. She took it as what it was, and never probed. It worked for her, feeling she was making progress with me. And it worked for me, in letting me deal with things on my own time, and not on a recommended schedule. I do think I would have benefited from being asked more in depth questions, but I did okay."

"Wow, that's a loaded answer." She turned to face me. "What do you mean they didn't probe far enough?"

"Well, she would ask me how I felt, and I would say sad, or scared, or hurt, and I would say why with the most obvious of answers, and she left it at such. I just had to pause a little when I answered. Or shed a tear. Hesitate like I didn't want to answer, and we were good." I felt a little odd and yet relieved telling her the truth. But it came out so easy. So easy, that I continued.

"Don't get me wrong, in that exact sense, I think it helped me. I needed someone to feel for me, and I didn't think I had enough to get the attention I needed, so I lied. In my lies she gave me what I needed. Now, years later, I know that if I was honest back then, I would have received that same attention even if I gave her what I was really feeling. Do I make any sense?"

"I think so."

"On the other front, with people in my life outside of therapy, I got more attention for saying that I was okay with what happened; giving them a little sadness, but overall a very positive outlook. I would crack jokes about myself, I would share enough emotion to be real, but not enough to be fully honest, and they loved it. The more people realized that I was okay, the more they wanted to be around me. No one wants to be around someone who is hurting. They don't know how to deal with it. They need you to be okay with what happened to you – to make them okay with what happened to you. Therapy made me better in that sense. I was able to keep the people I needed around me for support, even if I wasn't quite honest with them. Sometimes support is more important than understanding. Not healthy necessarily but you got to do what gets you through."

"Sorry Sadie, not sure if you are telling me that it worked for you because it didn't, or that it didn't work for you because it did, and you still need help."

I laughed out loud. "See, you are now as messed up as I felt back

Where the stream and creek collide

then. It took me a while to make sense of it too. The short answer is this – I had therapy and I like where I am today. So, it must have worked out, in some way because I am okay."

"Well that is always good." She said hesitantly seeming confused. She went on. "That seems to be sitting with me, on a different level. I am not sure how I feel. I am sure I will revisit this conversation with you. Especially once all you said sinks in a little bit." She smiled again in my direction. I smiled back and just shrugged my shoulders.

"Listen, I am sorry I have been such an ass to you lately."

"Thank you. I accept that."

"Really, that easy?"

"Yes. I will want to talk it out sometime soon, but not tonight. We don't have to sit in limbo until then. I know we will be okay, so let's start there, and talk it out later."

"Thanks Alex." I reached over and gave her a one armed hug, the other arm still holding onto my glass.

She finished her wine. Grabbed some gum from her pocket, offered me one, I said no.

"I need to go meet the police so we can talk to the Jackman himself." She made air quotes with her hand as she said his name. "I am sure he is expecting me at the very least. I can't wait to hear his side. This is a tough one, Sadie, since Julie was willing for so long, and on a self admitted high. Don't get me wrong, I do believe her. And I don't condone his actions," she paused. "Just wish me luck, okay."

I wished her luck. I had a feeling she would need it. I had looked into the eyes of evil, and I had felt its wrath. He was not the kind of guy I would have wanted to sit down with and asked questions to, especially when those questions were going to be accusations as well.

-21-

"I REPEAT, I DID NOT HAVE SEXUAL RELATIONS WITH THAT WOMAN!"

That morning I awoke to a message from Lonny asking me if everything went well at the conference. He also apologised for what Jessica and her friends had said to me. He said that she told him how they, "took care of me". He also furthered to say that he would not let them touch my face and that he would like to talk to me and start over as friends. The message was really quite lengthy; wordy. I erased it before it was over. I didn't really care to listen to the end, let alone follow up. He made his choice. He needed to keep it.

I had one class earlier but skipped it. I slept in until 11 in the morning instead. I hadn't slept that long in years. I think the tension and stress were starting to come out of me, in a good way. I was starting to not care about Lonny, and was almost able to see the dog for what he was - a dog. I had also resigned myself to the fact that father and Elizabeth were not going to be together. My dad was free to do what was best for him, without my manipulating.

And now, the conference was over, leaving me to concentrate solely on my school work and employment. The only other pressing matter was the situation with Julie. I felt for her. She obviously had a lot going on in her life. To first lie about her mother being dead, and now to get her self into a situation with Jack allowing him to hurt her in this way, showed she had a lot going on inside of her, both before and presently. She needed some attention for some reason. This I could figure out. But I didn't know why she needed it and what I could do to help her. A cry for attention, no matter how ill fated, was a cry for help. I should have paid attention to it when I found her in a lie about her mother because now not only did we have to get her help for some unknown need, we had to get her some justice for what had happened with Jack.

My phone rang. I was worried that it would be Lonny again, so I didn't answer it. I really wished the Greenbury residence would allow us to have call display. I hated answering the phone blindly. I showered and dressed before I checked the message. It was Alex

Where the stream and creek collide

asking me to come to her room when I had the chance. No time like the present. I called her to let her know I was on my way. I wanted to know how the rest of her night went.

As I left my room, I ran into Jack in the hall. "Apparently I have to leave. Not that you would care." He said with one hand holding a pointed finger towards me. "So don't wig out on me now, I will be out of here when I am done."

I just looked at him with a smirk and kept going. I really didn't want to start speaking to him. I wasn't sure I would stop.

Alex's room seemed like it was 3 kilometres away. I was anxious to know what had happened. She had obviously already talked to Jack because he was getting ready to leave. Alex had her door jammed open. I knocked once and went in. "You expecting someone?" I asked as I turned to go to the kitchen where she was sitting writing and drinking coffee. Caffeine addiction was one hazard of her job, I was sure. I bet I could count on one hand the number of times I had seen her without a coffee in her hand. Not including the times that she had replaced that coffee with a glass of wine, of course.

She looked up from her papers. "Yah, you!" She smiled softly.

"Oh, okay," I laughed lightly feeling slightly silly for the question. "Want me to fix the lock so it shuts?"

"Yes please. Coffee is on the stove if you want one." I did. I poured myself some in my favourite cup, added milk and sugar, and blew on it to try to cool it off. "Smells yummy."

"It is." She took another sip. "I am just finishing up my report from what Jack says happened. Give me a moment. I want to write this before I forget."

I decided to spend some time in her living room area, looking at her shelf of knickknacks. She had a little frog collection, with several mini statues of the animal in different positions on a lily pad. They were quite cute. The second shelf of the cabinet held many scented candles. I picked up one that smelt like oranges. I could eat it, it smelt so strong. The next one that I picked up was cinnamon and frosting. It reminded me of my birthdays from when I was little. Mother would wake me up in the morning with cinnamon buns slathered in frosting. It was my favourite part of my big day. It amazed me how a smell had the ability to bring you back to a place you hadn't been in years. I remember when I discovered that mother smelt like Vaseline. It wasn't until after the accident, when I bought myself a bottle of the jelly, did I realize that. When I was a child, mother would wear Vaseline on her lips to keep them from cracking. I never noticed the smell until she was gone. Now, I smell everything and everyone. I like to associate smells to moments, it helps me with remembering people and places. I also liked to smell people because it would let me know a bit about the person, before I got too far into a conversation with them. It gave me the upper hand. We all know certain smells when it comes to certain people. Men are the easiest. A motor oil and grease smell tends to mean a blue collar worker. Motor oil and aftershave would be a single blue collar worker. A guy with mild cologne wearing a suit usually was a pretty successful business man. But a guy with strong cologne wearing a suit tended to mean a newbie, or a CEO want-to-be. Women are slightly more complicated. Vanilla scent usually means catalogue ordered, and a catalogue shopper. No perfume typically meant married or a hospital worker. Light perfume means middle class average lady, whereas a strong perfumed person usually brought with it wealth and showmanship, and more often than not, older age. Skinny girls tend to smell fruity, bigger girls smell musky. Athletic women have a Pina Colada or coconut smell, and busy moms with young children smell like vegetable soup. The average senior smells wet with a touch of peppermint. Kids, smell like outside, dirt, air, and grass.

Smells are what classify us on first impressions. They are what tie us to others, to memories, and they are what connect us to the past. Smells are our links to what we are, and what we could have been. That was why I smell people as they walked by, why I smell them when they get close, and why I smell my surroundings when I am ensuring that I am mentally present in a situation.

"Penny for your thoughts?" I turned to see Alex plopping down on the couch behind me. Coffee held by both hands.

"Is that really how you want to spend your money?"

"Hmm, that doesn't sound to promising for juicy news. Do I want to know what you are thinking?"

"Probably not this time." I laughed, she did too.

"Did you hear the latest going around residence yet?"

"No," I responded a little unsure. There was always something going around residence, so there was a chance that I already knew. But nothing Alex would be talking about was anything I could remember hearing.

"Well, the latest is that the students are complaining that some of the culinary students who are now working in the cafeteria are threatening to put poison in the food. They say they were offered to get paid by the strikers to do it, so the deal would get approved."

"Paid to commit murder, sounds bright."

"We all know how bright students can be. That is why the Dean is taking it seriously. They are hiring security guards to watch over the cafeteria in the residence and in the college, as a precaution."

"Wow, that didn't take long to get messy, did it?"

I put my mug down on the coffee table and transferred onto the couch. It was nice to change positions.

"Not surprising. I am hoping it doesn't deter too many students from eating in the cafeterias. Although with the pre-paid meal plan being a required part of residence, most students won't have a choice, unless they don't eat at all."

At Greenbury, every student that was registered into a dorm room was also required to buy a prepaid meal card for the year that worked at both the residence and the college. We sell them in $1500, $2000, and $2500 increments, being our small, medium, and large plans. If you didn't have a meal card on opening day, you were not given your keys to your room. It was a way for the college to make sure that their students were getting properly nourished.

"I can see that happening. Is there going to be any signage explaining why the guards are there?"

"Probably. Most people know though."

"I hadn't heard until now."

"True. I will get signs to everyone soon. Want a refresh before we talk about Julie?" She asked pointing to her cup.

"Please." I handed her my cup. "Two sugars please, and milk."

"I know," she lifted her eyebrows in acknowledgement. "Two heaping, don't be cheap right? I've made it before."

Minutes later she returned with a plate of cookies and our coffee. I grabbed my cup and a chocolate cookie, biting into the soft chewy snack.

"I saw Jack as I was on my way down here. He was packing to leave. I take it you told him of the accusations, and that he has to move to a motel."

She held up her finger to show one minute, as she finished eating the cookie she shoved into her mouth. She chewed while holding her hand in front of her mouth.

"I did, but he is going to his Aunt's house, not a motel."

I interrupted her. "Isn't that a conflict of interest considering his aunt is the Dean of Student Services, and is in charge of deciding the truth here?"

165

"Well, yes and no. This is up to the police. We go by what they say. If they lay charges then he is out automatically. If they don't, then we have to decide what we think happened based on what they both have said happened, and if it warrants removal from the residence or not. And *that* my dear, is not only up to her, but up to the committee which includes the Dean, the Residence Manager, the President of the College, the head Counsellor who is Elizabeth, and myself. That is why he is allowed to stay there."

I rolled my eyes. "That doesn't mean anything. She still has a huge influence on the outcome. It is very prejudicial."

"I agree, but tell that to the committee."

"True." I conceded. "So what did he say?"

"Would it surprise you to hear he has a totally different explanation to what happened?"

"So he agreed that it happened? What was different?"

The differences of Jacks' interpretation over Julie's were quite large. Jack's story was similar to hers when recalling what happened at the bar, but changed once they got to the room.

"He says that she was the one pushing everything. That she wanted him to live on the edge, and even invite some friends over to participate in that evenings events." Alex made her famous air quotes with her fingers when she said participate. She continued. "Jack said he went to get his friends, and of course they said yes. When he returned, she was in her underwear and had Jackman's dirty whore written on her stomach, and a sash she was twisting around her wrists to tie them together."

I leaned forward on the couch. I was trying to consume all of what I was being told. "So let me get this straight. He says that it was her idea to have the guys there, and she tied herself up. Seriously, he thinks we would believe this?"

She puckered her lips and raised her eyebrows, shrugging her shoulders to complete the look. "He also claims that once the guys were there, that she took one of them," she grabbed the paper that had her notes from his talk on it and read it for a moment. "Pete. She had sex with him in front of everyone."

"Wow, I am speechless." I leaned back on the couch.

"He also said that she asked for the pictures to be taken, that she put her arms around Jack's neck in pose for them. He said that her hands were free, no longer tied for the picture. Oh yes, and he said that she brought the ecstasy pills."

"Can we get a copy of the picture to see?"

"Sadie, we can't ask a possible sexual assault victim to provide or locate a picture of their attack."

"I guess not. Wow, two very different ideas of what happened. Now what?"

"Now we wait for the cops to deal with it. They are taking statements as we speak. They should request the pictures. My only problem is that Jack gave his statement to me, without knowing anything that Julie said."

"What do you mean?"

"I mean, all I said to him was to tell me what happened that night. This was his response."

"That is odd that he would have a ready response. If you just suddenly asked me to reveal what happened on a night that I supposedly had consenting sex, I could promise you, that not only would I not have a story ready, I would be asking you what the hell you wanted to know about it for. Wouldn't you?"

"I agree. What you say makes sense. But there is a lot to consider here. And we aren't the ones with the say, at least not much of one. The other problem I see is that his friends are going to back him up with both the committee and the police."

"They would lie to the police I am not sure of that."

"First Sadie, I wouldn't be so shocked to hear they lied to the police. And second, you talk like you were there. We don't know what the truth is. It sits somewhere among what he said and what she said, and the truth."

I was shocked. I leaned forward again. "Do you really believe what you are saying? Are you really on his side in all this?" My face was heating up.

"I am not on anyone's side in this Sadie."

"That's the problem. You don't believe the girl in this. Just listen to what you are saying."

"Listen to yourself. You are counting someone as guilty before they are even convicted. Do you not remember Julie's lies about her mother? For crying out loud, you call her crazy Julie. You can't just automatically say everything she said is the truth. I believe it very well could be, but that isn't 100 percent for sure. Right?"

I took a very loud and deep breath before speaking. "This is bullshit, you know that right? Complete bullshit. I think he gets away with anything because of who he is."

"That may be. But it isn't up to us to decide now. It is out of our hands. We did our job." She finished up her coffee and used the spoon to scoop up the left over cookie crumbs in the bottom of the cup. I just watched her. I was stewing with my thoughts. "Let's not fight about this. We are allowed to see it differently. We should see it differently. That is the great thing about this job. We are all different people with different backgrounds and beliefs. I see where you are coming from, but see where I am as well. Deal?" She held out her hand in my direction. Her eyes seemed to beg for my agreement.

I smiled. "Okay, deal. But I still say you are wrong. I still think he is guilty."

She laughed. "I didn't say he wasn't. He may very well be. However, I will reserve the right to tell you, or in turn let you tell me 'I told you so' when it is appropriately required."

"Now that I will shake on," and I did.

"Want to watch a movie? I can be done for the day. Besides it's not like they can't find me if I'm needed."

We went through her movie collection and decided on a sappy dramatic comedy or as we say in class, a dramedy. She popped some popcorn and I went down to grab some sodas from the cafeteria. About half way through the movie, where the relationship between the two main characters was just about to get interesting, there was a knock on the door. Alex got up to answer it. It was my father.

"Jason, you're early." She opened the door slowly and turned to look at me. "Your dad's here."

"I see that. I would ask if you were looking for me, but by the 'you're early' comment, I am assuming you have found exactly who you are looking for." I wasn't sure how to feel about this. They were starting to spend more and more time together. I knew this was great for my father to have someone who he got along with, who he liked to spend time with, and who really knew him, around. I just wasn't sure it should be Alex. I wasn't sure I was okay with it being her. And mostly, I wasn't sure my opinion was going to matter too either of them.

"Yes, he is early. We were supposed to do dinner together. But that is okay, I am glad you are here."

"Do you want me to come back Graham?" He seemed to be asking me more than Alex, so I answered. It was awkward.

"No, I can leave." I pulled the blanket off my legs and lifted my feet onto the ground.

"Why does anyone have to go? We all care about each other here. No enemies. Why don't you sit down Jason and join us watching the end of this movie?" Alex said, taking a stab at easing the tension that

168

had erupted with father's arrival.

Father looked as though he had just been asked to touch the dead guy at a funeral. But he was a sport. He sat down on the chair and watched the end of the movie with us. I even think he laughed once.

* * * * * * * * * * *

"What are you doing still here?"

I had left Alex's room and decided to go to visit Piety for a while. I assumed since it was Sunday that she would be in Hal's room. That was where they usually hung out on the weekends, playing video games. I ran into Jack in the hall. He was walking holding hands with Bridgette.

"I moved my stuff already. Now I am visiting my girl here. And she is visiting Jessie. That alright boss? I am not allowed on our floor, but I am allowed in the building. Or are you going to re-write the rules today?"

"No need for rudeness Jack. I am just inquiring."

"And you, all wise and mighty resident assistant, do not know that I am allowed to visit?" Bridgette stood beside him. She stayed silent, smiling at every word he said, looking up at him like an adoring puppy. It made me nauseous.

"Just checking Jack, that is all."

I got to Hal's room and managed to shut the door behind me only moments before I lost my composure. "That stupid son of a bitch! Who the fuck does he think he is, some fucking Prince from the land of, of, ah who the fuck cares. Arrgghh!"

"Let me guess, Lonny?"

I punched the wall.

"No Jack." I filled them both in on what had been happening the last 24 hours in regards to Jack and Julie. They were equally stunned.

"And you just saw him with Bridgette. Does she know what is going on?"

"I am not sure how she couldn't." I guessed but I really was not sure of the answer. Then again, she was standing with him when he was saying that he was only visiting, I shared my thoughts. "She must, she was right with him when I was talking to him. Some girls never learn do they?"

"Nope!"

After two cans of cheap beer, and some great distracting video game playing, I headed back to my room. I wanted to make it an early night. I had a lot of homework to finish before school tomorrow. I would need all the time that I could afford to give myself. I had a feeling that I was going to be terribly distracted.

-22-

IT ISN'T TOO LATE TO CHANGE YOUR MIND.

The week went by awfully slowly. School work had been almost impossible to get completed. I had two spec scripts due and only a week to write them. A speculative script in its long form involved taking an active television show, and writing an episode for it as if we were part of the writing team on that day. It had to be done well enough so that it could air within the same year as you wrote it. So it couldn't be too far off from what was happening now. It was meant to show production companies. Not to sell as a script but to sell you as a writer. I picked two half hour shows, so it limited the amount of writing I had to do. I was not as much into the writing as I was into the editing. I personally thought you could have the best script, the best actors, and the best film, and it wouldn't matter if it wasn't edited properly. The editor was the one that prioritised the film and put the scenes in the order that they needed to be. The Editor had the final say in some respects, and the final vision in others. That was where I eventually wanted to be, in an editing suite for a major blockbuster film. Ah, dreams. They are great to have, and hard to pull off, especially on weeks like this one. When you had to get past the crap, or in this case the spec scripts, to get to what you like. But the good thing was that we all had a lifetime to get to our dreams. And I was well on my way. I had just handed my script in and it was only noon on Friday, leaving me the rest of the day off to enjoy.

    I grabbed a slice of cold pizza from my fridge. Piety and I had worked together last night and ordered some food to get us through the editing of each others papers. Wings and pizza was a college kids' staple food. Well, the pizza was a staple, the wings were a luxury. We ate them all, but split the last of the pepperoni pizza between us. The cold slices were my lunch. I actually preferred pizza cold.

    I was supposed to work tonight, but I was on call with Lonny. Tristen graciously offered to work it for me, and I took his next Fridays shift to repay him. It wasn't that I was really avoiding Lonny; I just didn't particularly want to spend the whole night trying to think of superficial conversations to fill up our time together. And I definitely didn't want to talk about what had happened between us. That was over now. I had moved on and I was hoping he had moved on as well, which, since he was now engaged, I was sure he had. It was a moot point anyway. The shift was no longer mine.

My phone rang several times this morning. I didn't answer it once. Assuming it was Lonny wondering why I had changed the shift. Considering there were no messages left on any of the calls, I knew I was probably right. This I guessed would count as job avoidance but I didn't care. It was short lived anyhow. A knock on the door told me that my avoidance was over. I had a role to play in the College. It could have been anyone at the door. And if it was Lonny, well, I had to confront him, like it or not. I put down the last of the crust I was munching on, wiped my face, and checked my makeup and hair in the mirror, before pulling the door open.

"Jack, what are you doing here? You are not allowed on this floor." I said surprised.

"I know, but I needed to get something out of my room."

"It doesn't matter Jack, you are not allowed up here." I said with exhaustion in my voice. Everything had to be told to him several times.

"Listen," he said with equal exasperation. He leaned his arm up against the door frame, crossing his legs in his stance. He was a good looking boy standing like he knew it. "I am here now and it will only take a minute. Probably less time then it would for you to argue with me about this. So, what do you say?"

He had a point. It would take less time, and less frustration to just let him go in a moment. He no longer had a key for his room. It had been confiscated right away. Alex had kept his key, but I, as senior R.A., had a copy of everyone's room key in my building; in case of an emergency. I of course, was not allowed to just enter any room, including his, as tempting as it was. But I could open it for him to quickly go inside. Other than an emergency, he was the only one who was allowed to give permission to open it.

"Give me a minute. C'mon in while I find your key, you can't stay alone in the hall and I need to shut the door to get into the closet."

He came in and I opened the closet doors to pull out the baskets of room cards. I thumbed through my floor keys and came across his card. At residence, our key cards had the student's picture on it.

"I tried calling all morning. I was just going to see if you would get it for me, but you didn't answer. Did you just get in?"

There went my Lonny theory. Obviously I care way more about him then he does me. "Yah! I was out all morning," I lied.

We went to his room and I opened the door. "C'mon in," he said, "it will take me a minute to get all my stuff. I need some clothes, and some of my knives that I forgot. Oh and something I have saved on the computer."

"I thought this was only going to take a second?"

He smiled his toothy grin. "Chill out Sadie, it won't take long."

He grabbed clothes from his drawers and shoved them in an empty briefcase. He pulled out culinary knives from the closet and sat them on top of the briefcase. Finally he sat at his desk and turned on the computer.

"Won't you need your computer at your aunt's?"

"No. She has one, and I have a laptop. I just need some things that are saved on this one. Besides, I am sure I will be back here in a few days."

I had to stop an involuntary laugh that was pushing to get out of my lungs. "Oh yah? I wouldn't know. I am not involved in the decision." I didn't know what to say in response. That was the best I could come up with. He evidently realized my predicament and called me on it.

"Yah, no kidding. Not unless you have been deputized recently. It is with the police right now. They haven't laid any charges. I am pretty confident that they won't either."

I just smiled a slight smile in acknowledgement that I heard him. Again I was speechless. I knew there was an invisible line that divided what I could say to him, and what was best left in my thoughts. I stayed silent. He didn't.

"I would even go so far as to say that it will probably be resolved as of tomorrow. In my favour of course, cause I am innocent." He continued to type on the computer. He turned and gave a pondering look. Finger to his lips first, then pointing towards me before he spoke. "No. I am confident that it will be resolved as of tomorrow." His disk popped out of his computer with as much confidence in its movement as its owner. He grabbed it and turned the computer off.

"I am glad you are so sure of that."

"I know you have me pegged as a perve, but I am not. You will see."

"Tomorrow right?" I smiled. Not sure if his poise was from cockiness or innocence.

"You will see. Tomorrow." He smiled. He went into his closet and grabbed another briefcase. "I am done." He grabbed all his stuff together. Turned off his light and shut the door. Before he got onto the elevator he turned to say that he would be in his brother's room if I needed him. Then he smirked, winked, and related: "See you tomorrow, Monday the latest."

* * * * * * * * * * *

My evening off turned out to be anything but relaxing. In fact the whole weekend was nothing of the sort. I spent it thinking about Jack, and what the hell he meant by it all being over on Saturday. I expected something to happen Saturday, but nothing did. I informed Alex of our conversation, and she said that she would let me know as soon as she heard something. I heard nothing from her all weekend. I tried to keep my mind off of things by hanging out with the girls. Piety, Ahslyn, Wanda, and I each rented 2 of our favourite 90's movies. We spent the majority of the weekend living in the past. Wanda even dressed in her best 90's clothes for the whole weekend. She wore purple Spandex pants, a ripped white t-shirt, a black leather jacket and high top shoes. We argued that it was more of an 80's style outfit, but she disagreed. She was always the entertainer.

It wasn't until Monday that I actually had an update, and an answer to Jack's comment. I was on my way to class when Alex had pulled me into her office.

"Well, he was right, he will probably be back today, or at least this week. But that is my guess."

"Why?"

"Listen." She sat down and picked up her phone. After she pressed several numbers she put the phone on speaker. It was her voicemail.

Hi Alexandria, it is Cathy DeGraff here. I am just calling on behalf of the review committee in regards to Jack Degraff.

"Man she talks like he is any student and not her nephew. Please, does anyone buy this?" I said over her voice reading off his student identification numbers, in case we didn't know who he was. Alex just shrugged her shoulders.

I just wanted to let you know that I got a message from Detective Carl Johanson, from the Criminal Investigations Division to inform me that there will be no charges laid in this matter. Apparently Julie Dabble has recanted her statement to say that she believes she was a completely active participant. More so than she had originally said, I guess. That she was just embarrassed about what happened. I don't know. I have to call him back and get more details.

I couldn't believe this. Crazy Julie strikes again. She cried wolf. Jack knew that she would recant her words because the asshole was telling the truth. I was shocked.

Now I have spoken to Rodney, and he agrees with me that we will have to now go over the situation as soon as we can, and see if we need to reinstate Jack with his residence privileges. Now on other business...

She went on talking about other residence stuff, so Alex hung up the phone.

"What do you think? He was right."

"I knew something was coming, but I didn't expect this. I guess he was telling the truth. I guess Julie was more of a willing player than she let us think."

"Well." She said shrugging her shoulders. There was a look of disapproval on her face.

"What do you mean, well? What are you thinking?"

"Common Sadie, put things together here. He told you Friday that it was going to be over this weekend, and now it is. Hmmm. You said he seemed pretty confident right?"

I nodded.

"And now what he predicted is true. You saw how broken up she was; now she says she was just as at fault as he was."

"You think he did something to change this. To make her recant?"

"Yes. Don't you?"

"That sounds like something out of a movie. A little too elaborate if you ask me."

"I don't know Sadie. He is a wealthy kid."

I let out a small giggle. "Listen to us. Can you believe it? You are sitting here accusing Jack of something and I am defending him." I hesitated a moment then smiled, "sort of." My eyebrows bowed at the end of my sentence.

"Who would have thought?" She smiled back.

"Not I. So you really think he what? bought her off?"

"Yup. I guess you can put it that way. Let me check something."

She picked up her phone and dialled a 4 digit extension. After a few moments she spoke. "Hi Candice, it is Alex here. Listen I need you to do me a small favour and check on something for me. It is kind of a personal request, so maybe when you get a chance you can call me back and I can let you know then. How is that for descriptive?" She laughed. "Anyway, call me when you have a moment. Thanks."

"What is Candice going to do?"

"Well, I am assuming that Jack is either going to give her cash, or pay her residence or tuition for her. I can't look into the idea of her getting cash, but I can the other. I want Candice to take a look into her account for me. Let me know if there are any changes."

"Sounds good. But again a little far fetched for me. But…" I just raised my eyebrows and shrugged.

"Ah, it is worth a try right? No harm done."

"True. I better go. I have class. I will try not to think of how annoying this situation is, while I am there."

"Good idea."

I left her office through the Residence Assistant lounge. No one was in there. I opened the other door and saw my father walk by. He was coming from the connecting hall.

"Dad! What are doing here? Were you just at my room looking for me?"

"No, I was just coming from Alex's room."

Of course. "Oh, well she is in her office. You should have checked there first."

"Um, yes, I guess I should have." He coughed. "Excuse me sweetheart. I have to see Alex quickly before my class starts." He bent down and kissed my head. "I will talk to you later. Maybe we can do dinner tomorrow night? I have a meeting tonight."

"I would like that." I said. And then he was gone.

-23-

EXCUSE ME, COULD I GET THIS TO GO PLEASE?

"So, I thought that we could all put these posters up on our doors, just to show the students that the strike doesn't have to completely ruin us around residence. A lot of students are going broke spending their money at the grocery store or pizza joints instead of using their pre-paid meal card to eat and all because of something so small."

Our R.A. meeting was held on a Monday night this week, instead of Sunday – due to many Resident Assistants throwing an Oscar party for their students. Many R.A.'s did a theme night for their students offering snacks, awards for those who guessed the most winners, and of course, the watching of the Oscar's itself.

"A threat of being poisoned is not that small." Hal responded to Jen's comment. Jen had made and printed off many signs that read 'I am not afraid to eat in the cafeteria.' She wanted all R.A.'s to post the sign on their dorm room door in hopes that students would read it and start eating in the cafeteria again. At least half the students had stopped dining at residence.

"Yah, so we have the sign, but we don't eat there…they will catch on eventually."

"Come on guys, have an open mind. Jen I think it is a great idea. And at the very least, it is worth a shot." Wanda came to her rescue.

We all agreed. Not that we would disagree. The boss had asked us to put up Jen's sign and so we would.

"As long as I don't have to actually start eating there, because I don't want to. Some of those kids are on my floor. I have seen their hygiene," Hal informed everyone.

This prompted a huge discussion on the strike, the students taking the employee's places, and the fight igniting between the cafeteria staff and the residents.

I sat beside Ashlyn. While the discussion heated up, she drilled me with questions about Lonny. She asked if I missed sitting beside him, if I missed talking to him, and if I was going to talk to him anytime soon.

I answered the questions with a no, a little, and another no.

"Really? You have no plans on talking to him again?" She asked quietly. We sat in the back of the boardroom.

"Well, I probably will talk to him again. Just not about this or us. He lied to me, and put Jessica ahead of me twice, after he said he loved me."

"He loved her too."

"Not helping. Nor are you getting any marks towards your point."

"My point is this. He fucked up. He is an asshole. But you guys were best friends for years. Do you really think you will never get past this and talk again?"

"Not sure Ashlyn. I am hurt. He said he loved me, that he was going to be with me. Then he came back engaged. And worst of all, I had to find out from others."

"I get it, but he isn't engaged anymore. He knows he screwed up, and he…"

"He isn't engaged anymore?" I interrupted. I was confused.

"No, didn't you know? He broke it off with her right after the conference." She stopped talking so she could look at me in the face. She had to lean forward onto the table to see my eyes that were hidden behind my hands. "Oh my, you didn't know, did you?"

I just shook my head.

"Well, see there's hope for you two yet."

"No there isn't. That is just my point. He broke off his engagement and again I heard about it from someone else. I am the last person on his mind." I tried to mask the tears. I didn't particularly want to spend anymore time hurt by him, but I couldn't help it.

"Sorry Sadie I thought you knew. You and I are like the best of friends, how could we not know that I knew and you didn't? You know?"

"Strangely I know what you are saying, and what you mean. How awful is that?" We both tried a smile.

Lonny was not engaged anymore. I wasn't sure if I was elated or extremely pissed off. How could he not have told me? It would have been nice to hear it from him. Although, I guess if he no longer wanted anything to do with me, then he wouldn't bother telling me. It wouldn't matter if I knew, because he didn't care what I thought. Argh! I didn't understand the opposite sex at all. Although I was not sure why that surprised me, I didn't understand my own sex, so why should I be aces on the opposite one. A spinster woman was my future self. And right now, it would be by choice.

I waited until everyone left. Ashlyn waited with me.

"Honestly Sadie," she said as we moved to the front to leave.
"No worries Ashlyn, seriously." I replied.
"Hey ladies, got a minute?"
"Sure Alex, what's up?" I was happy for the change in conversation.
She sat down, which usually meant that I wasn't going to like what I was about to hear.
"I talked to Candice. My hunch was right."
"No way!"
"What hunch?" Ashlyn asked. She was out of the loop. She knew what Jack had said about the situation with Julie. How he claimed that he was just one of two willing participants and not really the one in charge, but I hadn't yet told her about my talk with Alex in regards to a pay off to stop her from pressing charges. I felt that her theory was very soap opera like, and not something that would happen in Greenbury. Now, I see I was probably wrong in that thought. I quickly filled her in. She saw Alex's theory better than I did. Although she did also have the benefit of just hearing what Alex said about her hunch or a pay off being just as she suspected.
"So what did she say exactly?" I asked Alex after I finished informing Ashlyn.
"She said that late Friday night a large anonymous sum of money went into Julie's school account. Apparently not only are her last payments for this year paid off, but there was enough money as a credit to pay for the next 3 years of her housing and tuition as well, should she choose."
"But she won't be in residence next year."
"Probably not considering she will be in second year. We only take a dozen or so second years. However, it seems that when there is a credit the student is allowed to withdraw it out at the end of each year."
"Wow, so it is true, he paid her off. He can't get away with this, can he?"
"Well I will bring the situation up to the committee, but the problem is proving it came from him."
"Are all men assholes, or is it just the ones I am surrounded by that are?"
Ashlyn laughed. "Here we go again."
"Am I missing something?" Alex asked.
"Yah, Lonny isn't engaged anymore, and Sadie just found out."
"Ashlyn just told me. Not Lonny, but Ashlyn." Ashlyn shrugged as I spoke.

"Ahh. I see. Well to answer your question, no, not all men are assholes. Not anymore than all women are bitches. Some guys are rather sweet." Alex smiled very softly and drifted a little. "Very sweet indeed."

* * * * * * * * * * *

"J.P., got a minute?" I asked the custodian as I pushed up to the residence. The support personnel were standing out on the front picketing as they were every school day. They were good. They never stopped anybody from going in and out of the residence. They knew that it wouldn't help or hurt their cause to let the students in to where they lived. The battle was more on the College steps than on the Residence ones. J.P. was sitting on the bench having a smoke, his sign held between his boney knees.

"For you Sadie, I have an hour. What's the matter?" He drew a hard puff from his smoke.

"I need to ask you a question. Can you come in for a moment?"

"No I can't. With the strike and all." He stood up, holding the sign in his hands, message towards the ground. "I mean, I could go inside but I think they would hurt me, don't you?" He laughed a hearty and somewhat geeky laugh and pointed to the cafeteria ladies picketing behind him. "Some of those ladies are big."

"Oh right, I forgot. Guess not. A walk then shall we?"

"Sure, mind if I keep my smoke?"

I went inside and placed my back pack in the staff lounge. When I came out J.P. was lighting a second cigarette off of his first. He wore jeans and a blue t-shirt that looked more like a crumpled undershirt. On top of that shirt he wore a faded jean jacket. It worked for him.

"Where to?" He was no longer carrying his sign.

"Let's go towards the arboretum. We can walk along the college walk way, around back. Sound okay?"

"Sure. I remember as a kid I use to come here and play around the back all the time. It is now parking areas in the back but back then it was trees and water. Swamp like I guess. Maybe not, but you know what I mean. They saved part of it, the arboretum area, but the rest was turned into what they now call a concrete jungle. Without all the apes and stuff though." He laughed at his own joke. "Well, I guess we do have a few Tarzans here but…" He laughed harder, snorting 3 times and sighing once at the end.

I had forgotten how eccentric J.P. was. He was a fountain of stories, most coming from his own childhood. His memory amazed me.

"How long ago was that?"

"Oh, way before your time, Sadie. I was younger than you are now. I was only 12, so like half your age, right?"

"Uh-huh!"

"Anyways, we used to go back there and let off our pop guns. We would get the strip of caps, you know, that you can shoot the guns over and over, for like a hundred caps at a time. They're red. We did it back behind the school because our parents didn't give us the money to get them. They always questioned when we would use them. So we had to hide. You can't shoot them off now-a-days. Someone would call the cops in a second that is for sure. The first sound of a gun, boy oh boy."

"True, they would call the cops. So, you are from around here?"

He nodded. "A few blocks away."

"How did you pay for the caps?" We started to round the corner of the building. We were at the middle part of the back of the school.

"We would do people's lawns, or driveways in the winter, depending on the season."

"Oh, for sure! That's not bad, and you wouldn't tell your mother?" My voice went high at the end of my sentence, but I didn't correct it. There was no harm in him thinking I was more interested than I really was.

"No, because she would just make us spend it on other stuff like candy or carnivals. They would never let us spend it on caps. They thought they were too dangerous and too loud."

I smiled. "Eww! Stay away from those candies and carnivals." I teased.

He laughed. "She did not approve of caps. We were kids, we didn't listen. What was right and what was fun were two separate things, and we didn't much care. Or think about it."

"That's right. Sorry, you said that already. I get it."

He threw his smoke away into a machine created snow bank. We were now on the other side of the school on our way towards the front. I had to start talking to him about what I needed soon or we would be back before I got the chance. I didn't want to miss an opportunity.

"So I am sure you are wondering why I asked you to come out." He shrugged. Maybe he guessed already. It would be hard not to. "I need to ask you some questions about Jack."

"You are going to ask me why I was in his closet that day, aren't ya?" He seemed nervous.

"Well, no I wasn't, but since we are on the subject."

"I was in their room and the strike had already started, and I wasn't supposed to be in the residence. By the way, I am not mad that you told on me being there. I got a warning that is all for now."

"I see. And thank you. Not that it is my business, but why were you hanging out with them anyway?"

He seemed a little embarrassed, but answered. "I like those guys. I know I am not one of them. But they like me, they like my stories, and they don't mind my job here. I know they are younger, and I would never think that they are going to become my best friends or anything. But they pass the year along for me. Why not live vicariously through them for a school year, right?" He smiled innocently.

"I guess, but why them J.P.? They are bad news." My arms were getting tired of pushing my chair through the snow, not to mention the cold. We were almost back to the residence, completing the circle around the college.

"Oh, they are just college boys, Sadie. A pain in the ass maybe but not bad news."

I had a feeling he wasn't going to give me the information that I wanted about the boys, since he seemed a little protective of them. I decided to go for it anyway.

"Do you know if Jack mentioned anything about paying someone a large sum of money to get himself out of trouble?"

"Like paying someone off for something? Or what do you mean?"

"I guess just that, paying someone off to get himself out of some trouble."

"Odd question Sadie, but no, I don't know anything about any payments. Not that I can recall at all. Let me think." And he did. He slapped his head as he walked with his eyes closed. "Nope, nothing comes to mind. Who would he pay off?"

"I can't say. I just wanted to know if he said anything lately that could sound like he was trying to buy his way out of some trouble. Or even saying that he was out a lot of money, or complaining about someone really pissing him off. You know?"

"Not that I heard. I haven't been around him for a week or so though. Do you want me to ask him without letting him know why?"

I squirmed. "No! Please." It came out in a small shout. "Don't let him know that I even asked you, for any reason, okay? Please. Don't tell anyone alright?"

"Okay, I won't. You can trust me." I hoped that to be true, even after I had already broke his trust by telling on him when I found him in Jack's closet.

"I know. Thanks J.P." We were back and walking up the walkway to the residence. I thanked him again for his time.

"No problem Sadie. Hey did your dad get his car fixed?"

"My dad? There is nothing wrong with his car. Is there?"

"Oh, I don't know. Just figured it was broken. It has been here all weekend."

"All weekend? You sure?"

"Yes. I was on weekend overnight strike watch. It was here every night that I was - which was both Saturday and Sunday night. Come to think of it, it was in a different spot the one night, but still here, parked. Maybe it isn't broken if he moved it, not sure, you'll have to ask him."

"Believe me, I will." We parted ways and I went to collect my back pack.

Awesome! My Dad was here all weekend. He wasn't trying to find Alex to say hello, he was looking to say good-bye, see ya' later, ciao. Could life get any fucking sweeter? The world was coming together one group of people at a time, and not only was I not invited, I wasn't even allowed into the show. Go team Sadie!

ANGRY PEOPLE MAKE TERRIBLE NEIGHBORS - AND EVEN WORSE FRIENDS.

It wasn't until I was getting ready for dinner with my father that I had finally got my mind to relax - which wasn't an easy task. I would compare the chore to that of trying to tame a lion. Not that that has ever been a problem to solve for me but I was sure that if it was, again it would be comparable. I was jumpy, confused over which emotion I should express – anger or insult, and scared. I wasn't sure why, but the idea of my father with Alex made me nervous.

I put on a pink knee length skirt with a pink cotton t-shirt. I figured that would cover me for whatever style of restaurant we went to. It took me a long time to find this pink skirt. I had many testers. If the skirt was too long it made me feel naive and simple. Not helped at all by the disability. If it was too short, with sitting down and no leg muscle control to keep my knees together, you could imagine; beaver shots galore. But this pink skirt, it was perfect, just a tad over the knees in length yet not too much.

In my calmer moments, I had decided that I was not going to confront my father or Alex about the new information I had been given by J.P. I wanted my father to tell me. Besides, I wasn't even sure if what J.P. had said was the truth. Not that I thought that he would lie intentionally, but there was a great possibility that he was mistaken in the information. It could have been someone else's car that looked like fathers, or it could have been the wrong vehicle all together. I never thought to ask him what type of car it was to make sure that it was dads. But it was too late now.

I grabbed the mirror out of the closet and put it up on my counter. The square mirror banged the wall at least a half dozen times before it was placed properly. It wasn't really convenient but it worked. We had to supply our own mirror in Residence. I kept mine hidden in the closet because I wanted it loose and unattached to the wall. Things didn't always have to be accessible for me. That was a lot to expect. For things to be accessible it meant that they were in their simplest form; where it took the least effort to use. Even though it was great in theory, in practice it meant always getting someone else to fix it for you or to move it so that it was more accessible. For example; someone to nail in the bars in the bathroom or someone to make new cabinets lower down, or in this case, someone to screw the mirror to the wall so I could always have it to look at.

Not to say that people who love you won't do this for you, but why should they? And why should I, just because I was disabled, not have to work for anything in my life. Why couldn't I pull my mirror out of the closet where it was reachable, every time I wanted to put my make up on? If everything was easy, where did the challenges come in? People think that because I had a hard time at one point, when first getting into the chair, that now I needed things made easy. I didn't. Independence did not mean easy, it meant to learn to do it by one's self. If things were too easy in one place, it made it hard to function in another. If I didn't know how to adapt to situations to make them functional, then when could I survive in a new room, a new vehicle, a new bathroom, or a new situation, I wouldn't know how to help myself, and if I couldn't help myself, then I was no where near independent. Problem solving was no longer a necessary skill.

I know there are some things that are obviously needed. Things that are not negotiable when it comes to accessibility but come on, some things just didn't need to be fixed. Nothing was going to change when it came to me being disabled. But I could control how handicapped I was. Maybe in the end I would find out that my philosophy was wrong, but until then it worked quite well for me.

"Where do you want to go to eat?" Father asked after putting my chair in the back seat of his four-door Sedan.

"I am in the mood for Greek food. Are you up for that?" I asked.

"Yes. What about the Apollo? Mind a little ride to Sudbury?"

"Not with you I don't. I love spending time with you." I did. I was a daddy's girl through and through. A confession I would only make to him though.

Almost an hour and a half later we were at the restaurant and I was ordering chicken souvlaki and my father, a rack of lamb. For appetizers we ordered my favourite, saganaki. A fried cheese they serve on a platter. The treat was in the presentation. They poured Ouzo on it, Greek liquor, and lit it on fire right at your table. They extinguished the flames with a fresh squeeze of lemon and a cheerful cry of 'Opa!' It was hot, salty, and crunchy when you got it. Yummy!

"So I hear there is quite a mess again with Jack?" Dad asked, as he waved a hello over to Toula, the restaurant's owner and operator. She waved back with a smile.

"Yes. I guess you know about what he did and how he is trying to get out of it?"

"I do know. And about the possible pay off, if that is what you mean by trying to get out of it? I know I am not supposed to know, but Alex needed someone to speak to about it."

"So you were there to listen when she needed to talk?" I interrupted.

He nodded.

We talked for a while about Jack and the situation. Father didn't tell me anything I didn't know, so I guessed that Alex hadn't heard anything new. I did already hear that Julie was denying any payoff. She claimed her Grandmother gave her the money as part of an early inheritance. Once that subject was talked out, and our main course had come, I decided to address the Alex issue briefly to see if he would open up to me. I was never one for patience.

"So, Alex needed someone to listen to all this crap, eh? Did you spend a lot time with her this weekend?"

"Well she wanted to run it by someone who was on the outside."

"Well you are not exactly on the outside." His obvious avoidance of my second question was not lost on me. Nor was it going to stop me from asking it again in a moment.

"No, I guess not. But I am not living in residence. I am not affected by him living there. And I really don't know a whole lot about the guy."

"How does it not affect you Dad? He lives on my floor, affecting me. That concerns you a great deal. On top of that, I talk about how much of a jerk he is all the time. You are not exactly without knowledge of how much he annoys me."

"Wow, first that is one of my points - you can't stand the guy. And you are among many. I currently stand indifferent on that subject. Second, you're getting a little defensive about this. What's eating you Sadie?"

"This, this is eating me Dad." I grabbed my napkin from my lap and wiped my mouth. I was spitting rice as I spoke. I tried to bring my voice down. "Why are you getting involved?"

"Involved? I didn't know that bothered you. You have talked to me before about residence stuff and didn't care that I was involved. Why does Jack get to you this much?"

"He doesn't get to me. You get to me."

He looked confused, as he should be. I wasn't quite sure what I was getting at myself. I was angry at him.

"I get to you? Sadie, what is going on? This isn't like you. What are you mad at me about?" With his teeth he pulled some meat from the miniature lamb bones, using his fork to scrape off the remainders.

"Did you spend the weekend with Alex?" I went straight to my point.

He paused. Then he put his fork down on the table and wiped his face before returning his napkin to his lap. He looked up. "Yes."

I heard it. I expected it. Yet I was not prepared. "Yes? The whole weekend?"

"Yes, the whole weekend."

"Did you have sex with her?" He just looked at me. His stare had one eyebrow up and one down. His mouth stayed straight.

"I don't feel I need to answer that."

"Okay, then answer this, where did you sleep?"

"Sadie, you are out of line here. This is not your business." He folded his hands in front of his face. "I don't get you. First you are angry with me for not dating Elizabeth, and now you are angry with me for dating Alex. I am confused."

"What is there to be confused about? I liked Elizabeth, you would have been good together."

"And you don't like Alex? I find that hard to believe. I can barely separate the two of you."

"I do like her Dad, a lot. But I don't want you to get hurt." I started to feel bad. My anger was slowly turning into sorrow. I could feel a change of tide inside me.

"Why would she hurt me Sadie?"

"I don't know. Really I don't. I just feel it in my gut."

"Do you think you would feel this way no matter who I got serious with?"

"I haven't yet."

"Then why Alex?" His elbows left the table bringing his hands with them - away from his chin.

I had thought about that many times over the last few hours. I wasn't sure what it was. I just worried about him in this relationship.

"I don't know." I said through clenched teeth.

"Well, when you think of something, let me know. Until then…" He shrugged and ended his sentence. He picked up his fork and started eating again. He ate with a hurried hand and a heavy bite. I had hurt his feelings. I knew it. I wanted to apologise but if he asked for what part I wouldn't be able to give him a detailed answer. I was only sorry that it hurt him. I truly felt the way I said I did and I really was angry. I couldn't lie to him. And I couldn't take it all back. I did the only thing I could. I excused myself to the little girls' room so I could return and change the subject. I guess I owed him at least that. I owed it to myself as well. I was good at changing the subject, and my father was great at appeasing me.

* * * * * * * * * * *

I couldn't sleep. It had been days since I had a good nights rest. Now 9 at night, on a Friday, I was lying in bed hoping to finally get some zees. I was completely and utterly exhausted. Emotionally drained was how I would explain it. Father and I had three days of idle small talk. Both of us trying to keep in touch, to let each other know that we were okay with what had happened over dinner. We talked about the weather, the strike, and politics - things you would talk about with a stranger in an elevator. Not with your parent or child. I had nothing else to say. I was not feeling better by any standards, and from what I could tell, neither was he.

I hadn't talked to Alex at all. I wasn't sure what to say. I had many speeches rehearsed in my head though. I had the – 'I can't believe you slept with my father and didn't tell me' - speech. I also had one that went – 'you already had him once and he left you for my mother, so what makes you think he's changed or really wants you now' - talk. And lastly I had the – 'please don't date my dad. It can't end well for anyone.' I wasn't sure which speech would get my point across more clearly. They all had great dialogue in their moments of development yet seemed to become less effective once the sunlight came screaming through the curtains each morning. She had called a few times. None of which I returned yet. She was sure to let me know that she wanted to talk about personal matters not work related stuff, so I felt comfortable not returning any of the messages.

I rolled onto my side to try to get more comfortable. I also turned on the television to try to stop thinking. That had been my problem, I couldn't stop the thinking. And of course, the more I thought about not thinking, the more it made me think. It was the purple elephant syndrome. Tell someone not to think about the purple elephant in the room and that was all they would focus on.

Rrrinnnggg, Rrrinnngg. My eyes finally focused on my clock, it read 1:15 a.m.

"One fucking fifteen. Unbelievable." I said to no one. I recalled it was around 11 when I finally felt sleep setting in. I remembered seeing the first few opening scenes of a sitcom I had turned on but that was it. The butler had not yet had a chance to solve all of the children's problems. That was only two hours ago. A longer sleep than most nights these days I suppose, but I was kind of hoping for more.

Rrrinnnggg. It seemed louder than it ever had.

"Hello." I said in a sleepy voice.

"Hey Sadie, this is Mike from front desk."

"What's up Mike? You can't be calling me just to talk."

"As lovely as your voice is, no, I didn't just call to talk."

"I am not on call you know."

There was a knock on my door as I spoke. "Who is it?"

I heard Ashlyn's voice announce herself as the person behind the rap on the door. If she was also at my door, I knew there must be trouble.

"Yes, I know. Julianne and Brody are on call tonight. But they are dealing with a medical emergency right now on Wanda's floor. So when I paged them about the noise complaint coming from Jack's room, apparently there are a lot of people there, they asked me to page you and Ashlyn to go see and take care of it. I already paged her and now I am calling you. Your pager isn't working."

"I know. I turned it off in hopes for sleep tonight."

"Sorry."

"Not your fault that he decided to throw a party." I said sitting up, he was about to hang up when my mind finally caught up with me. "Wait a minute. What is Jack doing in residence? He is not supposed to be here."

"I guess you haven't heard. Jack was allowed back as of this afternoon. He moved most of his bags back around dinner time."

I had spent the afternoon and evening in my room. I even decided to make my own early dinner in the microwave. You can get pretty crafty with noodles and melted soft cheese when you really want to.

"Really, he is back and it is legal."

"Afraid so."

"Damn it." I rubbed the sleep from my eyes and accidentally poked myself in the left one in the process. *Ouch!* Yup! I was awake. Not a dream.

I heard Ashlyn ask if I was going to let her in. I had briefly forgotten about her. I shouted for her to give me a minute. I finished talking to Mike and then hung up the phone. It took me another minute or two to get in my wheelchair and get to the door.

"Come on in." I said to her. "I have to get a sweater on before we go to his room."

"Are you going to change out of your pyjamas?"

"Nope. Odd question from you though, considering you are still in yours."

"Yah, well, whatev's" she shrugged and smiled. "It is pretty loud out there. Once we turn the corner you will hear it. I didn't miss this while he was gone I tell you."

"I can't believe they let him back in here. It's a joke."

"Yah, well that is Greenbury College for you. Home of the blood rules. If you're blood related, you rule whatever you want. Let's go bust his party." She walked over to the door and held it open.

"Can't wait."

There were 4 guys and 1 girl inside Jack's room, and 3 girls and 2 guys hanging out in the hall. Jack was one of the students in his room. I wasn't quite sure I remembered all of their names. Two of the girls in the hall I was quite certain were not even living in residence here. Students are allowed to sign in up to 3 guests on the weekend, only one to sleep over, but 3 allowed in until 2 am. One hour after quiet hours end.

"A little loud there Jack." Ashlyn spoke first.

"Ah, the residence police. I was wondering when you were going to come crash my party. As for the noise, well, that is all relative isn't it Ash?" He spoke in his usual arrogant tone.

"There was a noise complaint Jack. Of course we are here. We are not your aunt we actually expect you to follow the rules," I answered for Ashlyn.

He lifted an eyebrow up and walked out of the depth of the room and to the door where we were. "I know what you are getting at, and I don't like it. Besides, privacy remember? I think you should keep your mouth shut, Sadie."

"I don't care what you think Jack." Some of the students in the hall had left to Pete's room. He was one of the guys standing outside, in fact, one of the only recognizable ones to me.

"You should my dear. I have…"

"The point is that it is past quiet hours and the music has to go off. The door needs to be shut, and the people need to be quiet. If that is not done then we will get security to come and assist you with these tasks." Ashlyn interrupted him.

"You want to be with me don't you?" He reached out to touch the cheek of Ashlyn's face.

"Please don't touch me." Ashlyn said with assertiveness. He moved his hand to the door way instead.

"Ahh, well, when you are ready to admit it, just let me know. As for the noise, I will turn the music down. This cd is over played anyway. And besides, I was about to close the door so my lady friend and my guy friends can have some privacy in here." He winked as he finished talking. He was such a prick. I knew he was trying hard to get me going, and it was working. I was pissed off. I couldn't believe he was making a mockery out of Julie's accusations towards him. True or not, he didn't need to make it sound like it was happening again. Arrghh! I could hit him, really. I wished this was the wild. We could settle this with some old fashioned brutality.

"Good. Have fun." Ashlyn said for both of us. He was right. I could not bring up the other stuff that happened with Julie. If I spoke anymore, I would say more than I should.

We were half way to Ashlyn's room when we heard a small voice calling out to us. "Do you have any Ibutylenol?"

We could hear the guys tease her because she got the name wrong. I was giggling myself until Ashlyn reminded me that Ibutylenol was our safe word on the floor for the girls. The safe word was to be used when you were in a bit of trouble, or wanted out of a situation and weren't able to safely or bravely remove yourself from the room, and it involved the opposite sex. The guys had a word, and so did the girls. It was unfortunate that we didn't have a system that would allow a student to inform us when they were in danger from someone of the same sex as well. Maybe that would come soon although I couldn't imagine how it would work. We turned to see the girl who was previously in the room, come out and walk towards us.

"Yes, there is some in my room. Come on." Ashlyn said.

As the girl approached I could see it was Bridgette. I didn't recognize her. Her hair was short and dyed black. She also had a ton of make-up on.

"Wow, Bridgette. You look great. I didn't recognize you."

"Thanks. I needed some change."

She walked with us. Jack yelled at her from the room to hurry back. She turned and waved at him. "Give me a minute will you?"

Once we got to Ashlyn's room, Bridgette informed us that she needed out of that room. The guys were getting too touchy feely and she was not liking it. Jack didn't bother her but she was uncomfortable with the other guys. They were making her feel awkward. When I asked if Jack was stopping them, or if she told him about how they were making her feel, she just responded with saying that she would be nuts to tell him that. We told her that she could stay with us for a while until the party was over and people had left. I wondered who had let Jack back into residence. Who had the final say? Was it Cathy DeGraff, his aunt and the Dean of Student Services? Was it a group decision? A unanimous decision? I also wondered where Alex stood on the whole issue and why she did not inform me of his return. I was sure I was not going to get anymore sleep that night. I stayed pretty confident in that as Ashlyn led us down stairs to the R.A. lounge. Sleep and I will never be one. It was sad, really. Although in contrast, the funny thing was, I didn't realize at that time just how sad it would end up being.

-25-

SORRY, CAN'T TALK. MY MOUTH IS FULL OF FOOT.

The lounge door was slightly held open when we arrived. All we saw was a hand on the outside. The body was still inside the lounge. It was Brody talking to Julianne before he joined some students in the hall. We passed in the middle of his agenda, ducking under his arm to get into the room. I, being the only one that didn't have to literally duck of course, entered smoothly.

Julianne was sitting in the corner filling out incident reports. She was a short girl with hair almost as long as she was. It went down to her knees. Most days she kept her hair in a braid. Tonight it was in a ponytail, with pink elastics wrapped around both ends. Her hair was a soft brown, which for me, was what kept her from looking like a teenage witch. She had the bumpy nose, the cackled laugh, and at home, the black cat.

"Hey guys, sorry about getting you to go to the noise complaint, had something to deal with that was a big priority."

"That is what Mike said. What happened?"

She was about to answer us when she noticed Bridgette sitting on the bean bag chair in the corner of the room. Once her eyes went towards Bridgette, Ashlyn and I remembered that we couldn't talk because of confidentiality issues, and decided to drop the subject. Bridgette must have realized this too because she kindly stood up and excused herself to the washroom. Once the door closed behind her Julianne answered our question.

"Calista, Wanda's cutter, well I guess she has had a rough week. She decided that she was going to cut herself as relief or whatever it is, I am not that well versed on the whole thing. Anyway, she cut herself in the shower and some girls, who were also in the bathroom showering, saw the blood on the floor in the water and asked her if she was okay. Calista apparently answered by saying leave me alone. That made her floor mates nervous and they called us immediately once they knocked on Wanda's door and had no answer."

"Oh my goodness, is she alright?"

"Oh yah, she made a few cuts on her upper forearms."

"Forearms?" I replied back, my emphasis was on the pluralizing of the word.

"Yes. Both arms. The blood mixed with the water I think, made the blood look like it was more than it actually was. Not that that makes it any better. It isn't her fault. Well it is I guess. Ah! I told you, I know nothing about this."

"It is a complicated, dangerous thing. She is lucky that those girls made a comment to her. Maybe that stopped her from cutting more than what she did of her arms. So what happened when you guys got there?"

Julianne got up from the corner desk and came over to the couch. She sat down by Ashlyn. I stayed in my chair and faced them both.

"She was out of the shower and in her room. We tried several times to get her to let us in and she wouldn't. That is when the page came in to go to the noise complaint on your floor. Brody went to get Wanda who he knew was at the pub at school. She went to watch the men's basketball team play London. They won by the way." She grabbed the lotion that was on the counter behind the couch. After pumping three squirts of lotion into her hand, she began to spread it up her arms. The smell of cucumber melon wafted through the room.

"Anyway, Calista finally let me in when I threatened to call security to open the door. I knew I could have gone to get my key but I didn't want to leave the door unwatched while I was gone. In case she left the room. When I got in, her arms were still bleeding slightly, but nothing much. The cuts were not that deep and they weren't near her wrists, but there were a lot of them. It was crazy."

"Bad choice of words," I interrupted.

"Sorry." It took her a second to get herself back on the subject. "Well, I got her to let me bandage them up, and that is when Brody and Wanda returned. Wanda talked to her for a while and Alex showed up. Brody and I left to come down and write this up."

"So what is going to happen now?"

There was a knock on the door. I could tell through the frosted glass that it was Bridgette on the other side. Her petite frame was highly recognizable. I went towards the door but hesitated before opening it, allowing Julianne to finish her idea and answer my question.

"Not sure. Wanda and Alex are still upstairs talking with Calista. They are waiting for Elizabeth to come. I guess she has to go into

194

therapy for a while or something to stay in residence. On her last warning maybe. Don't hold me to that. It isn't fact, more like a guess."

"Well, I guess we will find out soon enough." I opened the door for Bridgette to come in. She was holding a Pepsi, a chocolate bar and a bag of potato chips.

"I was hungry, is this okay?"

"No actually, no food allowed in here."

"Really, shit! I will eat it out here first then." She turned and sat on the ground.

"Get up Bridgette," I laughed. "I was joking. You can come in and eat that, we just ask that you sit at a table and not on the furniture. Manager's rules not mine, sorry."

As she walked in carrying her goodies I saw something sparkle from her wrist. She noticed me looking so she lifted her sleeve and showed me.

"You like?" It was a shinning diamond tennis bracelet.

"I do. Wow, it is beautiful. Is it new?"

"Yes." Her voice changed to a whisper. "Jack gave it to me. As a 'just because' gift. He won't admit that if you asked him of course, it would ruin his bad boy rap, but he did."

Probably a 'sorry I almost killed you, but thanks for forgiving me' gift, I thought. But I kept that to myself.

"It's very nice. You are a lucky girl." She agreed.

I considered filling out an incident report for the noise complaint call to Jack's room. I decided against it for two reasons, the first was that I was feeling lazy thanks to the lack of sleep. The second was because I knew that a noise complaint, by any other standards, was not a valid reason to fill out a form. Not for a one time call that ultimately resulted in the noise being turned down. I guess Alex was right. I wanted to constantly go after Jack for whatever I could. It was instinct, a gut reaction. Kind of like the wild I assume. He was my prey, and I, sat in wait, ready to pounce whenever I found an opportunity. I just wished, like the wild, I could rip his head off using nothing but my teeth.

The girls and I decided to put a Sex and the City DVD from season 2 on to watch. A late night television marathon was very much a College thing for me. I never watched DVD's with episodes of the same television show on it, one after another, until I came to Greenbury. Television on DVD, I was a fan of. What a great way to catch up on a season that you didn't get to watch or a show that you always wanted to see, and only got the out of order reruns. For tonight, it was a great way to pass the time with a student we hadn't planned on spending the evening with. Jack's girlfriend was not exactly my first choice as a hang out buddy, especially when all I wanted to do was sleep, not converse, but I could make do.

"What's going on ladies?" Brody came in the room, turning on the light as he entered. We winced at the light. Our eyes not use to the brightness. Hal, Piety, and Lonny walked in behind him.

"Ready for our last round Julianne?"

"Our last round? It is 3 in the morning. Our rounds are over Brod."

"Alex asked that we do one more round tonight if we were up." Julianne got up and grabbed her vest. Hal and Piety plopped down on the couch. Lonny sat on the arm of the sofa. "Long night?" Hal asked.

"Yes, you can say that." I answered. I looked over to Bridgette who was curled up on the bean bag chair. "What do you say we head upstairs and go to bed soon? I will walk you up there." I said. Bridgette stretched and nodded in response.

"Can we talk first?" Lonny asked me.

I wanted to say no. I didn't because Bridgette was there.

"I have a minute, and then I want to go to bed." We went into the hall. Bridgette stayed in the lounge.

"What do you want?" He looked great in his ripped jeans, white tight t-shirt, and unbuttoned blue collared shirt. His hair was a mess, a beautiful hot mess.

"I was out with Hal and Piety tonight. I told Piety that Jessica and I broke up a while ago, and Piety said that you didn't mention anything about it to her. That she was sure you would have told her. But you didn't, which only leads me to think that you are considering forgiving me?"

"I haven't had a chance to tell her. I have only known a week or so. And why would that make me want to forgive you? If you had broken up with her when you said you were going to months ago, then there would be nothing to forgive. But you didn't, you screwed me over instead, so no, I haven't and won't be forgiving you. But thanks for asking. Anything else?"

"Yes there is something else." He said in a whispered shout. "What do mean you have only known a week? I called you right after it happened. I left you a message."

"No."

No he didn't, did he? He left a message?

"Yes I did." He replied.

I pondered for a moment before I remembered the message, shit! He did call and leave a message. I erased it after only a few sentences. I couldn't believe it. I could have known several days earlier.

"Did you get it?" He asked when I didn't respond.

"No, well yes, but I erased it. I heard your voice and I erased the message. I didn't want to hear it."

"Damn it Sadie. Do you hate me that much?"

"Yes, actually, right now I do. You hurt my feelings Lonny. You hurt me. I don't want to talk to you, hear your voice, or see you for that matter."

"Thanks for the respect."

"Thanks for the respect? Seriously? Where do I even..." I was interrupted when Jack came bursting through the door of the connecting hall.

"Where's Bridgette?"

"Excuse me Jack; I am talking with someone right now." I barked back at him.

"I see that. Where is Bridgette?"

"I am talking."

"Just answer and I will leave you alone."

"Fine! She wasn't feeling good. She went to bed."

"Can you be more specific? How long ago?"

I spoke slowly and sternly in attempts to make my point at how insensitively demanding he was being. "We gave her some medicine and then we started talking to her about school. After some time, oh lets see, 20 minutes. Bridgette said the medicine was working and she was going to head to bed. It was making her sleepy. She stood up, scratched her head, and left," I lied. "Is that specific enough or should I have added our physical movements in there as well?"

He took a step towards me and so did Lonny. Lonny's step was more in between us then towards me. "Easy there pal." Lonny said to him.

Jack looked at him and then backed up. He winked and blew me a kiss. "That's alright doll. That was specific enough for me. Have you seen my brother tonight?"

"No."

"What an ass," said Lonny as Jack walked back towards the dorm rooms.

"Speaking of asses, I can't believe you just asked me to give you some respect. Do you really think I owe you any respect? You have to give it to get it Lonny, and you sure haven't done that. I love you, and you continually treat me like I am nothing of any importance to you."

"I'm sorry I made you feel that way."

I sucked in my bottom lip and looked towards the floor. "Me too Lonny." I pushed away and grabbed the lounge door handle. Just as I was about to turn the knob and open the door, Lonny grabbed my shoulder. I twisted my top half to face him.

"At least I have one thing going for me."

"Yah, what's that?"

"You just admitted that you still love me."

* * * * * * * * * * *

Bridgette and I left the Residence lounge a little while later. Before that, I had gone back in and talked with Piety and Hal for a while. They told me about their romantic dinner. Then talked about the movie that they went to and how they stayed in the bathrooms between showings and then snuck into a second movie; a small reliving of their childhood. They laughed like twelve year olds as they re-enacted the evening's crime. They told me that Lonny had joined up with them after dinner.

"Thanks for letting me borrow the Sex and the City DVD." Bridgette said on our way to her room.

"No problem. I have watched them all anyways."

Despite not wanting to, I actually did enjoy the part of my evening that was spent with Bridgette. She wasn't that bad when she was not around Jack or his buddies. I knew that Jefferson felt bad for her for dating his brother. He told me as much. Jefferson had a lot of love for Jack but did not agree with many of the things Jack said and did. In a small way I admired Jefferson for that. He was the good side of the twins. I could see why he thought Bridgette was not as bad as she presented herself to be. While we were waiting for the elevator, I told her about Jack's visit to the lounge. She seemed relieved to have missed him.

The elevator binged and we stepped off, immediately turning to the left hall and towards her room. I decided to walk her to her door.

"I never realized until tonight what exactly you guys sacrifice to be assistants. I always thought of you guys as brown noses, no offence," said Bridgette. I smiled. "I didn't really think that you guys give up so much sleep and time to do your job. It seems fun on the outside but I guess there is a lot more to it than that?"

I smiled. I appreciated her effort. "Yes, there is a lot more. It is still a lot of fun though."

"When do you guys take applications for next year?"

"We usually put out applications around the start of April. Are you thinking of applying?" I wasn't sure how I felt about Bridgette being part of the next generation of leaders in Greenbury College residence, but who was I to judge?

She nodded that she was interested.

"Thought you were in bed Bridgette? Or was that just a lie to get me to leave, Sadie?"

I turned to see Jack standing in the middle of the hall with nothing but a towel on; he was wet from what I assumed was a shower. Bridgette looked at me for guidance. I fumbled into it.

"She was, Jack. She is just coming from the bathroom."

"I just came from the bathroom," he pointed to the towel. I'm an idiot.

"There are three bathrooms on this floor Jack." That was better.

"So, you went to bed then got up and got dressed, just so you can go pee? I'm sure. How come you didn't answer your phone earlier?"

"I was sleeping!"

"And the door didn't wake you?"

"Guess not." She was snappy at first in her answer and then changed her tone. She walked over towards him, using a finger to make circles around his belly button. In a now playful voice she said, "I'm sorry baby, I was really tired, and the medicine they gave me was really strong. It knocked me out."

He looked down at her. He stayed quiet a moment, and then he looked at me. "You give her strong meds on purpose? Trying to keep her away from me?"

"What? Seriously?"

"I wouldn't put it past you. Trying to mess with me. Pit people against me."

"That's not what I meant Jack," Bridgette exclaimed. Playful voice gone.

"Shut up Bridge, you don't know what we are talking about. Keep to what you know. She wants me out of here, and is just using you to get it to happen. She probably kept you with her talking until the medicine kicked in. What did you give her?"

"I gave her a Tylenol, Jack." My voice was starting to rise. Bridgette looked at me worriedly. I wasn't about to rat her out. I was slightly entertained at what was going on in Jack's head.

"Sure, Tylenol. Whatever. I don't believe you. You are trying to drug her so she will do what you want. Is that it?"

"That's your trick."

"And here you are drugging students to manipulate them into staying away from me because you think I'm dangerous."

"You are not making sense Jack." I was beginning to lose the entertainment portion of this conversation.

"You know exactly what I am talking about. I am right, aren't I?"

"Jackie, I was not feeling good. I went to bed. That's all." Bridgette added in a whine.

"What did I say about speaking?" He pushed her to the side. "This is between my R.A. and me."

"Don't push her Jack. I will call security on you if I have to."

"Did I push you?" He pointed to Bridgette.

"No," she answered.

"You are just dying to find ways to get me out of here, aren't you? Just like that last cock and bull story you came up with."

"I didn't have to make up a thing Jack. Are we done here? I would like to get some sleep tonight." I turned to go back to my room. I didn't like the twist this conversation had taken. I learned a long time ago in residence that when being confronted by a guy that was adamant or drunk, it was best to let them sleep on it and revisit the subject in the morning.

"I am not done. I am tired of you trying to get rid of me. I am tired of your bullshit Sadie. Enough is enough."

"Would you mind keeping your voice down then so we don't wake everyone up?"

"I will speak as loud as I fucking want to bitch!"

"I won't speak to you anymore Jack if you keep swearing. I don't have to listen to that. And there is nothing your Aunt can do to make me." I had to stop antagonizing him, I knew, but I couldn't stop my lips from moving.

"Of course not. You are protected by the laws of residence right. How is that different than how my aunt protects me? She keeps it legal."

I laughed. "Hardly."

"Go to bed Bridgette." He barked. She looked at him, then at me apologetically. She kissed him on the cheek and then left.

"Goodnight," she said to Jack. "Thanks," she whispered to me. I nodded. "Goodnight," I replied.

"You jealous?"

"Jealous, of your aunt? No, I have an aunt of my own thanks."

"Not her. Are you jealous of Bridgette?"

"And why would I be jealous of her?"

"Then you are jealous of Julie." He smiled and sent two mocking kisses in my direction.

"Ah, I get what you are getting at." I shook my head. I couldn't believe what he was saying. "You're a creep Jack. You take advantage of women and you think that you are a stud for it. These women only come near you to use you. To get something from you."

"Are you calling them stupid? Maybe we should tell them how you feel. Shall I call Bridgette back?"

The way he twisted things around pissed me off. He was great at getting under my skin.

"You are twisting my words."

"No, you said it. You called these girls stupid."

"Not a chance Jack. I think you are a shallow, cheap thrill for these girls. They know that you are good for a night and not much else. They don't expect anything from you. Which is good because they don't get anything, just maybe a new shiny bracelet like Bridgette did but that's it?"

"You don't even know me. She got that bracelet from her father."

"I know your type."

"Do you now. And what type is that?"

The elevator rang and from around the corner came Hal and Piety. Piety was red in the face.

"Go to bed Jack, it's late. There have been several noise complaints from you guys. Time to put it to rest." She looked at me and quietly said "Alex is on her way."

"I am not done talking to Miss Sadie."

"Well, I am done talking to you Jack." The last thing I wanted was to see Alex, not when I was this pissed off.

"Go to bed guy." Hall added.

"Well aren't you high and mighty. You are just jealous Sadie, we both know it. You want a ride on the Jack-man don't you?" With this he re-adjusted his towel giving us a flash of his full frontal.

Hal stepped towards him. "Go to bed guy."

The elevator went again. Alex stepped around the corner.

"What's going on here guys? Sadie?"

"Your R.A. here is trying to get me into bed." He winked at me.

"Not even if I had a gun to my head Jack."

"Sadie, enough!" Alex walked over and placed her self into the 4 or 5 feet of space between Jack and me.

This time Hal put his arm up around Jack's chest. "Let's go to the room. I don't want to have to call security."

Jack started walking backwards. "Everyone keeps threatening security, yet no one calls. I just see the get-along-gang here." He smiled. "Later babe," was his last words to me.

"Have some respect for the boss at least, Jack." Hal demanded.

"Sorry Alex." He complied with Hal. She nodded in response. He left to his room.

"What was that all about and what were you thinking getting into it with him?" Alex bent down so her face was within inches of mine.

"He got me going." I was frustrated.

"Let's go to your room."

Hal and Piety followed behind us. My room had clothes on the floor, pop cans on the window ledges, and dishes on the counter. It wasn't really ideal for company.

"Now how did you get into that with Jack?"

I explained to her the whole night from the noise complaint, which seemed like hours ago now, to the interruption while I was talking to Lonny, and ended with our confrontation in the hall. She was not impressed with any of it.

"Did you not see it escalating to the point it did?" She was tired I could tell. She was in regular clothes, but I was sure she just got out of bed to go to Wanda's and now my complaint.

"No, I didn't. How did you find out about it?"

I was told that there was a noise complaint that went to the front desk, Mike had paged Alex but did not get through. It was after 3 in the morning so he assumed that she was sleeping, forgetting or not knowing she was up stairs with Wanda. He heard Piety and Hal leaving the R.A. lounge and asked them to come up. While they were at the desk getting the information on what happened, Alex returned the page and called Mike. Piety, and Hal, I guessed came running up to stop whatever they thought was going on, before Alex came up and got upset. It was a grand effort, but unfortunately not in time.

"You brought up Julie didn't you?"

"He did."

"What did he say?"

"He just said that I was jealous of her. He also said something about me making up the story of her and what happened. No great detail."

"That's it? No great detail?"

"No."

"I hope so. Are you okay?"

"Yes."

She sat down on the bed. "I can't believe this."

"Well believe it. He's an asshole." I laughed. So did Piety.

"Enough Sadie." She yelled this time. "I am tired of you versus Jack. I know he is a bad guy but you don't know what you are up against. Did this last situation with Julie not teach you anything? You can't fight him, them." She seemed exasperated.

"You don't have to yell."

"I think I do. You are not getting it. Get it through your head. Leave him alone." The last 3 words she said slow and concise.

Now she was on his side.

"So you're sticking up for Jack now? Is that why you didn't tell me he was coming back to rez?"

"I didn't tell you because I wasn't told. Somehow Cathy got everything turned over and he was allowed back into residence without the committee voting. He walked in and handed me a note. I did call you but as you can probably guess, you didn't answer, as you haven't for the past few days."

I have been hearing this quite a lot lately. I really must consider answering my phone at least in the afternoon.

"You really need to start avoiding him. Maybe I should move you to another floor." She seemed to be talking thoughts out loud.

"You can't move me floors. Not now. It is the middle of February. School is done in three months."

"That is a long time in Jack and Sadie land."

"You got to be kidding me. He is a jerk and I get punished for it. Nice."

"It isn't punishment, it is protection."

"Nice protection."

"You don't really have to move her do you? What about the other students?" Piety asked.

"Piety, this is not your business. You are not staff. You shouldn't even be hearing most of this dear."

Piety took a step back. "Maybe we should leave?"

"I am going to leave too. We will talk about the transfer tomorrow.

I'll expect you for noon. It really is for your protection Sadie."

"Sure it is, and you were really just *sleeping* with my father, right. I know he told you that I know. That's why you have been calling me like crazy. You want me to approve. You finally landed my dad; it only took my mother dying for it to happen."

"Sadie!" Piety said with disbelief.

"What? It's true."

Alex just put her head down and rubbed her forehead with her hand. After a few moments she looked up at me with a tear in her eye. Shook her head, and left the room without saying a word.

"What was that all about? Is she really sleeping with your dad?"

"Yup. She is."

"Even still, that was a little harsh wasn't it?" Hal added onto Piety's comment.

"Yup. That it was. But that is how I feel."

They said goodnight and left. It was after 4 in the morning and I was nowhere near being able to sleep. Although at this point a lack of sleep was the least of my worries. I managed to alienate my father, my boss and my friend, piss off my most challenging resident, and possibly give Lonny a signal that I really could have done without him knowing. Nope, with all that, sleep was not the priority; however, I knew, if I didn't get some soon, I could definitely add loss of sanity from sleep deprivation to my list.

But I was so pissed off! Protection my ass! Everyone wanted to protect me, but I didn't want them to. I didn't need them too. What I needed was my mother but she was dead. She should be here to fix this. She always said she needed me. Me! But I needed her and I need her now. I fucking needed her…argh! I grabbed the glass next to me and threw it across the room. It hit the wall with great force and shattered into a million pieces. "Damn you mother," I yelled hoping that somewhere, wherever she was, she would hear my anger and realize what she had done by leaving me. "Fuck you! And fuck me for causing it. I am my own worst enemy aren't I Mom?" I cried. "Aren't I?" I punched my fist into my bed. It didn't help. I took a big breath in. I needed to calm down. I had to calm down.

I decided to make myself a little night cap. Hopefully it would relax me to sleep. I was out of other ideas. All I knew for sure was that this was one day I didn't want to have again.

-26-

DADDY'S LITTLE GIRL, AIN'T SHE SWEET?

I awoke at ten. I could not sleep any longer. I did get some shut eye, not nearly enough, but what I did get seemed to have taken the edge off of me. The three quick glasses of half orange juice and half Peach Snapps worked the way I hoped that it would. I would have preferred something with a pound less of sugar but the Snapps was all I had in the cupboard. Who was I to be choosey? I needed sleep any way I could get it.

It was now 11:30 and I was still debating if I was going to show up to my meeting with Alex at noon. She told me to be at her office so we could discuss the transfer. I wasn't sure if our meeting was still on considering what I said to her before she left. Did she really want to see me today? I, myself, wasn't sure what I would say to her. I could not see a happy ending to this meeting. I had gone over and over in my mind, the events of last evening. How could I have lost my grip so quickly and so harshly? What bugged me the most was not what I said, but why I said it. I said it to hurt her, because I didn't like what I was being told. I tried to defend my position and my feelings, and in turn I hurt someone I cared about. It was becoming a running theme with me. There was a moment not too long ago that I had a lot of friends, a great job, a boyfriend or best friend at the very least, and a father who loved me very much, and now, now I had considerably less. I knew it was a brief moment, but I felt it. I could still recall it. With my eyes closed, it was there, everything I wanted. It truly amazed me how I could constantly mess up good things in my life. I must at all costs hurt those I love. More importantly, those I respect.

I liked the feeling when you first realized you respected someone. It was nice. It was how I knew that someone respected me as well. I don't believe you could respect someone properly, if they didn't have a mutual feeling for you back.

The point that I didn't like, was the respect turning into caring or loving. That was what scared me, because that meant there was something on the line other than your heart. Some people were worth it. They were worth putting yourself and your feelings out there. And others, well, others could only result in pain, either for you or for them. Why not skip the middle. Just get the hurt over quickly when you realized that you were starting to care for someone. That way you had control over the situation. You had power over your emotions. Was that why I was so mean to Alex? Was I afraid because she was getting too close to my father? Or was it because she was getting too close to me? Why couldn't I forgive Lonny? Was it really that bad that he needed more time to break up with Jessica? Was I self sabotaging my relationships? Or was I right in protecting myself? I wish life came with a manual. In trying to find answers, all I seemed to do was to find more questions. I couldn't handle a meeting right now. I didn't want to talk to Alex when I didn't know what to think of everything myself. I needed some time to hide out. I needed to be by the water to think. Water always helped me to make sense of my life, even now, when the creek and bush was still frozen.

Before that, I needed to drop off Alex's vial to her. She should have it back. I wanted mine in return but I could wait for that. I didn't want to have to see her, not now. I put it into a sealed envelope and decided I was going to leave it for her at the front desk. Hopefully she would do the same with my vial for me. I didn't want to be responsible for someone's secret, not anymore. I already caused her enough tears.

Bart Comet was working the front desk when I arrived. He was a short guy, around 5 foot 4. His skin was a dark brown. His head was shaved. He had a full head of hair at the start of the year, but for Halloween he went to the school pub as Mr. T. and shaved his hair down the two sides to give him a realistic Mohawk cut. He looked like a miniature version of the television character. Once the evening was over he decided to shave the rest of his head and left it that way ever since. I handed him the envelope.

"She is in her office if you want to give it to her yourself?"

"No, that isn't necessary. I have to run and she seemed to have someone in there with her. Can you just give it to her when you see her?"

"Sure."

I left the lobby and headed outside through the web of picketers. The cafeteria workers were on the task today. The support staff took turns on the weekends. Most strikers didn't picket on weekends but they figured since they were going to be kind about letting students cross the picket lines, they might as well make noise every day of the week in return. Even on Saturdays and Sundays.

"Hey kid, how are you? You look tired." It was Martin Ewell, the manager of Housekeeping.

"You could say that. What are you doing here? You aren't on strike are you?"

"No. I am management. We are not on strike. Just showing my support." I could not recall a time that I had seen him out of a suit and tie. Today was the exception. He was dressed in jeans and a v-neck sweater. The burgundy colour of his sweater went brilliantly with his long silver hair. Martin's frame was tall and thin, looking muscular but not overly done. He was one of those people who went to the gym to tone and not to build. His gait was light as if his limbs all flowed together when he walked; graceful. In that way, his body matched his personality. He was smooth, mellow, and kind, a true product of the 1960's.

"That's kind of you. I am sure that they appreciate it."

"I think so. I meant to be here when my housekeeping team was working, but I am enjoying myself. The cafeteria workers are a hoot."

"They are, and in good spirits considering the situation."

He agreed. We talked for a few more moments about the winter and the unusually warm weather. We shared our plans for when the cold thawed out. I was enjoying myself so much that I forgot about my trip to the creek in the arboretum. I also didn't see Alex walk out of the front door, my envelope in hand, standing behind me waiting for my conversation to end with Martin. It was he that brought her presence to my attention.

"Hey Alexandra, you looking for me?"

I turned around. She smiled a slight sad smile. My stomach dropped. "Actually no, Martin. Sadie is the one I wanted to see." She looked down at me. "Got a minute? We had an appointment."

"Um, I forgot. I was actually on my way for a walk in the arboretum. Can it wait?"

"No, I'll join you though. Let me go grab my coat. Hold this for a moment." She handed me the opened envelope and returned inside the building. I smiled at Martin.

"Are you able to get around the arboretum in the winter?" Martin asked filling in the time waiting for Alex.

"Yes. The paths are great, and the school keeps them quite clear. They have to, I hear. It is a city thing. Protected land, am I right?'

"I think so. I heard that as well, but we have full access because we use it as an educational arena for our horticultural students."

"Ready?" Alex bounced out with her spring jacket on. The warmer weather was allowing everyone to dress with fewer layers than before. I handed her the envelope. We said our good-byes to Martin, and headed out towards the nature path. There was no conversation until we got through to the creek. Alex sat down on the bench.

"That's not the spot I am stopping at. Up here."

"Oh, okay. I will follow." She stood up and walked behind me. I pushed myself about another 20 yards or so, to the point. The creek surrounded the arboretum, but, at this end, it gets fed fresh water from a small stream that trickles down into it. It was like a perfect corner to the arboretum.

"This is where I like to sit." I stopped once I was nicely placed at the point. I wheeled off the path and over some snow and brush. Alex kicked snow and branches away with her foot, took her coat off, and placed it on the ground. She sat on top of it.

"Talk to me Sadie, what's going on in that head of yours?"

"I don't know what you mean. I have nothing to say." I replied.

"Yes you do, you're just stalling." She looked up. "Start with something easy. Tell me why you like this particular spot on the creek." Not surprisingly, her tone was a little icy.

"I like this spot because it is a great metaphor for life and those who come to sit by the water."

"Interesting. How is that?"

"People come to the water to think; to figure out where they went wrong in a part of their life. They use solace to make sense of chaos. When people are trying to decipher what is good and what isn't, what is wrong and what is right, or what is to progress and what is to discontinue, they grow. They grow as adults, as people, as friends, as individuals. Even in confusion and frustration, they grow. We grow. This is where the stream grows."

"Grows into a creek. Something bigger and better." She said, still not seeming all that friendly.

"Well, something bigger at least. It depends on what part of the creek that something is, that determines if it is better or not. For a small fish the bigger water is definitely not a better thing but for the turtle it is."

"That is really thought out."

I smiled. "I have spent many hours here over the past 3 years."

"I never knew that."

"Not many people do. It is my space."

"Thanks for inviting me, or at least taking me along." She rubbed some snow off the tip of her running shoe. She didn't change into her boots for the walk. "So does that represent all the decisions you have made here as well? Some made you grow in good ways and others not so much?"

"You could say that. Some decisions didn't make me grow in a way that I am proud of. No matter what, there is always growth, but instead of smoothly going into a growth area sometimes I have collided with it."

"But that just means you have more growing to do right? We don't always learn the whole lesson or at least the right one on the first try. It just means you have taken the first step, enlightenment."

"I guess." I picked up a stone from the ground and tossed it into the water that was showing between the ice sheets that stemmed from the banks. "I'm sorry about yesterday."

"I know you are. You were upset with me."

"That didn't give me the right to hurt you."

"No it didn't. But it is done."

"You forgive me already? Your tone doesn't say that." I said.

"I care about you very much Sadie, and I know you feel the same. I forgive you. I am hurt but I forgive you. And I hope you forgive me."

I nodded.

"I know you are angry with me for wanting to be with Jason, your dad. But I don't get why? I have been going over and over it in my mind. Are you thinking I am going to hurt him? Do you think I am going to take him away from you? Do you think he is betraying your mother, because of our past together? Do you think I am not good enough? Can you help me out here?" She shivered a little as she said the last question. Her teeth chattered through the words.

I thought for a few moments on how to answer the question. I could tell her some story that she wanted to hear. Or I could tell her something that was easy for me to keep up. I knew though, that neither story was going to get me any further along in life. It was time I did some permanent growing and started facing the truth, with everything. I needed to stop fooling myself. I needed to be the stream and just collide with the creek or in this case, the truth. I could deal with the after mass later. I needed to go back to square one and tell her it all. Someone needed to know. She needed to know about my mother, about how I tried to make up for the pain I caused with my dad, and how she can't get involved with him, for her own good.

"Let's go back to the bench, you're freezing. It will be warmer for you if your butt is off the ground."

"I am okay for now."

"I know, but this may take a while. Can I have my vial?" I was shaking too.

She stood up to move towards the bench. She had a confused expression. I pushed over as well, taking myself out of the chair so I could sit on the bench with her. Alex held my chair still as I transferred.

"You really want to exchange them back don't you? I lost that much of your trust?"

"No, I want you to read it."

She looked at me awestruck. She placed her hands on her lap as she slowly sat down on the bench beside me. "Oh!" She hesitated. "Are you sure?"

I nodded. She took it off of her neck. "May I?"

I nodded again and she opened it up and read it.

The time between her opening the vial and her finishing reading the paper felt like an hour. I heard every sound there was to hear as we sat in the heart of the bushes. Birds were chirping, thawing tree branches were crackling, water was moving from the stream to the creek as it rushed by the ice that was still settled along the edges. I could even hear the wind rustle through the 60 or so strands of grass that poked through the snow in front of our bench. The one thing I didn't hear though was my breath. In fact, I wasn't sure I was even breathing. I wasn't sure I wanted to. I looked up at Alex to see if I could read what she was thinking. I couldn't. Her face seemed completely void of expression. I turned so that my back was to her. The bench had no backing so it allowed me to straddle it. My hands placed on the seat between my split legs to hold me up.

"Do you hate me now?" My voice came out in a whisper. Not sure I wanted to know if she was done. I turned my head in her direction, looking at her with only my peripheral vision.

She put the paper down on her lap. Her eyes still staring at the tiny letters inked on the sheet. She rolled it back up in her hands, straddled the bench as well and sat behind me. Hugging me tightly, she whispered back "not a chance."

We stayed there a few moments before anyone spoke. I couldn't stop myself from crying. "I killed my mother."

"I'm sorry but I don't know what to say just yet."

She squeezed tighter. I cried louder. I was scared. I was scared to talk her and I was scared of what she would say back. I also was afraid my father would find out, but I went this far, I needed to finish. I didn't know where to start. Luckily Alex did it for me.

"Turn around, talk to me. Tell me what happened that day."

I grabbed a tissue from my pocket. I wiped my face and turned around to face her.

"Do you have an extra for me?" Alex asked. I looked up. She had as many tears as I did. I handed her the bunch. I always kept a pocket sized package of tissue in my pocket, mostly to wipe snow or mud, depending on the season, off of my tires. It was small and easy to carry and in a pinch, it worked perfectly.

"Mother was a high profile lawyer. She defended a lot of murderers and mobsters. At least that is what I always heard. She was good at what she did, but wasn't well liked by the PTA and neighbourhood families." I moved my chair so it was facing the bench and placed my legs up on the seat. It was a great replacement foot stool. "She had been working on Armando Vitalli's court case. He apparently paid her a ton of money. He was a suspected mob boss that was up on many charges like extortion, running a prostitution ring, fraud, 3 counts of accessory to murder and other things like that. Well, she lost the case. It was the first case of this kind that she had ever lost, at this level at least. He went to jail for a very long time, and is still in prison now."

"I remember that. I remember the case. He was pretty guilty though from what I remember. Didn't they have a lot of evidence against him?"

"Yes. But you didn't know my mother in those days. She was a shark. She could get anyone cleared of any charges. That's what made her so popular, and I guess, as I mentioned so unpopular."

"For sure! It's a tough spot for her to be in."

"I guess, but not really. She chose that profession. She chose that side of the court room to be on. And she perfected her skill. She just missed this one."

"They always thought that it was her loss of this case that killed her. But it was never proven." She hesitated. "You know it was the case, don't you?"

I nodded. "A few weeks later I was in the park. Ironically it was a park mother used to always take me to as a child. I enjoyed it. It was a safety spot, kind of like this place. It helped me to think." I looked up, head in the sky so I could take a deep breath of air. When my lungs were full, I continued. "Anyway, I was there cooling off because I was angry with mom. I had wanted to go to a charity outdoor concert with Piety in Toronto and she said no. She said I was too young. When I argued about my age and that I was 17 and almost out of high school she said that if I could find a way to pay for my ride, my hotel and the concert, then I could go. It was two weeks away so the thought of getting the potential $300 that I needed was pretty unlikely."

"Did you not have a job?"

"I never really needed one, cash wise, so no, I didn't." She shrugged then nodded. I kept on.

"While at the park this guy came up to me and started talking. He said he recognized me as Sadie Coleman, and that if I didn't mind, he would like to ask me a favour. He told me that his brother was in a lot of trouble legally and really wanted my mother to represent him. He had called her several times and she had not called him back. The one time he got through to her, he said that she told him that she was too upset with her recent loss and was not taking on any more clients right now. That should have been my first clue that he was lying because that was not how mother worked. You knocked her down and she bounced right back up, twice as strong." I turned and straddled the bench again, this time facing Alex. I needed to change up my position to save my balance. A paraplegic on a backless bench was not always a good idea.

"Long story short, the guy offered me $500 to tell him where I lived, and to let him inside on a time and day that I knew mother would be home. He said he just wanted to talk to her and he believed that if he had a chance to plead to her face to face she would understand and take his brother on as a client. He said his brother's wife and kids depended on him. I needed the money and I believed him, so I set it up. I gave him the time and the day. I said I would be there to let him in."

"Wow Sadie, does your dad know any of this? The police?"

"No. And I don't want him or them to know. Please." I started to feel quiet anxious. Was this a mistake to tell her? Was this better off staying inside my head? Breathing was getting harder. Maybe I needed to stop now. "I am sorry, maybe you shouldn't hear this."

"Hey, don't worry. Calm down." She rubbed my shoulders. "I was just asking. It's okay. This will stay between us, just keep talking. Please."

"Promise?" She crossed her heart with her fingers once the words were uttered.

"Okay. That morning father left for work and mom, as usual on Tuesdays, went upstairs to her office to work on her latest case. Again this was a sign that I should have known that he was lying, mom was already in the middle of a new case only a few weeks later."

"Hindsight allows us to pass judgement on things we had no chance of tuning into previously."

"I know, but I still feel I should have been more in tune with everything," I responded. "Anyway, I called him to confirm that she was home like I thought she would be and that he could come over. She usually set up appointments for Tuesdays while she was home so a half hour later when the doorbell rang – she wasn't surprised. In fact my mother yelled to me that it was probably Mr. Gordini, her accountant and that I should let him in. She ended by shouting that he was early. I answered the door. It was Tim, the man from the park. I told him that my mother's office was upstairs in the den off of her room. I also informed him that she was expecting someone else soon. I walked into the kitchen to get my lunch ready. I was meeting Piety to go to the beach that afternoon. We were packing picnic lunches. I had only taken out the bread when I heard mother yelling upstairs. I knew she might have been upset that he was there, but it was unlike mother to scream the way she was, especially in the tone that she was using. That scared me. I ran upstairs and the two of them were in her room arguing. My mother said something to him about trying and that the situation was nearly impossible, I don't know." I shrugged my shoulders to emphasize my words. I continued. "My mother's lip was bleeding. I asked her if everything was okay. She said it was and that our guest was just leaving. He said that he wasn't, that he wasn't finished with her and then he started to beat her up. He was punching her and pushing her until she hit the ground." I stopped for a moment and wiped my eyes with another tissue. Alex took one as well.

"Sadie, I knew you were there but I didn't know you experienced all this. I am really, really sorry." She put her hand on my head. "Mr. Gordini was accused of the murder wasn't he, at least questioned at first right?"

"Yes, for a while. But he didn't do it. That was my fault as well. And don't be sorry. I did it to myself."

"Did what? This? What happened to Charlie, or sorry, your

mother? Oh, no you didn't kid. This was much bigger than you. You watched her die. My dear, no one should watch their mother get murdered. I always thought it was a possibility that you did witness it but not like this." She grabbed my hand. I pulled it out of her grip, patted the top of her hand and then removed my hand completely.

"Well, again. I did it to myself."

"No, you didn't. But we'll save that argument for another time," she said then paused a moment. "What happened next, between your mother getting murdered and you getting hurt?"

"Well, after he threw her on the floor mom begged me to save her."

"She what? She begged *you* to save *her*?"

I nodded. "She kept saying Sadie help me, please help me. Don't let him kill me. She repeated this."

"She did not say that?"

I was crying too hard to respond or speak. Did she not believe me?

"Oh, Sadie, what could you have done? You couldn't have saved her."

I disagreed. I caught my breath and continued my story. "He said that this was between him, Vitalli and her. I asked what he was talking about and he said that he was there to kill the bitch that put his boss behind bars. I started screaming and telling him that he was a liar. He just laughed and told me how easy I was to convince otherwise. How cheap I was too. He told mother that I had traded her life for $500. He then kicked her in the stomach and spit on her. She sat up and asked me what I had done. I apologised to her. It was all I had. She got up slowly in between us and told him to leave me the hell alone. She was bleeding so badly. I was in shock. I didn't know what to do, what to say. All I could do was relive our whole conversation in the park to try to find out what made me believe him. I couldn't talk, I couldn't move. I couldn't fight him with her. I couldn't save her. I could only think about the park."

"You were shocked. In shock. You did what you could. Your mind must have taken over your body."

"I didn't even try to help her, Alex. I didn't lift one finger. I couldn't protect the one person I loved more than anything in this world. She depended on me to protect her. I couldn't think any further than myself."

"Sadie, that is not true. That was not a normal occurrence. That was a horrible situation. Anyone would have frozen up. I probably would have. You can't blame yourself for that. And you are not responsible for protecting her."

"Who do I blame then? We are responsible for those we love." I sighed. She didn't respond right away. When she did she said "some times we help best by not helping. And besides, in a situation like this any human would react with fear, with the inability to fight off a big strong guy like that. I don't believe there was anything you could do to stop him from doing what he went to do. He was determined. He would have found a way."

"In the end she fought him for me. She even pushed me down right before he shot her in the head. As soon as she hit the floor something triggered inside of me. I called for her. She looked over at me and then her head dropped. I felt for a pulse, there was none. I looked up at him and he said to me 'you're next.' I yelled 'Dad' and made him turn around. My father wasn't there but he didn't know that. When he turned I got up and ran out of the room and down the hall. I got to the stairs and tripped over the banister. I went tumbling down to the bottom. He came running down after me. I felt him check for a pulse. I was in so much pain at first but then my legs just went funny. The sensations were odd. My legs felt like they were behind my head or through the floor. It was so weird and scary but not as scary as he was. So I stayed still and hoped he would go. He must not have been able to find the proper spot for a pulse because he said 'good dead, just like her mother' and he left the house. It was about 15 minutes later that Mr. Gordini came over. He helped himself into the house. He came straight over to me and checked me. I told him to check my mother. He ran upstairs to see her and call the police."

"They suspected him for week's right?"

"Yes. I wouldn't talk at first. I was afraid that Tim would come back and kill me."

"No kidding."

"After a while I decided that I needed to tell them that it wasn't Mr. Gordini. I told them that I never saw the guy. That he was wearing a mask the whole time but that he was taller and wider, you know? Mr. Gordini was cleared then."

"I am speechless Sadie. I wish I could take this away for you. I can't believe that you experienced this. That guy, did you ever see him again? You must have been so afraid? Still afraid? Holy shit!"

"No, I didn't see him again but a few weeks after the accident I received a letter at the hospital. It just read, 'I guess $500 buys your silence as well as your mother's life. Good girl. You don't tell on me and I won't tell on you."

She knelt down in the snow in front of me, her hands resting on my knees.

"Shit Sadie, how could you deal with this on your own? He was making you, or I guess *made you* feel guilty to keep you silent. He threatened you, and this wasn't your fault."

"You keep saying that, but you aren't getting it. According to the law I could be in jail right now as an accomplice. Not to mention just how horrible this makes me as a person. I did this to my self, to my mother. And once I knew Tim was lying, I didn't save her."

"You couldn't!" She softly yelled, then took a big breath to calm down. "I know that is the way you see it and I am sure nothing I say will tell you otherwise. I don't believe that it was your fault, not even an ounce of me feels that way. You didn't pull the trigger. You need to talk to someone about this. Someone, who can help you understand that this wasn't your fault. And at the very least, help you realize that what happened was not your intention. But again, I am sure nothing I say will change your mind on what you have been thinking for the past 6 years. Still Sadie, wow, this is a big secret. I don't blame you for not telling anyone. You must have been so afraid for your life and that he would come back after you?"

"I was more afraid for my dad. That the guy would come back and kill him or the knowledge of the truth would. At the very least, I knew the information would put me in jail and Dad would be left completely alone. I wanted to protect him."

"You couldn't go to jail over this. You were just as much of a victim as your mother."

"Thanks, but..." I couldn't help it. I was back to crying, out of control this time. What was wrong with me? Alex sat back on the bench and gave me another hug. This time we were both facing each other. It did feel good to have it out of my head. It felt good to have someone know my sins. It also felt good to have the person who knew the truth hug me.

Alex's pager went off. She looked at it and then placed it back in her pocket. She looked me in the eyes.

"Alex, I killed my mother, and I destroyed my father's life."

"Oh, Sadie. This is why you have spent so much time trying to fix up your father isn't it? You thought it would make up for what you think you felt you took away." She made a face of confusion over the words she just spoke. I understood her so I responded before she felt the need to reiterate.

I nodded and swallowed hard. It felt like a lump in my throat. "I can't get my mother back for him, but I can give him someone to love. I can protect him from more hurt. I don't know how else to make up for it. To give him back, not who, but what, I took away. No one could replace mother's personality, but someone could replace her duties. That sounds horrible doesn't it?"

She shook her head. "You didn't take her away Sadie. Someone like that guy would have got to your mother if you helped him or not. He was a type of hit man by the sounds of it. That was his job. You were just one method to the end he foresaw. You know?"

"Maybe. But it worked. My mother is dead. My father is alone."

"Not alone, he has you." Her pager went off again. She looked at it. "Give me a minute. It is the front desk. She grabbed her cell phone and called the residence. She had a lot of head nods, and okay's. She ended with saying that she needed another 15 to 20 minutes and she would be back.

"Everything okay?"

"Yes. Just Elizabeth looking for me. She needs to talk to me about Calista and last nights incident. I told them to tell her that I would be there in 20, so keep talking please."

I shrugged, "not much left to say."

"Sure there is. There is a lot to say. So much I wouldn't even know where to start." She said, looking surprised by my comment.

"I don't want dad to know about this. I don't want him to hate me." She made an attempt to speak. I held up my hand and cut her off. "I also don't want him to worry about me, and I don't want to have to tell others that I saw Tim, or that I know his name. If it is his real name. That scares me. I don't want to die." I could feel myself shake inside. "Please, Alex, I beg you, don't say anything."

"I won't. I promise kid. That is for you to do. I hope you can trust that I won't hurt you." She used her hand to wipe my tears. I believed her. I believed that she wouldn't tell him, and I believed that she didn't hate me for what I did. She honestly thought I was innocent. I was relieved and confused, both at the same time. Was she naive? It did mean a lot coming from her. Especially knowing how much respect father has for her and her opinion. It was as close as I was going to get to my father's input about the whole situation.

"Listen, what do you say we stop the confessing for one afternoon? Why don't I go talk to Elizabeth and you can go freshen up, then we will meet in an hour at my room for dinner and movies.

We will relax together. Sound good?"

"It sounds really good. But one more thing, I need you to know something."

"You won't convince me that you are to blame."

I smiled. "That isn't it. I want you to know something about my dad. Well about me. No, I guess about me and him and me trying to set him up with someone, or break him up with someone." I hesitated a moment to see if she was following me. I took a deep breath. After a while she nodded in a way that told me to go on. "Well, it isn't that I don't think you would be good for him, because I do. And I don't think that you waited until my mother died to get with him. I didn't mean all that."

"I know that," she reassured me. "No worries. That is old news and we are on to the new stuff."

"But wait, I need you to know this." I had to tell her before I lost my nerve. "I need you to know why I am having troubles with you and him being together. I want you to know that I wanted someone that he could love and someone I wouldn't have to."

"I don't understand."

"I don't want to have what happened with my mother, to happen again. And if it did, I don't want it to be to someone I love. Someone I would need to protect. Someone I would fail. How awful is that? It is so selfish."

"That's not awful, that is understandable after what you have seen. I am honoured that you feel that way about me but sad that you have been hurt so badly that that is the way you think. You have been through so much and you shouldn't have had to. And for the record, protecting someone is a gift when it happens, not a requirement to love."

"You are too kind. You are so willing to let me off the hook. My ego could use having you around more often. "

She laughed with me for an instant. "I am not going anywhere. I wish you gave yourself the same credit that I do. Now come on. Let's go inside." She bounced up off the bench.

We discussed meeting in her room around 3 or so. I wanted to take a shower and maybe lay down for a minute or 10. Then I would meet her downstairs in her room. I wasn't sure I was ready to be too far away from the person that held my biggest of all my secrets. Not yet. I wasn't convinced that it was solely between us two and I didn't know what to do, or how to feel about that. I had never been around someone who knew before, not since that night.

-27-

CAN I PLEAD THE FIFTH AFTER I'VE CONFESSED?

I was a little late when I headed down to Alex's room. I had a hot shower that relaxed me so much that when I got back to my room I had fallen asleep. It was a side effect to being paraplegic. I had to get into bed to get dressed. Once I was relaxed and lying down, I often nodded off. And this time, not just for a moment or two, but for an hour. It was now a quarter to 4 and I was just heading to her room.
   I knocked but the door was open so I let myself in.
   "Hey there! Little late aren't ya?"
   "Ya. Sorry. I fell asleep."
   She laughed, "I figured you did."
   "Hey Sadie." I looked over to the corner. Sitting on the left corner of the couch was Elizabeth. "How are you?"
   "Good thank you." I looked at Alex. I felt one of my eyebrows lift higher than the other.
   "Elizabeth and I were talking about some student stuff and I invited her to have dinner with us. I figured you wouldn't mind." She seemed to realize I wanted an explanation.
   "Not at all," I smiled tensely. I knew that it wasn't going to stay between her and me. I knew she would get someone else involved, especially the school counsellor. Why did I trust her? Well, it was my decision to talk or not. She could make me eat dinner with Elizabeth but she couldn't make me spill my guts to her. "What are we eating?" I asked.
   "Mashed potatoes, spare ribs with honey garlic sauce, yellow beans and a salad. I hope you like that?" she called from the pits of the oven. She was flipping the ribs over in their roasting dish.
   For dessert we had lemon cake with lemon icing. It was yummy. I ate a lot. I liked having a home cooked meal. Not a cafeteria special or a microwave dinner. The dessert was bought, but from a bakery not a box. We all had red wine with dinner. By the end of our dessert we were just starting the second bottle of Shiraz.
   "How is your father these days?"

"Pretty good. He has been really busy. At least I have found it hard to keep up with the happenings of his life." I looked up at Alex. She stayed quiet and took a drink out of her wine. I was so torn on the idea of her with my father. I couldn't help it. It was like a part of me that I couldn't control at all. I really didn't want to upset her. I was worried that no matter what - she staying with father or breaking up with him - it was going to result in her being hurt. Although, I guess hurt and dead were two different things, and I'd rather her hurt. And now that she knew the truth, it was more important than ever. It wasn't that I didn't want any other person father dated to die, it was just that I was afraid that if I was ever in that type of situation again, that I wouldn't be able to help someone I loved and especially not someone father loved so dearly and for so long. I worried that it would make me so nervous that I would freeze again. I was confident that that wouldn't happen if my emotions for the person were not so involved. And if I did still freeze I would want it to be with someone I didn't love, so it wouldn't hurt this much again. I was selfish – I knew, but I didn't care. Even though the odds of this situation happening again were non-existent, the guy was still out there. He still knew who I was. And I was sure he still had those eyes, those cold, dark, heartless eyes that were willing to kill anyone that they saw.

We talked for a little while longer. Elizabeth only stayed for an hour after we finished eating. She drank a couple of coffees to combat the wine, although she only had two glasses. She never once asked me about anything relating to what Alex and I had talked about. I was thankful for that. I was thankful to Alex for not saying anything and thankful to Elizabeth for keeping it to herself if Alex did. When she left, Alex and I decided on a movie and placed it in the DVD player. "Ready?" she asked.

"Not yet. Can we chat first for a moment?"

"Sure." She got up and sat beside me on the couch. She filled our wine glasses with more of the red that had been sitting on the coffee table. I was starting to feel the alcohol affects, not sure how much more I could take before being drunk.

"How involved are you with my father? I asked him and he said that it was none of my business."

She took a drink and then sat back, sinking into the couch. "I love him very much. I always have and I can't say I ever stopped. I am very involved with him. But I also always hold my breath when it comes to your father."

"What do you mean?"

"I have had quite a past with him." She took another mouthful. "Mm, think of it this way, if you and Lonny were to start dating again, how long would it be before you trusted him completely?"

I laughed a deep cackle. "A long time, if ever, but is it a trust thing with you? It has been a while since everything happened."

"Yes, a while, but only one try ago for us. You understand? This is our first try since we broke up because he met your mother, so I am involved with my heart, but I am still removed with my head. I am worried that if we were to get together officially, and he found someone better, that he would leave. So I keep some distance or at least I try to. You know?"

"I do. Thank you for telling me."

"It's a confession day I guess." She smiled, and I returned it. "What do you need from me Sadie?"

"Nothing." I was bemused.

"Of course you do. We all need something from someone. From my staff I need respect and loyalty, from my friends I need trust, from my family," she air snorted, "I need space, and from you I need your trust in me. What do you need from me?"

I didn't know. I was never asked that from someone. I always either expected too much from people leaving me disappointed. Or too little, and didn't care. I never ever told them first, what I had expected or what I had needed from them. "I guess I need your trust as well, and word that you don't hate me."

"Well, for the last time, I don't hate you. I love you." She looked me in the eyes to say this, smiling as she talked. "And also, you have my trust, completely, please know that. I do think with every fibre of my being that your father needs to know everything that you told me today, but I won't be the one to tell him. I will wait until you are ready. But I will probably bug you several times to tell him." She laughed. "Can you handle that?"

"I can. Now, how about that movie? And maybe some coffee?" We put in the best comedy we could find in her collection, grabbed a mug of coffee, and cuddled up in our own respective corners of the couch and prepared to laugh ourselves silly.

At some point I awoke and the room was dark with the only light coming from the blue on the television screen. The movie ran out and the television was still on the input component. I looked around. Alex was asleep in her corner. She must have been awake at some point when I was not because the wine glasses and mugs were cleaned up and both of us had a blanket on. I considered getting up and going back to my room but quickly decided against it. I put my head back down and went back to sleep.

    I did not get up again until I heard Alex's voice telling me that it was morning. In my moments waking up I remember that I had a shopping date with Piety. With all that had happened the past weekend I felt like I was on a reading week vacation. The two days seemed like 7. In my weekend I fought with Jack a million times, Ashlyn and I rescued Bridgette, I told Lonny that I still loved him, and I educated Alex on how I killed my mother. It was a busy two days. Two days that I was glad were over.

-28-

IF TABLES COULD TALK...THEY WOULD YELL, AND THEN SLAP ME!

To think of it, Ashlyn was right, when it came to guys I tended to tie myself to the tracks and wait for them to come and rescue me; the old fashioned damsel in distress syndrome. I allowed them to break my heart and then I waited until they came running with their tails between their legs begging for me to take them back, rescuing me from my heartache and my hurt. This was a pattern I wanted to change. I no longer wanted to allow them to hurt me, but when that was out of my control, and if it happened, then I wanted to be done with it. I didn't want to tie myself to any more tracks. I didn't want to have to wait in fear to see if they would come back for me. I didn't want to be disappointed when they didn't come, or when they did, and I realized that they weren't at all worth the risk. Here I was waiting for Lonny to be ready to come untie me from the tracks when in truth, he never will. All he was capable of was screaming for my safety from the side of the tracks. He wasn't coming any closer. He fought for me over the phone, he fought for me through our friends, and he even fought for me in front of others, but he never came to untie me. He never begged my forgiveness and he didn't tell me that he wouldn't leave when I kicked him out of a room. He didn't come to find me when I swore I would avoid him at all costs. I needed to untie myself. I needed to get off the tracks and walk away from the potential accident scene. I needed to walk away from Lonny. It hurt. I wasn't sure how I would do it. I just knew I didn't want to get to the point where Alex was. In a relationship with a guy that I loved that had my heart involved but not much else. I didn't want to love someone that I couldn't trust. At least not someone I hoped to one day say that I would spend the rest of my life with. This wasn't his fault, it was mine. I had come to depend on others in a way that they were not able to live up to. They shouldn't have to come rescue me from my own happenings, from my inabilities. He was the one that fucked up in the first place, but I was the one that gave him the chance to do it, even a second and third time. He wasn't coming because he was more into the end of the chase than the girl in the end.

I tried all of the month of February and most of March to work on one of my last major assignments of the year for school. All I could think of was Lonny. This, in one sense was a blessing, because it meant I finally stopped obsessing over Alex and if she would tell father what I shared with her. I really did believe her now that she would keep it to herself. I was relieved, but found a new crisis, finally dealing and getting over Lonny. I had successfully avoided him which helped me to think of our situation without getting so sad. Piety and I were working on our assignment together and she had told me that she wanted the night off. We had Friday and the weekend left to work on it, so we both agreed to take tonight, Thursday, and do some stuff of our own. I decided it was time to talk it out with Lonny. I asked him to meet me in the R.A. meeting room downstairs. I figured it would be the most private place to be. No one would come looking for us there, and no one would accidentally interrupt.

Lonny was sitting on the floor outside the room when I arrived. I had the key from front desk so he couldn't get in. He looked good. He was wearing slightly loose jeans with a belt and buckle showing. More a 'peeking-out' I guess. It was the only place around his waist that his shirt was tucked into his pants. His shirt was polo style, green with white stripes, the collar high around his neck. His hair was more perfect than I had ever seen it. It was his typically messy look. The - perfection in chaos - look. It was hot. It figured!

"Hey, I am glad you called me." I just smiled in response. I wasn't sure how glad he would be when we were finished talking.

"It is about time we talked don't you think?"

He agreed and stood up. I unlocked the door so we could both slip inside. The room's lights came on as soon as movement triggered them. They went off in similar fashion, after moments of inactivity. It was a great way to conserve energy.

We sat at the head of the rectangular table. The room was longer than it was wide. A window sat in the wall at the end of the room.

Behind us, on the wall that housed the door, there was another set of rectangular tables. We usually used those tables as buffet tables when we ordered pizza or Chinese food.

"Can you close the blinds Lonny? I would rather no one looked in and saw us. I don't want to be disturbed."

He got up and went towards the window. "I am not sure if I see this as a good sign or not." He looked back and smiled. His smiled faded as my silence lengthened.

"You are still upset with me aren't you?" He asked after he managed to close the blinds. "I can tell by your tone."

"My tone? I haven't said anything."

"Okay, then your lack of excitement, your silence. And now that you said that, well, your tone."

"Well, you are intuitive."

"Save the sarcasm, Sadie. I thought we were going to talk this out. Are we? Or are we going to just yell at each other? It's been several weeks. We should have cooler heads."

"I am sorry. You are right. I am just so damn angry at you still, Lonny. I did love you. I do still love you."

"Then what's the problem? We can build on that can't we?" He interrupted.

"I thought maybe we could. I thought that as soon as you came begging me for another chance, and saying how truly sorry you were, that we could move on with everything. And as you say build off of the love we had for each other."

"So why don't we?"

"Because Lonny. Because you never came begging me for another chance." I started to tear up. It seemed I was doing a lot of that lately.

"I did Sadie, I said I was sorry. I said it a couple of times. I tried to make it better. I broke it off with her for you, and I called you and told you. You are the one that didn't listen to it."

"But see Lonny that is the problem. You should have broken it off for you, and for us. Not for me. Only when I was hurt did you have enough in you to break up with Jessica. And then when you did, you didn't come to me. You called. And when I didn't respond you went to my friends. Not me. You never came to me. You never thought to come to me. You didn't fight hard enough."

"So then I am being punished because you don't like the way that I respond emotionally. Shit Sadie, we can't all deal with things the exact way that you do, the way that you want us to."

"No, but I can ask for someone who sees me in a more important role in their lives, can't I?"

He stood up slamming his fist hard against the table. "Damn it. It wasn't supposed to turn out this way. This isn't the end of our fairytale. You want me to beg? Fine, I'll beg."

"I don't want you to beg."

"You sure?"

He wasn't getting it. "Do you remember the time that Jessica thought you cheated on her with that girl from your basketball camp?"

"Vanessa, ya, that was a mess." He parked his butt on the table, one leg up and one hanging down over the edge.

"Do you remember the one night that you came over to my house because you were so upset? You spent the whole day on and off the phone with Jess trying to convince her that nothing had happened."

"Nothing did happen."

"I know that. But she didn't."

"You convinced me that I needed to talk to her face to face."

"Yes. You went up there that night. In a terrible rainstorm."

"I remember. We spent an hour driving around the city trying to find places that were open to get flowers and candy. Remember we finally found that 24 hour grocery store open?"

I smiled. "I do. That was a fun night."

"It was. The most fun was searching with you."

I shook my head and sighed. "My point is that you put a lot of effort into that. With our search, the lonely and scary drive up to Jansen College and even the trouble you had trying to sneak your way in to her all female building."

"That was hard."

"Yes. And you did it all for her. All to prove that you loved her beyond anything else. To prove that you didn't cheat on her. I just want the same type of effort from you Lonny. I know what you are capable of. I know what I deserve. And I don't deserve the way this has panned out. And you, you don't deserve expectations that you can no longer reach."

He stood up and started pacing. After a few seconds he spoke. "You missed the key part here though. I did all that with Jessica because you told me I should. It wasn't something that came naturally. You had to plan it out for me."

"But you still did it."

"Yes, I did. That is my point. If you would have told me what you needed from me, how to handle this to make it better for you, I would have done it. I would have done exactly what you needed me to do. I would have Sade."

What a dutiful guy I thought but I let him keep the heroics act anyway. "I know you would have but that is the problem."

I felt confused. I wasn't getting my point across very well. I decided I needed to be more direct. "Lonny, we are through. We can't do the friends thing either. It isn't working. I can't see it ever working."

"We have been friends for a very long time. I don't know how to not be your friend."

"We'll adjust." I assured him.

He paced more then stopped. He came rushing over towards me, grabbed my face with his hands and started kissing me. His lips were trying to force mine open. I tried to push him away, I tried to say no but when I opened my mouth to speak it just allowed his tongue to wiggle inside my mouth. His mouth was warm, wet, and strong. I kissed him back. I kissed him as hard as I could. My hands gripping his shoulders as an anchor. What was I doing? This was far away from the result I wanted. I couldn't kiss him. I pushed him away harder this time. His lip grip loosened and he backed off. I put my head down on the table.

"How could you untie me when I can't even untie myself from the fucking tracks?" I said to the piece of the table that my head was buried in.

"What?"

"Nothing."

"You don't want this Sadie. You want us to be together. You want me. I want you. Don't over think this."

I lifted my head from the table. I looked at him. His glossy crystal blue eyes stared at me. He was on his knees, eye level. All I wanted to do at this moment was kiss him. Nothing else. I leaned forward and kissed his lips gently. Once, twice, three times. He smiled and started kissing me back. Before I knew it we were back into our previous kissing pattern. The kisses came harder and faster. I couldn't get close enough to him. I couldn't get deep enough inside his mouth. He stood up and reached down to undo my seatbelt. Still kissing he picked me up in a fireman's lift and put me on the table. We broke the kiss only for him to get up on the table himself taking off his shirt before our lips locked again.

"I love you," he whispered. I responded by taking off my shirt.

He kissed my cheek, my ear, and down my neck. He felt amazing. He didn't have to say it, I felt loved. I went to lie back down but the table was cold against my back. Warm only where my bra strap covered. I sat back up slightly. He put his shirt down behind me. It was warmer on my back. His mouth warm against my stomach.

"I want you. I want you now." He whispered between kisses on my stomach. I smiled back at him, "I want you too." I wanted to rip his clothes off and feel him inside of me. I wanted to make love to him and forget about everything that happened, to forget about these past few months. Forget it all. He moved his hands down to the button on my pants. "Is this okay?" I nodded. He undid the button and the zipper. Standing up and undoing his as well. I reached down to start to pull my jeans off. "Make love to me Sadie; we can talk it out later." His words seemed to echo through the room. *We can talk it out later*. Here we were back into the old patterns. I stopped moving. Laying back I took a deep breath and put my arm up over my eyes. Lonny leaned over putting his hands over my stomach. Rubbing circles around my belly button, moving up to doing circles over my still covered breasts.

"This is easier if you don't fall asleep." He laughed and started kissing my stomach. He pulled my bra cup back and gently kissed my nipple. He felt wonderful.

"Stop!" I couldn't believe this. I got caught up in emotions again. "This can't happen."

He stopped. He removed my arm from over my eyes. With his hand he wiped my hair away from my face. "What's wrong?"

"We are doing this again. We are doing it all wrong."

"What do you mean?" His face was inches from mine.

"We should be talking first, making out after." I sat up.

"If we are going to be doing this after anyways then why not now?"

"Why not now? Because there is no guarantee that after we talk, that this would be the result."

"But we are very attracted to each other. That should count."

"Sure, for a one night stand. Not for a relationship. We need more than that. I want more than that, don't you?"

He stood up completely. He pulled his shirt out from under me. He was angry. He picked my shirt up off of the ground and threw it at me. I couldn't catch it because my hands were busy doing the button and zipper up on my pants. They hit me in the face.

"I am sorry Lonny. We shouldn't have done this. We keep going in these circles, don't we? It is like we are in a boat with only one paddle. Even though we take turns paddling, we keep going only in circles. We are never both able to paddle at the same time, in the same direction."

"Your analogies are giving me headaches. It can't just be simple with you can it? Maybe you are right, maybe I can't live up to your standards. You win. I give up. Although I guess to you I never really tried, did I?"

"Don't put this on me Lonny."

"Don't worry Sadie I won't put anything on you anymore. I am through. Happy?" He ran his hand through his hair, turned, and left the room. The door slammed shut and I was in stillness. I stretched back out on the table. I didn't really know what just happened. I knew I loved him, and that he loved me, but I also knew that right now, we were not good for each other. We couldn't be together and we couldn't be friends. We would either rip each other's clothes off like savage beasts, or fight like spiteful enemies. We had no middle ground. I wanted to forgive him. The frustrating part was I also wondered many times just exactly what I was so angry about. What did he really do wrong? Most days I had an answer to that. Some days I did not.

Ten minutes after Lonny left the room the lights left as well, thanks to their automatic system. An hour after that, I left the room myself. I needed to try to go work on my part of the assignment.

SHALL WE CALL IN THE HOUNDS?

"Okay, so we are now taking applications for next years set of R.A.'s. Please put signs up on your doors and on the bulletin boards on the floors. If there are any students that you strongly feel would be great for the job, please make sure that they get an application personally and really work to have them apply. We want a large and diverse group of applicants to choose from. I want some quiet staff, loud staff, male, female, extroverted, introverted, athletic, academic, you get where I am going with this don't you? I want to have it all. And I want to be able to pick from a group of say athletic staff my two or three best ones, not to be stuck with filling a space for a personality by settling with what is left."

It was the beginning of April. We normally would have put out the applications before now and started the hiring process this week, but we were behind on the procedure. We had to wait to hear from the management on how many staff members we could hire. With the strike going on, it seemed to slow every deliberation down. This was a connection I didn't understand at all. However, it was the reason that we were given and who were we to argue?

Because of the delay, we had one week to get applications and one week to do the hiring carousel. It was called that because on one day, the interested students would circle around from one job interview to another. For instance, in one room, two or three Resident Assistants would be mocking a scenario that sometimes occurred in residence, like an underage student that came back to residence drunk, or a normally academic student failing out and segregating themselves from others. We would test the potential new hires on how they would approach and handle the situation. We kept in mind, of course, that they had no formal training. But we still liked to see what their common sense and gut reaction told them to do. In another room we do group assignments where we would test applicants on how well they could work together with other potential co-workers. It was a long day, but a fun day, for us as staff members at least. I remember being a ball of nerves when I was going through it years ago.

"They have to have their applications in no later than midnight a week from today. Next Sunday is the absolute deadline. Well, I guess technically the deadline would be by when I get to my office Monday morning but you get the drift. All got it?"

We all agreed to what Alex was asking of us. We were in the meeting room. It was my first time back in the room since I made out with Lonny. It was awkward only because Lonny was in the room as well. He had yet to look at me. I had gotten what I wanted. I had him agreeing that we were no longer a couple. I just wished it didn't feel so awful.

"Are all the applicants going to do the carousel?"

"Good question Tristen. The answer is no, not necessarily. We are hiring nineteen staff members, two of which will be returning staff who are placed as senior members and three as regular second year staff. That is between Manny, Wanda, Jen, Jonathan and you Tristen, who are returning next year. All five of you will be on staff but I will decide who will be hired in what position at the end of the month. That leaves us with fourteen students to hire. With that, I will cap the applicants at forty of our best, with your help of course, to go on to the carousel. If we get that many applicants, of course."

"We usually do don't we?" Hal asked.

"Usually." Alex answered.

We were in the middle of going over the changes in the quiet hours and rounds schedule for the next few weeks prior to final exams when someone knocked on the door. Jen Lee jumped up with her usually bounciness and answered.

"Sadie, Ashlyn, for you girls." She announced to the room.

We got up from the table and went to the door. It was Bridgette. I still was not used to her new look. The dark hair made her face look so tiny and serious.

We walked out into the hall. "What's up?"

She looked upset, nervous even. Her hands were shaking. "Are you okay?" I asked.

"Yes, of course, sorry. It isn't about me. It's about Jack."

"I am not surprised." Ashlyn retorted.

"You know when I collapsed? When I had problems with the ecstasy? Well, it was Jack that gave it to me. He gave it to me to take so I would be nice and ready for when he got back from the bar. His words not mine. He was just going to have a drink with his brother he said. He was coming back to spend the evening with me."

"Why are you telling us this now?" I was a little confused. This was her boyfriend that she was ratting out. Why? And why now?

"Because now he is giving it to other girls. I know about Julie, he told me. He said that he gave her the drugs."

"She admitted that."

"Sadie, not her information to know." Ashlyn reminded me.

"Sorry."

"Listen, he is giving it to other girls and then spending the evening with them. It is like all these girls just want to be with him and this is how they get their way."

"Does he sell it to them?"

"No, he doesn't need to. They want to spend time with him, I guess in hopes of impressing him or whatever, and he convinces them to take the drug before hand. He gets a thrill on it. On how many girls he can get to take the drug."

"You are his girlfriend aren't you? This doesn't bother you?"

"Not really. So girls like him, who cares. He gets them high and then lets his buddies laugh at how stupid they get. How much they fall all over him. He doesn't do anything with them, just make fun of them. But it is getting too much. He does it like every night. I am afraid for the girls. I am afraid that the next one that collapses will not be as lucky as I was."

"That is smart of you. Are you not afraid of what Jack will say to your confession?" I asked.

"Well, I am kind of hoping you don't tell him that it is coming from me. He needs to be stopped. He is going to hurt someone. I just don't want backlash. I can tell you that he keeps it in his room."

"We can't just go in his room without permission. We have to see him deal to force our way into the room. We will talk to him about it though. You are certain that there are a lot of girls involved?"

She nodded. "Absolutely! I know of at least 2 dozen."

"Wow!" Was all I could say back to her. I looked at Ashlyn. "We should get Alex involved in this now," she strongly suggested. "You wouldn't want another assumption that you are going after him because of your hatred for him."

I agreed with her. Ashlyn went back into the room. Moments later the door opened and everyone started to pile out. Ashlyn was last. "Come on in ladies."

We got Bridgette to repeat to Alex what she told us. Alex asked a lot more questions than we did. She got Jack's phone number and room number from Bridgette and then let her go. Alex told her on her way out that we wouldn't break her confidence. We would look

into this without saying that the information came from her.
"Where do we go with this now?" Ashlyn asked Alex.
"Well, we call him in and talk to him about it."
"Now?"
"Can you think of a better time?"
"No, but what if that gives Bridgette away?"
"I don't think that now or later would stop or start any different rumours about how we came across this information, no?"
"No," we agreed.

Alex stood up and went to the house phone in the corner of the room. She picked it up and called Jack's room. There was no answer. She then tried calling the front desk. We heard her address Bart by name and ask if Jack was in the lobby or the cafeteria. I guess he informed her that he wasn't because she hung up the phone and said to us that she would be right back. She told us that he was outside with his brother talking to the support workers that were picketing, and she was going to go to get him. She returned minutes later with Jack in tow. Jefferson came along with him.

"I should have known it would be something involving you." Jack said to me.

"Of course it would, I am your R.A." I answered sardonically.

They sat down on one of the chairs to our right. Alex started asking him questions. She said that we have had some students complain that he was passing out ecstasy pills in and around residence.

"That's bullshit!" He responded to her. "Let me guess, Sadie told you that some girls came up to her right? She hates me." He turned and looked at me. "You hate me. You wont be happy until I am kicked out will you?"

"I don't want you kicked out Jack. And I don't hate you. I disagree with you and your choices a lot. But that is it."

"Ya, okay. Whatever. The point is I don't have any drugs here. I have taken drugs elsewhere and came home to residence. I have been around girls who have taken drugs and come to my room. Some whom I am even convinced took the drugs while in my presence by the way they started acting strange after their arrival. But I don't give drugs out. I don't sell them and I don't use them as a weapon." He started to get loud. Ashlyn asked him to keep it down a little. Oddly he did. He sat back in his seat and let his head rest in his hands. His elbow rested on the side arms.

"This is quite an accusation guys. My brother may not be the most responsible guy, but he isn't a drug dealer and not a pimp,"

Jefferson said in his brother's defence.

"We aren't calling him a drug dealer or a pimp."

"Oh, I am sorry. You are right. You said that you were told he gives girls drugs and then laughs at how they react. That he does it for the thrill. So are you saying then he is a drug pusher? Is that a better way to put it?"

"Again, that is not what we said. We are concerned about the accusation that he is in possession of drugs here on campus. We have a no tolerance policy here. If we know that there are drugs being used we have to investigate it."

"I don't have any drugs I told you."

"Then why don't you search his room. Jack, do you have a problem with that?" Jefferson asked. I couldn't believe this. I wanted to search his room so bad but thought it would never happen. I thought I would have to fight to get that to occur and now here was his brother offering up Jack's room for inspection.

"That's fine. I have nothing to hide. You go with them though. I don't want Sadie stealing any souvenirs of mine for her personal use." He stood up and handed Jefferson his key card. We all got up and left the room. "I'll wait in the lobby." Jack said as he parked his butt on the couch. Alex went to the front desk. "Can you page security? Ask them to come over."

"Marco is in the back. You want him?"

Bart went to the back and returned with Marco. He was the newest security guard to join the Greenbury team. The guard that he replaced left for personal reasons, which was a nice way to say he quit. The position had a high turn over rate. Many people came in and out of the position. It was often boring and inactive, and then when you did have a call it was generally to deal with drunken students who didn't want anything to do with any security guards or rules and regulations. It was a tough position for little pay.

Alex told Marco what was going on and asked him to come with us as a separate witness. He agreed and we all headed up stairs. Jefferson let us in once we got there. I stayed in the door way and watched everyone search around the room. I figured with all the bodies already there, they didn't need me and my chair getting in the way. Jefferson stayed in the far corner. Alex searched the closet, Ashlyn the desk, and Marco the counters and shelves. They lifted jar lids, opened drawers, and moved papers. They were coming up empty. Jefferson moved himself over towards the doorway where I was watching.

"Come on, you can be honest with me, you are a little disappointed aren't you?" He smiled as he asked me.

"We aren't done yet. And if he is guilty of this, then yes, I am going to be disappointed if we don't find them. And if he is innocent, well, then I am glad nothing is turning up."

He smiled. "Good answer Sadie." He laughed. "Oh, that is a picture of our mother. Jack holds that statue dear. He got it from an ex girlfriend. Let me help you open it up." He walked over to where Ashlyn was holding up a figurine that was connected to a picture frame. It looked cracked in several areas. It held a small cup in the back of it, almost like an area to put a candle except it had a lid. Jefferson grabbed the statue. "Let me open it for you. It is a little tough and if the statue breaks it will be a lot better if it comes from me." He grabbed the statue from her and sat on Jack's bed to open it up.

"Any luck anyone?" Alex asked the group. They all answered with a no.

"Here. It is open. And...ah," he fisted something then quickly placed his hand down at the side of his leg.

"What's in your hand Jefferson?" I asked. Alex heard my tone and turned around. "What is in your hand?" She backed me up.

He didn't say a thing. He just stared at her.

"Jefferson, show me your hand." She was getting upset. "You don't want to get in the same trouble that your brother is getting in, do you?"

He still didn't move for a few moments. Alex stared him down and he finally lifted his hand and opened his fist. In his palm, he held a clear plastic baggy, with little white pills inside of it. None of us could speak. Alex grabbed the bag and shook her head. "Damn it," she said in a huff. "Son of a bitch!" She rubbed her forehead with her free hand. "Alright everyone, let's go."

We headed downstairs and to the main staff office. Alex went to her room and called Reggie Austin the Front Desk Manager, Rodney Maigny the Residence Manager, and Cathy DeGraff, the Dean of Student Services, and also Jack's aunt. She had sent Marco to go get Jack. It only took moments to hear him yelling. The shouting got louder as he approached where we were. The slightly opened door smashed open further as he entered. "Let me see them. Let me see what you have. They are not mine. I don't have any drugs here. I have nothing. You planted that bitches. I know it." He said mostly towards me. Alex came running out of her office.

"Calm down Jack. I don't want to have to call the police. Do I need to do that? Right now this is just a residence offence. Let's keep it that way."

"Those aren't mine." He said looking past her, pointing to the bag that was on Alex's desk. "Seriously, they aren't mine. I am not the monster that bitch seems to think I am." He was pointing at me. Our feelings of mutual dislike were clear.

"This has nothing to do with her. Sadie wasn't even the one who found them."

He looked around the room, staring down each of us for a moment or two. I stayed silent. I may have made some questionable choices lately but this one I was certain would work in my favour. I couldn't think of anything that I could say that would make this situation better, for anyone involved. I sat silent.

"Jack, the residence committee is coming in for a meeting to discuss what is about to happen. You will be asked to leave residence immediately. Normally we would escort you out now but as a courtesy to your aunt we will allow you to wait in the lobby until she arrives and the meeting is over. She has informed me that she will be taking you home with her."

"I am not going home with her."

"That is between you and her. Now please, if you wouldn't mind leaving this room. You can wait in the lobby and I would suggest that you do wait there, to not make it worse for yourself."

He looked as though he wanted to say something in his defence but he didn't. He turned around and walked out of the room shouting profanities as he left. I kind of had the feeling he was not impressed with what was about to go down and I couldn't help but smile at the thought.

* * * * * * * * * * * *

"So how do we know these are his; he says that they aren't his?" Cathy DeGraff asked as she sat at the meeting table. I got a chuckle when she sat down at the part of the table where my ass was just a month ago. Every time she put her hands down on the table and started rubbing the wood as she talked, I laughed. I tried to keep it in as best as I could but I knew my smile showed every once in a while.

"Of course, he says they aren't his. Do you really think he would admit it?" Alex rebutted.

"Well there is something to be said about trusting a student's word."

"Yes but how long are we going to take his word before we stop believing him? Before we stop asking his opinion on the subject and just follow the facts." I added to the conversation. "Man, we give him so many allowances, really, what is the problem here?"

"Excuse me young lady but I would appreciate some restraint. You don't know Jack very well at all."

"Actually, besides you maybe, and that's a big maybe, she probably knows the student in him best out of all of us. He has been in residence for three years and Sadie has been his assistant that whole time. She does know him and she knows the trouble that he has been in. So she has valid input." Alex stuck up for me. Cathy backed down. I smiled at Alex as a thank you.

"The point of the whole meeting can be summed up easily. Jack was caught with drugs in his room and we have a no tolerance policy. He is out. We have the hard evidence that was in his room." Rodney Maigny added. He was the residence manager. Alex's boss. He had the ultimate say. If for some reason there were a tie in the committee vote, he would break it. I was glad to hear that he felt the way he did. Cathy wasn't. She continued on about reasons why this was not up to code. She started with the fact that we went up there to search his room without probable cause, even though he gave permission. She had many other arguments as well, saying she was just trying to play the devil's advocate. I disagreed with her.

I got kicked out of the meeting about twenty minutes after it started. Apparently they didn't like it when someone who wasn't on the committee constantly threw out examples of incidents from Jack's past that were completely inappropriate; even if they were the truth. Ashlyn was asked to leave with me. I suspected it would be the last time that they would let R.A.'s in the room while they were discussing a matter of this nature.

The meeting went on for almost an hour after that. Elizabeth had been called in as well to talk with Jack and Jefferson. She only stayed with them for a half hour and then joined the rest of the gang in the meeting room. In the end, Jack ended up leaving with his aunt. She informed him it was his father's wish. Jack didn't want to argue with his father considering he held his wallet strings. This was according to Jefferson at least, who was talking to me in the lobby for a few minutes after his brother left. He informed me how his brother still insisted that the drugs were not his. We both agreed that Jack needed to start taking more responsibility for his own self if he was going to get further in this life. Jefferson said that he was like this as a child as well. He was always blaming someone else for his mistakes. He never claimed responsibility for anything. He didn't need to. Everyone was willing to either take the blame for him or give him an excuse out. I wasn't surprised to hear that. After all, at first even Jefferson tried to hide the drugs from us when he found them. We all had our skeletons that caused us issues I guess. For Jack, his issue was accountability. But, I didn't have to worry about it anymore. Jack was now out of residence for good. No more crappy calls in the middle of the night to go to his room, no more yelling and arguing in the hall, and no more fighting him over every little thing. I couldn't help being happy. Ding-dong Jackie's gone. I just hoped it stayed that way. I hoped that this time, Cathy DeGraff, or any other DeGraff couldn't and wouldn't have this one fixed for him. I was sure they couldn't but I was not going to bet my life on it.

-30-

FORGIVE ME FATHER, FOR I HAVE SINNED.

Hey Sadie, it's dad. I was hoping that we could get together Thursday night and go for dinner. It has been a while. I think we could use some catch up time to talk. I was thinking some seafood but it's up to you. I would like your permission to invite Alex along with us, or at least we bring dessert back to residence afterward and we all eat it together. That is if you are alright with that. Any-who, I guess we can discuss it more when we talk and not when it is just me and your machine conversing. He laughed at his own joke. *Okay kiddo, give me a call when you get in. If that day doesn't work, we can pick another, and if it does, well we will just pick a time then. I love you Sadie. Talk soon, okay? Bye.* He laughed again, and then hung up.

    He was such a ham. No matter how upset I was, he made me smile more times than not. I really looked forward to our dinners together. It was Monday afternoon. A full week after Jack had been kicked out. It was so quiet on my floor, on every floor for that matter. I was actually able to concentrate on other students as well as my studying which was important as we rounded the last three weeks of school; especially since the hiring carousel started in the next two evenings from now. That made Thursday the perfect night to meet with my father. I called him back on his cell phone but he didn't answer. He must have been in class. I picked up my cell phone and I sent him a text. I said the day was good and that I would be up for getting dessert after we ate, bringing it back to residence to eat with him and Alex. Hours later, he text me back to say we had a date.

    Tuesday and Wednesday went by fast. I was paired with Jonathon on the interview session that dealt with floor meetings. This was where we asked students to plan a floor meeting about a certain subject and present it to us and the rest of their group. This tended to be the least popular of all the stops. I had asked for the student scenario room but was not granted it. This was fine except Alex seemed to be particularly upset with me and with every one, I guessed. She was moody. I knew that she had a lot of emotional stuff to think of lately but she was beyond distracted. She was almost mean, which was truly out of character for her. Once, Manny had asked her if she wanted him to hand her the applicant's score cards right away after the session or hold on to them. She answered by saying that she wasn't sure how he expected her to be able to hold on to everyone's score cards from every stop if we all handed them in to her after each session. She ended up by asking Manny to think next time before he spoke. Not a normal response for her. I wanted to ask her what was wrong but she never made herself available for a chat. The one time she seemed free, she told me that she was tired and wanted some time alone and then she walked away. After all she had done for me recently I figured that I owed her some time free from issues or chats.

After the two days of hiring we all sat down and went over the results of the tests. People were impressed with Julie and Bart from front desk. They also, not wanting to, liked how Jefferson held himself in most situations. In addition, six or seven of the other students really seemed to sparkle over the others. That left us with around four or five really tough choices. We all put our opinions in on our own set of sheets and handed them in to Alex for deliberation. The comment of the night was, 'if you don't know who they are by their names, than they obviously didn't make enough of an impression with you.' We stuck to that.

"I will have answers by next Monday. Tell any inquiring students that please."

We all agreed and got up to leave. Lonny was the first one out. He managed to go through the whole meeting without a single glance in my direction. I knew this because I stared at him the whole time. I was not sure why this bothered me. I was finally getting what I wanted, an end to the Lonny and Sadie show.

"Do you have a moment Alex?"

"Not really." She answered.

"Oh, okay. I guess I will talk to you some other time." I started to wheel away. Something was definitely up with her.

"Sadie wait, what do you need?" She looked exhausted. Her voice sounded weak.

"Are you okay?" I wanted to find out why she was so distracted.

She smiled a fake looking smile. With more enthusiasm than was necessary she responded by saying that she was great and then thanked me for asking.

I got the impression that I was not going to get any further with this inquiry tonight so I said okay and I left the room. It looked like the Alex and Sadie show was also on a hiatus.

* * * * * * * * * * * *

"What are we getting for dessert? Did Alex put in a request for what she wanted?"

"No she didn't. Let's just have dessert here. We can continue our conversation that way." He smiled one of his fake smiles.

"I thought we were going to bring some to Alex. I am okay with it dad, really."

"I am glad. Let's order here."

"I would rather not. Why are you changing your mind about dessert?"

"She broke up with me, Sadie," he said not looking me in the eyes. Instead, he took a swig of his beer and looked inside the bottle as if looking for a sign or a life preserver.

"She broke up with you?"

"She dumped me, Monday night. Said it was complicated. That she loved me but couldn't be with me. The timing was wrong. She was worried that someone would get their heart broken. I asked her to elaborate but she wouldn't. She just said goodnight and hung up the phone. She was crying the whole time, Sadie. I couldn't calm her down or change her mind. I tried calling her back, even left messages, but she hasn't responded yet. I figured I'd give her some space now."

I was shocked. I was also ashamed. I knew she must have broken up with him because of me. I put her in that position. I felt awful.

"I know she has been really busy and stressed. She didn't say anything else?"

"No. Nothing. She probably got scared. We have a history as you know and I think we were really getting close. That's adults for you. We love to complicate things that are important, eh? I would tell you to stop growing up but I am sure you won't listen."

I smiled. "Wouldn't much matter if I listened or not – I can't stop growth. Besides to most, I am an adult already."

"Yes you are. But always my baby."

"That I can handle. I am really sorry dad."

He shrugged his shoulders and drank the rest of his beer. He was sad. I could see it. I felt it all night but never asked. I just assumed he was tired. I was torn. I wanted to fix this for him and yet I didn't.

I ordered the chocolate cake, my dad the cheese cake. The

desserts were huge. I was glad I didn't get the ice cream on mine because in the end I opted to have the cake packaged up instead. Seeing its size only emphasized how full I already was and how little room I had left. Father ate his. We left right after.

I rolled down the window a crack in the car. "You mind?" He shook his head no.

"Dad, this is my fault." I said. It was a pretty common confession for me these days.

"What's your fault?"

"Your break-up."

"This isn't your fault. Why would you say that?"

"Because it just may be. In fact, it probably is." I looked at his profile through the reflection in my window. I considered rolling down the glass further; it was quickly heating up in the car.

"How is that?"

"I did something."

"What."

"Well…" I paused.

"Spill it. What did you say?" Funny how he assumed I was at fault because of my mouth. Although he was right this time.

"I may have told her that I didn't want you two to date. Not really in those words though."

"What words did you say it in then?" He was getting more upset.

I hesitated. I didn't want to tell father the context in which their dating came up. I wasn't ready to tell him about that day mother died. So now I was caught in the middle of my own doings. I needed an out and I didn't have one.

"Sadie, if you felt the need to say something to her please have the decency to say it to me."

"I just said that I was afraid of the two of you dating. I was afraid to get hurt." I trailed off at the end of my sentence. He caught it.

"Hurt, how would you get hurt? You have been pushing for me to start dating and to find someone to love for years. I mean just recently with Elizabeth. Now that I do have someone I can feel that way for, you are against it? I am confused."

"Join the club." My eyes began to water.

"Talk kid." He kindly shouted. He pulled into a parking spot at residence. "I am getting upset now and you are scared. Talk! We need to work this out."

"I'll tell you what I told her but don't ask for more. Don't ask why. Not tonight anyways."

"I can't make that deal." At least he was honest. So was I. "Then I won't tell you." He rubbed both of his hands in his hair. Vigorously rubbing back and forth before stopping and facing me. "All right. Fine. Tell me. I won't ask for more."

"Are you sure?"

"Sadie!" he was yelling now.

"I told her that I was afraid that if you started dating, what happened to mom would happen to her. That we would get into a situation that I couldn't save her." The water became tears that flowed down my cheek. I turned away at first, then changed my mind and faced him. I was hoping that the sight of my tears would force him to keep his word. He was silent for a few moments.

"What do I say to that?" He turned his body in his seat to face me better. His tie wrapped around the steering wheel. "Why would you think that kid? That's way out in left field."

"Dad, you promised. I don't want to talk about it tonight. Not now. I am not ready."

"Ready? Ready for what?" He sighed then put his right hand up in a stopping motion. "Okay, then tell me this. Why do you worry about this with Alex and not with any of the others?"

"I am sure it may have come up with some of the others. Especially with Elizabeth if you two got serious. But it didn't before because my heart wasn't as invested. I work closely with Alex, I have for years. This is a tough job where you have to constantly rely on each other. Other staff have come and gone but she hasn't. I have bonded with her. She is my friend."

"And you don't want to lose that?" He interrupted.

"No, I don't want to hurt her." I retorted.

"Like you think you hurt your mother, Sadie that is ridiculous. You had nothing to do with what happened to your mother. That was some crazed madman."

"But I didn't stop him from hurting her. And I am afraid that it will come up again and I will fail another person I care about."

"Well, first, that situation is not going to happen again. And second, in residence you are faced with all sorts of characters, something dangerous could happen there and you might not be able to protect her and anyone else you cared about. That is life kid. We take those chances everyday. Do you think Alex will try to replace your mother?"

"No, I don't think she would and I don't need her to. I have so many amazing women in my life that give me the motherly advice

243

when I need it, that I don't feel I am lacking in the parental guidance area. But I do care about her and don't want to let her down."

"How did you fail your mother? Do you remember more from that night?"

"Stop Dad, please. I don't want to talk about it. I mean that. Let me out of the car please." I reached for the handle. I hated not being able to leave without assistance or approval. I couldn't get to my chair nor could I walk back to my room.

"Wait. Sorry. I won't ask again. I just wish you would think about this a little more. I understand your fear but I don't agree with it. Although it isn't my emotion to approve of I guess. But Sadie, if you are too afraid to get hurt, you'll never have love. I loved your mother so much. It killed me inside when she died. But if I knew now, the outcome of our relationship and couldn't change her death, with the exception of your injury, of course, I would still do it all over again. The love, the fun, the pain, and the ending. I would go through it again just to feel the love she offered. It is worth it kid. People are worth it. Besides, if we had the power to kill people just by loving them we would be something pretty rare wouldn't we. Loving someone doesn't sentence them to death, it gives them life. You get what I am saying?"

I nodded. "I guess." I must not have convinced him because he continued.

"Love cannot be passive Sadie. It isn't enough to just not cause harm you must actively love as well. So even if your worst nightmare were to come true again – you must be actively invested in love to save someone. Evil is proactive. You can only fight it by being the same in love."

I reached over and hugged him. I wasn't sure the last time I held him so tight. "I love you dad."

"I love you too, Tootie."

I laughed backing out of the hug. I wiped my nose on a tissue. "I haven't heard that from you in a while."

"You haven't heard a lot from me in a while. We need more of these heart to heart talks. No more me telling you that it isn't your business. My life is your business and I am sorry. Now your chair, you ready for it?"

He went to the back trunk and put my wheelchair together. I got out of the car and into my chair, turning to face him once I was settled in nicely.

"Dad, you'll work it out. You'll see. Like you said, you guys have a history together. That will bring you back to each other. It already has. Just wait it out. I am sure I just scared her temporarily. I am really sorry."

"You know how to make me feel better kid." He reached over and messed my hair with his hand. "Thanks."

And even though I wasn't quite sure why, ten minutes later I found myself outside Alex's door with two plastic forks from the cafeteria and a Styrofoam container with chocolate cake.

"Make some time, we need to talk. And grab the wine." I said as she led me in to her room. "I was wrong about you and my father. I am sorry. You guys should be together. Chocolate cake?"

-31-

FORGET THE SCISSORS, SHE'S RUNNING WITH THE DAMN HEDGE CLIPPERS!

"Did you get the email?"
"What email?"
"The one from Jack?"
"No, I didn't. Why would he send me an email? You hit your head or something?"

Ashlyn made a mocking face and verbalized a fake laugh. "He sent an email last night to Alex, Front desk, you, me, and some others. It said he was tired of all the games and the accusations and that he was sorry for it. He said he has proof that he is not the monster we pitted him to be and that we will see this soon. I don't know. It was something to that effect."

"Yikes. What has everyone been saying about it? I haven't heard a thing."

"Well he just sent it this morning so I haven't heard much. I was just downstairs in the office and Alex showed me the email. I was copied on it. I haven't actually looked at mine myself yet. I think they did already put a block on his email address though. So nothing else could get through." My heart sank in my chest. He was the only guy I knew that could keep coming back. Gone, yet he still remained.

I was in my room getting ready for the day. My Friday classes were either cancelled or completed, with the exception of the one last assignment that we had. The professor wanted us to use the normal class time to get the assignment done at home. I was never that organized. My old class time was replaced with my now titled 'free time.' I slept in this morning and it was now noon. I was just getting out of my sleep mode and into my day mode. I had spent a long time in Alex's room the previous night talking to her about my father. I was somewhat right about her breaking up with father because of me. She said that she respected my feelings and that if they were meant to be together, when it was all right and I was ready, they would work it out. She said 'that's what happens when things were meant to be'. Otherwise, there would always be things coming up to keep them apart and maybe that was Mother Nature's way of stepping in and taking control. Stopping what shouldn't be. I told her that I thought that was a crock of shit and that I had made those excuses up before as well. That prompted many other conversations and by the end of it, we were still friends and she and my father were still broken up. However, she did say that she was going to rethink the whole thing. She was a little worried with my sudden change in outlook and I admitted that I was as well. I was honoured that she took my feelings into consideration. But I was saddened by this as well. She took me into consideration and all I did was think of myself. I was trying to avoid some future pain and all I managed to do was cause some present pain, in myself and in others. Now that's talent!

"Hurry up, I am hungry. What are you going to eat?"

"We are going to the cafeteria. With those students cooking, I am sure that everything will taste exactly the same, no matter what I pick," I said to Ashlyn.

"True. Although I am much happier with what is behind that yummy taste now that Jack is not working there anymore."

"Um, right, Jack. Let me check that email." I had almost forgotten. I finished throwing my hair back in an elastic band and I turned on my computer. The Windows screen popped up and so did my email. It signed me in automatically. The epitome of lazy, I didn't even need to remember my passwords anymore.

The email came up and it read just as Ashlyn had said. A few words different here and there but that was it. I was shocked both at his apology and at his claim to have proof.

"That son of a bitch has balls doesn't he?" Ashlyn laughed as I closed up the email.

"No kidding. Just let me read this one from Alex addressed to everyone. Give me a minute."

In light of this past email from Jack McGraff titled, 'Sorry to inform you,' I am requesting that we all get together and meet tonight at 7 to discuss what actions need to be taken in regards to this breach. I have already put a stop to his address being able to send emails to any of ours with a Greenbury College address line; however, more needs to be done. Please email me if you are able to make this timeframe. A secondary time would be tomorrow at 9 am.

I look forward to your responses,
Alexandra Ward
RLC Greenbury College
705-555-9661

Ashlyn read it as well. We decided to go down to see Alex. We were curious to find out if there was more information. When we arrived, her office was empty. We decided to eat first. I had the chicken Caesar wrap and Ashlyn the poutine. We figured those two items had the best chance of not being totally screwed up in the making. We took our food back to the R.A. lounge to eat so we could catch Alex when she returned.

"So, you and Lonny are done?"

"Yup."

"For sure this time?"

"Yes."

"You don't want to talk about it?"

"Nope."

"Well, you are going to be in the midst of it soon."

"And why do you say that?" I asked as I struggled to keep my wrap attached.

"Because he is on his way into the building and he is with Piety and Hal. I am sure they will stop in here, at least to get their mail." Ashlyn was looking out the window to the parking lot. She could see the three of them walking over from the school.

"Awesome!"

"Want to leave?"

"No."

"Doesn't that bother you?"

"Seeing him? No, not anymore than not seeing him. It hurts in the quiet moments, not in the ones where he is around."

"Hmm, interesting. I meant though, does it bother you that Piety and Hal still hang out with him?"

"Oh, no. Piety, Lonny and I have been friends for years. She doesn't throw it in my face so it doesn't bother," the door flew open, "me."

The three came in with their usual enthusiasm. Jen Lee followed behind them. Hal grabbed a few of Ashlyn's fries and then went over to check the mail for new letters.

"What's happening ladies?" He asked.

Lonny had left quicker than he arrived so we could only fill the other three - Hal, Jen, and Piety in with what had been going on in regards to Jack. We agreed that we were all ready to be done with anything to do with him. The two and a half weeks left of school could not come fast enough for that purpose alone.

We all sat around talking for nearly an hour before we noticed Alex back in her office. She must have entered through the front door connected to the lobby. Ashlyn and I went to her door and knocked. She opened it right away. We went in and shut the door behind us. Despite what was going on, her mood was drastically improved. At least there was one good thing that came out of our talk last night. Maybe she and father had made up. Or maybe she just became okay with the idea. Who knew? All that mattered was that she seemed a little lighter.

"So I guess you were filled in about the email. Oh, what fun!" Her voice sang.

"Has anyone else responded?" I asked.

"Most of the committee members have. We are going to meet tonight to discuss what we are going to do. Security has a meeting at the same time over at the college so everyone but them will be involved. Elizabeth will be there late as well. Other than that, I have everyone on board."

"What are you planning to accomplish?"

"Well, I would like to have him completely banned from residence. Not just physically but any contact, to students and staff, via email, phone, whatever."

"Do you think you can have that?"

"No, probably not." She smiled. "But it is worth a request. It is a 'no' if I don't ask right?"

As we were talking a little box showed up in the right hand corner of her computer screen that read, 'message received.' It said that it was from Pete Lagois and the subject read: from Jack.

"Oh, oh, here we go again." I said to them both, pointing at the screen. Alex turned to see her monitor.

"Shit! What now?" She opened up the email. It said *FYI – look and see*. There was a picture attached. She clicked on the attachment.

"What the hell?" Up on the screen popped a picture of Jack and Julie standing in the naked pose that they both claimed took place the night of the incident.

"Son of a bitch!" Alex whispered as she pulled it up. She turned to look at us with a completely horrified look. "What is he up to? I don't know what…" She turned back towards her computer.

The pose had Julie standing in front of Jack with hardly any clothes on. She had 'Jackman's dirty whore' written on her stomach and her legs were posed just as they both said they were.

"Now how is this going to help him? We see everything that they both said was there. I don't get it. This makes him look worse because it shows just how tasteless he is. Really? I don't get it." She was shaking her head. "Who did he send this to?" She looked up at the address bar. Only her name appeared. "Well at least he was smart about that. I have to call Pete down here immediately. I don't get this. What is his point?"

I got it. "His point is clear. Look at what is not in the picture Alex?"

"What?" Ashlyn asked. She didn't know many of the details about what had happened that night.

"Just wait. Look closely Alex."

She did, literally. She put her head closer to the picture on screen. "What's not there? I see the marker comment, I see most of their clothes not there but that is expected, I see a smile on her face. Is that what you mean? The lack of remorse on her face?"

"That too, but there is something key missing."

She shook her head. "I don't get it, tell me?"

"The sash. The sash is missing."

"The sash?"

I nodded.

"That's right!" She put her hand over her mouth as she spoke masking the words slightly.

"So, what does that mean?" Ashlyn asked.

"That suggests that she was not forced to take this picture. She said that her hands were tied and she was forced to pose with him. She said that she was forced to do many things. But here, her hands are not tied. She could have fought them, moved, walked away, or even turned around." I replied.

"Well that doesn't really mean she wasn't forced does it?" Ashlyn responded.

"No, it doesn't. But it proves she lied to us. Why would she lie about that? It definitely changes things a little."

"A lot in my books," said Alex.

"Either way, he was caught with the drugs so he is out of here."

"Yes. But this could give him grounds to say that they were planted. Damn it!" Alex shouted, lightly punching her fist on the desk. "I wish I knew what he is up to?"

Alex looked up Pete's room extension and then picked up the phone to call him. No answer, so she left a message for him to come to see her as soon as he got the message. She also informed him to have the front desk page her if she was not there.

"It's Friday, he is probably gone home for the weekend."

"But he just sent it."

"He could have sent it from anywhere."

"Maybe." She added. "But I have to make the effort to find him." She closed the attachment and went back to the email.

"Wait, scroll down a minute." She did. We could see the bottom of the email. There was a message from Jack to Pete and back again. The first read:

P, send the message to A for me this afternoon. My email won't go through. You have a copy don't you? ~J

The response read:

Of course I do. I will send it around 1'ish, between classes. What time will you be here tonight? Call me and let me know.

Pete.

There was no response to the last question asked by Pete.

"He is planning a visit tonight. Who is working?"

"Jen and Wanda I think." I said.

"Okay, I will have to talk to them. Ashlyn, I need you to find Julie and tell her what is going on. Convince her to go home for the weekend. I am not going to deal with her until after I speak to Jack and find out what he is up to. I am also going to call security and let them know what is happening so they can keep an eye out." She stood up and grabbed her coat. "I am going to go see Elizabeth and ask her to come over so we have her on stand-by. I also should get this email to the police."

"And me?"

"You, I need you to go upstairs to Pete's room and to Jefferson's room and see if you can find either one of them. If you do, bring them down here."

"You're leaving though."

"Crap that's right! I will be back in a half hour. If they are there, try to get them to come to Elizabeth's office to meet me. If they won't, then entertain them until I get back, okay?"

We accepted our jobs and left. I found neither Jefferson nor Pete. Ashlyn called my cell and told me that she found Julie and she was willing and ready to leave residence for the weekend. Apparently, her Mother, of all people, was on her way to come to get her. I couldn't help but laugh with Ashlyn as she informed me.

Our tasks kept us all the way until supper time, where we were invited to Alex's to eat. Elizabeth joined us. Alex asked her to come over for dinner and to stay at residence as much as she could that night, just as a buffer. We needed her help in understanding the emotions of all the parties involved. We were glad to know that Julie had left for the weekend but other than that, we had no idea what to do to prepare. We were not sure what Jack had up his sleeve. We were worried that if he did get into residence and he either decided to do something like be with a girl, or party with a keg, or utilize any of his other great tricks, that he would cause damage to other students trying to finish off their year. We didn't want any one caught up in his drama. We worried that if we had to escort him out that he would put some of his friends in a bad position of choosing between him and the rules - causing the friends just as much disciplinary harm as Jack. We hoped to utilize Elizabeth here as well in de-escalating any hot heads that might try to play hero. We couldn't do anything other than that. We had no real threats from him, just the one that said he was going to prove himself innocent. He was in a heap of trouble for the email but not punishable by us since he was already kicked out of residence. And Julie, according to Ashlyn, had no desire to go after him for anything in relation to this picture. She said that what was done was done. That she wanted to forget it. She also said she didn't want to comment about the sash not being there. We couldn't push the matter. So here we were, all in anticipation of what silly prank Jack was going to be up to tonight.

"You know, there is a chance that he is going to show up outside of residence and his friends are going to meet him. If so, there is nothing going on at all. We are a little dramatic at times." Ashlyn said, wiping her face from the spaghetti splatter that happened just after she sucked in her last noodle.

"I thought of that. It is possible but I doubt it. This is Jack. He'll want to come in and play with us." Alex added.

"I agree." Elizabeth shared.

"Awesome," was all I could add to the conversation.

We ate dinner and had a few laughs. Elizabeth shared with us some stories from when she was a young girl growing up in a small town south of Greenbury. She said as kids they would do things like hold their necks in a certain area and breath real heavy, in a desire to make themselves pass out. She said they actually thought it was funny. She also told us about the high school initiations she was a part of - like being taped to the gymnasium wall and having to race down the street by pushing a peanut with their nose. We talked about how different, with only twenty years between us, her, and Alex's initiation pranks were from Ashlyn's and mine. Ours were more dangerous and complex. They typically involved underage drinking as well. Schools had put a stop to most of the initiations around Ontario because of how dangerous they were getting. One school that Ashlyn's friend went to had students go as far as tying the new batch of grade nines to tree's, deep inside the woods. When parents started complaining that their kids didn't show up home that first night, an inquiry went out. The students were found tied in the woods beside the school, dressed in the home team cheerleader outfits. They wore hard hats that had cup holders on the sides with rubber straws that could go from any liquid to the student's mouth. The only drink the students were given was Vodka. Most of the kids were completely drunk by the time that they were found. One almost died. They were found roughly 16 hours after they were tied up. After that, a lot of the petitions went out to get the high schools to start banning any initiation activity. We had that here at Greenbury and so did a lot of other Colleges because of the danger to their students. Universities; however, had not seemed to have adopted that way of thinking yet.

So what do you like most about your job, Elizabeth?" Ashlyn asked.

"Helping the kids. It is very rewarding."

"And what do you hate the most?"

"No real improvement. It is frustrating."

"What do you mean?" Alex inquired further.

"Well, the same issues come up every year. And every year we counsel the students on these issues. We finally get a grasp on it and civilize the group, then the next year comes and we have the issues again. They are different students but it is the same thing. I don't ever feel like I am getting ahead of the game. That frustrates me to no end."

"I can understand that completely." Alex agreed.

"Let me help you with the dishes?" Elizabeth asked standing up.

"I am just going to make sure the food is away and pile the dishes on the counter. I will load them and clean the rest up later. It is six o'clock or a little after right?" We nodded but she checked her watch anyway. "I want to get down stairs and grab my sheets so I can make some photocopies before the meeting."

We put the food in plastic containers and piled the dishes on the counter.

"Go ahead if you two want Alex, I will load your dishwasher for you before I leave," I offered.

Alex liked that idea and left with Elizabeth whose schedule had recently cleared so that she was able to make the meeting on time. They decided to go together.

"Page either one of us if there are any problems with Jack tonight while we are in the meeting, okay?"

We said okay and got to work on the dishes. It took us about ten minutes. When we left, Ashlyn took the stairs to run up to her room quickly. She needed to make a phone call before it got too late. I was headed downstairs to the staff lounge, where she would join me later. I pressed the elevator button and waited patiently for the doors to open. As the sound of the elevator arriving rang out so did a familiar voice. It came from down the hall.

"Sadie girl, miss me?"

I twisted my head around the corner to see.

"Jack! You are not supposed to be here."

"And you, you're going to stop me?"

"Jack, you have to leave." I moved towards him.

He stood there and looked at me for a moment or two. I was getting closer to him. He smiled his toothy smile again, "Okay, I'm gone. Bye!" And he turned around and left.

I didn't trust him to leave. Not this obediently. I had to watch him get out. The only problem was that I just saw the door to the stairs close. I had lost him to a hallway I had no access to. Although I expected it, I couldn't believe it. Jack was back.

-32-

COME OUT, COME OUT, WHEREVER YOU ARE.

Where was he headed? Jack was so unpredictable. Who the hell knew where he would go and what he had in mind. I hit the elevator button to head down, pressing it at least a hundred times in hopes that the lift would realize how important I needed it come, and open faster. I needed to catch up with Jack. He said that he was leaving so I thought that would be my first step to try, the main floor. Who knew, maybe this was one time he decided to tell the truth. I felt like a lioness stalking her prey.

The elevator opened to the first floor and as it did, I saw Jack leaning against the wall in front of me. He was waiting for me. Alex was right. He was playing a game.

"Jack, this isn't funny." I said to him. I tried to find my pager. It wasn't in my pocket.

"I'm amused. Not my fault that you aren't." He said back to me as he ran down the hall straight toward the McGregor building. Maybe I wasn't a Lioness after all. The way he had me running, I seemed more like the prey at the moment. How lucky would I be if he went straight to the lobby and then out? Hopefully he was headed towards Alex's office? I knew that she said she was heading to the residence office to get some photocopying done but she should be finished that by now. Surely she was in her own office. I hoped she could catch him off at the pass. She would make sure he left. I reached into my sweater pouch and grabbed my cell phone. It wasn't on. Damn it! This phone always took forever to turn on. As I pushed I kept opening and closing my phone to see if it had a signal yet. I was in a hurry to have it ready to call out. By the time it actually was ready; Jack had passed Alex's office and was headed toward the lobby where Jefferson was there to greet him.

I relaxed my push a little. I gave them both a look and Jefferson responded back with a smile and his index finger pointed up. He was asking for a minute. Jefferson usually had a calming affect on Jack so I went over to the security desk and gave him that moment. "Having a fun afternoon?" Bart asked. He looked down at his watch.

"Evening I guess."

I nodded my head and then leaned it towards the brothers.

"I already paged Alex and Security when I saw him come in. He is kicked out of residence, isn't he?"

"Yes he is. No one answered their page yet?" He shook his head no. I shook my head as well. "Crappy. Well, I think he is leaving anyways. At least that is what he said he was doing."

Bart winced. "I forgot all security guards are with Trent in the managers meeting, in the Dean's office. Starting about now I guess. The bulletin went out about 30 minutes ago for the changed location. It should only be an hour or so. I can send someone over to get a guard if you want?"

"No, not yet. I forgot about the meeting. How convenient! They still should answer the page though." I sighed. "Why is the Dean not going to the meeting here? Why was the location changed?" The look on his face told me that he had no clue to either question. I should have known he wasn't up to speed on what the meeting was about. "Let me use your desk phone so I can try calling Alex. I'll see if she will answer her cell. Can you try Elizabeth Warrender's pager on the other line in the back?" Alex's cell phone didn't pick up. I paged her to the front desk line.

"You called her office right?" I shouted to him hoping he could hear me back there.

He returned and nodded. "To be honest, I didn't see her come back from the residence offices. She went there with some papers and hasn't returned. Maybe you should go check there."

"Her meeting is there but I guess if she won't answer the page, then I will need to knock on the boardroom door and get her personally."

I looked over at where the two boys where once standing. They were gone. Crap! I moved over to the girls sitting on the couch.

"Did Jack and Jefferson leave? Like outside leave?" I pointed out the door.

"No, they went down that hall." One pointed towards the residence office.

"Argh! I wish Alex was dealing with this." I said to no one in particular which was good because no one around me seemed to care that I was speaking.

"You can always call the police." Bart called out.

"No, I am going to go and see what they are up to first. See who they are trying to con into letting the little weasel stay this time. I am sure they are just trying to plead their case at the meeting that is about to take place. Page Wanda and Jen for me and tell them that I may need some back up. Get them to bring Hal or Tristen. And if Alex returns my page, please let her know that Jack is back in residence and that we are trying to get him to leave now. Hopefully she is in that meeting and the committee is already dealing with it. And if no one answers and I don't return in 15 minutes, then call the police to come in and help us remove him. He is in violation being here."

"Okay, first I will page Hal and Tristen but Lonny is already in the residence office I think. I saw him go there about 15 minutes ago. Maybe he is in the meeting."

I couldn't see how he would be in that meeting but I wasn't about to argue. I pushed my way down toward the residence office. The hallway was bleak. I was sure the walls had not been painted in years. With all the resident fee's the office collected, you would think that they could, at the very least, afford to put a fresh coat of egg shell white up on the walls.

I opened the door and went inside. It was quiet. I said hi to Candice who sat rigidly behind her receptionist desk. She didn't respond to my greeting. She just looked at me, face still, eyes shifting back and forth between me and the door behind me. I looked back half expecting a television set to be playing a tennis match between the two Venus sisters. There was only a white paint chipped door with a piece of green construction paper taped to cover the window. The whole room seemed frozen. Candice, whose desk normally took up the majority of the entrance way, seemed to have her emotions overtake the room instead. The office to the back left of the room belonged to Rodney Maigny, the Residence Manager. It was empty. Beside his office was the supply room and beside that was the boardroom, both with a closed door. Voices could be heard coming from behind the boardroom door, the meeting I supposed. To the immediate right when coming into the office area was Julie Raymer's office. She was the Coordinator of Student Services. Her door was open and also empty. The last part of the room that occupied space was the wall between the back of Candice's desk and the front of Rodney's office. That was where the photocopier, fax machine, and printer were kept. The room seemed different, yet I couldn't tell you why. I was puzzled.

Moments later Jack DeGraff came stumbling out of the boardroom with an evil smile on his face.

"Well, well, well, if it isn't Miss Sadie. How nice of you to join us here. You know you shouldn't follow people. Although in this case, we were happy you complied so easily." As he approached me closer I could see a shiny object tucked to his side. It was the blade of a knife from his student culinary kit. He saw me looking and held it up so I could get a better look.

"You like?"

"What's going on Jack?" Was all I could muster up the voice to say. I felt frozen now too.

Jefferson came out from the boardroom next. "She arrived? You were right" He was looking at me. His eyes were tired and his expression void of much emotion. Did he know about Jack's knife?

"She just strolled in here a moment or two ago. She was just looking at my blade Jeff but I don't think she is a fan."

That answered my question. Jefferson broke away from our stare. He looked at Jack and then looked at the blade. I couldn't stop looking at Jefferson's face even now when it was turned to the side. I was in shock. My eyes were magnetically stuck in his direction. It felt as though, if I made the slightest eye movement in any direction, it would result in my being stabbed by Jack. After a few moments a jolt of sudden realization hit his face and Jefferson returned to my attention.

"Not liking it. Well, it isn't your only option Sadie. What about this, is it more to your taste?" I broke my glare one more time and looked down to see a gun, gripped tightly in the palm of Jefferson's right hand, with a metal barrel glaring straight back at me. I didn't get to see if he approved of my shocked expression or not because the second I saw the gun, was right about the second before the one where I passed out.

* * * * * * * * * * *

When I awoke, it took me a minute or two to realize where I was. I looked around the room to see no one but me and a still very quiet Candice. My heart felt like it had a rabbit inside, with his little foot thumping hard and fast against my chest. I wanted to run away. I wanted to forget this whole thing. How did it get this far? How did I not see this coming? What the hell was going to happen now? Jefferson? I took a deep breath. I had to relax. I closed my eyes. I no longer cared that Jack was in residence. I no longer wanted to get him out. I wished I never saw him on my floor. I wished I didn't follow him. I wished he didn't exist. I wished I had a damn Genie for all these wishes. My only saving grace at this moment was that people knew where I was headed. It wouldn't take them long to figure out what was happening. At least I hoped. Surely Alex would figure it out.

I couldn't see the guys. I could hear Jefferson's voice. He was busy yelling in the boardroom. There must have been other people in there. Of course there was. It was almost seven. Most of the committee must have been there. I was on the ground by the copy machines. One of the boys must have placed me on the floor, before removing my chair to the other side of the room where I couldn't access it. This, I assumed was a power tactic and it worked. I was stuck. I was held hostage not only by them but by my own limitations. Running was not an option. I felt a tear fall down my face. Strange, it didn't feel like I was crying. I was thinking. I was thinking hard about my life. How I never had a chance to fully make up for my past mistakes. How I will never get to fix things with my dad. How I never let myself actually see, or take advantage of the chances when they were there. How I will never get to see Lonny. *Shit!* Lonny, he was possibly in here. That was what Bart said. My stomach went queasy. Where were Alex and Elizabeth?

"Hey there darling, you didn't answer my question earlier. Did you miss me?" Jack came out from the supply room slamming the door behind him. He knelt down in front of me. His face only inches from mine. I could smell his cologne. I was still.

"Cat got your tongue?" He paused to pick his teeth with his pointer finger. "You know Sadie, I was thinking back to that night that you accused me of, how did you put it, umm, assaulting Julie. Sorry, sexually assaulting her."

"I wasn't accusing, I was stating. And I didn't bring it up, you did."

"Not as I recall."

"Then you recall wrong."

He smiled. Not a happy smile but a devilish smile. It was more like the kind of smile you would expect to see from a bird right before it was about to devour its first worm of the morning.

"Potato, Patato. My point is that that night, you informed me, that I was creepy and eerie and that I was nothing to be desired at all. That women only liked me because I was a shallow cheap thrill and nothing more. My words of course, but close to the same meaning wouldn't you say?"

"Close enough." I wasn't sure if I was angry or afraid. Either way, I was shaking.

"Ah yes, close enough. Then I offered you a shallow cheap thrill of your own. You know a little ride on the Jackman. Give you a little taste of why the girls really liked me so much. Do you remember?"

I wanted to spit in his face. I wanted to scream, hit him, claw at his skin until the blood was no longer in his veins. My training told me otherwise. I knew the only thing that could help me now was my strength to stay calm. I took some more deep breaths.

"Answer me please."

"I remember."

"Thank you. And do you also remember what your response was to me?"

"Absolutely! I said no to you."

"Well, yes you did. But do you remember your exact words?" He knelt in closer. I could feel his hot, toothy smile on my face. For a moment, his nose brushed against my cheek. I closed my eyes and tried to recall that night.

"I don't remember my exact words." I said.

"Think."

"I don't remember."

"Think damn it!" He was getting angry.

I thought back to our conversation. Back to the words that he now so desperately wanted to hear again. Why couldn't I remember?

"Well, come on now. You must recall what you said."

I tried to replay our conversation in my mind but it would always stop at his request for a ride on the Jackman. Why couldn't I remember more? I looked at him. I looked at the intensity in his face - his white teeth, his almost fully darkened eyes.

"Think hard now girl. I will not give this answer to you."

He held up his right hand. He must have exchanged his knife for Jefferson's gun because the barrel was now inches from my face. It was almost square from this angle. I could read the word Glock on the side.

"Does this help?" He asked.

I looked harder at the piece of metal dangling in front of my eyes. I thought harder as well. And after some time it did help. I remembered. I swallowed hard before barely speaking out. "I remember. I said no, never, not even if you had a gun to my head."

He grinned from ear to ear. He placed the gun at eye level. "And look here, what is this?"

I didn't answer. I just started to cry.

"What is this?" He yelled louder. Shaking the gun from side to side.

"A gun. A gun that is to my head." I whispered.

"Yes." He seemed satisfied. "Hmm, guess this means you are ready for your' date with the Jackman now aren't you sweetheart?"

He scared me. At that moment all training and common sense went flying out of the window. It wasn't helping me. It wasn't going to get me out of this one. I could only fight. I put my chin up high. In a loud voice I said, "that gun doesn't change a thing. I want nothing to do with you." I spit in his face.

He stood up slowly, wiped his cheeks with his arm. He was quiet for a moment. All was quiet. The only movement came from his top middle teeth when they clamped down on his bottom lip. He chuckled a nasally laugh. I couldn't read him. I was expecting him to lash out but he just walked away. He got up and walked back into the supply room. Had I scared him off? I didn't think so. Did I insult him? Again, I couldn't believe that either. I was lost. Confused. There was so much silence. Just a slight sign of whimpering in the air and Jefferson's voice mumbled through the wall. He seemed to be pleading with the resident manager. I heard Rodney's voice as well. It was not a desperate plea though it was more like a bargaining plea. I tried to listen to what was happening in the boardroom but the silence in the main room where I was, was too important. It was almost too loud. I could not concentrate.

The supply room door opened again. Jack stepped out. He was struggling with something, or someone. I couldn't tell right away. Not until he pushed the person from behind him onto the floor in front of me. He grabbed her hair pulling her head back and placing the gun beside her temple. I gasped. "No," I shook my head slowly, "please!" I put my hand up like a stop sign, losing power as it hung in the air. I relaxed it to my forehead, rubbing my skin back and forth. "Alex," I cried but my voice was all breath.

Her eyes were soaked in tears. Black mascara ran down her face. She had blood on her shirt. She mouthed the words, 'I'm sorry,' then placed her hands to her face and cried more.

"Does this change anything Sadie?"

"Yes Jack." I said, no longer tearful and with more voice than I have ever had before. The back of my hand now wiped the last remaining droplets of tears from my cheeks. I was not frozen this time. And I vowed I would not become frozen. "This changes everything."

-33-

LOVE, UNLIKE LIFE, CAN COME THROUGH ANYTHING.

The sound of his zipper could have been heard clear across two continents. I was sitting on the floor. My head and back against the wall, my legs crossed in front of me. Jack got on his knees, pulled my legs straight out, and then sat one of his legs on either side of mine. He placed his gun to my head and his empty hand to my jaw.

"Open your mouth." He said in a soft yet determined voice.

I looked at Alex, whom he left sitting on the floor a handful of feet away. I opened my mouth. He hesitated a moment, then he placed the gun into my mouth. The cold, hard metal barrel tasted bitter on my tongue.

"Jack, don't do this. Once it is done you can never undo it."

He ignored Alex. The blood on her shirt seemed dry. It didn't seem to be getting bigger either. I could tell now, it wasn't hers.

"Let's talk about this, really. If you are looking to get back into residence, this isn't the way to go about it. I saw the picture Jack. I know you didn't force her. There was no sash. That's what you wanted me to see right?"

He continued to ignore her. He was starring at me, running his fingers over my lips and around the gun. I started deeper breaths through my nose. My lips were trembling under his callused finger tips.

"That will get you back into school Jack. Not residence but school. That's the main thing right?"

He continued to ignore her. "Jack?"

He licked his lips and winked at me.

"Don't you fucking touch her, Jack!" All rationalizing and pleading had left her voice.

"I swear, I'll kill you myself if you don't stop hurting her." She was now angry. She was angry and panicked.

He just laughed.

"Sadie, close your mouth. Spit it out and close your mouth." She was back to pleading, this time with me. Her new tears started to

Where the stream and creek collide

clean up the running mascara the earlier tears caused.

I didn't spit it out and close my mouth. I couldn't. The gun was too far in.

"Let me change places with her. Please Jack?" She took a deep breath. "Please?" Alex finished speaking then opened her mouth for full emphasis. Hoping he would place the gun in hers instead.

He finally indulged her with a look and a smile but that was all. He didn't speak until he turned back in my direction.

"What a bunch of martyrs we are ladies. What is the saying?" He bit his bottom lip to imitate the look of someone deep in thought. "Ah, yes. Something like, we have to sacrifice the lion to save the lamb. Do we not agree that that is what you want?"

Who was the lion? Was it Alex or I? I didn't understand. I needed to understand. I needed to know what he was thinking. I needed to concentrate. I needed to calm down and think rationally. "Alex, it's okay. Just close your eyes." I said. Although it came out more like, "Awix itth ophay. Dith koth yar ith."

Fwack! Like a thousand bees stinging at once, I felt Jack's gun rip from my mouth and hit hard across my face. My cheek bone felt hot and heavy. I bit my lip to try to stifle the scream. I didn't succeed.

"You shut the hell up and stop talking to her or I'll put a bullet in your head first. Then I'll put one in hers." He was talking to Alex. "And you!" Eyes now focused on me. "Open your fucking mouth and shut the fuck up."

Again I obliged his request. It was harder this time, with a mouth full of blood and an ache that went straight from my jaw into my eye. I took one more look at Alex and then felt the gun back inside me. This time the gun didn't lay dormant, it moved back and forth in a slow stroking manner.

"Now that we are done with our little game, I am going to play one of my own in your mouth. Stay still. We wouldn't want my trigger finger to slip now would we?"

I closed my eyes. I didn't know where to put my hands. Should they stay on the side of me? Maybe across my stomach? No, my side. I left my hands on my side. He continued penetrating my mouth with the gun. In and out. My head was hitting the wall. I was getting a headache. My eye and jaw were swelling. My tongue was feeling raw.

"Do you like it?" He moaned.

The room was fading away, nearing complete silence. My ears

seemed water logged. Everything muffled.

"Do you want the real thing yet?" He was getting excited. The penetration was getting harder and faster. The gun was warm feeling now.

Besides his voice and Alex's cries, the only sound I could distinguish was the crashing of my head to the wall. It was the sound and the rhythm - back and forth, back and forth. It reminded me of a rocking horse I had as a child. Mother got it for me on my 5th birthday. She was beautiful. Rocky, was what I named her. How original.

I moved my hands to across my stomach. Maybe they would be comfortable there. They hit Jack's left hand that was settled inside his pants.

"You do want the real thing don't you, you little slut? Well you will have to wait."

"Stop it please! Leave her alone." Alex couldn't hold her tongue any longer. Her voice sounded painful.

"Are you jealous sweetheart?"

I moved my hands back to my side and then together in front of my chest. My fingers intertwined. I closed my eyes again. Rocky was white. She had blue painted eyes that seem to show so much glee. Around her neck was a painted red bow. The second I got her, I hopped on for my first ride. My legs slipped smoothly over her sides, my butt fit comfortably on the saddle. I sat. It was a perfect fit. I held onto her neck and I rocked. I rocked for hours. She was my horse, my comfort, my place to get away. She sat near the corner in my room. Her hind legs would hit the wall on the back part of the swing making a clunking sound every time. Yes. The rhythm definitely reminded me of Rocky. But Rocky was safe. Jack was not. Jack hurt. My jaw was aching. My head was aching. Mostly my heart was aching. I separated my hands and placed them under my legs in attempts to keep them still a while. Please, I prayed, let this be over soon.

I opened my eyes. All I saw was raw flesh in a jungle of hair. I wanted the gun out of my mouth, even if it meant taking the jungle in replacement. I stretched my eyes to the right. Alex was sitting up. Eyes shut tight. She was singing a song. I strained to hear. *"Life for me is a river boat fantasy..."*

I wanted to sing with her but I couldn't. My mouth was full of metal. I wanted to throw up. I wanted to stop gagging. I wanted to find a fucking place for my hands.

A door slammed shut. The singing stopped.

"What the hell are you doing?"

"It hasn't been that long has it bro?" Jack replied between gasping breaths of air. "Surely you can figure out what I am doing."

I opened my eyes.

"You son of a bitch! You are ruining everything. You always do. This isn't the plan you selfish asshole." Jefferson sounded angry. I couldn't see him. It was in his voice. I was so surprised to hear Jefferson speak the way he was. I was surprised he was here. I wanted his help. I wanted him to end this. I wanted this gun out of my mouth. But Jack didn't stop. He didn't seem to care about his brother.

"Come on Bro, you can be next. Just give me a minute here. I will even let you blow the bitch's head off when you are done." You could almost hear his smile. He finally pulled the gun out of my mouth.

"Stop it Jack, I mean it. We have more important things to accomplish here. It would have been hard for you to convince them before to let you back in but now it will be impossible."

"Relax Jeffy. Quit the game. It's over. You don't have to look like the hero. I made myself into the bad guy. Just sit back and let me take care of it all. We will get the same result."

"Not now that you did this." Jefferson said as he pointed towards me.

"Oh, come on Jeff. Have a little fun. Or is this part of the plan, you looking all innocent?" He grabbed himself. "Now open up your mouth wider Sadie, and just ignore little Jeffy over there. He may have a soft spot for you but I don't."

"Jack, I am not joking. Stop it! Father won't want me if I end up in jail with you. This is not the way this was supposed to go."

"If you can't be his little mini-me, you will settle for being his lap dog wont you? Even if this goes wrong, you won't get the time I am going to get. He will forgive you. The only thing he ever required from me was to be better than I am. And I am not. Now enough talking, my little soldier is going to go soft."

I was lost in their logic but I didn't care. The more they talked the less the gun or the flesh entered my mouth.

"You gonna let him ruin your plans?" Alex asked Jefferson, interrupting.

Jefferson shot her a look then laughed. "Isn't that ironic. I get to be anything I want and the only thing I want to be is Dad and that is exactly what he wants from you," he addressed Jack again. "And only you. But you don't want it. You won't even let me have it you son of a bitch." He laughed a breathy giggle. "It will never change will it?"

Jack didn't answer. I felt his penis touch my lips.

"And you don't even care do you?"

Jack again had no answer. He went inside my mouth. The rocking began again.

"Well, I care." Jefferson whispered. He walked into the boardroom slamming the door behind him. Seconds later the door opened again.

"Get away from her." It wasn't Jefferson but the angry masculine voice was familiar. I couldn't see his face.

Alex screamed.

Bang! Bang! Bang!

My mouth was empty. I could see straight ahead now. No jungle of hair. I looked down to see Jack lying on the floor beside me. Motion-less. Rhythm-less. Alex jumped over him landing inches away from my side. Her hands were quickly searching my whole body for remnants of a bullet wound. There was none.

"Are you alright?" She was crying. I looked down. I was red. Jacks blood was covering my whole body. My heart seemed to be beating from my head.

"There are two guns?" My mouth was still open. It was stuck. I was dazed.

Alex grabbed me and held on tight. My face pressed against her shoulder. Her one arm was around my torso, her other holding my head to her body. I felt safe. I felt calm. I felt I finally had a place for my hands. I held on tight as well.

"Is he dead?" Alex asked eventually.

The gunman looked up from where he was sitting beside Jack. His two fingers pressed against his neck.

"He should be." J.P. answered. "I shot him many times, just like he said to do. Are you okay Sadie?" He asked pulling a pack of cigarette's out of his pocket and lighting one. He picked up Jack's gun.

"I am now, I think. Just like who said to? How did you get the gun away from Jefferson?"

"Away from him? No. It isn't his. It's mine. This was my duty." He pointed the gun to Jack's lifeless body. "And the boardroom." He drew in a large puff of smoke.

"Your duty?" Alex asked.

He just shrugged. "I got to go before he gets mad." He walked away pausing before the door. He covered his mouth with his hand for a moment and then scratched his head immediately after. "I couldn't let him hurt you Sadie. That was my deal."

"Deal? With who?"

But he didn't answer. He just went back inside the boardroom.

-34-

EVEN THE ANGELS HOLD THEIR BREATH SOMETIMES.

Bbriinnngg! Bbriinnngg! The phone screeched across the room. Candice, still at her desk went to answer it out of habit, then decided better of it when she saw Jefferson look up at her and shake his head no. Her face looked like it aged 12 years in the last hour - her wrinkles now seemed more prominent around her forehead and chin.

"Why did you make me do this to you?"

Jefferson was sitting on the floor next to his brother. He had come out of the boardroom minutes after J.P. returned to it. Had J.P. been told to come out and shoot Jack? Was he forced to? If so, why did he not shoot Jefferson as well? Why didn't he let us get out? It sounds like he was part of this. Was that possible? I had a hard time believing Jefferson was a part of it, let alone J.P.

Jefferson's knees were up with his elbows resting on them. His hands were crossed over each other causing the guns he was holding to just hang down towards the floor. He was talking to Jack. Jack for once, had nothing to say. He was breathless.

The phone stopped ringing.

"You had to make my life hell didn't you? All you thought of was yourself. What would make Jack happier? What would make Jack more popular? What would make Jack be Jack?" He ran his hand through his hair. He was crying. "Why couldn't you just flunk out? You didn't want this, I did. But you couldn't give it away could you?"

I couldn't help but feel a little sorry for him. He had so much desperation in his voice. I wanted to say something but I had no words. I had nothing to say that would change the situation. I was torn between my sorrow and my anger. I didn't know this Jefferson in front of me.

"I need to call my father." He got up.

"The phone won't work." I said

He spun around to look at me, as though my facial expression alone would elaborate on my last sentence.

"The cops are here." I pointed to the window. The blinds were drawn but a glimpse of blue and red flashing light snuck between two broken plastic strips. I could see the top of an ambulance, a part of the school and the side of the arboretum. Even the trees looked restless tonight.

"So? I called them. I know they are here." I gave him a quizzical look but moved on.

"That was probably them that just called. The police would have taken over all the phone lines in the residence by now and that includes cell phones. If you pick up that line, it will go directly to some negotiating officer either outside in a command center or at a nearby police station."

Alex loosened her grip on me slightly, choosing to sit at my side instead.

Jefferson's eyebrows bowed. He was thinking about what I said. He turned around and picked up the phone. He started to dial his father's number. He stopped after 5 digits, slamming down the phone.

"How the fuck do you know this?" He approached me, gun waving in my direction.

I looked up at Alex, her face asking the same question. She moved closer to me again. I looked back at Jefferson.

"Earlier this year we were working on a script involving a hostage situation. I interviewed a cop about policies and procedures and that was something he told me."

"How fortunate for me. What else do you know?"

I debated how much to say. I was worried that I would give away something that would hinder us from being rescued. I was also worried that I would be wrong about something and cause him to lose any trust he might have had in me.

"Just randomly, I know that they limit negotiations with you. If you ask for something in return for something else, they won't do it, unless you are giving up hostages in return. And they won't barge their way in unless someone is in direct danger of being shot or killed. They will give you a chance to surrender and come out peacefully."

"So, that means no helicopter and no pizza, without a person being freed, got anything helpful?"

"Well, they will give you food if you ask."

That didn't help him. I tried to think hard of something more concrete but I couldn't think of anything else. My mind was full.

Apologetically I said, "Not right now. I will tell you if I think of anything more."

The phone rang again. Jefferson stood still. He was now leaning against Candice's desk with his hip, elbow in one hand, and thumb holding his chin with the other hand. The phone stopped and then started again. After a few rings he finally picked it up and spoke.

"It's Jefferson." He paused, looked up and right with his eyes, bit his lip and then spoke again. This time in a whisper. "J.P. has a gun. He is holding us all here. He thinks that I'm on his side but I'm trying to get us out of here safely. I want to talk to my father."

I looked at Alex.

"What is he saying? Why is he blaming J.P. for all this?" I whispered.

"J.P. came in with them Sadie. He was here when they first arrived and held down the fort until they came back. Up until just minutes ago, I thought that this *was* J.P.'s heist."

"That doesn't make sense!"

"None of this does kid."

"I want to talk to my father." Jefferson repeated. "J.P. is making me talk to you guys. No I can't get him. He won't come on."

He was quiet.

"I want to talk to my father now." He waited. "Of course, he is not around. Does he know that Jack is here too? That should make him come."

He paused and looked around. He looked at his brother and then at the doors of the rooms where other hostages were.

"They are all still alive. I will see if he will let you. Now? No, you cannot talk to any of them. Give me some time." He hung the phone up.

"Shit!" He rubbed his hands through his hair. He did this often. A nervous twitch I guessed. Jefferson went into the Resident Manager's office.

"Who is all in here?" I whispered to Alex.

"Most of the committee members. Rodney, Julie, Reggie, Martin, Elizabeth, us." She motioned to me, Candice, and herself. "Trent and Cathy got called to an emergency security meeting so they have not arrived yet. But Sadie, Lonny is in here too. He's in the supply room. He was in there when I came in to do the copying. They must have put him in the supply room earlier. Sadie, they stabbed him. I was in there with him trying to help when Jack pulled me out to see you."

"Is he alright?" I was afraid of the answer. I looked at her shirt and made the connection. "Oh, please tell me he isn't dead." I started crying.

"Hurt but okay. I gave him some blankets from the shelves and he is holding them tight to his wound to try to stop the bleeding. He needs a doctor. They stabbed him in the stomach but to the side. He should be okay."

I wanted to see him. To know he was okay. I knew it was impossible right now. But I didn't want him to be next to Jack on the floor. "Who did it?"

"J.P."

"J.P? Why?"

"I don't know." She admitted.

"I don't understand this at all."

She just shrugged in response. She couldn't have understood either.

"How are we going to get out of this Alex?"

She put her head back against the wall and took a deep breath. "Not sure how. But we will." She smiled at me for assurance. I smiled back, not sure either of us really felt the confidence we were trying to portray.

"I think I am going to faint." Candice was looking very ill. Her voice was meek and hoarse. Alex got up and assisted Candice off her chair and onto the floor.

"Don't worry we'll get out of this. Just hang in there, okay. Do you have any candies or drinks in your desk? Something with a little sugar?" She was whispering.

Candice pointed her to the drawer with all the snacks in it. Alex set her up with a Cola and a sponge toffee bar.

"This should help with the fainting feeling."

"I am not sure she is going to make it. She looks terrible." Alex whispered to me when she returned to my side. "I am worried about her."

"Me too."

The phone began to ring again. Jefferson came out of the office and answered it. He looked sad and confused at the same time.

His expression reminded me of a boy I once knew named Cole who lived across from us. I remember, when we were around seven years old, both of his parents were killed in a car accident. His

Grandmother, who was quite close to the boy, came to live in his house with him. I recall my parents saying that it was a blessing because then he wouldn't lose his friends, his house, his schooling, or anything else familiar, along with his parents. Anyways, I remember weeks later we returned to school. The first day, when the bell rang, I had clean-up to do in the classroom so I left late. When I did leave, he was standing outside on the corner, just off of the school grounds. He was standing motionless just staring down the street. I asked him what was wrong and he answered by telling me that he didn't remember which way was his home. In full silence, I walked him the 3 blocks home. He just kept staring. The look on his face was one I never saw on another human until today. It was a look of complete uncertainty and loss.

"Did you get my father? Well, work harder please. I am begging you. No, I won't let you talk to anyone. You can't talk to him. Fine! Fine, I will talk to him again." He hung up the phone. "Fucking pricks. J.P., get your ass out here." He looked at Alex and I. "And you both and that bitch behind me, better follow my lead and do as I say or I will shoot you all right now. Got it?"

We got it.

-35-

IT'S TIME TO LEAVE THE ROOM AND THE MEMORIES BEHIND.

"What do you mean you told them it was me? This isn't my show, it is yours. Did you tell them that I shot Jack too or that I stabbed the kid?"

"Well you did stab the kid."

"Not the point."

"I didn't tell them anyone was hurt. I don't plan on it."

"So what did you say?"

"I said that you were holding us hostage. That you trusted me and that I was going to help get you out of here."

"I can't believe this." J.P. started to pace. "How did I get into this?" He seemed to be asking himself. "Why the hell did you blame me?"

"Hey, you were with us on this. You were just as much a part of this as we were. You said you would help. Buddy, I need you to bail me out here now. I need your help. Come on, you're one of the guys. We watch each other's back."

He stopped pacing. "And who is going to have my back?"

"We are. We will tell the cops that Jack was in on this with you. That he stabbed the kid and then shot himself because he couldn't handle the pressure. The girls will back up the story, won't you?" He pointed towards us. J.P. looked over.

"Yes." Alex answered. They looked at me and waited for my response. I didn't want to give one. I wanted to tell them that the kid had a name but I didn't want to tell them that I would back up their story. Alex nudged me in the side. She obviously wanted me to say so.

"Yes." I said to appease her nudge.

"I don't know about this." J.P. said. "What would my mother think?"

The phone started to ring.

"Well you don't have much time to think about it. That is the cops and they want to talk to you. All you have to do is talk to them briefly and then say that you would only talk through me. Then pass me the phone." He seemed really confident until he asked me if I agreed.

"That might work."

His looked hardened. Clearly that was not the response he wanted. I tried again.

"It should work for sure. Especially after we corroborate the story when this is over. You will just have to work hard at convincing them that J.P. won't talk and that they will have to go through you and you only, Jefferson. But you both can do that. You're good with words."

J.P. looked at me and gave me a trusting nod. I momentarily felt bad for lying to him but that quickly vanished when I remembered that he was the one who stabbed Lonny. I needed to get to Lonny to see if he was alright. I had to figure something out. It broke my heart to know he was fifteen feet away possibly bleeding to death.

"This is J.P." He answered the phone. Not wanting to speak but forcing it out anyway. "Everyone is fine. Yes. I want you to speak to Jefferson. I don't like the phone." He put his hand over the mouth piece and whispered to Jefferson. "What do I say?"

"Say that I will speak and if they want you to keep me alive then they will talk through me. Otherwise you will keep putting people on the phone until you find someone they will talk to."

"I can't say that." J.P. replied.

"You have to. It is our only way out of this."

"I will just never be able to say it in a way that they would believe." He was starting to be louder than a whisper.

"Give me the phone you idiot. I will deal with this. Give me your weapon and go back into the boardroom." He obliged.

"This is Jefferson again. J.P. said he was done with the phone. Well, he won't speak. Please talk to me. He said that if I can't convince you to deal with me, he will kill me. He said he will keep trying other people until you find someone you will talk to. Okay?"

He hung up. "The police said they would call me back. Does that make sense?"

"I don't know. I only had a few minutes for my interview. I am not an expert. Sorry."

"You may be sorry."

He walked behind Candice's desk and reached into her drawer and grabbed a candy bar. "Thanks for the snack gorgeous." He got up and went into the boardroom.

"You should go to the boardroom. It is probably safer there. Especially now that J.P. has no weapon." I said to Alex. Her breath seemed a little shallow.

"Or not." She looked at me. "We don't know what is happening."

"You have to be safer in there than you would be out here with me."

"Okay, mama bird, thanks but I doubt that."

"I am serious. You are safer away from me. Believe me, that is my track record." I put my head down. I was feeling sorry for myself again and I knew it. But I was okay with it. I needed to protect her. I couldn't protect my mother, or Lonny, or my father from what I did to them. But I could protect her.

"Again, what happened with your Mother was not your fault. I am one hundred percent certain of that. But let's say for some odd reason it was, that you did kill her, one time does not count as a track record."

I smiled out of the corner of my mouth. "How doesn't it? That makes it one for one, one murder for one mother. Listen, I am okay with what I have done. I have accepted my past and who I have become because of it. Besides, it is not like you have any ties to me, really. We are friends but nothing that is worth dying for. You can leave at any time. That's the way life is. We show up for the party and if we are smart, we leave before the dance."

"Well that's encouraging." She didn't budge. I tried again.

"I'm serious."

"I don't doubt you are."

"Just go then would you?"

"This brave act is not becoming of you."

"Whatever!" She was upsetting me now.

"Is some old leftover teenage angst coming to surface?"

"What is your problem? Why so sarcastic?"

"What do you want me to say, Sadie? Okay, I will leave? Not going to happen, love."

"Please don't stay out of obligation. Maybe I don't want you with me. Maybe I don't like you."

"First of all, like I told you before, the opposite of love is not hate or dislike, it is apathy or indifference. As long as you are arguing with me, claiming to dislike me, I know you care."

"Maybe I don't care."

"Wow, you are just all over the map aren't you? You're not even making sense anymore." She turned to look me straight in the eyes. She put one hand on my shoulder. "I am staying here beside you because I care. Just like you let that fucking creep touch you and not me, because you care. Like I just sat and watched so he wouldn't hurt you more, because I care. Like I am sitting here and arguing with you now because I care. And like you're sitting here trying to push me away, because you care. Don't you get it, we care."

"I don't care." I murmured.

"Fine!" Alex stood up and walked towards the boardroom. "Then I will tell them I am next.

"Next for what?" My heart began to race.

"I don't know. Next to fight them. Next to have sex with them. Hell, maybe I will say that I will not go along with this farce of theirs and that they might as well kill me next. That's what you want isn't it?"

"That's not what I want at all. I want you safe."

"But you don't care right?" She moved close to the door. I was worried that they would open it and find her standing there.

"Stop! I want you away, not hurt. You should have some more respect for yourself. Why wouldn't you want yourself safe?"

"I do. I want both of us safe." She walked back over to me and sat down. "People who care stay together and fight together. They are stronger that way. We are not better off apart my dear, we are better together."

"You sound like my father."

"Hmmm. Not sure how I feel about that." She smiled.

I had no more argument left in me. I didn't want her in another room but I didn't want her dead. I was not sure what would be the best for either of us anymore.

"I just want you safe. I don't want to hurt you like I hurt my mother. She was in the room with me fighting for her life and I just stood and watched. I didn't protect her but I can protect you."

"Sadie, I know you idolized her but she didn't fight. You were not the only one who froze."

"But I could only control myself."

"It has been six years Sadie. Let yourself out of her room."

"What?"

"Let yourself out of her room. It is over, it is done. Stop living it over and over again. It is okay that you survived and you are not destined to repeat it. This is a different time and a different place. We'll be okay. You have not frozen mentally yet and you won't. And it isn't your job to protect everyone you love." The phone started ringing again. It rang three times and then stopped. There was a phone in the boardroom. He probably picked it up there. "I've learned a long time ago that family isn't blood, it is love. You are my family Sadie, I am not going anywhere. Even if you say you hate me or you physically try to remove me. I am not moving from your side. I love you."

I went to hug her but I was stopped by the boardroom door opening again. Jefferson came out and sat in front of us.

"Are you hungry? We are going to see if they will bring in food."

"No thanks." I replied.

"Yes, get us both some." I looked up at her. She convincingly nodded her head yes so I left it alone.

"Good choice. We could order pizza, burgers, or Chinese, it is up to you. After all it is your last meal."

"Pardon me?" Alex asked. I could feel my eye lids receding into my head.

"Your last meal. You know the food you eat before I have to shoot you."

"Why would you shoot us? You need us? Don't you?" It was my turn to ask questions now.

"For now but not once I am on my way out of here. I can't take the risk that once we are out and two or three months or a year has passed, that you won't decide to tell them what really happened."

"Believe me I am the queen of hiding killer's identities." I mumbled.

"What?"

"Never mind, besides they wouldn't believe me that many months later." I wasn't helping, I knew it. I just couldn't stop my mouth from moving.

"How do I know that you are going to even back me up in the first place?"

"You can trust..."

He interrupted me. "Nah, don't go there. And don't make me shoot you now. At least live out your last few hours. And believe me there is nothing you can say to change my mind. You are going to die tonight ladies. Sorry! Oh and remember, if either of you leave while I am in there, I will shoot everyone in the boardroom dead. Just so you could live with the guilt." And with that, he got up and went back into the boardroom to order our last meal. Making the decision himself on what it would be.

-36-

HAVE SOME WHINE WITH YOUR BURGER?

The burger wasn't going down well but it tasted better on my tongue than the gun did. Jefferson ate dinner in the main room with Alex, Candice and I. Candice seemed to be recovering more now that she had some real food in her stomach. Alex had explained to me that she thought we should get some food and eat it to help with our strength. That was why she said yes and not 'no' like I wanted to. It made sense to me to eat now that I knew he was planning on killing us. We needed to fight or die trying. It was just really hard to eat with my cheek bone as sore as it was. My eye was still swollen and sore, my cheek bone hot and aching and my jaw, stiff and bruised. Not to mention the pain I was getting in my teeth as I chewed. But I guess it was better to be in pain than to be what my future fate was. Pain meant I was still alive.

"What does J.P. think about your plan to kill us?" Alex asked once Jefferson was nicely settled into his spot, eating his second burger.

"He doesn't know."

"How come?"

"Because he will die as well and if he knew that than he wouldn't be helping me now."

"What makes you think that we won't tell him?"

"Because you don't want to die now. If you tell him then I would have to kill you all now."

"Well if we are going to die anyway?" I added.

"Yes. But as long as you are dead then you have no ability to fight. Keep yourself alive and you will always have a chance. I know the way you think ladies. You're fighters, not passive players. Besides I said I was going to kill you three. I said nothing of the people in there. You talk, I kill them too."

He was right. We didn't want to die and the more time we had the more we could think of ways to get out of this mess.

"I want to see Lonny. I want to make sure he is okay."

"He's fine."

"I want to see him."

"That's right. He's your boyfriend isn't he?"

"Not exactly. But I care about him very much."

"Young love. Got to love it. Maybe when we are done, I will let you see him. For a moment."

"Thank you." I didn't expect his answer but I took it. I wanted to be near Lonny, to know he was alive and okay. It would have been almost 3 hours now since he had been stabbed. That is a lot of blood loss.

"What was the plan?" Alex continued with her questions.

"What plan do you mean?"

"The one you were talking about with Jack."

"Don't say his name." He looked straight at us. "I don't want to hear it off of your lips."

"Okay." She backed off quickly. I had a feeling she was looking to gain something through all of this questioning but I don't know what.

He started eating some of his fries. Three or four strings at a time.

"The plan was to get in here, hold everyone for a couple of hours and then leave. Jack would just get a slap on the wrist thanks to father's lawyers and I would get off." He ended there.

"I don't get it. How does that benefit you? How would you only get a slap on the wrist?"

"He kept eating.

"Is this because of your father's business that you want and that Ja…your brother didn't?" I remembered him talking to me about this when we were talking about law school.

"Yes. He didn't want to be a chef, I do. My father; however, wants his first born to follow him not his second. It's the way. You know? Jack didn't want it. I tried to convince him to drop out or say no to father. He wouldn't. He was afraid that if he said no to father that he would get completely cut off of the money, cars, everything. And that is what Jack is…or was all about. The money and the possessions."

We nodded to show we agreed. He continued.

"He needed to find a way out without father knowing that he wanted out. But he never came up with a plan. Too lazy to sit down and think of something. Once I started College here I brought it back up with him and he told me that he was just going to go with the flow. That he had given up. He was going to give in to his destiny as a chef and that was that. I told him that I wanted to be a chef and we agreed that father only wanted one of us."

"So that is when you hatched this plan?"

"Nope. We didn't, as you say, hatch any plan. The selfish bastard just laughed and said that I would have to get over it. I would have to succumb to my destiny as a corporate pig dog just as he would succumb to a culinary career."

"Wow. That must have hurt?"

"Don't shrink me?"

"I am not shrinking you. I am just talking with you. I meant that your brother pretty much ignored your feelings and your troubles. He was not willing to give you something he had and didn't want. That must have pissed you off."

"It did. What is it to you?"

"Well, I want to know. We are going to die anyway so why can't I learn how this fate of mine came to be? What would it hurt you?" I asked.

He scrunched up his wrapper for his second burger. Grabbed his cup and drew in soda from the straw.

"Okay. Fine! I'll tell you." He opened the lid to his now empty drink and stuffed the crumpled wrapper and the fry container into it. He pushed them to the side and stretched out his legs. "I tried to take care of it myself. If he wasn't going to quit school, then I was going to have him flunk."

"So you sabotaged his schooling?" Alex asked.

"Sort of. I sabotaged his school year. I took control of everything. I controlled his friends - his girlfriend - and I use that term loosely. I even controlled his activities and his rebellious ways. I caused a problem, he got the blame."

"What did you do?"

"I did it all. I controlled you both as well."

"Give me examples." Alex probed.

"Just think of all the stuff you blamed Jack for this year."

"What happened with Julie?"

"Sure, for starters. That was me. I got her to go in that room and set it all up. Right down to the picture. The little bitch almost screwed it up on me with the sash talk though."

"You paid Julie to drop the charges didn't you? You set that up to happen and then you paid her to make it go away so that you wouldn't get caught in the middle of it?" I added. He just smiled.

"Did you control his girlfriend Bridgette as well?"

"You mean my girlfriend?"

"No his."

"Right, mine."

"Bridgette is your girlfriend?" I clued in.

"That is what I said, isn't it. She and I have been dating two years now. She was helping me with my brother. It only cost me a ton in jewellery and clothes. And, of course, a lot of promises for the future."

"I can't believe this." I said almost to myself.

"So Bridgette was in on this all? But she was hurt at the beginning of the year. Sadie, you saw her, you did CPR on her." Alex asked through clenched teeth.

"I did, and she was out like a light."

"Yes, that was an accident. Thanks for saving her by the way. She took more than she was supposed to. The idea was to put it in your heads that he had access to drugs for a later use."

"Well, it worked. We did think that."

"I can't believe she almost died for your cause."

"Well, she almost died and you didn't kick him out."

"I couldn't. I had no proof that it was him. Besides, your aunt was a thorn in my side anytime I tried to do anything to reprimand him."

"She was a pain in my side as well. When that didn't work and when the incident with Julie didn't work, then I had to plant the drugs."

I felt a thousand light bulbs going off in my head at once. "You came to his room with me. You got him to get you to come represent him. There were no drugs in his room were there? You brought them with you didn't you?"

"I lucked out with my brother trusting me. They were in my pocket. That was an easier plant than I thought it would be. Man, you were a joke. You were so angry and so convinced that he was a complete ass that you could only see what I allowed you to see."

I felt horrible. I looked over at Jack's body. I couldn't help but wonder how much I contributed to his death.

Seeing my remorse Jefferson added, "don't feel too bad Sadie, in the end, he did force you to have sex with a gun."

I didn't know how to respond. I felt a cold shiver run through my body.

"I really liked you Jefferson."

"Liked? As in no longer like?"

"You are going to kill me. That tends to dampen things."

"I guess." He conceded. He was quiet. Almost the Jefferson that I thought I knew.

"Can I see Lonny now?"

"No more questions?"

"I have a few still," said Alex.

"I want to see Lonny."

"Give me a minute. I want to know the idea behind this, behind J.P."

"We were going to come in here and hold hostages, as I said before. Leave after a few hours and blame it all on J.P."

"And J.P. would willingly take the blame?"

"He wouldn't have to. We were going to kill him before it was over. Tell them that we had to do it to save everyone. Make it look like that to you as well. Like he talked us into coming in here and when we realized his plan we stopped him. We would be the heroes."

"Of course, he never knew your real plan did he?"

"Would you go through with a plan if you knew your partners were going to kill you off in the end?"

Alex shook her head.

"He became one of us. He trusted us. That simple minded fool. We even convinced him to stab Lonny. That was part one of our plan. Until my brother fucked it up."

That reminded me. "Can I go now? Can I see Lonny?"

"If you can get there yourself. He is in the supply room."

"I want Alex to come with me." She started to move forward with me.

"No. She stays." I turned to look at her.

"Why can't she come?"

"She stays. Choose! You stay with her or you go to see him."

"What does that mean choose? If I leave what are you going to do to her?"

"Choose!"

I didn't know what to do. I felt I was choosing between two lives - two lives I cared about. I wanted to see if Lonny was okay but I didn't want Alex to pay for it.

"Go Sadie. Go see Lonny. I am okay. You don't need to choose."

"Okay. Don't choose. Live with the consequences." Jefferson taunted.

"This isn't fair. You said I could see him."

"I still do say that."

My chest felt heavy. I couldn't breath. I started to gasp for air. I needed air. I needed a window. My shirt was too tight. I pulled on it but it didn't loosen. It didn't give me more air. "Alex, *humph!* I can't *humph!* breathe. I can't get any *humph!* air." I started to cry.

"What do you mean?" She looked frightened.

"I don't *humph!* know. I think *humph!* I am having *humph!* a heart attack *humph!* or something. *humph!* It hurts, and I *humph!* can't get any *humph!* air. Do *humph!* you feel that *humph!*?"

She abruptly grabbed my shoulders and laid me onto the floor putting her face inches from mine. "You can breathe, you're okay. You're not having a heart attack." She looked deep into my eyes. "Just breathe. Are you in any pain?"

"What's going on?" Jefferson asked.

"I don't know. I am trying to figure that out," Alex responded.

"No pain, I *humph!* don't think. *humph!* I don't *humph!* know. Maybe *humph!* I do. My chest *humph!* hurts. *humph!* It's heavy. My *humph!* hands and face are feeling *humph!* numb."

"Calm her down." Jefferson yelled. "Calm her down now! She's freaking me out." He stood up and started pacing.

"I am *humph!* scared Alex. I *humph!* can't *humph!* breathe. Did he *humph!* poison me? *humph!* Am I dying *humph!*?

Alex kept her hands on my shoulders but looked up at Jefferson as though looking for answers to what was going on.

"I did nothing to her. I didn't!" He was still walking back and forth, biting his nails with great force and little care. "Shut that bitch up or I will kill her now."

"Give me a moment Jefferson, please." Alex brought her attention back to me. Did she find an answer? He said nothing. "You're okay. You won't stop breathing. You won't. If you stop breathing, if you *ever* stop breathing, I will breathe for you. I will put every breath into you, for as long as you need it, I promise. So relax. Just relax."

I looked into her eyes. She was focused. I believed her. She wouldn't let me stop breathing.

"You need to take some deep breaths. Sadie. It is very important. It will help you feel better." Alex said to me. I no longer worried about what Jefferson was doing. I was only seeing her. She was softly rubbing the corner of my forehead along my hairline. She reminded me of my mother. My mother would do that often to relax me for sleep. I felt comforted; safe.

I took some breaths. Deeper and deeper. I was starting to get some more air in my lungs. My heart beat slowed down slightly. Alex talked me through it for another few minutes.

"How are you doing?"

"Better." I said with less trouble speaking than before. "The chest pain is gone. My fingers are still numb."

"Good. The fingers will come the more you breathe." She smiled. Still calm and focused. I was calmer as well.

"What the hell was that?" Jefferson asked still yelling and pacing.

"She is having...er...had a panic attack. You gave her an impossible choice and she panicked. Anyone would." She looked back at me. "It's okay. You're okay."

I took a few more deep breaths. I closed my eyes to try to stop the tears from falling. I failed miserably. For many moments I stayed there, breathing, crying, and listening to Alex hum. She was still rubbing my head, only stopping the odd time to wipe away a stream of tears before they hit my ear. In that moment I decided.

"If I have to choose, I stay here. I won't go see Lonny." I directed my statement at Jefferson. But it was Alex that responded.

"You can't do that Sadie; you need to go see if he is alright."

"He may be dead. You are alive. You told me earlier that I need to leave the room. Metaphorically leave my mother's room. Well, I can't do that if I don't learn any lessons from what happened in that room. I am not leaving you like I left her. I won't leave a friend. I won't leave someone I care about. We see Lonny together or not at all. He will be okay. He's a fighter." I wiped the last of the tears from my eyes. "You're alive and I love you. I'll stay here with you."

"Are you sure about this?" Jefferson asked.

"Positive." I sat up and gave Alex a hug.

Jefferson stopped his pacing. He walked over to his brother. He stood looking over him for several seconds and then kicked Jack's right leg. "Go ahead. Go check on him."

"I already told you my choice."

"I mean both of you. Go."

"Are you sure?"

"Don't give me a chance to change my mind."

We didn't. We went towards the supply room. Alex opened the door. I butt crawled my way into the room. Lonny was on the floor, sitting against the wall. He had a blanket pressed against his side. "Lonny, are you okay?" He didn't' answer.

Alex walked over to him and gently lifted his head off the wall. His head rolled into her arms. "Lonny," she called. He didn't answer. She lightly slapped his cheeks then checked his throat for a pulse.

I felt tears welling up again. "He's dead isn't he?"

She turned and looked at me with sad eyes. "I can't find a pulse anywhere, Sadie. I am sorry."

LOSS COMES IN ALL FORMS...ESPECIALLY IN THE SHAPE OF A BROKEN HEART.

"He's dead?"

"Let me check again." She pulled him up so he was lying in her arms. His head fell back exposing his neck. She took her right hand and placed it on the left side of his neck. She stayed still for several seconds. She turned and looked at me. "He's alive. I have a pulse. It's weak, but it is there."

I breathed for the first time since I went into the supply room. I crawled myself over to him. He looked awful. He was white. What parts of him that weren't white, were red. He was covered in blood. His blood.

I put my hand on his face. I rubbed his cheeks with my hands. I pushed his hair back. He was still lying in Alex's arms.

"Lonny, wake up."

"Alex put her hand on my shoulder. "It might be best if he doesn't wake up. I am no doctor but if he is awake, he will feel the pain."

"Yes but he will also be able to put pressure on his wound if he is awake."

"Good point. But I think this one is out of our hands. He will wake up or stay out without our opinion no matter what kid."

"I am still angry with him but I love him. He is my best friend. I want him safe. I want him okay. I want him to know that."

"I know you do." She pushed my hair away from my face. "You can be angry with those you love, remember the opposite of love…"

"Is not hate, I remember. You say it enough." I interrupted with a slight smile.

I grabbed the blanket and found a dry spot. I moved his shirt and pressed the blanket onto his wound. It was still bleeding, not heavily but it was still flowing. It didn't seem like the cut was too far into his body. It was really far to the side. I wondered what organs it may have hit. I couldn't remember what was there on the left side.

"Is Romeo alive?" Jefferson was in the doorway. He was leaning against the frame.

"Barely. He needs to have someone press the blanket to his cut or he will bleed to death." Alex informed him.

"That's a shame."

"Jefferson, please. I don't want him to die."

"You're going to. Someone has to go first."

"Can we stay in here or let him come out with us? I want to make sure that…" I realized that saying the word death here was not going to have an effect of Jefferson. "That he stays comfortable until he passes." I barely spoke the words.

"I could shoot him. That's how they put animals out of their misery."

I looked at Alex. Her eyes got bigger and she shook her head no. She knew I was about to yell my head off.

"I want you both out here. He stays inside. I don't need another distraction."

"I can't leave him." The phone started ringing in the other room.

"Are we really going to go through this again? Another choice? Because we are going to need an oxygen tank brought in if we do. He is staying, you girls are coming. You made your choice, live with it. You have two minutes. I need to answer that."

"I am sorry Sadie." Alex whispered.

I started rubbing his face again. I wasn't sure if he could feel me or not. "I am sorry Lonny. I am sorry I didn't forgive you. I am sorry I didn't give you more time to work out what you needed to work out. I had this idea of a knight with a white horse and metal armour, coming to sweep me off my feet. Someone with no other cares for anyone else. I wanted a fairly tale romance. I still do. And it isn't you who can give it to me. I should have seen that and moved on. We could have worked through it and stayed friends. I didn't fight for you. I fought against you. Now, I would do anything to have you back again. For you to tell me that we will be able to figure this out and be friends. I will take that and forget the rest if you would just wake up and make this go away. Please Lonny. Make this go away." I slapped his chest. I cried. I cried loud and hard.

"Quiet Sadie. Don't make him come back in here."

"Make this go away. Make this not happen, Alex, please." I begged her.

"I would if I could, love." She cried with me. "I would fix," she paused to take some breaths in. "I would fix it all if I could."

I put my head on Lonny's chest. I could hear his heart beating. I didn't want to leave. I didn't want this to be the last time I heard his heart beat. I needed to hear it.

"Don't you dare leave me Lonny. Not now. I will forgive you all your mistakes and you will forgive me and we will work it all out. We will. You got that?"

"Come on Sadie, we have to go. Let's get him comfortable. We should lay him down in a way that helps the blanket put pressure on his gash."

We manoeuvred him into a position that would do just that. I rubbed his head and kissed his face. "I don't want to leave him."

"I know. You can stay if you want to. I mean, what is he going to do, kill you? He is planning that anyway."

"Comforting."

"If you want I will stay with you as well." Alex offered.

"So we can what, all die together? He isn't my Romeo you know. Well, at least I am no Juliet. I won't stab myself in hopes of living with him forever. That isn't how we work. I don't want him to die but I won't go down with him if it is already too late. I appreciate that you would stay. But this isn't over. We are not going to die."

"No."

"No. We will get out of this. We will not let him win."

I heard Jefferson hang up the phone and call for J.P. He came out of the boardroom like an obedient puppy and went running towards Jefferson.

"That's it."

"What's it?"

"I need to get J.P. on our side." I decided.

"Do you think he will help? What do you have in mind?"

"I don't have anything in mind yet. But I know that J.P. will help us. At least I hope he will. He shot Jack for me right? I know that he will help."

"Are you sure? We didn't think he would be a part of this but he is."

"I just have a feeling about him. I need to talk to him."

"Then let's make a plan. But we have to start by getting out of the supply room before he freaks out. Let's go."

I turned around and looked at Lonny one last time. I kissed him again. "Don't you..." I couldn't say it. Not right now. "Don't you do anything I wouldn't want you to do. I love you." I touched his lips with my finger.

Alex grabbed my arm. "Come on. We have to go."

"Good-bye Lonny." I squeezed his hands.

-38-

FIGHT OR FLIGHT.

We were back in the main room. Jefferson and J.P. were talking in the corner between the boardroom and supply room. Candice was in her usual place on the floor. We quietly moved to our previous area by the copiers.

"Have you thought of your plan yet?" Alex asked.

"No. But I am missing something. I know it. I just can't figure out what. We can do this, I know it. I just need to think."

"Well, I am game for whatever you come up with because I have nothing."

The guys came over to Candice's desk again. Jefferson picked up the phone. "He said he would let two people go. Give us twenty minutes and we will send them out of the door." He hung up the phone. He looked at J.P., "Go get Elizabeth."

I forgot all about Elizabeth being there. I turned to Alex. She seemed to be reading my thoughts. "It's okay. I forgot too."

She should have been okay in there.

I felt bad that I had forgotten about her. I cared about her a lot and I didn't even remember she was in the boardroom. J.P. went to go to get her.

"You! You are going too." He pointed to Alex.

"No I am not." She said confidently.

I looked at her. "What are you doing?"

"I certainly am not leaving." She was adamant.

"He's letting you go. Go." I said, torn between wanting her to leave and wanting her to stay with me.

"I am not leaving unless Sadie comes with me." She said to Jefferson.

"She is not leaving. My brother had an obsession with her for some reason. She is staying."

"And so am I."

"That isn't your say." He growled. "Besides I am giving you a chance to live. Take it!"

The door opened up and J.P. came out with Elizabeth. She

Where the stream and creek collide

looked rough. Her hair was a mess, her clothes dishevelled and her expression was that of fear.

"Are you guys okay?" She asked.

"No talking." Jefferson shouted. I nodded in response to her anyway. "Now you, let's go." He pointed to Alex.

"I am not going. You would need to kill me if you wanted me to leave this room without Sadie."

"Alex!"

"Take Candice. She needs to get out of here." Alex offered.

"That isn't your say." He repeated as he walked towards us. He grabbed Alex by the hair. "I said you are leaving."

"Please. I want to stay. I will do anything you want. Anything."

He stared at her. The glare lasted a long time. When it finally broke, he threw her to the floor. "Candice, it is your lucky day girl. You get to leave this joint."

Minutes later the two women were hurled out of the office door and into the residence hall. J.P. was the one at the door with the gun to shove them out. Jefferson was good at making J.P. look guilty. Although, he did just let Candice go - who knew the whole truth about what was happening inside the boardroom. She was after all, in the room when Alex asked Jefferson all of the questions.

I was very happy to see Elizabeth leave the room. And greedily I was happy to see Alex stay.

"Now you," Jefferson pointed to Alex. "Now it's time to cash in. You said you would do anything to stay."

"Yes."

"That's fine. I want you to shoot your friend here."

"You want me to what?"

"You heard me. I want you to kill her. It won't be me, it will be you."

Alex looked at me horrified. On her knee's she moved into the few feet of space that was between me and Jefferson. She grabbed my hand. "I will not shoot her. I will not kill Sadie. That's absurd."

"That's anything. And anything was our deal."

"That I won't do."

I had to think of something. This was getting too much. I needed to fix this. I needed to end it. I needed to keep us alive. I was blank.

"You will. It was a deal." Jefferson said rather calmly. And don't think about saying yes and them trying to turn the gun on me, it won't work. I would shoot you first and Sadie would watch it all."

"Listen, I know that you don't want them to know that you are in

289

here controlling things but to get me to kill her, that won't get you off the hook."

"That's not it. They already know that I am in charge here. They said they figured it out last phone call. Said that they are able to see through the walls with some infrared technology. I don't know. They gave me some things we did, places we were sitting and standing. They also said they could hear through the walls. The cop gave me some lines that I had said. They were bang on."

Now I understood why he didn't care that Candice was leaving.

"I will not shoot her."

"Do you see this boys? Better come quick. The hostages will be killing each other soon." Jefferson said to the walls. "They are probably listening too."

Was he on a suicide mission? He came over and grabbed Alex by the hair again. This time he pulled her away from where she sat. He threw her into the corner and kicked her in the stomach.

"Stop it!" I cried. "J.P! Stop this please." I begged him the best I could. He looked like he wanted to assist me but he didn't budge.

"You stupid bitch, you think you can just make your own rules don't you?" He slapped Alex in the face before he grabbed her by the hair again and screamed into her face. "You ruin everything." He started slapping her more. Her nose started to bleed. I had to think of something. I had nothing left to lose. His back was to me but J.P.'s wasn't. He was to the right where he could turn his head in my direction.

"J.P. Jefferson is going to kill you when this is done. He always was going to. You were just his pawn. You were the one that could take all the blame. He told us this."

"You know that isn't true." Jefferson yelled to J.P. He was listening to us talk. I didn't care. It stopped him from hitting Alex. "You are my friend, I wouldn't do that."

"Yes he would. He said that he was going to hold everyone here for a few hours and then shoot you so he looked like the hero. You were always going to die. Don't let him win. Don't let him kill us, you, or any one else."

Jefferson got up from kneeling. He walked over to me very slowly. "You shut up. You said enough. You don't know what you are talking about."

"If I am not telling the truth, how come you are getting so upset? J.P. why is he getting so upset?" I felt his boot hit my mouth. I tasted blood. Jefferson only kicked once.

He turned towards J.P. "You know she is blowing smoke out of her ass right? You know that I would never do that to you, right, buddy?"

"I know." He answered. "I know you wouldn't do that."

Damn it. Jefferson just smiled at me and went back to Alex who was still on the floor in pain. She was holding her stomach. He kicked her again in the same area.

"Stop it!" I couldn't yell anything else. I didn't know what else to say. I wiped the blood from my lips. I need this over. It was too much. With what happened with Jack, Jefferson hurting Alex, and Lonny being stabbed...

Lonny was stabbed! That was it! The knife!

That was what was missing in this puzzle. The knife had not been around since before Jack died. What did that mean? It had to be somewhere. Did he leave it in the boardroom? Someone would have used it. Did Jefferson or J.P. have it? I was sure if they did they would have shown it over the last few hours for some reason. It had to be on him. It had to be still with Jack. I looked over at his body. He was only two feet from me. Jefferson was busy yelling in Alex's face again, his back still to me. I pushed myself over to Jack. I checked his waist band on his pants. There was nothing. I checked his shirt pocket, again I came up empty. Where was it?

"Are you ready yet bitch?" Jefferson yelled.

"No." Alex said through a mouth full of blood.

Jefferson asked J.P. for a cigarette. He handed Jefferson a lit one and then lit one for himself. Jefferson put the smoke in his mouth. He tightened his grip on Alex's hair. He took a deep breath of smoke in - coughing on the exhale. When he settled the coughing he pulled Alex's head back and pressed the lit end of the cigarette to her chest. She screamed in pain.

"Stop that!" I yelled. "You said you would not hurt me. You promised. How can you think that this isn't hurting me? There is nothing you could do to me that would hurt me more, than what this is doing now." I cried to J.P. He continued to stay where he was. "Why are you only responding to Jefferson?"

He still didn't respond and when I heard another scream from Jefferson putting the cigarette back to Alex's chest, I realized I needed to get back to my task at hand. I looked back at Jack. I checked in his shoes. No luck. I pulled down his socks. The knife was there. It was nicely tucked into his right leg. I pulled it out. J.P. saw me. I put my finger up to my lips to ask him to stay quiet. He still didn't move.

I pushed over towards Jefferson. I wasn't sure how I would reach him or how I could stop him. I just knew I was not going to do it from over here.

"You are trash you know that right?"

I tucked the knife into my sock. "Leave her alone." I scooted my butt across the floor. "Take me instead. Leave her alone."

"I see patterns developing here with you two."

I looked at Alex. She was trying hard to stay alert. Her face was full of blood from her nose and mouth. Her neck and chest stained red with burns.

"Stop, please."

"I will stop when she agrees to shoot you."

"Never." She whispered through the bloody mess and another cigarette burn. He threw the smoke to the floor after it went out on the last press to her skin.

He leaned over and pushed his hand to my forehead, knocking me down. He twisted back and reached to put his hands around Alex's neck. "Then you can die watching Sadie's face. Seeing her torment over having to watch you get murdered - knowing she was the cause."

She squirmed under his hands to get away. Trying to kick him with her feet. She kept missing him.

"You son of a bitch." I yelled. "I will kill you first." I reached the knife out of my sock and I lifted it up. He saw it, let one hand off of Alex's neck and turned to me. The move left him wide open. I jabbed the knife straight into his stomach. It went in like a thermometer to a cooking turkey. I pushed it and pushed it until it wouldn't go any further. I let it go. He gasped hard. Jefferson sat up straight, letting go of Alex's neck completely. He grabbed onto the knife handle. Closing his eyes he made a wincing face then opened them and glared at me. His eyes were wide and evil. He took another gasp and pulled the knife from his chest, lifted it high above his head and aimed it at me.

"Sadie, move!" Alex called out.

But I didn't need to. He didn't get a chance to stab me. As soon as he lifted the knife in my direction J.P. shot him dead. Jefferson fell forward, flat onto his face just inches away from me.

I took one look at the back of his head and then climbed over him as fast as I could. I reached Alex and wiped the blood from her face with my sleeve. "Are you okay?"

"I am now. It's over Sadie. We did it. You did it. It's over."

J.P. came over to where we were. "I am sorry. Don't hate me. I am sorry."

"We know," I replied. But I was mad. I did hate him. I was angry. "We would be dead without you," I said. I didn't really want to be nice but I didn't trust that is was truly over. Not until we were out of the room. I was afraid to start any more fighting.

"You wouldn't be here if it wasn't for me."

"I am really not in the mood to be comforting you right now but I will say this, we don't know that for sure. You were just as much of a player in their sick game as we were." Alex said. She had the same thought as I had.

The phone began to ring.

"You are going to let us leave aren't you?" I asked J.P.

"Yes, of course," he replied, dropping the gun to the ground.

I got down on the floor beside Alex. I was facing her. "I have never been so happy to hear that phone."

She smiled and grabbed my hand. "Same here."

-39-

IT WILL ALL COME OUT IN THE WASH.

Police Officers and Ambulance Attendants filled the room. Lonny, Alex, and I were taken out by stretcher. The others left on their own feet once they were untied. I went out first as Lonny and Alex needed much more prep work than I did. The outside air was nice to feel on the face. It was amazing how several hours felt like several days.

"Sadie!" My father cried running up the walk. "Sadie, I am so glad you're okay." He grabbed my hands and held them tight. He kissed my cheek. I winced in pain. My jaw and eye still very sore and very swollen.

"Sorry. Sorry for this," he rubbed my injured face. "For this," he pointed at the residence. "For not being there for you, for not believing you that this could happen again, for…"

"Dad, it isn't your fault. It isn't anyone's fault, right? Isn't that what you said about what happened with mom? That sometimes things just happen? I am okay."

He just smiled holding my hand and walking fast to keep up with the paramedics who decided to continue pushing my stretcher to the ambulance.

"Lonny, he was stabbed Dad. Pretty bad. Can you check on him?"

"Yes, but I don't want to let you go just yet." I smiled. I didn't want him to let go either. We stared at each other for a few moments. Once we arrived at the ambulance bus, father asked the paramedics to let me stay for a while. At least until I saw Alex and Lonny come out. They disagreed at first but father reminded them about the big ordeal that had just happened and how a few moments would go a long way in reassurance to both me and him. They said okay since my vitals were acceptable, and considering the circumstances. They even let him wash some of the blood off of my face while we waited.

The doors to the residence opened up. "Alex is coming out dad, go see her."

"Are you sure?"

"One hundred percent. Please go. I am okay. I want you to make sure she is okay too."

He kissed me on my other cheek this time. It was in considerably less pain. He turned from me and ran to Alex with great speed and intensity. I saw him practically throw himself on top of her and her arms reach up and around his. He kissed her head several times not able to kiss her lips because of the oxygen mask she was wearing. They were talking. At one point father pointed over in my direction. Alex's head moved towards me and I waved a small wave. She waved back.

The scene was surreal. There were police lights flashing around us. There were sounds of sirens and people talking over police radios. Many people were scurrying around with individual duties of their own. And several people were starring. They were starring and smiling at me. People I have never seen before in my life.

"Excuse me, Miss. Coleman. My name is Officer Gentry. May I talk to you for a few moments?"

I looked over at my dad. He looked up at me and kissed Alex on the head again then started walking over towards me.

"Yes," I took one more look at father approaching, "I will answer all of your questions."

For the next twenty minutes I filled the officer in on everything I knew about Jack, Jefferson, J.P., and their plan.

* * * * * * * * * * *

"Hey come on and hurry up. They were expecting us a half hour ago. You wouldn't want to be any later would you?"

"Oh come on, it helps your father to practice some patience."

"Don't you think he did enough of that lately?"

Five weeks had passed since the hostage situation at residence. School had ended and the residence was emptied for another year, all without Alex, Lonny, or my attendance. We were pardoned out of our work contracts with full pay. Lonny and I also received full credit for our courses. I personally, never wanted to see the inside of that residence or school again. Father collected all of my personal belongings, as well as helped to pack up Alex's apartment. He moved us both into his house. He and Alex officially got back together about 5 seconds after we were released.

Mr. DeGraff, who lost both of his children in the situation, tried to sue the school for what had happened to his sons. He was going for the 'negligence causing death' defence. He didn't get very far with that lawsuit.

J.P. went to jail for his part. He pled down to a lesser sentence after we told them how he turned on Jack and Jefferson and ultimately saved us. We learned that the cops didn't hear into the walls using special devices at all. It was actually Rodney calling the cops from his cell phone in the boardroom, feeding them the lines from Jefferson's conversations. That was how they also knew that Jefferson was the mastermind behind this and not J.P. Rodney informed everyone that J.P. was actually allowing him to call out. This also helped J.P. get a lesser sentence.

Alex ended up in the hospital for two weeks. She had a bruised jaw, a bruised kidney and three broken ribs due to the beating. She also had some 2nd degree burns from the cigarette. As she said, she would take it over death any day. After Lonny was released, I spent the rest of the time in Alex's hospital room. The nurses let me sleep nights on a cot beside her bed. No one really asked about it, they just let me. Father didn't argue.

"Okay, I am ready. Let's get out of here." Lonny said to me.

We had just gone to my therapy appointment at the hospital. He usually spent the hour in the cafeteria eating and reading or chatting with patients on my appointment days. He had been making new friends every week and this week he was playing a game of Chess with Bob, a senior from the cardiac floor. He met Bob when he was in emergency with him, the night Lonny was stabbed. Bob had had a mild heart attack the day before but was still in the ER waiting for a bed on a floor. Bob kept Lonny company during some unpleasant moments.

"Can we finish next week?" He asked Bob with a plea in his voice. "I am actually winning this time."

It was nice to be around Lonny again. He was in the hospital for three days recovering from the blood loss. The wound didn't cut any organs and healed nicely. It was just on the scary side of a flesh wound.

I came away with a bruised jaw and black eye. I was released the same night after a psychology consult and a promise that I came back for therapy as an out patient. Lonny and I talked a lot about our relationship and what had happened. We agreed that nothing from any of the previous fights seemed to matter. Nothing that happened was due to malicious intent – it was all emotion driven. I didn't care about the drama. I was just happy to still have the chance to get past it. We did agree though, that we would just stay friends. We did friendship much better than we did romance.

We were later than we said we would be getting home. We had called from the hospital so they would know we were late and could hold off dinner for us. They were just putting it on the table as we came in.

"Hey you two, how are you?" Alex asked as she placed hot plates onto the wooden table.

"We are good. How are you?" I went over to give them both a hug hello. I made sure not to squeeze Alex too hard so I didn't irritate her ribs.

"Never been better," father answered. "How was your session?"

I told them that it was good. Father asked me last month to start therapy like I said I would when being released - to talk about what had happened with Jefferson but mostly for what happened with Jack. I fought it for awhile but now I agreed. I needed it. The first week we were home I didn't sleep unless I was in the same room as Alex and my father. I would start out in my bed but my dreams and my nerves would get so intense that I couldn't handle staying alone. In the night I could feel Jack on me, or see him around me, sometimes strangling me, other times dead beside me. I would sneak into their room and sleep on the floor. One night Alex woke up and nearly stepped on me on her way into the bathroom. Father picked me up and carried me back into my room. That was when we had the therapy talk. Alex bunked with me that night and for the next week. She and Piety took turns camping out every night after that. When I would wake up from a nightmare, they would remind me of where I was. It helped me to get back to sleep. I was indebt to them both, I knew. After three sessions with the psychiatrist I was finally able to sleep alone. Which was a huge feat; I never do anything alone anymore.

We all sat down to eat our dinner. Father poured us all some wine. "Shall we open our gifts now?" He asked. "Or do you want to hear my announcement first?"

Alex gave me a look that asked if I was ready. I just shook my head. I planned to come clean to father about everything in regards to my mother and her death after dinner. Alex said she would stay by my side the whole time for moral support. Lonny said he would be there too although he had no idea what he was being there for.

"Why don't we eat first? Then I think Sadie has an announcement that she would like to get out first. Then yours, if that is okay Jason?"

Father looked at Alex and then back at me. "Okay. Don't argue with the ladies right, Lonny?"

"Not these ladies, Jason." We laughed.

When dinner was over we removed the plates, grabbed the dessert, and sought out more wine. Alex sat beside me on the bench, filling up my glass before I spoke. A little liquid courage I assumed.

"Alright ladies, I feel a little ganged up on. What is up?"

I told him everything. I cried through the whole story but I got it out with Alex's help. He sat and listened without interruption. Father was shocked. He was a little upset that I had told Alex and neither of us had told him before this but he understood. He said he didn't like what I did but he didn't blame me for mother's death. He agreed with Alex that they would have found a way to get to her with or without me. He also said that he didn't want to go to the police with this information, at least not right away. He was worried that if it came out that I remembered this guy that I might be in danger as well. We all agreed to wait the weekend before we decided on what to do. He held me for a few moments when we were done talking. It was such a relief to know that he didn't hate me. I was convinced he would.

"We'll figure it out, Tootie. Don't worry about it anymore. You have done that long enough." Alex and Lonny came over and joined our hug.

"Now, I would like to make an announcement." He said as he stood up and walked back towards his seat and dessert.

"Dad, there are three of us here besides you. Do you really need to be so nerdy?"

"Yes. Actually before my announcement I think we all need to give each other the gifts that we brought to dinner tonight."

"Is that your announcement, because it stinks? We knew this was happening."

"My announcement will come later."

"You go first Lonny," I said. "I got your gift. He opened the box to find a notepad and a pen. "This is to write in. To write all those stupid little facts that you hear and say. So you don't forget them."

"Thanks." He said. "And they may be stupid but you like them." I nodded in agreement.

I opened mine next. It was from Alex. "Your vial?"

"Yes." I want you to keep it. One of these days when I am ready, we will open it together. That was the deal right?"

I smiled and placed it around my neck. "Right! Thank you. I am honoured."

Father opened his gift next. It was a pipe from Lonny. Lonny said that it was his grandfathers and very special to him. Dad, who never smoked a pipe before in his life, was elated by the gift. "Thanks so much Lonny. Wow, I feel special."

"You're welcome Mr. Coleman."

Last was Alex. She opened her box from my father. I didn't need to see what was inside to know the contents by the way the box opened up. She cried instantly. Father walked over to her and then got down on one knee.

"This is long overdue. I have loved you for decades. Alex, marry me?"

She picked the ring up out of the box and placed it on her own finger. "Yes," she said simply.

They shared a kiss and a hug while Lonny and I cheered them on. Father stood up and cleared his throat. "Now, my announcement. Alex and I are engaged." We all groaned at how cheesy this all was.

"You're too much dad." I was embarrassed for him and proud of him all at the same time. I was happy. I had everything I wanted. Life was good. Maybe growing into the creek was not so bad after all. I could handle it, or anything.

On Monday, I went to see the police to tell them what had happened with my mother.

CPSIA information can be obtained at www.ICGtesting.com
Printed in the USA
LVOW062359151111

255135LV00001B/24/P

9 781926 635613